The Dream Eaters

A Legacy of Devils novel

Viktor Bloodstone

FORTRESS PUBLISHING, INC.

WWW.FORTRESSPUBLISHINGINC.COM

The Dream Eaters
© 2023 Fortress Publishing, Inc.
ISBN: 978-1-959797-90-6

Edited by: Catherine Jordan

Cover by: Jay Fife

This book is available for wholesale through the publisher,
Fortress Publishing, Inc.

PUBLISHED BY:
Fortress Publishing, Inc.
1200 Market Street
Unit 17 / Box 137
Lemoyne, PA 17043

WWW.FORTRESSPUBLISHINGINC.COM

CHAPTER 01

Nila leaned her forehead against the window, the glass cool against her skin burning from agitation. The sensation felt good, but the view from her tenth-floor apartment didn't tell her what she needed to know; *Is this real, or is this a dream*? Lights speckled the darkened city from illuminated windows of towering apartments and office buildings. The rain didn't tell her anything either, tiny drops aided by gusts of wind making thin, glinting streaks on the glass. At times it seemed as if it rained upside down. If that were the case, then Nila would know this was definitely a dream and she'd have a better idea about making it through the night alive. Right now, she couldn't tell the real world from the dream world.

The prudent thing would be to wait until she could confirm reality, to wait until she felt safer before ending her relationship with Billy.

No, she couldn't wait. Guilt swirled the acid in her stomach, the nausea now greater than her fear. She'd have to take her chances and dump him tonight. If she backed down now, then when would the next opportunity arrive?

Frustrated and scared, she turned away from the window. There had to be some hint within her apartment that would help her determine if this was reality or dream. Billy had been here enough to know the layout as well as she did, enough to make it *appear* real. The cold cloak of hopelessness draped over her slumping shoulders.

No! she snapped at herself. *This isn't the time to be fatalistic. Look around*! Was there a knick-knack that Billy didn't know about, a new decoration, a recent crack in the wall? Were the dishes in the sink dirtied last night or the night before? Had the empty wine glass always been on the coffee table? *Fuck*!

Why hadn't she taken more control of her own world? Because she had been too enamored with riding the wave of righteousness. God, the feeling was so intoxicating. She rationalized so much in the name of that feeling. Too much, she now knew. But no matter what she did at the time, no matter how evil, she was in the right.

Not Billy.

The children. So much blood from such tiny bodies. A guerilla news outlet that prided itself in showing what the mainstream media was "too afraid to show" had uploaded the grisly images this morning. Their reporters sported tattoos, facial piercings, and hairstyles that screamed counter-, sub-, anti- culture. The news outlet encouraged their correspondents, and their readers, to cross any line necessary to get to the truth, including lines of good taste and social responsibility. It took less than an hour for higher authorities to take down the images, but an hour on the internet was a lifetime and Nila had seen the pictures, seen the blood-covered bodies of the siblings, two boys and a girl, all under the age of ten. Seen whose children they were.

Their father had been murdered a week ago, his body slaughtered in his own bed. His children's gruesome deaths were not a coincidence. There had been too many reports of other murder victims' children being subsequently murdered. Nila had read every article.

Trying to piece together her day, she marched to her kitchenette and looked in the trashcan. Staring at the mostly empty plastic containers and paper plates stained with food bits, she wondered, *Which ones had she eaten from, if any?*

Nila closed her eyes and used every muscle in her face to squeeze them shut, hoping the childish effort would bring forth a blip or a shadow of a memory that might help her recall her day. Colorful stars burst behind her eyelids, but no recollections. Damn it! The wasted attempt only succeeded in her making her dizzy. She took a moment to regain her balance, then walked over to her coffee table, to where her laptop had sat all day.

She sat on the couch, then immediately popped back up. Deep inhales through her nose, long exhales from puffed cheeks, she shook her hands as if trying to air them dry. Paranoia strummed her nerves like a harp, the macabre tune created from misdeed, and she couldn't sit still. Plus, she had been sitting in that very spot all day. At least she *thought* she had been.

This was too much, too many questions. She'd end things with Billy tomorrow, not tonight. Yes, tomorrow was better. *Close the laptop and stop being so nutty*, she told herself. But as she went to close her laptop she glanced at the image on the screen.

The blood.

Shaking her head, she changed her mind again. The breakup had to be tonight.

A heavy and familiar knock at the door made her jump.

Had to be him, Billy. No turning back now.

She opened the door and Billy wheeled inside, his toned forearms taut, his hands rolling his wheelchair forward. "Good evening, Nila. If you didn't have anything in mind for tonight, I thought we could..." Billy parked himself beside her coffee table, eyes glued to her laptop. He winced. "What's this?"

Billy was a thin young man with a serious face, sharp features, yet handsome. He never let his disability hinder him and that warm confidence radiated from him. Had circumstances been different, Nila could have imagined him having walked through her door with a rock star's swagger accompanying the fierce intelligence raging behind his eyes. But to feign ignorance like this angered her.

Nila slammed her door shut. "Don't play dumb with me."

She stomped around the couch, grabbed the computer, and dropped it in his lap, pointing to the highlighted names of the children in the article.

Billy squinted. His eyes moved as he read, becoming misty with each paragraph. He looked up at her with wet eyes. "I didn't do this."

Nila huffed, snatched her laptop back and returned it to the coffee table. "Fine. You didn't do it. Will did it. I did it. *We* did it. We did this, Billy."

Billy frowned, confused. "Okay, I agree that what happened to these children is unfortunate, and it makes us look guilty, especially after what the three of us did to their father."

"Cut the shit. There are others."

"Others? What are you talking about? You're not making sense."

"What am I talking about? I'm talking about taking things too far. I'm talking about one of you or both of you going beyond vigilantism.

And… I'm done with what you and Will and I have been doing. I'm done with *you*."

Billy's eyes widened with surprise. "What? Nila, the three of us have accomplished so much good together. We're ridding the world of truly evil people."

"But why have you taken it beyond that?" Nila yelled, tears of frustration rolling over her cheeks. "Why have you and Will been killing their children?"

"We haven't!"

"Stop lying! Stop talking. Stop rationalizing. Stop pretending to be God. Stop. Just stop. In fact… just leave."

Billy looked away, his eyes wandering around the room as if Nila's words had been written on the wall. Then, what Nila had dreaded this entire time, he shifted in his seat and reached into the right pocket of his pants.

This is it, Nila thought.

Billy pulled out his hand, fingers closed tightly into a fist.

If he has a gold quarter, then this is a dream and I'm dead.

Billy held out his hand and uncurled his fingers. Resting in the center of his palm was a gold quarter.

Fuck!

She should have been prepared. She should have had a better plan. A laundry list of things she should have done rippled through her mind. But still, she had power, and now that he confirmed this was a dream, she tapped into her limited abilities.

She stretched her hands out in front of her – the motion helped her focus. Concentrating to the point of a stabbing sensation between her temples, she commanded the coffee table to fly through the air and wrap around Billy as if rubber. She willed it to constrict tighter. Tighter.

It wasn't enough.

Billy stood up and out of his wheelchair, and the table crumbled and fell away like sand.

Turning toward the kitchen, Nila focused on anything that could be used as a weapon. She used her thoughts to send utensils and appliances through the air, shining missiles with one target. Each exploded into a puff of harmless ash as they neared him.

Paintings, wall hangings, plants, the laptop, lamps, anything Nila focused on turned into a projectile. But they all fell to dust around him.

Billy smirked. "Nila, I'm so disappointed."

She grit her teeth in anger. The couch – it was the last thing left to throw at him, and her mind launched the shitty brown sofa at him, imagining it smashing him into a bloody pulp against the wall.

The piece of furniture exploded into hundreds of golden butterflies.

Hands behind his back, he took a step closer.

Nila always hated when he struck that arrogant pose, a harbinger for something pedantic.

"Throwing things at me, Nila? Here? You're displaying the limits of your imagination. I thought I taught you better. Let me demonstrate."

The robin egg blue walls rippled, undulations flowing together to form bubbles. Two, three, four hands popped out from the bubbles and grabbed Nila by the wrists, lifting her off the ground. The carpeting below her twitched and fluttered, discontented things underneath wishing to break free. More hands reached for Nila, fuzzy and strong fingers latching onto her ankles and pulling.

Billy was right; she'd never imagine doing this. The soft carpet under her bare feet was heavenly after a long day of classes. She had painted the walls the week after she moved in, a memory she never failed to cherish. This apartment held nothing but happiness and comfort for her. Billy considered the entire apartment a weapon, something Nila could never have done.

Fibrous hands crushed her ankles and light blue jagged fingers dug into her wrists, drawing blood. The wall-hands pulled. First, her joints popped and then muscle separated from bone with meaty rips. She screamed her throat raw. Pain coursed through her eternal – no beginning, no end – and she tried to kick and thrash, but since her joints had been pulled apart her actions were impotent.

"I thought you were the one," Billy said, studying her as if she were a museum sculpture.

Pain-induced darkness closed in around her peripheral vision, blurred from tears. Nila swore she saw Billy wipe at his eyes as if he were crying. Throat hoarse from screaming, she struggled mentally to summon her powers, but to no avail. "All... all about... you... Right?"

Nila screamed again as the hands pulled tighter.

"It was about *us!*" Billy yelled. "About you and Will and me making this world a better place. About us doing to those who have done to others! You said you understood. You said you understood my pain. You lied! You ripped my heart out. So..."

A pop came from within Nila's chest. A crack. She released a deep exhale as a jagged rib poked from her chest. Another crack and Nila thrashed her head, swore, pleaded, spat, and screamed. One by one, a snap, a crack. Her ribs now hovered in the air in front of her.

Exhausted and praying to lose consciousness, slimy strings of bloody mucus dripped from her mouth and nose. The rib-holes in her chest formed gashes, fleshy strips of raw skin hanging from her like the torn rags of her shirt. "Puh... puh... please...," she whispered, not even knowing what she was begging for.

The twenty-four sinew covered ribs floating in the air converged and joined together to form two hands. Newly formed bone-fingers dipped into her skin and pulled, splaying her chest.

Nila screamed. Not from the pain this time, too immersed in agony to feel anything new, but the shock of seeing her own heart float out from her chest. Still attached to veins and arteries, it pulsed. Mercifully, it shriveled, and Nila's world finally went black.

*

Billy awoke in his bed, unrested. The usual mental debate around going back to sleep presented itself, but it was brief. His mind was too active, needling him about all the work he had to do.

CHAPTER 02

Today was the last day of Shinko Dangan's current job. Working as one of Mr. Tanaka's housekeepers hadn't been as awful as she had thought. She'd heard the rumors about his cruelty, but in the past three weeks, spending eight hours a day in Mr. Tanaka's spacious and extravagant home, Shinko hadn't witnessed anything beyond him yelling or belittling other people. It had been her experience, though, that if she heard a rumor often enough, there was some truth to it. But it wasn't her place to ask questions, simply to do her job.

"Shinko! Where are my tie choices?" Tanaka called out from his changing room, the alcove between his bedroom and his closet.

Shinko stood in the center of his closet. Just as the house was a shrine to western culture, the closet was a shrine to excess, bigger than many apartments in Japan. Tanaka's tie choices had been arranged yesterday evening by Karin at the conclusion of her shift. Three ties lay on a black velvet covered tray. With the agility of a street magician, Shinko switched out the tie on the far right with one she had tucked in her pants pocket. She symmetrically aligned the three ties on the tray, and then adjusted her own tie, not wanting to incur Tanaka's wrath should hers appear crooked. Despite the non-traditional notion, Tanaka insisted his hired help wear slacks, long-sleeved, button-downed shirts, and ties. Not for the appearance of progressiveness, rather his personal attitude – since he had to wear business clothing to work, then they, too, should wear similar clothing. Satisfied with her tie presentation, Shinko brought the tray to Tanaka.

The changing room was simple, the only modest room of the house. Tasteful patterns decorated the fusuma – sliding walls – separating the changing room from the bedroom. The ranma above the fusuma was plain. A full-length mirror adorned a permanent wall while an upholstered bench sat in the middle of the room.

Tanaka finished buttoning the top button of his shirt.

"About time," he mumbled while looking over the ties.

As Shinko predicted, he reached for the tie on the right, colored red at the bottom with a conservative pattern weaving into a mustard yellow at the top. Unfortunately, that was when Karin entered from the bedroom and asked, "Are you sure you don't want the silver tie? It matches the pinstripes in your suit."

Tanaka's hand drifted toward the silver tie until Shinko countered with, "The tie on the right represents the rising sun. Which do you believe would be viewed as stronger – the energy of the rising sun, or the laziness of the silver moon?"

Tanaka snatched the tie on the right.

Karin frowned. "But, the silver—"

"Enough, Karin," Tanaka snapped. "I made my choice. Be gone."

Glaring at Shinko, Karin gave a slight bow, then turned and left the changing room.

With agitated movements, Tanaka worked his tie into shape around his neck. He glanced at Shinko and said, "Your presence is no longer needed either."

"But it is," Shinko replied. She waited until he had the knot complete and was ready to slide it up to his neck. "I need to make sure your incompetence doesn't interfere with the simple act of dressing yourself."

Eyes ablaze with anger, Tanaka tightened the tie with a forceful pull, driving the knot into the base of his throat. He turned to Shinko. She assumed he wanted to deliver a tongue lashing, but when he opened his mouth only the raspy sound of vowels escaped.

Hands behind her back, Shinko strolled closer to Tanaka with no fear of him reaching for her.

Eyes bulging, he pulled at his collar. Too tight, he couldn't put his fingers between his collar and neck.

Shinko looked him in the eyes. "I'm sure you're too panicked to understand me, but I will share pertinent information with you anyway. This was done by your children. I'm not sure what it was you did to them, but my being here is their decision. After you realize there is no escape, you might begin regretting all *your* decisions. There is nothing you can do; your death is inevitable. I worked a simple, notched garrote into your tie. I designed it myself, so I know it works flawlessly."

A purple hue bloomed across his face as his tongue lolled from his mouth. Fingers desperately worked the knot of the tie, slipping impotently over the fabric. Bubbles formed at the corners of his mouth as he dropped to his knees. His hands fell away from his neck, the whites of his eyes turned pink, and blood-red freckles sprouted along his cheeks. After a slight wobble, he fell to the ground, and his head hit the floor loud enough to draw Karin's attention.

Just as Shinko had hoped.

Shinko allowed a moment for Karin to assess the situation. She could have killed Karin as soon as she stepped into the changing room, but she needed Karin to play a specific part in this theater. She also savored Karin's reaction as she realized she had failed her assignment of keeping Tanaka alive.

Karin turned to Shinko, and lashed out. Her hand, elbow, and knee strikes were sloppy, ungainly, her ki disrupted, and Shinko deflected her attacks with easy forearm blocks. After all, when one loses control of their inner energy, then their outer actions are sure to follow. The changing room was not where she wanted Karin, though, so she needed to move her.

Shinko threw a few strikes, landing none – not that she was trying. A few kicks to Karin's left side and a few to the right.

Karin used her legs to block, her stance widening after each block.

When Shinko deemed Karin's feet wide enough apart, she took a step and dropped to the ground. She half spun while sliding between Karin's legs, popped back up to her feet, and faced her opponent's back. She allowed herself the indulgence of planting the heel of her foot squarely on Karin's backside before running from the changing room.

Shinko sprinted through the bedroom into the hallway. She turned, expecting to see Karin behind her. She did *not* expect Karin to release a throwing star. Shinko could have ducked it, but then it would have embedded into a wall, and that was unacceptable. A hole in the wall was evidence she didn't wish to leave. She twisted to catch the shuriken, throwing herself off balance enough to stumble into the dining room.

During her tenure, Shinko visited this room only to clean it, though it was her favorite, the decorations far more elegant than the tigers and dragons in many of the other rooms. The dining room featured cranes; one in flight along the ranma, others perched gracefully in water on the fusuma and tapestries draping the permanent walls. The room was too delicate for Karin's anger.

But as the other ninja stormed in, Shinko backed away in a straight line, stepping on one of the zabutons around the chabudai – pillow seats circling a short-legged table. As far as Shinko could tell, Karin held no other weapons. Good. Shinko only needed to maneuver Karin out of this room. Still backing away, Shinko hopped on and off the chabudai, wincing at the disrespect of her toes daring to touch the table even though she left no mark.

Karin kicked the zabutons at Shinko. The pillows were an obvious distraction ploy and Shinko swatted them away with ease, readying herself for Karin's real attack. Karin picked up the chabudai and charged, leading with the table's short legs. Shinko spun and crouched. When she popped back up, she stood between Karin and the chabudai. She whipped her head backward, connecting with Karin's cheek. Hopefully she left a bruise, congruent with what she had planned for later.

The impact was hard enough for Karin to release the table.

Shinko snatched the chabudai and set it back down where it belonged. This room needed to look untouched, so she kicked the zabutons to their original placement while blocking strikes from Karin. Now, to maneuver out of the room, Karin standing between her and the door.

Shinko didn't want to fuss with the furniture again, so she engaged Karin in hand-to-hand with a flurry of quick strikes. As Karin blocked each strike, Shinko stepped backward. Several more attacks to Karin's shoulders and waist, but Shinko's hands purposely never made contact. She kept moving backward, toward the corner of the room. Exactly where she wanted.

Shinko repeated the sequence of attacks to Karin's face, encouraging her to recognize the pattern and launch a counterattack.

Finally, after Shinko's fourth missed jab to her throat, Karin returned a volley of jabs and stepped forward. Speed, agility, focus. Shinko jumped and took two quick steps up the walls that formed the corner of the dining room, and launched herself at Karin. Hands on Karin's shoulders, Shinko flipped over her adversary, simultaneously pushing her away while landing behind her. Shinko sprinted from the room.

The hallway led to the great room. Enormous for any house in Japan, this room felt even larger by the color scheme. White furniture held pops of embroidered silver. Most of the tables and cabinets were glass, trimmed in silver. A lone wood cabinet, waist high and painted white, stood along the wall between the hallway entrance and the stairs leading to the first floor. On the cabinet was a Baccarat crystal vase filled with clear marbles that held the stem of an opulent orchid between two thin bamboo reeds. It had been Shinko's daily duty to dispose of the old flower and replace it with a new one.

Satisfied that her plan would work perfectly from here, Shinko entered the great room and turned. Karin launched into the room and attacked with a flurry of hand strikes, all of which Shinko blocked with ease. Shinko spun, dropped to one knee, and pushed with both hands, careful not to strike. Karin's hip connected with the corner of the cabinet hard enough to slam it into the wall. Perfect. The cabinet left a mark on the wall and a bruise should form on Karin's hip; all part of the narrative Shinko intended for future investigators. The final piece fell into place. Literally.

The Baccarat with the orchid toppled over, spilling the marbles. Her feet firmly planted, Shinko gave Karin another push, hard enough for her to lose her balance. Desperate to regain her footing, Karin stepped on a few of the rolling marbles, just as Shinko planned. Cognizant of the marbles, Shinko took a few well-placed steps and gave Karin one last shove toward the stairs.

Arms windmilling, Karin succumbed to gravity. Two shoulder-hits on the stairs, one final head-thud on the first-floor landing. Mindful of the marbles, Shinko made her way down the stairs to check on her adversary. Dead from a broken neck. Perfect.

Shinko withdrew Tanaka's rolled up tie from her pants pocket and tucked it into Karin's pocket, completing her mission. The scene was set. Karin killed Tanaka, but wasn't familiar enough with her surroundings, accidentally running into the cabinet during her retreat and knocking over the vase of marbles. The police would have to assume the clumsiness of their murder suspect, but police always liked a simple answer. Should they decide to investigate further, they would find no signs of struggle with a third party.

Job done. She brought honor and financial gain to the clan. Once news got out about Mr. Tanaka's demise, then his children would pay the clan. After all, it was they who hired Shinigami's Helper.

The garden path led away from the house, toward the driveway. Shinko followed it to her car and left the estate the same way she entered, careful to avoid the range of the external security cameras, just as she did on the way in. There was no recorded evidence of her being there today.

She thought about Tanaka and his children for the entire trip back to her home. What kind of monster must he have been for his children to unite in his demise? She sighed. If they were nothing more than soulless monsters looking for an inheritance, then they were products of the man who taught them how to be monsters.

As soon as she stepped through the door of her house, she grabbed her cell phone. It had been about a month since she last spoke with her daughter, but they texted often. Fearful that her lack of communication could lead her daughter down the same path Tanaka's children followed, Shinko typed and sent: Hello, My Dream. How are you?

CHAPTER 03

Yume Dangan strolled along the sidewalk, enjoying the late afternoon. Not quite as warm as one might infer from the sunshine, but it was a welcome break from the recent stretch of dreary days. March in Pennsylvania could be fickle, so Yume made a conscious effort to get outside as much as possible when invited by nice weather. She had no more classes today, only an upcoming appointment with a tutor, but first she wanted to meet her best friend and pseudo-sister, Shanna, for a quick snack at their usual café.

About two blocks away, she got a text from her mother: Hello, My Dream. How are you?

Yume smiled. Words spelled out completely, proper grammar and punctuation. Her mother refused to text any other way. For the sake of her mother, Yume replied in kind. I'm wonderful, Mother. How are you doing?

I find myself missing my only child. I would like to visit you in a month or two. Are you able to talk later?

Yume took a couple quick little hops, excited by the news. Embarrassed that she had skipped in public, she glanced around to see if anyone was laughing at her. Too engrossed in their own lives, no one on the Philadelphia sidewalk took notice. Yume answered, I'm very busy today. Would it be okay if I called you tomorrow?

Perfect. I look forward to it, My Dream.

Yume all but ran the rest of the way, excited to share the news with Shanna.

Less than half the tables inside the Grain-N-Bean café were occupied. It was almost three-thirty, and the people in line were probably grabbing a snack or a caffeine boost to get them through the rest of their day. A unique mixture of caraway and ground coffee floated through the air. Shanna sat in their usual spot – a square table for two in the front corner of the café – inspecting a lock of her long, blonde hair.

As Yume approached, Shanna held out a section of her locks and ran her fingers through as if searching for something.

"Digging for gold?" Yume asked as she sat.

"Hey, Sis," Shanna said. "I don't know what I'm digging for, but it's definitely not gold. I felt like there's been a clump of something in my hair all day."

"Probably food. I keep telling you to pull your hair back when you eat."

Running her fingers through it one last time, Shanna stopped fussing and delivered a full body sigh. With a roll of her eyes and a tone of sarcasm, she said, "Yes, yes, if only I listened to you like I should…"

Giggling, Yume flicked her brown, ruler-straight hair over her shoulder like a runway fashion model. "If only."

Shanna sat up straighter and offered Yume one of the two plates in front of her, each with a bagel cut in half. Shanna groaned. "Yeah, yeah, yeah. You can't help that you're not only a brain, but also friggin' gorgeous."

Yume chuckled as she spread herb cream cheese on her everything bagel. "Oh, please. Not only are *you* gorgeous, but you also have those." She pointed her plastic knife at Shanna's full C's.

"Yeah, well I needed these to keep at least a few of the guys in high school from falling in love with you. Can you believe that it's been five years already?"

"I was just thinking the same thing," Yume said. "God, five years. I remember being so nervous when I moved in with your family as an exchange student. Everything I knew about America was through the internet and sometimes that view is less than flattering. My mother visited the states a few times before, but these lands hold sad memories. Her brother, my uncle Kamu, went missing six years ago, right at the turn of the century. But you were awesome – you swept away my fears when we met with your gift of gab."

Shanna talked a lot, as most Americans did, and mostly about herself. Yume learned later that stemmed from Shanna's own anxieties about the experience, needing to fill the silence to keep fearful thoughts at bay. No matter, because Yume thought Shanna was great. And rather than putting Yume off, Shanna's constant talking helped Yume feel contented. The feeling was mutual, Shanna declaring that Yume was her sister immediately after meeting her, and she'd always love her as such.

Thanks to Shanna and her parents making her arrival comfortable, Yume fell in love with America and hadn't gone back to Japan since. This upset her mother, but she respected Yume's wishes and supported her to the point of pulling a variety of strings so Yume could stay an extra year until she could attend college. Yume never asked her mother about the "pulled strings," since the act of a foreign exchange student staying past her allotted time was nearly impossible. Her mother never shared more information than needed, even when directly asked about it, so Yume didn't waste her breath questioning her.

Shanna tilted her head and her eyes glinted with the joy of looking at a puppy. "You've been the best part of my life! Despite stealing the attention of all the boys."

"Ugh. Boys from our high school were lame," Yume said before enjoying a bite of her bagel.

"College boys are better. They're still lame, but they buy me drinks. The sex is better, too."

"I'm guessing you hooked up last night?"

"You guessed correctly."

"Do you remember his name? Did you even get his name?"

Mouth half full of bagel, Shanna pointed at Yume as she chewed and said, "No lectures, Sis. I know you think I sleep around a lot to fill a hole inside of me made when my dad left, but I like to think of my promiscuity as a form of empowerment, using men the way they use women. Smashing down the walls of the patriarchy with my vagina. Plus, sex is fun."

"I can't disagree with that. I just don't want to see you get hurt."

"First of all, I'm not into that kinky shit. Second of all, all condoms all the time. I know you psychiatrists think I have daddy issues. If anything, I have mommy issues. I want to make sure I'm in control of my life, you know, be nothing like my mother. She has zero confidence in herself, and I never want to be like that."

Yume had heard this before. Shortly after Yume and Shanna started college, Shanna's father left. The divorce was ugly, accusations made, secrets exposed. Shanna's childhood home had to be sold, forcing her and her mother to move from a two-story house in middleclass suburbia to a doublewide in an area where she felt the need to carry two cans of pepper spray and a lock-blade in her purse.

Yume didn't think Shanna's bold personality was an issue of confidence, rather one of relevance. Shanna's father had left. Why? No one truly knew, but Shanna believed that if her mother would have been more relevant, then her husband wouldn't have noticed other things – women, careers, hobbies, places to live. If her father's eyes had been on her mother, then they never would have seen anything else.

Shanna feared being irrelevant and subconsciously craved attention. Her curve-emphasizing clothing got her noticed, her bright smile and willingness to converse about anything kept a man's interest. Once her cravings had been sated, then her obvious intimacy issues kicked in and she turned away from whom she originally sought attention before they could turn away from her.

Yume started on the other half of her bagel, spreading around a dollop of cream cheese. "There is nothing wrong with having an active sex life. Forget this country's backwards, double standard, Puritanical view of a woman's sexual rights. And how about you let me get through junior year before calling me a psychiatrist."

Shanna gave a twisted smirk. "Oh pah-leez. I can't imagine you not becoming a psychiatrist."

"Me neither, but I don't want to jinx my entire future by counting unhatched poultry."

"Yeah, yeah, yeah," Shanna moaned. She took a large bite from her bagel and scrutinized Yume as she chewed.

Yume crossed her eyes and stuck out her tongue.

Both women giggled and Shanna said, "You're extra smiley today. Did you get some, too?"

Instead of feeding into that comment by denying it, Yume said, "My mom texted me and said she wants to visit in a month or two."

Shanna smiled and reached across the table to grab Yume's hand. "That's so awesome! How long is she staying? I'd love to see her if that's okay with you two."

"Of course. She would love to see you."

"Great! How long has it been since you saw her? About a year? You'll have so much to show her."

"Yep, you're right."

The women went back to eating until Shanna sighed and said, "I feel like I've been talking about my dating life too much again. How's yours? Any dates? Any new guys? Used guys?"

Yume chuckled. "No, nothing new. No contact with any exes either."

Shanna shook her head, and with a tone of apprehension said, "What a shame. Don't forget, if you don't use your goods on a regular basis, they'll fall off."

"My goods appreciate your concern, but no need to worry."

"Okay. I trust you know what you're doing with your goods. You can get any guy you want, when you want, especially with that cute little accent of yours."

Yume had spoken English all her life. When she came to America at sixteen Shanna and her family complimented her on how well she spoke and how quickly she picked up on conversational English, idioms, and puns. "For now, my focus is on my classes. Plenty of time to worry about boys later."

"Focus on your classes? Good grief. You have A plusses in everything. You're the only student in the history of this college who meets with tutors in classes you have a four-point-oh in."

Yume shrugged. "I like to learn. I'm meeting a tutor for my Psychology 351 class. It's all about dreams and the subconscious, which you know I find fascinating."

"Weirdo." Shanna wiped her fingers with a napkin and dropped it on her plate. "Is he at least cute?"

Yume finished her bagel and wiped the crumbs from her lips. She shrugged. "No idea. His looks aren't important."

"I know, I know. I thought it'd be nice if you could meet someone who enjoyed all the weird things you enjoy, someone to spend the rest of your life with."

"The rest of my life? God, Shanna, I just turned twenty-one. Waaaaaaay too young to think about that."

"One of us has to land a mature relationship and I'm sure we're all aware that it isn't me."

"We don't know that. Your Mister Right might be out there some-where."

"Doubtful." The severity to her word matched the hopelessness in her eyes. Her expression only lasted a second, replaced by a bright smile after a quick head shake. She then grabbed Yume's crumb filled plate, put it on her own, and wiped the tabletop clean. "Okay, so I'm gonna head out. I know your tutor will be here any minute."

"Thanks," Yume said. "Are you going home?"

"I don't know. I went home last night after my hookup."

Shanna rarely spent two nights in a row at her own house. Her mother had married Gus six months ago; Yume met the man three times and liked him less with each meeting. It irked her to her core that she had to remind Gus they had already met. As much as she wished her pseudo-sister would handle it differently, Yume under-stood why Shanna didn't want to be anything like her mother. The poor woman probably saw Gus and his steady managerial job at a lo-cal warehouse as a way for her to move out of the doublewide. The variety of reasons Shanna's mother gave as to why *he* instead *moved in* masked her own disappointment and her fatalistic views of being trapped.

Yume asked, "Is anything getting any better?"

Shanna stood, plates in hand. "This morning he made eggs and bacon for Mom and me, so that's a step in the right direction, I guess. But, God, he's such an ass. Mom still refers to you as her other daugh-ter while *he* refers to you as my 'Oriental friend.' Such an ass."

Yume couldn't disagree, but she didn't want Shanna to leave up-set, primed for self-destructive behavior. She placed a hand on Shan-na's forearm and squeezed. "He's just undereducated. After he and your mother settle in, maybe he'll open his mind."

Shanna patted Yume's hand and smiled. "You always know how to make me feel better. You're gonna make a great shrink."

"Thanks." To encourage Shanna from getting too wasted tonight, Yume added, "Let's meet for breakfast tomorrow and I'll detail my hot tutoring session?"

"Wouldn't miss it for the world, Sis." With a chuckle and a wink, Shanna left.

Yume stared out the window, the life along the sidewalk blurring together. She tried to think of ways to help Shanna. Since they only had about a year and a half until graduation, patience was her best option. Hopefully, Shanna would then start a career and move out. That thought made her smile, until a voice interrupted it.

"Yoo-mee?"

The voice belonged to a young man, the tutor she was scheduled to meet. Thin, but handsome. She greeted him with a cheerful smile, and almost laughed out loud at his pronunciation. "Very close. It's YOO-meh."

At first glance, he seemed serious, but his sharp features softened when he smiled. Yume's heart fluttered at that, and she decided to keep that lovely little detail to herself during breakfast with Shanna tomorrow. He extended his hand to shake, and Yume noticed he was already sitting. Not in a café chair, though, rather in a wheelchair.

Yume took his hand. His handshake was firm, warm, and inviting, as if ready to pull her closer to him. "Nice to meet you, Yume. I'm Billy."

CHAPTER 04

Picasso walked into the pawn shop with Anthony, Sal, and Mort behind him. Picasso wasn't his birth name – that would be Harold Michael Varvaro – rather it was his street name. After thirty-five years in the business, he no longer gave a shit about street names, long past the seventeen-year-old thug on the corner who worried about things like that, when he was called Harry Knuckles. Times changed, nicknames no longer a priority. He once had a "Fat Mikey" and "Little Big" in his crew. Fat Mikey always had a cannoli in his doughy mitts, his undoing, of course. The Japanese made a statement a couple years ago and slipped poison sugar to Demarco's in Little Italy. Poor slob's palate was so desensitized that he couldn't taste the arsenic as he wolfed down a half-dozen cannoli. Little Big was cut littler when the Japanese chopped him to pieces and delivered him in a box to Picasso's boss.

His boss didn't like this new organization moving into his territory, nor did he like the way they communicated with his people. Harold received the none-too-pleasant task of taking care of it. But hey, he took care of it. He blended old school with new thinking and decided to climb up *their* ladder. He did it quietly, though, no busting skulls on the streets. A few Benjamins here and there, some old-fashioned snooping and spying. It took only weeks to find the big boss. Then came the old school – he brought a few of his closest friends with baseball bats and brass knuckles to welcome the new guy to the neighborhood. The next day's newspaper said the ten dead bodies looked like Picasso paintings. The following week, Harold Michael Varvaro became "Picasso." He didn't give a shit about the nickname, but that's what everyone called him now.

And that was only part of the reason behind his new name.

For doing such a great job removing the competition, Harold got a promotion. The boss made him management. Drugs, weapons, numbers, prostitution. Keeping his guys in-line was easy with a simple and enforced punishment-reward system. It was the law that was tricky. Not the cops he saw around town, but the big law – the federal government. Two rules to follow with them: don't get too loud, and pay your damn taxes. Picasso made sure no one's voice went above a polite murmur.

He needed a way to launder money, so he took over the art gallery his boss owned. And thus, another reason for his nickname.

Picasso's business cards read: "Harold Varvaro, Proprietor, 8th Street Gallery." What better way to collect a 100K legally than by taking the cash and handing over a crappy painting that a three-year-old could have made? Feds came sniffing around wanting expert opinions to make sure the sales kept in line with the larger market. The experts were critics, agents, and talent managers. Critics were easy to pay off. Agents and managers clamored to get their artists into the 8th Street Gallery. Didn't matter if the artist pissed on a canvas, just that Harold Varvaro, miracle-worker art connoisseur, could move it for a quarter million dollars, and the agent or manager got fifteen percent. Picasso never met anyone more steeped in their own bullshit that an "art expert." But hey, they told the feds he was legit. Who was he to criticize the "art" that he moved to launder money?

Picasso did good business, ran it smart and quiet. Every once in a while, he got his hands dirty, but even then, he was smart, like with the owner of this pawn shop. A classic case of making a bad bet followed up with three more awful bets while trying to dig himself out of the hole he dug with his own hands. No more bets. Time to pay.

The shop was small, one aisle from the door to the counter in the back, but not too cramped. It held a little bit of everything: practical shit like bicycles and scooters to get around Philadelphia, stupid shit like radios and CDs. The valuable shit, like jewelry and antiques, was locked in the case that the pawn shop owner – a middle aged man named Yanni with thick black hair, extra pounds from his wife's good cooking, and bags under his eyes – leaned on while flipping through the pages of Modern Cat magazine. A lazy glance to see who entered turned into wide-eyed fear as he dropped the magazine, the cover of a green-eyed tabby now looking at him with pity as he backed away from the counter. "Pi… Picasso? I… uhhh… was getting ready to contact you."

"I bet you were," Picasso muttered as he approached the counter.

"Yeah… yeah, I just wanted to tell you I needed a little more time to get you the money. Twenty thousand's not easy to get so fast, but I got people who owe me. It's just that… they ain't… umm… liquid. They need some time to get me *my* money, so I can get you *your* money. A week. All I need is another week."

Picasso stepped aside to allow Mort access to the counter. The short man had gray hair, a bit of a forward slouch, and always wore a suit. Today's blue jacket accompanied a plain white shirt and blue tie. Mort hefted his black briefcase onto the counter, thumping it down on the magazine, crumpling Fluffy's face. He popped the two latches and opened it up to pull out a four-page document. Flipping it to the last page, he slid it on the counter toward Yanni.

From within his suit jacket – a dark shade of gray with barely visible pinstripes – Picasso withdrew a pen. He slapped it down on the document and said, "One week? Perfect. Now sign here."

Yanni let out a nervous giggle, a cross between relief and suspicion. "Yeah? Really? Ummm… Thanks, Picasso. Thank you for being so reasonable." Trembling, he shuffled closer to the counter in small, timid steps, ready to jump back should anyone try anything funny. A couple glances to the papers, struggling to keep an eye on Picasso and Mort. "So, uhhh… What's this? Like a payment schedule?"

"Close," Picasso answered. He nodded toward Mort. "He's your lawyer and this is your will."

The words were so unexpected, so out of place that Yanni stopped shaking, his lips slack. "My… my… My what?"

"Your will. Your lawyer here drew one up for you today. It states that should you die, all of your assets are bequeathed to me. So, let's say in a week, you have a catastrophic misfortune, then this store and all its inventory becomes my property. As does the money in your bank accounts, should you have any. As does any kind of savings you might have for your two kids' future schooling. As does all the furniture in your two-bedroom apartment. As does the very fucking wedding ring on your wife's hand."

Yanni started to tremble again, harder, faster, so strong it locked his jaw closed. Tears flowed over his cheeks as he whimpered. He was attempting to scream, but couldn't, trying to awaken from a nightmare that wouldn't let him go. Exactly the reaction Picasso expected.

Other people in the non-licensed gambling business would've tossed the place, or broken Yanni's bones, or even shot him to "make an example." Picasso found that approach spiteful and a waste; he'd never get his money. Breaking up Yanni's store would hinder his ability to make the money he owed, as would busting his knees. Killing him and grabbing the valuables? A quick ten thousand, at best. Picasso wanted his money paid in full, if not more. Yanni probably kept his gambling issues a secret from his wife, using store money and nothing from their personal funds. They had to have bank accounts, maybe something squirreled away for the kids' college fund.

Yanni shook his head and backed away from the counter.

"No?" Picasso asked. "You don't have to sign it, but don't forget, if something cataclysmic were to happen to you, then your wife gets all your assets. And all your debts. Day after your funeral, I'm having this exact same conversation with her. Is that what you want? Is that sound estate planning?"

Yanni's whole face quivered as the dam burst, tears and spit and snot flowing as he let loose. Big gurgling sobs with every pained inhale. But he signed the will.

Mort signed it and then Anthony stepped forward to sign as witness. Sal finished the process by notarizing it.

"Okay, I'm done here," Mort mumbled with boredom. He paused at the door and glanced over his shoulder. "As your lawyer, I advise you to quit being stupid. Mazel tov."

Ignoring the tear drops and snot stains on the pages, Picasso took the will, folded it up, and tucked inside his jacket. "Your lawyer's a smart man, Yanni. I'd suggest contacting all the people you know who owe you money as soon as possible. You seem to be experiencing a lot of stress and studies have shown people with too much stress are apt to lose focus. They make mistakes and become prone to life-ending accidents."

Yanni cried and quaked so much that he all but lost control of his hands. They dropped to the counter, then he tried reaching for Picasso, but then pulled them back to his chest. Spittle started to foam at the corners of his mouth from his incompressible blubbering. Picasso wondered if Yanni's will would have to be read tomorrow. No matter. He'd get his money one way or another.

Picasso opened the door to leave, and Yanni barked out, "Wait!"

"Wait" usually meant begging or bartering or some other non-sense that included empty promises. He thought about ignoring Yanni, as these kinds of pleas from people in this kind of situation were always backed by fairy tales, dreams, and wishes; nothing substantial.

"C'mon, Yanni. I'm a busy man. And you should be, too."

"Information!"

Props to Yanni for bartering with something concrete. Picasso doubted it was anything more than, "The Easter Bunny ain't real." But hey, he admired the effort. Since Picasso had no immediate plans, he closed the door and turned to give Yanni his full attention. "I'm listening."

Yanni rushed from around the counter so hurriedly that Anthony and Sal moved defensively in front of Picasso. Yanni stopped, his fingers reaching as if to hug Picasso while his arms jerked, as if fighting to rein himself in. "Yeah. You want information. I got information. You'll wipe away what I owe?"

"Look, Yanni, cut the bullshit." Picasso tapped Anthony and Sal's shoulders. He wanted Yanni to feel perfectly at ease and talk without hindrances. "Don't you try to haggle or bicker. If the information is good enough, I'll be fair. And before you start barfing out names, I got 'em all, don't you worry about that. I don't care about other bookies or pimps. I doubt you have anything important to say about any kinds of drugs or guns shipments. I ain't interested in complicated heists, so I don't care about banks moving cash in armored cars or museums getting valuable jewels or what have you. If you think you still got something, then I'm listening."

Yanni started to fall apart again, back to hugging himself to keep his body parts in one place. His face contorted from the pain of failure and fear, and somehow the poor bastard still had more tears. Picasso shrugged and shook his head – Yanni had nothing. He turned to leave.

"The Chinese place, two blocks down!" Yanni yelled.

Picasso reached for the door.

"They... They got a girl!"

Picasso opened the door.

"Oh, Jesus! Oh, Jesus, Picasso! They say... They say she can... She can go inside people's dreams! I know... I know it sounds crazy. They... They got this girl from an island from Indonesia or Philippines or one of them countries that's nothing but islands. Could be Hawaii for all I know, but about a month ago, they got her and she... She can get inside your dreams."

Anthony and Sal snickered, and bumped into Picasso when he stopped.

Picasso's boss was into this sort of nonsense. Weird stuff. Anything from monsters in campfire stories to ancient mysteries that history books couldn't explain. Creepy tales spread by whisper in shadows. Just in case it was real, no matter how slim the possibility, Picasso owed it to his boss to take a moment and hear Yanni out, no matter the fairy tale bullshit.

Picasso turned around once more, allowing the door to close behind him. "Last time I'm stepping inside *your* store, Yanni. Next time I do, it will be my store. Now keep talking."

Anthony snorted and looked from Yanni to Picasso. "You gotta be fuckin' kiddin' me."

Picasso eyed Anthony, signaling for him to shut the hell up. To Yanni, he said, "What, exactly, do you know about this girl?"

Gaining control over his right hand, Yanni wiped away his tears and drool and snot.

"Two of the kids who work at The Dragon's Blessing. Cousins, just outta high school, family members of the owners, so they bus the tables. They came in here one day with a couple friends. You know how boys are at that age, shooting their mouths off, bragging about how they got this girl and how she could control dreams. A week later, one of them came in by himself, looking at a bicycle, a flashy red one. I asked him about her, about the girl. Told me she was legit, that he got her to give him any dreams he wanted. I told him he could have the bike for free if I had a dream about fucking ten girls. That night. That very same night, ten of the most beautiful girls…" Yanni's eyes glazed over as if he were seeing them again right there before his eyes. "I woke up with wet underwear. Kid got his free bike."

Anthony elbowed Sal, and the two of them smiled like they were in on the joke.

"That's the dumbest bullshit I ever heard," Anthony said. His mouth hardened, the smile wiped clean off his face. "You wanted to dream about fuckin' ten bitches, so you dreamt about fuckin' ten bitches and because of that you think the Chinese got some kinda dream witch or whatever? You're either fuckin' stupid or you think we're fuckin' stupid."

Yanni stepped forward, lucidity in his bloodshot eyes. No tears, no shaking. "Picasso, I'm not stupid and I know you ain't. I'm not lying. The dream… The dream was *more* than a dream. The color, the sounds, the touches. Jesus, Picasso, have you ever had a dream where you could feel *everything*? And it lasted hours. Hours and hours. You ever dream like that, Picasso? Ever?"

No. No he hadn't. He doubted anyone had and he was especially confident that Yanni didn't have the acting skills to be so compelling under pressure. "Tell me more about the two kids who work at the Chinese place."

CHAPTER 05

Yume returned to the table with lunch, a flat bread topped with gouda, prosciutto, and arugula and a three-meat club sandwich slathered in artisanal bacon jam, cut in half to share. Billy smiled because she smiled. It was infectious, her smile. He hadn't expected a tutoring session to turn into... He didn't know what this was. A date? A meet cute? Was there such a thing as a pseudo date? Usually, his tutor sessions were with freshman who took Psych 101 because they couldn't find anything better for their required science credits. He had been curious when he saw that his appointment was with a Junior who held a 3.93 GPA in Psych 351. So why would she need a tutor? And he hadn't expected to be sitting with this girl for over an hour, talking about everything but psychology.

"She's pretty," Will said, Billy hearing the words inside his own head.

So surprised by Will's comment, Billy jerked and looked down, upset that he made such a random twitch in front of Yume. Billy composed himself and readied an apology for his behavior, but she was dividing the food as if she hadn't noticed. She was sweet and smooth like that, Billy had been learning. Deescalating an embarrassing situation by ignoring it. Allowing the people around her to be themselves, no matter how cryptic their actions. She was going to make a great Psychiatrist. Maybe more?

Within the privacy of his own mind, Billy asked Will, *What are you doing here?*

Yume slid the other plate of food to Billy. She licked her fingers and said, "I gave you more because of insert-your-own-archaic-stereotype answer for why girls shouldn't eat what they want to in public."

"She's funny, too. I love the low-key sarcasm," Will said.

Seriously, what are you doing here? We never talk like this.

Billy accepted the plate and said to Yume, "It looks like you portioned everything out evenly."

"Hmm. Maybe I did." Yume moved a piece of prosciutto from her flat bread to his. "Now you definitely have more."

"I know, I know," Will said to Billy. "We usually leave notes and emails for each other. And it's hurting me, too, to talk like this. Like a spike digging into the front of my head... our head. But the levels of emotions stirring within you this past hour have been even greater than with Nila."

Don't say her name. We just broke up with her.

"Come on, Billy. It's been two months. It's time we move on, and Yume could be more than just a rebound. At first glance it seems like she's fair and giving. Great qualities for a girlfriend, but also great qualities for a partner in our mission."

You've skipped a few steps, don't you think?

"Then ask her why she's doing this."

Billy ate a slice of the flatbread, contemplating Will's words. As he used a napkin to clear away the oil and crumbs from his fingers, he said, "I apologize if this kills the conversation flow, but I believe you hired me as a tutor."

"It doesn't and I did."

"I must confess that I'm more than a little perplexed as to why a student who has such a high GPA would need a tutor."

"Much to the chagrin of advertising execs the world over, there is a difference between want and need. The reason why your statement didn't kill the conversation flow is because I love talking about psychology. I like to hire tutors so I can discuss a topic with them and learn more about it, and gain different perspectives, through conversation."

"That's really interesting," Will said to Billy.

"That's quite fascinating," Billy said to Yume.

Still seated, Yume half bowed. "Thank you. I do like to think of myself as a fascinating person, despite whatever any ex-boyfriends might say."

"Oooooh, did you hear that?" Will asked Billy. "She's telling us that she's single! You don't need to be a student of the mind sciences to pick up on that obvious hint. You should let her know that we're single."

The pain between his eyes grew from talking to Will – the effort required significant concentration, and Billy ignored his suggestion.

He asked Yume, "You like psychology that much?"

"I do."

"I must apologize for the next question's lack of originality, but why do you want to be a psychiatrist?"

"You're forgiven. And then I must apologize for my answer's lack of originality. I want to help people."

"She wants to help people," Will repeated.

I heard her, thank you.

"Nothing wrong with that answer," Billy said. "I like helping people, too, or else I wouldn't be a tutor. Any particular motivation behind your desire to help others?"

"You mean like a superhero origin story?" Yume asked.

William laughed, sending ripples of pain from Billy's eyes to the back of his head, and said, "This is bordering on fate. You should tell her about the superhero we created as a kid."

That was a coping mechanism for what you and I went through. And just because she said the word "superhero" doesn't mean anything is fated.

Billy chuckled at Yume's comment. "Yes. Exactly like a superhero origin story."

Yume shrugged. "Nothing that exciting. I don't know who my dad is, and my mother never talks about him. Your first thought might be that she and I struggled, or that his leaving devastated her. Quite the opposite, really. She's a strong woman who has done very well for herself. Back in Japan, we lived an upper-middle class lifestyle. Maybe I used her as inspiration? She found all the answers within herself and encouraged me to solve my own problems."

"You think people should solve their own problems?"

Yume's eyes widened. "I didn't mean to sound callous. Obviously, people need help. We *all* need help from time to time. Tell me – how do most therapists start off an initial meeting with a first-time client?"

"They usually say something like, 'I don't have the answers to your problems, you do.' Or some variation of that."

Yume nodded. "Exactly. And who is most likely to be the biggest hindrance in your life?"

"The person you see in the mirror."

"Also, exactly. I want to help people stop hurting themselves."

"Now," Will said with excitement, his words making the pain in Billy's head worse. "She set up the next question perfectly."

"But what if someone else is hurting them?" Billy asked.

Yume frowned. "Then I'd help them find a way out of the situation, or a way to make the situation stop permanently. I have zero tolerance for abusers, predators, users, or bullies."

"Perfect answer!" Will yelled. "Tell her that was a perfect answer!"

Billy winced. *Communicating like this is quite painful.*

"For me, too," Will said. "But she's kind of amazing."

"Very admirable," Billy said to Yume.

Yume held up her index finger. "But wait, there's more. Helping people become better versions of themselves is the shiny veneer. My true master plan is thus – Once I help my clients reach Maslow level of self-actualization, I will then write my best-selling self-help book, be a guest on every radio talk show, get my own TV show, and launch my own line of high-end pens."

"Pens?"

"Duh! Every shrink needs a good pen."

All three of them shared a laugh.

Billy took a bite from his sandwich and waited for Yume to finish chewing before asking. "Okay, so how does 'Psych 351, The Psychology of Dreams' fit into your plan for world domination?"

"I want to learn more about the bonds between the conscious and the subconscious. I mean, the most restful sleep happens when we dream, when our brains sort through the happenings of our waking day. Without dreams, we'd go insane. Dreams are a biological necessity that somehow links the conscious and the subconscious."

"You view dreams as purely biological?"

"Hey, don't be a dick," Will warned. "This isn't the time. She's one smart cookie, so let's hear her out."

Yume shrugged as she wiped the corners of her mouth with a napkin. "Technically all psychology is biology. If you really wanted to drill down, then all biology is chemistry."

Billy smiled and erased his last words by gently waving his hands. "I apologize if my statement seemed snobbish. I meant to say that most of the world's population view dreams through a more mystical lens."

Yume's eyes went wide, and she sat up straight. "No, no, no. You weren't snobbish at all. My comment sounded dismissive, and again it's my turn to apologize. See, this is why I like to meet with tutors, to hear different viewpoints. How do *you* view dreams? Mystical? Biological? Somewhere in the middle?"

Billy took a breath, pushing past his headache, trying to sound more articulate. "No doubt that dreams are biological, but I'd define the dream scenarios we find ourselves in as mystical because we wake up and wonder why we even had that dream, especially the weird ones, and the scary ones. But my main interest lies in how dreams shaped the world."

Yume's eyes sparkled as if his words had set off fireworks in her soul. She leaned forward. "How dreams shaped the world? Okay, you've elevated my curiosity. Please continue."

Billy also leaned forward, their faces now less than two feet apart. "Every culture has a different viewpoint about dreams. There are villages around the world that believe the dream world is more important than the waking one, that dreams unify the world more than cars, planes, boats, or the internet. The further we travel back through history, the higher the percentage of people seeing instances of oneiromancy."

"Oooooooh, big fancy word! I love those. What's it mean?"

Billy's eagerness to talk fed off her enthusiasm. Even Will had held his tongue. "Oneiromancy is divination based on dreams. I believe the Japanese word for it is *yumeuranai*. I also find it 'mystical' that I'm discussing dreams with a woman whose name means 'dream.'"

Yume's jaw slowly dropped as her smile widened. "Very impressive, sir. Look at you, slinging Japanese at me."

A warmth bloomed within Billy's cheeks. Will piped up and said, "Oh my God, you're blushing!"

Billy shrugged. "Like I said, every culture has different theories and interpretations and superstitions around dreams."

Yume nodded. "I completely understand. Back home, we have the concept of *masayume*. I'm sure you already know this, Dream Master, but it means 'dream that comes true' and according to superstition, your first dream of the year is *masayume*."

"I think that lends itself to my early comment about dreams shaping the world. If we use Japan as an example, I have no doubt that the superstition you just mentioned came from the Jomon Period which, by no coincidence, is the same era that Japan's creation mythology came from."

Yume pushed her food aside to lean even closer. "Okay, we're going to circle back and discuss how you know more about my native country's history than I do, but first I want you to clarify – you're saying that you believe dreams are the reasons for our mythologies?"

"First of all, I only know a tiny portion of your native country's history in regard to *dreams* and I'm sure you know more than I about the *general history* of both Japan and America. Second of all, yes, I am saying that mythologies and religions have derived from dreams."

Yume jutted her jaw and looked to the side, contemplating his words. "I never read the Bible, but I do know there is a lot of communication via dreams."

"Even before that," Billy continued. "Way before."

Yume offered a dubious squint. "I'm still intrigued."

"Primitive humans were scientists. They wanted to understand the world around them to better their quality of life. Lightning strikes a tree and starts a fire. Primitive humans studied the fire, learned how to perpetuate it, harness it, use it for heat and cooking. They studied the patterns of animals they hunted for food to put on the fire. But what they studied was tangible, external. Early humans had zero ways to study dreams or understand them or interrogate them with any kind of rudimentary scientific process. Let's not forget, we dream about what we can conceive, what we know or have seen or have learned. Primitive humans didn't dream about living in mansions or riches. They didn't have nightmares about showing up to a surprise test in class, or about plane crashes. They dreamed about being inside dark clouds throwing lightning bolts, about controlling fire, running and flying with animals. Imagine all the fear and excitement and wonder of doing these amazing things and having no context as to the subconscious."

Yume exhaled slowly through pursed lips. "So, they assumed that something bigger yet similar to them – gods – lived in the clouds, controlled the fire, and dictated what the animals did. Then they believed that these gods communicated with them while they slept. That's pretty deep. I've always thought dreams were cool, but the way you look at them has taken it to a whole new level."

"Okay Billy, you have to ask her," Will said.

She'll think I'm insane. As much pain as I'm in now, I might be.

"Ask her and I'll leave. Promise."

Deal.

"So," Billy started. "What do you know about lucid dreaming?"

"Not much. Just that the person experiencing a lucid dream is aware that they're dreaming. I've never had one, so what can you tell me?"

"Hook, line, and sinker," Will said. "I'm outta your head for the night. Leave a detailed report for me."

Will's departure alleviated Billy's headache and he smiled. "How much time do you have, Yume?"

She planted her elbows on the table and rested her chin on her hands. "I have until my next class tomorrow morning."

Billy's smile grew wider.

CHAPTER 06

Shanna got home a little before 10:00 P.M. with barely a buzz to show for it. The sunny weather earlier in the day primed people to ditch the confines of their home, and they all wound up at the bars. A little too packed for Shanna's tastes. One guy pointed to her and then pointed to his crotch. Effective communication in a room full of thumping music and a cacophony of voices, but she preferred a bit of conversation first. Bored, she decided to call it an early night.

An ache between her eyes started the moment she opened the front door. She walked through the living room and Gus's burgundy armchair was empty. Her mom sat by herself in the kitchen at the small aluminum legged table, smoking a Camel and drinking a can of Budweiser. Shanna asked, "Where's Gus?"

"Pulling a double shift at the warehouse. Too many guys from his second shift crew called off."

All her pain disappeared. Shanna smiled as she opened the refrigerator. "He worked a double yesterday, too, right?" Gus was obviously cheating on her mother. It was hard to pity a woman who willfully put herself in shitty situations.

After a long drag on her cigarette, her mom spoke through a plume of smoke. "He did. Said he's gonna fire a few of them if they keep this shit up."

"Go get 'em, Gus." Hopefully he'd work another double tomorrow, then another, and another until her mother finally got smart and kicked his sorry ass out.

Standing, her mother said, "I'd appreciate it if you started calling him, 'Dad.' He would, too."

"I'd appreciate it if his heart exploded and his eyes popped out of his head," Shanna mumbled into the refrigerator.

"What'd you say?"

Shanna moved the milk, the ketchup, and the six pack of beer – the few items that seemed to be perpetual – to get to her PowerBlaster. The only thing more ridiculous than the obnoxious levels of caffeine found within the twelve-ounce bottle was the comical quantity of whey protein. She closed the door hard enough to rattle the glass containers. "I'm pissed that you're making me say this cliché, but if you really need me to, then what the hell – he's not my dad."

"He provides for you more than your real dad does."

Shanna shrugged and opened her drink. "Doesn't matter."

"It doesn't matter that your dad didn't pay a dime in child support? It doesn't matter that he spent all the money he should have given you on some fucking tramp?"

Shanna's dad left when she turned eighteen. And so, her mother never received a dime of support, and she had been too timid to push for alimony. One hundred percent sincere, Shanna answered, "No, it truly doesn't."

"You just wait. You just wait until the man of your dreams turns into a nightmare!"

As she so often did, Shanna pushed past her mother and headed to her bedroom. She closed her door gently, not wanting to slam it and give her mom the satisfaction of knowing how pissed she was. Enough to grab her favorite hoodie – the soft pink one, cropped to show off her midriff – and give the night another try.

Hand on the doorknob, she stopped herself. No. Good chance she'd wind up hung over tomorrow and she had promised to meet Yume for breakfast. Her bonus sister always made a great shoulder angel, considering Shanna's shoulder devil was the person she saw in the mirror. In a year, Shanna would graduate with a degree in Business Administration. Nothing special, but the general degree allowed her to move anywhere Yume needed to go to further her schooling or career. Hell, she would follow Yume no matter what. More than once, Shanna had fantasized about Yume marring a handsome doctor, having insanely beautiful children, and living in an almost-mansion behind the metaphorical palisades of a gated community. Shanna would live in the closest low-rent neighborhood and ask Yume's insanely beautiful children to call her, "Eccentric Aunt Shanny." *Just another year or so,* Shanna reminded herself. *Just another year of this bullshit.*

Hoodie off and tossed onto the bed, Shanna plopped down at her desk and turned on her laptop. A quick email check and then a few cat videos would calm her down before bed. But one email caught her eye, one with the subject line, "I'm sooooooo sorry!!!!!"

Shanna smirked as she opened the email. It was from her oldest friend, Charles "Chez" Sumpter. An eternal prankster even back in kindergarten when he poured three bottles of glue into a cup and told other students it was milk. Getting caught and punished never deterred him from messing with people for the next decade and a half. Sometimes he went too far, and Shanna felt this was one of those times, especially since his apology email included a link to a porn site.

Getting ready for a show, she crossed her arms and slouched. All too often he'd send her thinly veiled, bizarre metaphorical links. "Playing with adorable kitten" took her to a video of a woman's vagina being fingered. "Test your concentration" displayed a picturesque scene of a babbling creek running through a forest accompanied by soothing music, then a scream blared and a grotesque monster face unexpectedly appeared on the screen, inducing a cheap jump scare. "Splitting headache" equated to a B horror movie clip of a man's head chain-sawed in half.

Shanna prepared herself for something equally tasteless when the video – what she assumed was a cellphone recording – started in a dark bedroom, the camera approaching the bed. The person holding the phone panned down to his right hand stroking his erection.

Shanna rolled her eyes and wondered about Chez's mental stability. Why would he send this to her? Did he really think this was funny? She hoped whoever was "asleep" in the bed would suddenly roll over and punch the phone holder's dick. *That* would be funny! But the sleeping woman – judging by her long, blonde hair and the title of the video as "REAL daughter" – didn't move, even when the man stroked her hair with his curved, furry worm of a dick. Then the man whispered, "Here she is. My slut daughter."

Volume low, the man's voice wasn't clear, but it sounded familiar. Shanna shifted, uncomfortable as the man's rhythmic breathing sped up and his stroking became faster. Shanna gulped hard.

As her gut tightened, Shanna shifted in her chair again and twisted a lock of hair in both hands. She didn't want to watch this but couldn't stop. There had to be a punch line. Finally, the phone holder finished, glob after glob spurting onto the girl's hair. Shanna sneered so hard that her cheeks hurt. He gave his deflated dick a shake and then slowly panned the camera toward the girl's face.

Shanna understood that this was not an anonymous person, even though the camera showed nothing more than blonde hair on the pillow. There hadn't been a face yet, but the joke would be revealed once the man showed that he just masturbated on a mannequin head. Or a cantaloupe with a blonde wig. Or a balloon with the words, "Ha Ha!" written on it. Or a football with a smiley face sticker.

The camera kept panning.

It wasn't a mannequin head.

It wasn't a cantaloupe.

It wasn't a balloon.

It wasn't a football.

It was a person.

Her.

CHAPTER 07

The elevator ding roused Yume from her euphoric stupor. The doors started to close, and she laughed as she hit the "door open" button. She finally gathered her wits enough to exit the elevator. She couldn't believe it was almost 11:00 on a school night and she was just getting back to her apartment. Very unlike her. But her time with Billy had been amazing.

After a loud yawn and a quick shoulder shimmy, she headed down the long hallway toward apartment 506. She couldn't wait to tell Shanna tomorrow at breakfast how her tutor session turned into a date. Was it a date? They had lunch and then went to dinner when the café finally closed. They opted for a sleepy diner that the locals frequented, and the college kids eschewed. As long as their food order was enough to justify their reason for being there, then the diner staff didn't care about two college kids discussing everything from the socio-economic conditions of Asian countries to the latest movie released last week to the newest internet cat videos to favorite restaurants to dreams, dreams, dreams. The night ended with her leaning down to deliver a kiss. No tongue, but her lips lingered on his long enough to be considered a solid date kiss.

Key hovering in front of her door's lock, she replayed clips of their conversations about dreams, especially lucid dreaming. Fascinating. Billy's knowledge was unfathomable. She felt like she had just met a member from the new band she'd heard for the first time, and they were immediately her favorite.

Tired enough to fall asleep as soon as her head hit her pillow, she hoped that when morning came, she'd remember her dreams. Unlocking the two deadbolts, she pushed the door open only to have it stop short – she smacked her face against the door. Rubbing her nose, she stared at the gold braided chain strung from door to wall. Sloan, her roommate, had latched the chain.

"Sloan." She knocked on the door, the chain rattling. "Sloan! It's me."

Nothing.

Yume didn't want to yell any louder, so she sent a text, knocked again, and sent a second text. Right as she was ready to tap the icon to call Sloan, the chain fell away, and the door flung open.

A couple inches taller than Yume, Sloan was a statue carved from anger. Tight, straight posture. Clenched fists. Scowl with more angular lines than a girl so new to age twenty should have. Even her mussed brown hair seemed irritated. "Jesus Christ, do you know what time it is?" The oversized rainbow Care Bear tee shirt and baggy pajama shorts kept Yume from taking her too seriously.

"A little after eleven," Yume said, sliding past her miserable roommate and toward her bedroom. "Which is too early for you to be this upset at me for waking you up, which I wouldn't have had to do if you hadn't chained the door."

"You're usually home before now. Some of us take our college career very seriously. I wanted to go to bed, and my schedule doesn't revolve around your social life. You should have texted me if you knew you were coming home late."

"I did."

"Well, I didn't get it." The statement came out with the speed of someone expecting to say those words.

"Sure, Sloan. Good night, Sloan." Yume entered her bedroom to the sound of Sloan's door slamming. Not that she really cared – she wasn't going to let her anyone else's anger ruin her giddiness.

She basked in the awesomeness of her date as she dressed in her night clothes.

Yume padded down the hall to the bathroom. She brushed her hair and pulled it back. Elasticity long gone in her black hairband, it was now perfect for holding her hair at bedtime; she didn't want it too tight while sleeping. Constant, dull ponytail pain might give her nightmares and after learning more about lucid dreaming, she certainly didn't want those.

The last step of her nighttime ritual was to dampen a half dozen sheets of toilet paper and wipe the sink clean, removing a few stray hairs. It was easier than arguing with Sloan again. An only child of a real estate salesman and a lawyer, Sloan was the sole focal point for her parents' unattainable high standards. Yume couldn't help but feel bad anytime she overheard Sloan justify a 3.90 to her parents over the phone, but that didn't justify her borderline antagonistic "sink-ruler" argument. Yume did her fair share of cleaning, but not enough according to Sloan when she proclaimed through clenched teeth that she "always" cleaned Yume's hair out of the bathroom sink. Since Sloan also had straight, brown hair, Yume deemed the specificity of the accusation preposterous. Sloan found a ruler to measure a random sampling of hair she pulled from the drain to prove her point – Yume's flowed past her shoulders, while Sloan's stopped at the base of her neck.

Yume tossed the toilet tissue and stray hairs into the trash. She turned off the bathroom light, its click perfectly timed with a knock on the apartment door. Loud and rapid, with a desperation behind it. She hurried through the darkened living room and when she reached the door the person on the other side knocked again. She almost jumped out of her skin. Through the peephole she saw Shanna. Crying.

"Shanna? Are you okay?" Yume asked as she hurried through the three locks to open the door.

"No," Shanna replied with a sniffle. "I'm really not."

"Oh my God, come in. What happened?"

"It's Gus. He… That piece of shit. He… God, I wish he was dead. I just… I don't…" Shanna rambled.

Yume grabbed Shanna's hand and pulled her into the apartment. Sometimes when Shanna sought attention, she dragged out the story before getting to her point. But Shanna wasn't stammering to add drama; something happened and if it involved Gus, it wasn't going to be good. Expecting the worst, Yume said, "You're safe now. I'm here and you're safe."

Shanna's whole body straightened with every inhale, slouched when she exhaled. Tears rolled over her cheeks as she tried again. "He… He… Oh, God, he's disgusting."

This was bad. Very bad. Yume rubbed Shanna's back between her shoulders and guided her to the couch.

"Jesus Christ," came from Sloan's bedroom. Door open, she leaned against the jamb with her arms crossed. "Can you be any louder?"

"C'mon, Sloan. Can't you see what's going on?" Yume snapped.

"Yeah, I can see the drama queen doing what she does best. Just keep it down. I have a big day tomorrow." Sloan punctuated her statement with a slam of her door.

Yume huffed. Turning her attention back to Shanna, she continued to rub her back. "Don't listen to her. When you're ready, we can talk."

Shanna's body quaked with one last inhale. "No, I'm sorry. I'm ready now. Sorry for being so disruptive. But I can talk now."

"Okay. I'm listening."

"A friend of mine... Chez... You know Chez, right?"

"I do." Yume found him enjoyable in small doses.

"Yeah. Yeah, I knew you did. He emailed a link to a video and... and it took me to a porn site. I thought it was gonna be a prank of some sort. You know how he likes to kid around and stuff, right?" Yume truly hated his pranks, but she nodded to encourage Shanna to continue. "So, I got ready for a stupid porn video or maybe some kind of horror video because I was expecting porn, but..." Shanna exhaled, a shaky stream of breath over pursed lips. "It was of *me*."

"What?" Yume kept her tone even, calm. She thought of murderous ways to deal with Chez, but she didn't want to usurp the narrative. Instead of sharing any of her vengeful thoughts, she asked, "Of you... having sex?"

"No. Worse. I was sleeping and... and Gus... It was Gus filming me sleeping and then... and then... And then he jerked off in my hair."

Shanna's words put Yume's guts in a blender, and she had to fight to keep her dinner down. This was beyond disgusting. It was criminal. She wanted to let her anger out and plot plans for revenge, but would that help in this moment? If Shanna were a patient rather than a family member, what would she do, what would she say? "Then what happened?"

"I went to my mom and... And I showed her the video."

"What did she do?"

Tears started again, streaming faster than before, drops of anguish flowing from her chin. "She didn't believe it was Gus. She accused me of being a pervert and that it was one of my 'many perverted boy-friends' and that I hated Gus for no reason and that it was me and one of my many boyfriends trying to frame Gus for being a pervert and… and… and…"

Yume heard enough. She widened her arms and let Shanna fall into her. As Shanna wept, Yume held her tightly. "You're safe now. You're safe here. You're staying here tonight."

"What about Sloan?" Shanna asked between sobs.

"Fuck Sloan."

Shanna's body went limp, her crying slowed as Yume stroked her hair. Shanna had been an important part of her life for half a decade now. Without her acting as a sister, Yume wouldn't be poised to grad-uate next year and begin living her dream. She wasn't going to fail Shanna now.

Gus was going to pay.

CHAPTER 08

Picasso walked into The Dragon's Blessing Chinese restaurant. He always liked this place, despite the furtive glances the wait staff gave him. Many of the area Chinese places shifted their business models to permanent buffet style. Picasso didn't like that, didn't like the din of banal conversation happening all over the place all the time from the customers constantly in and out of their seats, wandering around every available space in the restaurant. Dipping their grimy hands in and out of the food pans, ignoring the sneeze guards. The décor of those places was always tacky or boring, monochrome walls with framed paintings that were probably purchased at a flea market. He never liked the gold or white or black beckoning cat perpetually waving its paw next to the register. He liked the elegance of a more traditional, sit-down restaurant where meals were meant to be savored, not shoveled down one's gullet in the shortest amount of time possible. The Dragon's Blessing was elegant.

Booths and chairs were upholstered in a shade of rich red, the softness of the cushioning apparent at first glance. Beautiful murals on the walls of rolling green hills, a golden sunrise and sky full of white birds, flowing blue streams, with the eponymous dragon watching over. And no plastic cat on the counter.

A sharply dressed woman greeted Picasso with a forced smile, unable to hide the look of distaste in her eyes. But he was a customer, and she treated him as such, escorting him to a table while informing him of the daily specials. After pouring him a glass of water, she left to fetch a server.

Picasso ordered General Tso's chicken. Nothing beat the tang of a plump pepperoncini, but he enjoyed the heat mixed with a nice sweetness in their General Tso's sauce. Didn't matter if anyone from the kitchen spat in his food, the sauce was delicious enough to hide any kind of goober. The night's atmosphere held a certain familiarity, as if he had recently ordered this dish. But it'd been a couple months since he last ate there.

Fifteen minutes from seating to service. Not too bad. It gave Picasso plenty of time to watch the restaurant happenings.

He counted twenty patrons in the place, ranging from families enjoying a cooking reprieve to couples enjoying each other's company. Picasso had no interest in any of them, just the owner of the flashy red bicycle chained to the rack by the dumpster in the alley – the only bus boy on duty tonight. He was good. Fast. Quiet. Normally, he would have gone unnoticed. Not tonight.

The couple dining at the table next to Picasso left, and the bus boy swooped in with an empty bin, ready to fill it with dirty dishes. Perfect, as if Picasso knew he'd be coming. Before the kid started wiping the table, Picasso said, "Hey. Come here."

The young man looked around, then said something in Chinese to Picasso.

Picasso chuckled. "Look, I know you speak English. Your buddy Yanni from the pawn shop told me."

Eyes widening, the bus boy stepped closer to Picasso's table. "Yeah?"

"You know who I am?" Picasso asked, using the napkin to dab the corners of his mouth. The cloth felt familiar.

The young man nodded curtly.

"Good," Picasso said. "That your bike in the alleyway?"

Head cocked and frowning, the bus boy took a step back. That was enough of a confirmation for Picasso. "Don't worry," Picasso said. "I don't care that Yanni gave you the bike. I care about why. He says there's a girl here who is special."

Upper lip twitching, the young man looked around to other staff in the restaurant. None of them paid him any attention.

"Hey," Picasso said, then snapped his fingers to get the bus boy's attention. "Look, I'm not here to start anything, as long as you do a favor for me. You tell that special girl to pay me a visit tonight. That's all. Nothing crazy like she did with Yanni. Just pop in, say, 'hi,' and pull a rabbit out of a hat or whatever. That's all I'm asking. Can you do that? Or do I have to tell one of your family members that you've been shooting your mouth off about her?"

The young man relaxed a bit, but he still looked ready to jump through the front window at any moment. He gave a simple nod and hurried away through the kitchen doors.

Picasso took his time finishing dinner. Not only did he want to savor it, but he wanted to give the bus boy's family members plenty of time to peek at him through the doors, and maybe stop by his table should they want to discuss his request. None of them did. Odd, but not too unusual. He assumed that meant they were going to ignore his request and make phone calls to his rivals for assistance. That was even if the girl was real. Picasso didn't care, but Yanni would. What he didn't expect was for a little girl to exit the kitchen and make her way to his table.

"Hello. You wanted to meet me?"

Picasso was expecting a teenager, not a child. A wisp of a thing, at that, arms and legs so thin her floral dress looked like a white cotton bag with flowers on it. Her skin just as golden as the restaurant's employees, her straight hair just as black, her expression just as earnest. No little girl should look this serious, like she was a participant in a business meeting. Caught off guard, Picasso muttered, "Umm... Yeah."

Hands folded in a relaxed manner in front of her, she said, "Here I am."

Picasso straightened his posture and wiped his fingers clean. For some reason he felt as if he was meeting with a high ranking, important individual. He wanted to make a good impression, yet felt like a fool when he asked, "So, what's your name?"

"They call me Maya. You can call me that."

Picasso grunted. "That was my daughter's name. How old are you, Maya?"

"How old do you think I am?"

"You look like you're eight."

"Then I'm eight." Her voice was tiny and soft, but she wielded it with more control than any eight-year-old, her answers far more formed. In fact, her words punched Picasso right in the gut when she finished with, "The same age as your daughter when she died."

Had he seen the statement coming, he would have been angry. Instead, he was pained. "How did you —?"

"I know everything that you know about yourself. Tell me about her."

Picasso frowned, his anger starting to assert itself. "If you know, then why do you need me to tell you?"

"I want to hear your thoughts when you tell me about her."

"Butterflies." The word rushed from his mouth like a prisoner breaking free from a cell. "She liked butterflies. She drew them all the time, went through entire boxes of crayons drawing and coloring. Except the black crayons. She never liked that color, said it was too dark and not pretty enough."

The slightest twitch of Maya's lips seemed to indicate a smile. "That's nice. How did she and your wife die?"

Picasso's frown deepened. This girl was rude, no matter if there was an unfathomable depth behind her dark eyes, no matter how cute her butterfly print dress.

Wait, weren't flowers on her dress a second ago?

"There's a butterfly house just outside the city. My wife and I took here at least twice a month during Spring and Summer. One day, I couldn't make it. On the way there... There was an accident."

"Accident. That's what you tell others, but they were gunned down by a rival gang. You feel very little on a daily basis, usually anger and apathy, but the guilt for not being with them that day eclipsis all else."

Like the flame on a candle, his anger burned until there was nothing but a thin layer of hot wax coating his insides. He looked around to see if he was being observed. Employees stared at him, hardly reacting, completely unmoving. None of the customers moved either. Everyone else in the restaurant remained frozen in time. Picasso understood now – she was demonstrating her power.

Less flustered, he turned back to her. "So, they let you use your abilities?"

"They demand that I do. That is why they took me from my home."

"Where is your home?"

"A small island between Philippines and Indonesia. I wish to go back, but they won't let me. They make me do things for them. They want me to kill you."

Picasso balanced between mirth and fear at the threat coming from a frail figure. Yet her matter-of-fact tone triggered something primal deep inside. "You've killed for them before?"

Everyone in the restaurant exploded.

The families. The dates. The staff. Popped water balloons filled with guts and bone.

Picasso ducked in his seat and buried his face in the crux of his arms, but none of the gore touched him or Maya. He peeked from the protection of his arms and his breath hitched at the horror. Rivulets of blood flowed around him as if over a glass dome. A set of ribs tumbled to the floor. A pair of lungs slid along slowly, leaving a streak through the crimson film.

"Jesus Christ," Picasso whispered. "You killed them. You killed them *all*."

"No," Maya replied. "They weren't real. *You* are real."

He didn't know what she meant, but he knew he was alive only because she deemed it so. If he got out of this unharmed, there would be a few extra Benjamins in the church collection basket this Sunday. An eyeball rolled along the dome, the dangling nerves flopping like streamers.

"If you can do this, then why do you stay with them?"

"I can only kill one person at a time. I need help to go home. If I went with you and helped you, would you help me get home?"

Only kill one person at a time? Picasso couldn't stop staring at the blood of more than twenty people flowing around him on the other side of an invisible fishbowl. He didn't understand her perceived limitations, but he understood power. It was meant to be used. She had it and offered to use it for him. "You'll help me if I help you get home?"

Picasso finally looked back to the little girl, completely at ease with sheets of blood flowing around her. "Why me?"

51

Through a thin veil of desperation, the look upon her serious face implied, "The enemy of my enemy." However, she answered, "You'd have done anything for Maya, your daughter. I remind you of her."

A pinch stung him behind his eyes, a pain he hadn't felt since the funeral. "I will help you, Maya. Shall we go now?"

"This isn't real, remember? Mr. Chen is away on business and will return in two nights. Come for me then. Through the kitchen are stairs to the apartments above the restaurant. Mr. Chen usually falls asleep by 9:00. He will die one hour after that, when the restaurant closes. Be here for me. If you're not here and they find out what I have done, they will kill me and probably kill you."

Two nights? Picasso held out his hand. "Why wait? Let's go now."

"Remember what I said."

Picasso reached for her, but she burst into dozens of different colored butterflies, their paper-thin flapping wings tickling his fingers.

Picasso jolted awake, panting as if he had run a hundred miles. He brought his hands to his head, gliding them over his sweaty face. It was a dream. It was real. It was both. And she wanted him to rescue her!

He jumped from his bed and tore off his soaked tee shirt. Moving too fast, he stumbled for the lights and ran to his closet. Rescue Maya. Get her out of there. He had to get there at 10:00. He had to get... New shirt in hand, he looked at his clock. 2:52 A.M.

Picasso dropped to the floor and leaned against the wall, still panting. Soreness tugged at his joints. He closed his eyes and focused on controlling his breathing, relieved it was only a dream. Relieved that he had forty-three hours to prepare.

CHAPTER 09

Yume pushed the food around on her plate. A slight awkward-ness touched her sense of presence; Billy had finished his dinner a while ago and she hadn't even hit the halfway mark. Then she felt bad. She wasn't being the best date at the moment.

The second date started well, her meeting him for a casual dinner at Ruby Apple Fridays against her better judgment. She didn't like leaving Shanna alone, but she had been upbeat all day long and insisted that Yume go out and have fun. It was difficult trying to relax while thinking about what happened to Shanna two nights ago. All the tingles were in all the right places when she had first seen Billy this evening, and she was excited to share the good news from the afternoon – she had talked to her mother, and they set up dates for her to visit.

The conversation moved on from there, Billy doing most of the heavy lifting. Yume appreciated his efforts, and he certainly was great company, but thoughts of Shanna kept creeping into her head, punctuated by the disgusting and inhuman things she wanted to do to Gus. The bastard deserved to go to prison for what he did to Shanna. Maybe even worse.

"Is… Is everything okay?" Billy asked. "You seemed very excited when you first got here, happy that your mom is coming to visit, but you… kind of faded away. It's making me wonder if my deodorant's potency has diminished."

Yume chuckled. "As far as I can tell, your deodorant game is on point. It's… It's just something happened a couple days ago that's been bugging me."

"I'm no psychology major, but I've heard talking about it would help."

"No, no, no. I don't want to bog down our date with my problems. Bog it down any more than I have. Starting now, I'm alert and attentive."

Billy smiled and shook his head. "You don't need to soldier on for my sake. Look, Yume, I am absolutely enjoying your company, but I do want to get to know you as a person, and people have problems. No matter how heavy or weird it may be, you can tell me and it won't scare me away. In fact, I'm not going anywhere unless you tell me to."

Yume smiled. "That's sweet of you, but..." *Why not? He's been patient, and he's right. I need to talk to someone and if this relationship goes anywhere, he's going to end up being that someone.* "...You know what? Okay. Here we go. It's about Shanna."

"Your sort of sister?"

"Correct. Okay, short version. Her piece of shit stepfather publicly posted a video of himself jerking off in her hair while she was asleep."

Billy's eyes widened and his skin paled. "Oh my God, that's disgusting. How is she?"

"Upset, but she's handling it well. Better than I am, actually. Anytime someone tells her about the video, she plays it real cool and says she's seen it, but it's not her. Says the girl in the video kind of looks like her, but it's not her. If they don't drop it, then she jumps all over them about being a deviant for watching a video about a creepy dad who cums on his sleeping daughter. I think... I think she's said it's not *her* so many times that she actually believes it."

"Everyone has coping mechanisms to deal with trauma. Some as extreme as creating another personality."

"I don't think she's gone that far to cope. But she feels like she has no recourse, and unfortunately, I agree with her. She can't go to the police, because she has no real evidence, and her own mother doesn't believe her."

"Her own mother? That's awful."

"It is. Unfortunately, it's not surprising. Her mother is not an individual I would describe as a strong independent woman. It burns me up that Shanna can't get justice."

With a level of theatrics Yume never expected, Billy took a drink, used his napkin to dab the corners of his mouth, and then folded it before setting it back on the table. He took a breath as if preparing his thoughts for an uncomfortable conversation. "I can give her the justice he deserves."

Yume frowned. Billy's humor was varied, but this didn't sound like a joke. There was an earnestness in his voice that concerned her. "So, you and your redneck buddies are gonna grab a six pack, jump in a pickup, and head over to beat on Gus?"

"No, nothing so draconian."

"I have certainly fantasized about lopping off his balls, but that daydream stays in my head."

"This would stay in his head, too."

"What are you talking about?" Yume asked, and Billy said the exact same words she did at the exact same time.

"What the hell are you doing?" Again, Billy mimicked her, perfectly in time.

Reeling back in her seat, she held up her index finger. "Billy." She paused to make sure he wasn't talking at the same time. "I don't know how you're doing that, but you're being really weird."

"We've had this conversation before."

"There is no way we've had this conversation," Yume started, but heard Billy saying the same. "And what the hell is happening?"

"We're in a dream. Your dream."

Yume had been on plenty of dud dates, but she usually figured that out within the first hour. Up until now, Billy displayed all the qualities she was looking for in a guy. Then he dropped this bombshell. Obviously, he was into the topic of dreams, but apparently, he was obsessed enough to blur the line between reality and fantasy. "Jesus, Billy. I mean—"

"How else could I know what you say before you say it?"

"That doesn't prove anything other than you can accurately predict..."

Damn it! He did it again. Frustrated from hearing his words piggyback off hers, she blurted out, "Banana pudding, cumquat, rodeo clown, Declaration of Independence, electroencephalogram!"

Billy had said the same.

Yume slouched down and rubbed her eyes. "This can't be happening."

"It already happened. You felt better after you told me about Shanna, then we had a great conversation. We ended the night with a nice kiss."

"Why don't I remember any of that?"

"You will when you wake up."

"Why am I dreaming this?"

"You started to dream about the date and then I jumped in and took over. I need to explain to you – show you – what I can do. Fifth time's the charm. The first time, you threw water on me and stormed out, but each subsequent meeting has gotten a little better. This has been the best one so far."

"So, the previous four times, something went wrong and then you restarted at the beginning of the date?"

"Yes."

"Why? Why start it at the beginning?"

"Because it's a natural starting point. It's less jarring than starting in the middle of our entrees. I apologize if this makes me sound like a troglodyte from last century, but you're a beautiful woman. The way the light struck you when you first entered the restaurant created something magical. It's not something I will soon forget. Plus, more importantly, I enjoy talking to you. Repeating the same hour-long conversation is a joy."

Yume closed her eyes and took in a deep breath. At least she thought she did. The world went dark, but not pitch black like it would in a room without lights. She felt the air flow into her nostrils as her lungs expanded. She heard the ambient noises of the restaurant – conversations, the soft music, silverware clacking against plates. This felt real. But so could dreams.

She opened her eyes, and everything was as she expected. "Okay, that's… kind of a creepy chocolate coating around a sweet, creamy center, but I appreciate the sentiment. If this is a dream, I should be able to do amazing and fantastical things like turn the walls and tables into butterflies. I'm trying right now. I'm thinking and concentrating about the walls falling away into thousands of butterflies, yet nothing is happening."

"You're trying to sprint the Boston marathon before learning to crawl. It takes practice. Hell, you need to believe you're in a dream before doing something like that."

"But you can?"

"Yes."

Yume crossed her arms over her chest and leaned back in her chair. "I'm pretty sure you're smart enough to know what I'm going to demand next."

Billy nervously ran his hand through his hair and glanced away. "I tried that in meetings number three and four. It didn't turn out so well."

Yume squinted. "What exactly did you show me in meetings number three and four?"

Billy shifted in his seat. "In meeting number three, I did what you were trying to do. The walls turned to butterflies. Then you freaked out. For meeting number four, I made the walls fade away and showed you we were in Japan. Then you freaked out. Again."

"How about you stop making the fucking walls melt away and show me something a little less grandiose?"

Billy nodded and offered a faint smile. "You are absolutely right. Okay. Start small. Ahh... You mentioned butterflies, so I'll start with this."

He held out a fist over the center of the table and then unfurled his fingers. Resting on his palm was the rare, great purple emperor, the national butterfly of Japan. With a black abdomen and black-rimmed purple wings speckled with white spots, it fluttered from his hand to Yume. She extended her hand and the butterfly landed on her open palm. After a few seconds, it flew away and out the restaurant's door with a group of customers. "Ooooohkaaaaay. That was... was interesting. But logically, that could have been an elaborate magic trick. I think I need to see something more substantial."

Billy looked around the restaurant and then back at her. "Okay. Please try not to freak out."

Yume didn't know what to expect. She had been muting the date, too focused on Shanna. Then the impossible happened. Everything in the restaurant stopped. Petrified in time, the wait-staff had halted in

57

mid step. Patrons froze within their conversations. No one breathed or blinked. A man at a neighboring table dropped his food from his fork right before it made it into his mouth, and now it hovered in the air.

This was no magic trick, no sleight of hand. There were no wires or mirrors or misdirection. This had to be a dream. What Billy had been saying was true. "Make it stop. Or start. Or whatever, just make things go back to normal."

Activity returned to the restaurant. Blissfully unaware, all the other people went back to whatever they were doing with a smile, except for the man at the neighboring table, frowning at the new stain on his shirt.

"What the fuck, Billy?" Yume snapped. "Is this some kind of grooming process?"

Eyes wide, Billy held out his hands as if they would protect him against Yume's words. "No, no, no, nothing like that. I want you to make your own decisions. I wanted to make sure you had the necessary information before you came to any conclusions. I just needed you to believe that this is possible."

"I believe I'm dreaming. I don't believe that you, Billy, are actually in my dream, doing weird dream things. Maybe I'm dreaming this because you and I have been talking about lucid dreams so much lately in the real world that this is my mind's way of sorting through all the information. And if you, Billy, are somehow in my dream and controlling it, then I'm demanding that you stop and let me wake up."

"That is a very reasonable request. To let you know that this is real and what I've been saying is true, I'll prove it to you. I promise that Gus will get retribution."

"Retribution? You still haven't explained—?"

Yume sat straight up in her bed, shaking. Her sweaty night shirt clung to her body. It had been a dream. Only a dream. After taking a few moments to catch her breath, she then flopped back onto her pillow. *I need to monitor my spicy food intake before bed from now on.*

CHAPTER 10

Shanna slid the key into her house's front door lock as quietly as she could. She had sworn to herself that she wouldn't step inside if there was any chance that Gus might be home. No, it wasn't her house anymore; her piece of shit stepfather made damn sure of that.

The door usually creaked when opened, but over the years she had learned to circumvent that by pulling up on the knob while opening or closing it. She slipped into the dark living room without so much as a squeak, just like old times.

Tiptoeing toward the hallway, she hated to admit that this house never felt like home. Home had been a two-story cookie cutter house in the suburbs. More than just that – what was inside the home. Family. Comfort. Memories. Not this doublewide, two-bedroom dump. Three years ago, her mother took "home" away. More specifically, let it disappear.

Shanna was worldly enough to know that it took two to tango. The divorce was equally Dad's fault and Mom's, and he wasn't winning any father-of-the-year awards for how infrequently he communicated with Shanna. When a boulder rolls down a hill and crushes someone, a lot of different forces are at play – gravity, momentum, mass, and the dumbass at the bottom of the hill who didn't move out of the way. And it was Shanna's mother who pushed it.

Shanna's mother had to have seen the signs, had to have known that her husband was drifting away, yet she did nothing. Nothing; inaction the worst form of action. Any decision on her part would have been better than no decision. She did nothing to keep him from "working late" in the office. Nothing to save her marriage, nor Shanna's home.

Three years in this place hadn't been long enough to build any fond memories. The walls were painted with arguments, the floors shellacked with tears, the rooms trimmed with insults.

She opened her white, hallow bedroom door.

She blinked, momentarily confused by walking into an empty room with plain gray walls. Empty except for one thing.

Gus.

Tied to a chair.

"Shanna? What the hell is going on? How did I get here?"

The anger in his tone increased with every word. Shanna knew he was going to be yelling within a sentence or two.

"You did this somehow. Slipped something in my beer. This is bullshit, Shanna! Untie me! Untie me now!"

Shanna had nothing to do with his current situation, but she liked watching him squirm, helpless and angry. The thought of stomping her foot onto his crotch crossed her mind, but that wouldn't hurt him the same way he had hurt her. His physical pain could not compare to her emotional anguish, her betrayal.

"Get me out of here, you bitch!" Gus screamed, face reddening. "Get me out of h—"

The clunking noise of gears engaging cut him off as the back of the room lifted like a garage door, rolling into the ceiling to expose a wall of glass. Featureless dark figures milled about behind the glass, murmuring indistinct words.

"What the fuck, Shanna? What the fuck?"

Gus finally sounded afraid.

Then another door opened in the room, and a naked man walked through, stroking himself. Smiling longingly at Gus.

Then another. Taller, broader than the first. He leered at Gus.

And another man, this one fat and sweaty. He stared at Gus's crotch and licked his greasy lips.

Man after man entered the room, at least a dozen, circling Gus.

The crowd behind the glass cheered. So did Shanna.

The men closed in on Gus. As he pleaded and shouted at them, kicking and twisting, Shanna stepped out of the room and slowly shut the door. She didn't need to see what was about to happen. The gurgling noises of his mouth being filled satisfied her enough.

Shanna woke up and immediately looked to her digital clock on the nightstand. It was a little after 8:00 A.M. She sighed, then smiled, remembering her dream, a wonderful dream.

She wanted to share it with her sister, but Yume had already left for class.

After a quick shower, Shanna grabbed a premade breakfast cup. Add one egg, stir, microwave. As she ate the overly salted potatoes and egg combination, she replayed her dream with tremendous glee. She rarely remembered her dreams, and even when she did, they were fragmented. This one… This one played in glorious three-dimensional Technicolor and Dolby surround sound. She remembered it from start to finish, every movement from the members of the crowd to the stink of Gus' sweaty fear.

The replay ended when this morning's nightmare, Sloan, stomped into the kitchenette.

"Oh, you're still here," Yume's roommate snipped.

"Yeah, sorry. The breakfast bowl is Yume's and I used one egg. After my classes today, I'll run to the store to replenish. In fact, I'll even stock the freezer with the boxed meals you like. As a thank you for letting me crash here."

Sloan shut the cabinet door with authority. "It's not like I have a choice. This is Shanna's world, we're all just living in it."

Shanna frowned and dug deep to remind herself that she was legitimately intruding on Sloan's space. "Sorry you feel that way. I don't mean to be an interloper, but I have no other place to go."

"You do. You're a townie who lives with her mom, yet you choose to run to Yume every time you have a problem. If you're so anxious to get out of your mom's house, then why haven't you and Yume found a place together?"

"I can't afford it yet. And I ran to Yume because… She told you why I'm here, right?"

"Yes. I feel bad that it happened and I'm just as disgusted as everyone else, but I'm not surprised."

Shanna wanted to punch her, but that would only make the situation worse, jeopardizing not only her future, but Yume's. She couldn't do that to Yume. "Wow! Way to blame the victim."

Sloan opened the refrigerator and started to root around. "As a woman, I have the same fears as all other women. I know there are women who have been assaulted while wearing sweatshirts and no makeup. I know there are women who have been assaulted on a first date after they've spent months talking to a guy online before meeting him. I know women have been targeted even though they go out of their way to bring no attention to themselves. *You* aren't those women." Sloan took a strawberry yogurt from the refrigerator, closed the door, and sauntered back to her room without even so much as glance toward Shanna.

Stomach twisted in knots, Shanna tossed the rest of her breakfast in the trash. The phrase, "You aren't those women," repeated in her head. She finished getting ready with the alacrity of being whipped by Sloan's words. The faster she got out the door, the faster she could make them stop.

Shanna had been accused of being a cock tease more often than she could count. Men blamed her for arousing them on purpose without following through with her inferred promise. She hated that. Wearing a short skirt or showing cleavage didn't imply anything, and there was literally no way to satisfy "an inferred promise" to every guy who saw her. *Fuck that logic, and fuck Sloan for saying it was my fault that Gus was a degusting piece of shit!*

But Sloan was right about one thing – Shanna ran to Yume every time there was a problem.

If she got a job, she could easily afford to split a shitty apartment with Yume. Obviously, a job would cut into Shanna's partying, but it was time to reprioritize, time to grow up. Time to take more control of her life.

Taking control meant dealing with fears and anxiety. Taking control meant not running from her problems. She was going to limit her time at her mother's house, but she couldn't let Gus's perversion control her life. She'd lock and barricade her bedroom door, maybe set up a simple trap. Keep her pepper spray under her pillow and her window unlocked for a quick escape. Maybe just start with a night or two per week. Take control and count this small intent as a triumph.

Other than a defiant act to take her life back, she needed to go home to get her art history book. It was still before 9:00, so Gus should be at work and her mother should still be asleep. Easy in and out. Easy first step to life reclamation.

Life was never that easy, though.

Like in her dream, she slid the key into the front door lock as quietly as possible. She even pulled up on the doorknob as she opened it, her heartbeat asserting itself throughout her body.

Gus was in the living room. Naked.

The adrenaline must have been pumping, because Shanna had her pepper-spray out of her purse and primed within half a heartbeat before she realized Gus was on the floor. His back and head were on the ground, but so were his toes and knees, his body folded in half. Blood-shot and glistening, his eyeballs bulged outside of his head. His testicles were still attached to his body yet rested on his nose.

Shanna screamed.

CHAPTER 11

Apricot blossom sweetness filtered through the gardens and Shinko breathed it in. Sitting on the bench with her feet drawn under, ankles crossed, she waited for her boss Fumiko. The sun warmed her back, the garden peaceful, the people wandering its paths limited in number.

So why did she feel tense? Ordinarily, her assignments came without her boss acting as a middleman.

When she was about five years old, during a visit to a garden, she had turned for only a moment and got separated from her mother. But her mother had found her, brother Kamu in tow, Shinko seated just like this, ankles crossed, trying so hard to be fearless and adult. Choosing to find a bench, her decision to stay in place and wait until she was found was the first responsible move she'd made on her own.

The memory was of an event over four decades ago; time to focus on the here and now.

With that, Shinko pulled her feet out from under the bench and planted them firmly in front of her, hands resting on her knees. What was she thinking, sitting in a position like that? She'd allowed her memories of the past to distract her. At least Fumiko hadn't caught her sitting in a way that prevented her from taking quick action. Jaw tightening, she pushed her shoulders back, smoothed her blouse, and tightened the silk sash at her waist, working to regain her composure.

When she raised her head, she caught sight of Fumiko strolling around a bend in the path. The candy floss pink of her wig accented with two ornate amber hair-sticks was in opposition to the formal black power suit. The constant change in wig and style made Fumiko deliberately hard to identify, but Shinko knew that gait anywhere.

A young woman walked alongside her boss. Shinko jerked back. Yume? *How had Yume gotten here?* After a second look, she realized that the young woman was a stranger. The resemblance to Yume faded with proximity, the young woman too poised. Why was Fumiko bringing an unknown to their meeting?

Shinko stood and considered the girl as she approached. Her walk possessed a graceful balance and her calves were toned under that short student-length skirt. She kept her shoulders carefully in line. Obviously, someone had spent time with her. It then occurred to Shinko, the purpose of this meeting – she was to receive an apprentice.

Fumiko raised her hand in greeting, deftly playing the part of an ordinary woman catching the attention of another in a public garden, and Shinko caught the way her boss watched her for any betraying emotion or reaction. Shinko's mind raced a step forward. How could she do her job effectively and spare the time to train another? Or was Shinigami's Helper taking her off active duty? Certainly, she was older than several their operatives, but she was still one of the best.

When close enough, all three bowed, and Shinko contemplated her actions. Should she accept this apprentice? Gritting her teeth, she closed her eyes, completed the bow and rose, only opening her eyes when she stood balanced once more. It was a subtle symbol of trust, submitting her will to Fumiko. Shinko gestured for Fumiko to sit on the bench, another non-verbal test since there was only room for two women.

After settling, Fumiko nodded toward the young woman. "This is Aika. Your new apprentice."

Aika, having spent the last few seconds studying the sand of the path, looked up at the mention of her name and gave Shinko a small smile.

"She came to us as nobody," Fumiko continued. "Now, she is somebody. She is a Helper. There is a possibility she could become exceptionally valuable."

Perhaps it was that memory of the garden from Shinko's past, perhaps it was her still not accepting the possibility of her new role, but she decided to test this new recruit before offering acceptance.

Shinko made a sudden flex of motion that had Aika dropping back before giving herself room to move. But Shinko wasn't attacking – this was a far too public a place. Instead, she pulled at her sash, unraveling it. Then with a brief consideration of the wind, she held her arm straight up and let it go, satisfied that the black silk floated on the small breeze over the pond. It snagged on the tallest reed at the center of the water feature. "Would you please retrieve that for me?" she asked Aika.

The young girl looked back and forth, considering her request. When she appeared to be steeling herself for a wade through what had to be ice-cold water, Shinko interrupted her. "This is a formal garden. It is disrespectful to damage or disrupt the peace here. Please bring my sash by means of least disruption." With that she returned to her seat beside Fumiko. Shinko was surprised to see her boss suppressing a smile.

Fumiko grasped the arm of the bench and pulled herself to her feet. "The sun and the blossoms are pleasing, but perhaps we should walk as we give Aika time to reflect on her task?"

Shinko took the hint and joined her boss. Together the two women walked the path circling the pond. Dead leaves crunched underfoot and gave off a spicy scent of rot.

"How far do you want me to take her training?" Shinko asked.

"That one," Fumiko stopped and looked back. "She has a destiny. You will give her every skill you can impart." Fumiko grasped Shinko's shoulder to capture her full attention. "I can see that you are aware Aika has skills, but she lacks your focus and familiarity, your balance necessary to move onward. She has potential, like any piece of steel. I need you to forge her into a weapon."

Shinko looked over her shoulder at Aika. The girl made her way around the pond, her black hair flicking back and forth in the breeze as she studied her target from various angles.

Fumiko pulled an apricot branch closer to inhale the blossoms. "I know you wish to visit your daughter in Philadelphia in two weeks? Perfect timing. While there, you will have a mission and Aika will join you. We understand that a low-level Chinese crime lord is trying to improve his status by seeking out a new weapon. An unusual weapon. While we do not know its nature, it's definitely causing concerns." Fumiko released the branch, and it snapped back into place.

Shinko risked another glance back at Aika. The girl had chosen her spot. Now she reached behind her back and pulled something out from behind her skirt's waistband. A blade glittered in the sunlight. She turned the blade over in her hands while Shinko watched. "Two weeks is not enough time to prepare her for the field. Is she ready for something like this?"

Fumiko's dark eyes looked Shinko up and down. "I am pleased that you are accepting responsibility for your student already. But time is of the essence. I don't trust anyone else with this. Besides, she's not going to slow you down. In fact, she might actually be quite helpful." With that she pointed towards Aika who stepped into motion while they watched.

Aika's throw was fluid and well-aimed, but it had not gone as planned. True, the blade flew cleanly through the stem of the reed and Aika had judged the wind correctly, freeing the sash from its entanglement. The silk lofted into the air and the young woman ran towards it as it drifted over the pond. The knife, however, struck another reed and spun away at an angle. It dropped into the pond instead of landing on the shore. As the ripples of its passing widened, Aika caught the sash from the air at the edge of the pond.

Fumiko and Shinko's eyes met, both acknowledging Aika's split second of hesitation before her throw. "Perhaps too attached to that knife," Fumiko said as she crossed her arms.

"She will need to commit fully," responded Shinko. "If there had been no hesitation, she'd have the sash *and* the knife." After a moment, she continued. "I will give her credit for completing her objective. She has also accepted the loss." Shinko found herself already making plans about what to work on with Aika since they would be in the field within a short time.

Fumiko stared at Shinko. "You will do well with her now that you have gotten past your own hesitation."

There were many tests that afternoon, Shinko realized. Fortunately, no one had failed.

CHAPTER 12

Yume's eyes stung. It had been a long time since she had been exposed to this intensity of cigarette smoke, but Millie had every right to chain smoke while sitting at her kitchen table. Shanna sat next to her mother, smoking as well.

I'd kill for some eye drops. Though the words were a private thought, Yume felt disrespectful, considering that Millie had just lost her husband and Shanna had lost a stepfather.

Slouched back in her chair, Millie stared at a wall a few shades darker than its original color after years of ambient grease. Her hair a cartoonish mess, she cocked her hand near her face as if bringing the cigarette to her mouth, but paused in the moment, the length of ash a prehensile appendage. Yume had no idea what Millie was thinking. Probably a hundred questions starting with "why, when, how?"

As if reading from a script, Millie mumbled to her daughter, "Sorry you had to find him... like that."

"Me, too. Sorry he's gone," Shanna mumbled back, her tone just as lifeless. Yume had a much better idea of what Shanna was thinking about.

Millie finally brought her cigarette to her lips, the long ash falling to her lap, and took a drag. As she exhaled, she stood and tossed the butt into the ashtray on the lopsided kitchen table. "Gotta shit."

The floor gave up soft groans until the bathroom door shut with an audible click.

Yume placed her elbows on the table and asked, "How you doing, Sis?"

It had been seven hours since Shanna had called Yume in a panic, nearly incomprehensible. The only words she made out were, "Gus, dead, house, naked." Shanna mumbled a few other phrases, but made no sense. Yume said she was coming right over, but Shanna said the police were on the way, so she'd call her after they left. Yume gutted out her next two classes – normally fun but turned torturous as she waited for her sister to call. Four hours later, she got the call and went right to Millie's house. The body removed, the ambulance and police gone. Just two women with blank looks on their tear-streaked faces.

Now, staring at the wall, Shanna said, "I'm a fucking terrible human being."

The burgeoning psychiatrist within Yume wanted to ask, "What do you mean by that statement?" Yume tamped down that instinct. She was here as a sister, and already knew what Shanna meant. "No, you're not."

Shanna took a hard drag from her cigarette, the tip a blinding orange, and then a deep pull from her beer. "I am. I really fucking am, Yume."

"It's perfectly natural to feel—"

"To feel sad? Angry? Confused? I don't. That's what I'm trying to say – I don't. I actually... I actually feel relieved. Almost... almost glad."

Yume leaned forward and put her hand on Shanna's. Waiting until Shanna made eye contact before she spoke, Yume said, "And I'm telling you that's okay."

Shanna sniffled and wiped away a new round of tears. "That's a fucking weird thing for a shrink to say."

"You're not my patient, Shanna. You're my sister. What Gus did to you is inexcusable and unforgiveable. He deserved..." Yume paused and looked over her shoulder to make sure Millie hadn't stumbled her way back into earshot. It also gave her an opportunity to soften her tone as she turned back to face Shanna. "What I'm saying is, I have the same feelings you do. I feel relief for you and your mom. I'm... I hate to say it, Shanna, but I'm glad two people I love don't have to live in discomfort. In fear. Under someone else's control."

The smoke plume stuttered from the corner of Shanna's mouth, her breath hitching as if she fought back the urge to sob. Two streams of tears flowed over her cheeks, though, and she made no effort to wipe them away. "Jesus, Yume, I don't *want* to feel this way. It isn't *right*. I should be sad. My stepfather died. I found his dead body. I *want* to be freaked out. I *want* to be as upset as my mom, but... but...

fuck, Yume, for the life of me I can't. If anything, I feel really, really guilty for feeling relieved."

"There is nothing inhuman about that. I swear on my life, Shanna, you have every right to feel those things. I can't stress enough that you're not alone with these feelings. I feel them, too. Okay? Do you hear me?"

Lips quivering, Shanna struggled for a smile as she squeezed Yume's hand. "I hear you, Sis. I hear you. You're the best humanity has to offer, and I hear you."

"Good." After a pause long enough for Shanna's breathing to return to normal, Yume said, "When you called, you said you found his body."

Regret punched Yume in the chest when Shanna's skin turned pale.

Eyes widening, Shanna all but whispered, "It was so fucking weird, Yume. Disgusting, and just... just fucking weird. I mean, he was a freak. We knew firsthand he was a deviant, but... no fucking clue he was into doing... that... to himself. I don't know... I don't think I'll ever get that image out of my fucking head, the way he folded over on himself..."

"Wait. What you said on the phone was true? I wasn't sure what you were saying; it didn't make any sense."

"It's true. How I found him. But... I don't know..." Shanna paused, confusion on her face. "This is gonna sound crazy, Yume, I'm sorry for sounding crazy, but I almost think this is my fault."

"Shanna, there is nothing—"

Ashes flying everywhere, Shanna waved her hand at Yume to stop talking. "No, not what I mean... I don't know what I mean. But, Yume, I had a dream last night."

A chill moved through Yume, as if she walked through a cemetery and the tombstones started whispering to her. "A... dream? You had a dream that you found him... dead...?"

"No. Not dead. But tied to a chair and... I dreamt that I came home to find him tied to a chair in front of an audience of people and then these naked guys came into the room with their dicks ready to go.

You don't need to be a shrink to interpret it, but… It makes me sound crazy, Yume."

"I promise you, Shanna, you do not sound crazy." Yume thought *she* was going crazy, her own dream from last night replaying in her mind, the memory vivid and in color. Billy's words crystal clear, telling her that he was in her dream. That he controlled her dream. And that Gus would pay. "What else happened?"

"That was it. That was all that happened. I didn't want to see what the guys did to Gus, so I closed the door and heard gagging. The part that is freaking me the fuck out, the more I think about it? Gus sounded like… Gus. I mean, it felt like more than a dream, like he was really right in front of me. The way he said his words, the way he moved, the way his right eye closed a little bit when he gets really angry. I can't imagine dreaming that level of detail, Yume. I can't."

So wrapped up in Shanna's story, both women jumped from the ringtone of Millie's phone. Shanna fumbled with it and answered, on speaker. "Millie Chesterfield's phone."

"Umm… Millie Chesterfield, please." Yume overheard the caller. A man, soft spoken, nervous.

"She's unavailable," Shanna continued. "This is her daughter, Shanna."

"Umm… My name is Doctor Phillip Walderhaus. I'm the coroner and I need to—"

"I'm here!" Millie yelled as she hustled through the living room to the kitchen. Sitting down at the table, she repeated, "I'm here. This is Millie Chesterfield, I'm here, go ahead."

"Ma'am, this is regarding the death of your husband. I would recommend taking me off speaker phone."

Millie frowned. "Nonsense. My daughter has every right to know about the death of her stepfather."

"Ma'am, the circumstances of his death are rather peculiar—"

"She's the one who found him, so she knows the peculiarity of the circumstances."

"Okay, for procedural purposes, I have your permission to discuss the details I found regarding the death of your husband with your daughter present."

"Yes!" Millie and Shanna yelled.

"Okay. Okay. Umm… First, I need to say that it isn't often I examine a body so soon after death, but there were no other bodies in the queue and the circumstances were curious."

"So, you stated already," Shanna said.

"Okay. I did. You're right. I read over the statements you gave the police, but I must ask the following question again – Did you hear anything out of the ordinary last night?"

Millie blinked rapidly and reeled back. "No. Nothing."

"Did you take any form of medication that would put you in a deeper sleep than usual?"

Now Millie frowned. "No. And before you ask, I didn't get drunk and pass out or get high or do any other kinds of drugs last night."

"How about your husband? Was he taking any medications he normally hadn't taken before? Or mixing medications? Or… recreational drugs?"

"He drank a lot, but that's it."

"Was… Was he a practitioner of yoga or other forms of exercise designed to improve flexibility?"

Shanna laughed. "Gus would describe any man who does yoga as a homosexual. Why are you asking these questions? What are you getting at?"

"Umm… Okay, whenever a man comes into the hospital for an accident involving auto fellatio, it's for severely strained back muscles. The worst cases being pain and difficulty walking."

"You get a lot of cases for accidental… what you just said?"

"We're close to Temple University ma'am. You'd be surprised by what we see and how often. But these are usually healthy, young men. Gus was… umm…?"

"Old with a beer gut."

"That is one way of putting it, yes. The way he was found, with his… penis… *entirely* in his throat… Well, it's impossible. Even if he were cooperative, it would still take hundreds of pounds of outside force, more if he were resistant. There are absolutely no signs of struggle. So…"

"This wasn't an accident?" Millie asked.

"I don't know what this was," Dr. Walderhaus continued. "I've sent blood samples to the lab, and I'll know more soon."

Yume's phone buzzed in her back pocket. As Millie and the coroner wrapped up, Yume checked her phone. A text from Billy: `Let me know when you're ready to talk. I'll explain everything.`

CHAPTER 13

Billy centered the candle on his coffee table and lit it. Was this a time for a candle? Maybe not, so he blew it out. In this stage of his relationship with Yume, a candle meant romance, and he doubted she'd be in any mood for romance.

Now the situation seemed too sterile, like the setting for a business meeting. He lit the candle again.

"Oh, for God's sake, Billy, don't overthink it," Will said.

Pain tingled and stabbed through his head as if someone dragged a jagged chunk of metal across his brain. *Ow! Fuck! Will! What are you doing?*

"Helping you, obviously. Ditch the candle. Wait... Why do we even have a candle?"

Thumbs rubbing small circles over his temples, Billy replied, *We have candles because we never know when one could come in handy. Like now. It might add a sense of comfort, make the situation less business-like.*

"Candles are romantic, Billy, and she's not coming over for that. This is an apartment, not a board room. She won't view it as a business meeting. No candle."

Billy pinched the flame. He wheeled to the kitchen, tossed the taper in the junk drawer, and reached for the refrigerator's handle, but stopped. *We have a bottle of wine chilling. Leave it or pull it out?*

"I think wine is neutral enough. As long as it's a screw cap and not something stupid expensive, then I don't think it'll send the wrong message."

Billy grabbed the Josh Chardonnay and two oversized white wine glasses, then wheeled back into the living room. *Thank you, but you can leave my brain now. I'll write up a report letting you know how it went. If she stays with us or dumps us.*

"No way. It's my brain, too, so grab some aspirin because I'm staying."

Why put us both through this pain? How are you able to do this?

"Because... because I really like her, too. Just in case she leaves us..."

I understand. Billy wheeled to the bathroom to get the aspirin. After he downed a few tablets, he went back to the living to pour the wine. *But we need ground rules. No yelling!*

"Sure. Yep. Got it. No yelling."

After tonight, don't do this again. It's... unsettling.

"Okay, but *only* if you tell her about us."

There are more important things to discuss with her.

"Dude, you and I both like her more than any of our exes. I want to be upfront with her. The conversations became quite awkward when we waited a month or two after revealing our plan, remember?"

Billy remembered. He also remembered what always happened next – the betrayals. The accusations of taking their plan too far. The breakups.

"Yeah, the breakups are the worst."

It's frustrating – the downward spiral always starts the same way. The women see something horrible in the news and then think it was either you or I who did it.

"Yep. Nila was the latest. Was she the third?"

Fourth.

"Wow. That's... What are the odds that our last four girlfriends saw the same phantom correlations?"

Now that you mention it, it does seem odd, doesn't it?

"What if... What if there's someone else? Someone like us, but more brutal? 'There can only be one person of power' is too Christian of a mindset for us to dismiss the possibility."

I always assumed that we caused too much psychological stress on our exes, leading paranoia and delusions, causing them to accuse us of crimes we didn't commit. But you might be right. Tonight, no matter what happens with Yume, we'll start exploring the general dreamscape.

"Sounds like a pl—" A knock at the door cut Will off. "She's here!"

No yelling!

"It's open," Billy called out. He locked his wheelchair and used his arms to relocate himself to the couch, then exhaled his nervousness.

Yume opened the door and peeked in. After a quick glance around the apartment, she entered and shut the door behind her.

Billy's apartment was set in a simple layout; the television against the same wall as the main door with a coffee table between it and the couch, a loveseat against the one wall, and a kitchenette on the other side. Behind the couch were two doors, one for the bathroom, the other for the bedroom.

Never once taking her eyes off Billy, Yume opted to sit on the loveseat. She embodied both predator and prey, her movements tight and cautious as if ready to flee, yet a glint of anger shined in her eyes. Or perhaps it was a hunger for more information. "So..."

"Would you like a glass of wine?" Billy asked, gesturing to the half-filled glasses on the coffee table.

"No." The word was accompanied by a frown, but after a beat, her expression softened slightly. "Sorry. No, thank you. I think I want you to explain your text first."

"Okay, understandable. What happened to Gus...? That was me."

The soft expression disappeared as she leaned forward to rest her elbows on her knees. The look in her eyes told Billy she wasn't going anywhere until his answers satisfied her questions. "I need you to elaborate on that statement, please."

Billy cleared his throat, actually intimidated by her pointedness. Will chuckled and said, "Don't forget, her direct nature is one of the reasons we like her."

Billy said to Yume, "After you and I finished our shared dream, I went into Gus' dream and brought Shanna along. It only took seconds for me to assess what she wanted to happen to Gus, so I made it happen. The theatrics took place in his dream while the results took place in the real world."

Almost snarling, Yume said, "Yeah, your explanation is the start of a few more conversations, the first about you saying you and I shared a dream last night."

"We did. Well, I entered your dream and manipulated it."

"Do you know how fucking insane that sounds, Billy?"

"Yes. But it's just as insane to think that we can watch entire movies via radio waves on a plastic rectangle carried in our back pockets, or that we transport ourselves from here to there while sitting in metal boxes on wheels powered by the remains of dead dinosaurs, or that structures the size of a small cities float along the ocean, or that humanity set foot upon the surface of the moon."

"Those examples are culminations of smaller steps leading to a bigger journey. One person didn't just say, 'Hey, I'm going to invent the cell phone.' It evolved over the decades of other technological improvements that, themselves, evolved from *other* technological improvements. I mean, do you have some sort of contraption you hook into at night? Some kind of dream machine?"

"No."

"Okay, then. It's like someone who's really into jogging thinking they can do a one-minute mile."

"But if you witnessed that jogger run a one-minute mile, then how can you deny the possibility?"

Yume frowned and exhaled through her nose, working her jaw muscles as she leaned back. She crossed her arms over her chest and looked away. Retaining the frown, she turned back to Billy. "What did I dream about last night?"

"Our date from earlier in the evening. We had to repeat the process five times before you accepted what was happening."

"How did I react?"

Billy chuckled and brought his fist to his mouth to stifle it. "Not well, to say the least."

Yume looked away again, this time crossing her legs, her foot tapping. Her expression softened. "How is it even possible?"

"I honestly don't know how I am *capable* of doing it, but the *how* is brainwaves."

"Bullshit."

"Not so. I enter people's dreams by syncing my brainwaves with theirs. Our brains register and interpret different wavelengths. Our eyes register light waves and the color spectrum. Our ears pick up and funnel audio waves into our brains. Brainwaves are the same concept – they're physical, they can be seen, heard, processed."

"I've taken sixth grade science, so no need to mansplain. I meant, how it is possible for brainwaves to travel the two miles we live apart? They're not strong enough."

"They can be. People exercise to become stronger, faster, gain more endurance. No, the brain isn't a muscle – it's an organ, but it's not static – it can change and grow and needs to be exercised. Use it or lose it, just like a muscle, to stave off cognitive degradation. Think about how strong and fast and durable a professional athlete is, and how much more intense their training is compared to the average individual's trip to the gym."

Yume frowned again. "So, one day you said to yourself, 'I want to jump into people's dreams,' and then trained yourself to do so?"

Billy shifted in his seat, unsure how to continue.

Will said to Billy, "You have to tell her about us. The conversation is headed there."

She's really angry right now, Billy replied.

"But she believes you. Okay, I'm eighty percent sure she believes you. She's just trying to wrap her mind around the 'how' of the situation. I'm willing to wager she'll be sympathetic. Loser does dishes for a week."

You're not helping!

"Ummm, sort of?" Billy answered Yume's question. "I don't know exactly how I started getting into other people's dreams, but I practiced… exercising to be stronger with it. Be more efficient, extend my reach."

Yume squinted. "You don't know how you started? How is that possible?"

Billy's sphincter tightened.

Will said, "Damn, she can be scary."

Shhh! Billy snapped at Will, causing pain to spike behind his eyes.

Will said, "Okay, now you have to tell her."

No. Not yet.

"Tell her! C'mon, buddy, you gotta tell her now!"

No yelling!

Billy cleared his throat and stiffened his posture. "There is one more thing I need to tell you about myself. It's... It's really big. A huge part of me that I have... I have a hard time talking about."

"I'm listening," she said, her tone dubious.

"I... I have multiple personalities. Well, one other personality. His name is Will."

Yume reeled back as if to avoid being splashed by water. "Are you messing with me right now?" She chuckled as if Billy might chuckle along, but stopped when he answered emphatically.

"No. I'm serious."

Yume's jaw muscles worked as her frown faded. "Are you... are you being... treated... for that?"

"No, not at all, because there's nothing to treat. We get along, have a great relationship. A two-member team."

Will shouted, "Fuck yeah we are!"

Billy winced, and continued. "He can be brasher than I."

"Easy there, buddy," Will warned.

"And I'm more intelligent."

"Dick!"

"But he is stronger than I am. Braver."

Will sighed. "Love you, too, Billy."

"An amicable split personality," Yume mumbled to herself as she ran her hands through her hair. Her eyes darted from side to side as if she were reading an article about the condition. She then gasped and sat forward. "Usually when someone develops multiple personalities it's to deal with unspeakable trauma. Did...? Oh, God, Billy. Did... something... happen?"

Billy fought back tears, his voice quivering. "Yes."

Yume's anger, skepticism, and apprehension melted away, her face a visage of sympathy, as she moved from the loveseat to the couch next to Billy. She took his hand in hers. "I'm so sorry, Billy. I apologize for pushing and pushing and making you feel bad about... everything. You don't have to say any more. We'll enjoy that bottle of wine and talk about something else."

Will shouted, "Ha! Told you! And so now you gotta do dishes for a week!"

Shut up! Billy replied.

Billy squeezed Yume's hand. "You did nothing wrong. I present-ed a rather fantastical fact about myself and I'm sure I could have done it in a better fashion. I want to continue because this is important. The reason I don't know how I first got into people's dreams is be-cause Will – my other self – is the one who created me."

Yume looked surprised, but didn't let go of Billy's hand, didn't move from away from him. "Oh! Well, that's... *He* created *you*?"

"Yes. I won't share details about what he had to endure, but it wasn't a one-time event. He had a bad childhood. At first, he tried es-capism. Reading comic books and playing video games to pull his mind away from reality. He even created his own superhero, named Bigby. But none of that helped. One day, I woke up and realized I could travel into people's dreams."

As if enraptured by a compelling campfire story, Yume leaned closer. "Then what happened? How did you help?"

"I taught Will how to do what I could do. This sounds like an irra-tional conundrum, and even though I can't remember my first time – like learning how to walk – I taught Will how to enter people's dreams. He made the people who were hurting us stop."

Yume exhaled and looked away but didn't let go of Billy's hand. "Like what you did to Gus, I assume?"

"Yes. Like what I would like us to do."

Yume's eyes widened with surprise. "What? Us? Us do what?"

"Us do to others the same thing I did to Gus."

Yume released Billy's hand. She jumped from the couch and paced in a tight circular path. As if talking to someone else she said, "That... that... That's not going to happen. I'm still not one hundred percent sold on your ability to enter other people's dreams... Yes, I witnessed it, but... It's mind-boggling, and then to suggest you want me to help you *kill* people using this ability... God, I don't even know where to begin with how wrong that is."

"Let's start with Gus. Let's examine him and decide if I did any-thing wrong."

"What?" Yume stopped pacing and whipped around so fast that she needed both hands to brush the hair off her face. "Yes, it's wrong. If what you're saying is true, then you *murdered* Gus."

"Or executed justice. Tell me something, Yume, and please be honest. Are you mad that Gus is dead?"

"I'm..." Yume stopped herself, closed her eyes, and took a deep breath. When she reopened them, she calmly replied, "Of course I'm not mad. But it wasn't up to you to decide if he lives or dies."

"No? Then who? The law? The authorities have limitations, and that's even if they're involved in the first place. You expressed your frustration that Shanna couldn't go to the police. Like you said, even if she did, then the investigation would be brief because they wouldn't be able to prove it was Gus in the video. Again, be honest, didn't you want Gus to pay for what he did to Shanna?"

"Yes, obviously. But not murder. This is *murder*, Billy."

"By definition, murder is unjustified. I didn't pick a random person and decide to end their life. Gus was a blight on this world. He was quite literally torturing your sister and her mother. When was he going to stop? And if sexual assault isn't enough to get him arrested, then what is? What would he have to do to Shanna or her mother, how badly would he have to *hurt* someone to garner that kind of attention? Unless you think he had potential for redemption. Do you believe a good person waited inside Gus for the right helping hand to come along?"

Yume flopped down on the loveseat, shoulders sagging as if defeated, admitting a factoid she didn't want to believe. She wiped away tears, but more followed. "So. What do you want me to do? Want me to kill people in their dreams? Do we kill all the criminals on the planet?"

"No. Nothing like that. I believe in the justice system, but it's not infallible. When police investigate a crime, they're only looking at what they can submit as evidence. They interview, but they presume everyone they talk to is an unreliable narrator. I'm sure you've learned in your classes and have seen plenty of studies involving memory. It's faulty, and police often piece together a puzzle using faulty data. They investigate tip-offs before a crime is committed if the info is reliable, but how many times does that happen when the perpetrator is a cunning monster? They lie to the police, they manipulate evidence. They discredit those who speak out. I'm not talking about criminals, Yume. I'm talking about monsters."

A tremor started in Yume's hands. She wiped away more tears and then folded her fingers together to stop the shaking.

Billy didn't need to enter her dreams to know how his words weighed her down, how she wrestled with indecision. She could reject his offer and walk out of his apartment or ask for more time. One of the things he liked about her was how fast her mind worked, how effectively she processed information, so he shouldn't have been surprised when she said, "You're right. You're right about the psychology of abusers. They're not... They are *not* people. Gus would have continued to abuse Shanna and Millie. Even after Shanna left, he'd abuse her *through* his abuse of Millie. And there are so many, many more monsters like Gus."

"Monsters that we can stop."

Leg jack-hammering the floor, Yume shook her head. "This is the Trolly Problem. A real-life Trolly Problem."

Will asked, "What's she talking about? Did we break her mind already?"

Shhh! Billy replied. *No, we didn't.*

"What's a trolly problem?" Billy asked Yume.

"A hypothetical ethical question designed to create conjecture. A trolly car is running out of control. You notice it's going to hit and kill five people, but you're standing next to a switch that can make it change tracks where it will hit and kill only one person. What do you do? The question is designed to examine fundamental pillars of ethics. It's easy to say that you'll flip the switch until you realize you're assuming responsibility for someone's death. If you do nothing and let things play out, five people will die, but you're not the one killing them. You can alter variables to question other fundamentals. For altruism – would you flip the switch if the person who dies is someone you know, just to save the lives of five strangers? For societal hierarchy – would you flip the switch if the person who dies is a young mother of three and the five in the trolly path are convicted criminals?

I tried to view the question in its purest form – one life or five. It's so easy to say one, but now I'm standing at the switch."

Billy nodded. "I've always heard, 'It's easy to say you'll run into the burning building to save people until you feel the heat of the fire.'"

Yume frowned, her lips pursed. Staring at the center of the coffee table, she cracked her knuckles one finger at a time. Time slipped by interminably, and she finally broke her reverie with a long sigh and relaxed. She looked Billy in the eyes and said, "So… Oh, God, I can't believe I'm saying this… So, what do we do next?"

CHAPTER 14

Picasso walked along the beach, wet sand squishing around his feet.

A little girl's giggles – his daughter.

She skipped and splashed beside him. He was dreaming. Same one he had before, a vivid memory from the summer before she died. They were at the point where the beach tamed the roaring waves to watery splashes no stronger than ones made in an overfilled bathtub. Any disruptions in the sand were immediately washed away. They walked along for half a mile, the precious melody of his daughter's laughter ringing in his ears.

He loved this dream.

But this time it skipped onto a different track.

"Daddy? Are you okay?" his daughter asked. "You look super tired."

Unusual, but he went along with it. "I am."

"Why?"

"Daddy has a lot going on, and he hasn't slept for a long time."

"Is it because of the other little girl named Maya?"

Picasso stopped walking. This dream wasn't like the others *at all*. "How do you know that?"

"Because she's all you've thought about."

"I've been thinking about her because I... I need to rescue her."

"I know. And they know why you're here."

Picasso's heart revved like the Ferrari he had in his garage. "What are you talking about?"

His daughter's hearty facial features tightened. Her belly and chubby arms rippled and thinned. His daughter was gone, a faded image. The frail girl he needed to rescue with the earnest eyes stood before Picasso and said, "You need to wake up!"

Picasso awoke with a jolt, a small twitch accompanied by the embarrassment of falling asleep in public. He straightened himself in his chair, trying to act nonchalant, and then glanced around the dining room of The Dragon's Blessing to see if anyone was staring at him. No staring, but plenty of quick glances.

Coming here as a customer was a mistake. Like many mistakes people made, he knew it was a mistake as he was doing it. The restaurant closed at 9:00, the time he told Anthony and Sal to meet him with a crew. Them and ten guys would have made short work of this place. But Picasso was tired – ambling corpse-level tired from forgoing sleep and stewing over data to plan this hit – and hadn't been thinking straight.

He had showed up across the street at 8:00. He paced, reviewed his plan, fretted. After half an hour, it hit him – he'd never have their General Tso's chicken again. He should have put that stupid thought out of his mind, but the rational part of his brain fell asleep at the wheel.

Hey, they'd have no reason to suspect an upcoming hit, so he crossed the street and went inside. Crooked thinking, he knew, but fatigue blocked him from straight thinking. He sat. He ordered. As he waited, he must have fallen asleep. But he was awake now, and very aware that the restaurant employees were discretely ushering out the last few remaining patrons.

Five employees fluttered around the dining room. Three he'd seen before, one being the kid he talked to last time he was here. Stupid! Of course, the kid told Mr. Chen what was going on! The two he didn't recognize wore loose fitting clothes and moved like two tigers among house cats. Something odd about their backs, like they were smuggling baseball bats under their baggy sweatshirts.

There was a sixth – a man in a suit, probably a bodyguard for Mr. Chen. If so, he undoubtedly packed heat, and was number one trouble.

Picasso instinctively patted the nice chunk of metal with a thirteen round clip tucked inside his jacket's inner pocket.

The last two customers were a white couple, bitching about being asked to leave early. The man in the suit and one of the waiters escorted them to the door, all smiles, intermingling Chinese with rapid fire apologies in English.

Door latched shut behind them with a click, and the blinds were drawn with a swoosh.

Damn it. Shit is about to get real and I didn't even get my dinner.

The man in the suit whipped around, reaching inside his jacket. Picasso was ready.

Too old for the game he played, he was still a quick draw, and more importantly, an accurate shot. Pushing his chair over with his left foot, he drew his weapon and fired one round into the bodyguard's chest. Of course, Picasso felt his age as his right shoulder slammed into the floor.

Get up! The adrenaline helped him move faster, but getting to his knees winded him. The three waiters kept their distance, obviously not bringing the right tools to a gun fight. But the other two... They moved like lightning.

Both men ripped off their sweatshirts, revealing what they were poorly trying to hide. Swords. Thin with a long, wrapped handle, they looked exceptionally sharp. Picasso knew nothing about swords, just the general concept of slice and stab. Weapons raised, the two men swooped in.

"Jesus!" Picasso yelled, throwing himself backward. Bad luck, he thought as pain shot through his back, but ultimately realized he had backed into the corner of a table. He flipped it toward them – no purpose behind the move, just a flailing reflex born from panic. No force behind his kick, launching it at his attackers. It made enough of a commotion for them to hesitate and pull up. From his back, he fired three more times, but hit nothing. He hated to be sloppy.

A few muscles he forgot existed in his abdominal area pulled away from each other as he sat up. He needed help from the nearby booth to get to his feet, shooting two more times to distract his assailants as he did so. On his feet, gun in hand, he assessed the situation. The three waiters had ducked behind booths, poking their heads out far enough to see what was happening. The other two men still clutched their swords with both hands, ready to swing. This would have been their chance to take cover, but instead they moved away from each other to opposite sides of the restaurant with the grace of trained dancers.

Picasso didn't like the looks of things from where he stood. "Look, let's all calm down and no one gets hurt. All I want—"

The man on the left rushed forward. Picasso targeted him, and the man hopped to the right. Just as suddenly, the man on the right rushed forward. Picasso wasted no time and fired but missed when the man hopped to the left. The man on the left started running again, and this time Picasso shot and hit his bicep. But the bullet didn't drop him. Then the man on the right rushed at Picasso.

Picasso moved along the row of booths, backing toward the flimsy kitchen doors. Two more trigger pulls. *How the fuck do I keep missing them? Are they fucking ninjas?* As one of the men brought his sword down, Picasso burst through the kitchen doors and flung them shut as the blade slid through the gap between them.

Picasso reared back, slamming into the metal prep counter. By now, both sword bearers had kicked open the doors. Picasso spun out of the way of a sword, and it clanged against hanging pots and pans, creating an orchestra of metallic chaos. He rapidly squeezed off three more rounds – *So fucking loud in this cramped space!* – then several impotent clicks. Silence fell along with one dead swordsman.

The second swordsman wasted zero time mourning his fallen comrade and leapt into a ballerina split over his partner's body. In need of a move that his opponent wouldn't expect, instinct took over for Picasso. He lunged toward his attacker and grabbed his wrists.

Half a foot taller and a hundred pounds heavier, Picasso used his size advantage to squeeze and twist. He smashed the swordsman's hands against the wall. It took two whacks for him to drop the sword.

But larger meant slower, and susceptible to being outmaneuvered. The ninja slipped free and moved at speeds Picasso couldn't fathom, taking fingertip jabs at his ribs. The pain! He'd been hit by baseball bats a few times and a crowbar once, but preferred those to the hell this ninja inflicted upon him.

Arms up to protect his face, Picasso swung and missed by a mile. More jabs to the ribs and Picasso reached and grabbed for his assailant, but missed each time, instead smacking his hands into skinned ducks and utensils and hanging pans. Half of what he hit clattered to the counter and floor. He couldn't get ahold of this fucker.

He raised his fists and charged.

The ninja ran backwards faster than most people could run forward.

Even when the ninja stopped running, Picasso couldn't grab him. Foot on the wall, foot on the counter, foot on the wall, and suddenly he stood behind Picasso. *No! Never let your enemy behind you!* Picasso spun as fast as he could and was met with a foot to his knee. A nasty pop he'd heard before from others came from *his* leg, and he dropped to the ground amid an explosion of pain. He wanted to puke, the agony crashing through his entire body in waves. No. No puking. No stopping. *Fuck this guy!*

Fighting, pushing through the agony, Picasso lurched forward when the ninja attacked. Catching him by surprise, Picasso grabbed ahold of the ninja's pant leg – he wasn't letting go this time – and gave his leg a yank.

The ninja fell to the ground, but landed like a clumsy cat, retaliating with a rapid series of kicks with his free foot to Picasso's face. Blood sprayed from Picasso's mouth with every exhale, but he didn't let go. He stood, and then came down with all his weight on the ninja's knee. Payback came in the sound of snapping sticks wrapped in wet cardboard.

The ninja still squirmed, fighting even when Picasso wrapped his fingers around the man's neck. Finger jabs and pokes to Picasso's face and ears. A jab to the temple made him dizzy. This had to stop.

The thought of Maya energized him. Picasso grabbed the counter for leverage and stood on his good leg. He roared as he lifted the ninja off his feet and slammed him down on the counter beside the hanging ducks. A meat cleaver hung close enough for Picasso to grab.

The first swing was to the forehead. The blade didn't cut deep, but enough to slow this guy down. As soon as the ninja's hand flopped onto the counter, Picasso took it off at the wrist. Then at the elbow. Washed in warm blood, Picasso cleaved off the other hand. He ended the struggle by plunging the cleaver back in the bastard's forehead, sinking it all the way.

Picasso staggered backwards against the wall, sliding in the thick blood. He clawed at his chest as if it would help with his breathing. If only he could slide down the wall to the floor and rest. No! *Maya needs me.* The sword on the counter glinted in the light. Just what he needed, and he didn't need to bend over to pick it up.

He had to climb the stairs to rescue Maya. Picasso was in no shape to take on whoever might be waiting for him at the top of the stairs. Then he remembered the three waiters. Maybe they ran off. Maybe it'd only be a matter of time before they got brave enough to investigate.

Hurry. Got to hurry.

Stumbling to the stairs wasn't the challenge as he thought it'd be, but taking each step up brought a blast of nausea inducing pain. It'd have been easier to climb Mt. Everest. His ribs burned, every inhale started a fire, every exhale fanned the flames. That was nothing compared to his right knee. Using the sword as a cane, he put just enough weight on his right leg for balance. He doubted he could bend his knee if he tried, and the broken glass scraping inside his skin discouraged him from trying. He'd need surgery, he was sure of it. Last step. *Come on, old man, come on.*

Once he reached the small landing, he leaned against the wall to catch his breath. He sounded like a worn-out engine – the pistons chugging along with parts that still worked, but the valves coughed and sputtered. He should wait for Anthony and Sal and the others. They could handle whatever lay on the other side of the closed door. They could handle Mr. Chen's other bodyguards if there were any.

No.

Maya was his to rescue. Her life was his responsibility. He had to save her and bring her back home. And no way Mr. Chen slept through all that racket.

Sweat and blood smeared the wall where Picasso rested his head. Inhale. Exhale. He pushed himself off and put his weight on his left leg, then a little on his right. It almost gave out and it hurt like a mother, but he didn't fall. He needed the sword. Never used one before this night, but he'd swung a baseball bat plenty of times. Same concept, right?

He opened the door and entered the apartment wielding the sword with both hands.

The room looked like any other apartment. No lights except for the ambient city light seeping in. Couch, armchair, coffee table, bookcase, television. A white beckoning cat, a bronze feng shui gong, and a multicolored gemstone tree sat in compartments on a Chinese rosewood flower-shaped shelf. A silk landscape painting with the ubiquitous waterfall. A framed Buddha canvas. Typical displays he'd seen in common restaurants. He imagined something more opulent but remembered that Mr. Chen and his family were merely grunts for a larger organization. Picasso made a mental note to check with his accountant to see if he was paying his own underlings a living wage.

As quietly as possible, he limped through the room, ready to swing the sword at more ninjas or anyone else who might jump out of nowhere.

An opened door stood at the other end of the living room, probably the bedroom. Mr. Chen had to be there. Maya had to be there. God, Picasso wished he could breathe quieter, his raspy breaths like a dull handsaw gnawing through a log. Nothing he could do about it, so he kept shuffling forward.

Once he got to the door, he paused. There was no plan, never had been, and he felt stupid. As much noise as he was making, there was no formulated element of surprise. In his mind's eye, he saw Mr. Chen holding Maya with a gun pressed to her head. *Might as well be a man and get this over with.* He entered the room.

And dropped the sword.

What the fuck?

It was the bedroom, and Picasso had to assume it was Mr. Chen on the bed, because what was on the bed looked like a human flesh and bone and blood pretzel.

Movement. He regretted dropping the sword and considered grabbing it to swing wildly. But the movement was subtle. The hesitation of a scared child stepping forward.

Maya.

She looked just like she did in his dreams, only smaller, frailer. Her eyes were sadder, more sunken. Her face seemed like it had never smiled before.

Picasso limped over to her and dropped clumsily to his ass. After a struggle to sit with his back against the wall, he took her into his arms. Limp, like a ragdoll. He held her, hugged her, cried while he petted her hair. "It's okay, Maya. I got you. I'll protect you better this time, I promise."

A creak from the living room.

A shadow passed across the light from the outside. In the doorway stood the bus boy who had informed Picasso about Maya. His features were hidden by the darkness, but Picasso felt the kid's anger, tasted the sour rage in the air. The kid stepped into the bedroom, a butcher knife in his hand.

"I promise, Maya, I promise," Picasso repeated, holding Maya tighter.

A pop of thunder. Two. Three. Each noise was followed by bursts of blood and brains and bone from the kid's face, slops of red and gray goo splattering Picasso's cheeks.

The kid fell over like a tree, revealing Sal behind him in the doorway. He rushed into the room, confusion plastered on his face like a tattoo. "Jesus, boss!"

"I promise, Maya, I promise," was all Picasso could say.

CHAPTER 15

Was there another person out there capable of infiltrating people's dreams? Evidence pointed to yes. But how to find this person?

Billy and Will had been trying for two weeks now. It was Billy's turn to spend the night looking into random people's dreams.

A swipe of his hand to the left and the image on the wall slid away to reveal a new scene. A classroom. All the students were taking a test and doing well, answering questions with ease and then moving on to the next. Except for one student who had forgotten about the test. Billy felt a general sense of anxiety, but nothing out of the ordinary. Living this close to Temple yielded many nightmares like this one. Tonight alone, Billy had witnessed three dreamers who forgot where their classroom was, three more who forgot the notes to an important presentation, and one classic – standing naked in the classroom. Actually, two dreams started that way, but one dreamer showed up naked to class on purpose and all the other students were beautiful women. Billy assumed the dreamer fell asleep after watching porn.

He swiped to the left again to display the next dream. A woman in a large house filled with expensive furnishings. A black hole opened in the polished hardwood floor and slowly pulled all the surroundings into it. Just another testament to upper-middle class existential angst.

Billy felt no outside presence in this dream either.

Frustrated with searching for a needle in a haystack, he swiped left again.

Without a link to someone specific, he reached blindly into the general dreamscape, but had to narrow the playing field by conceptualizing the process. When he and Will were fifteen, they had turned his personal dreamscape into a fantasy backdrop. Thick forests carpeted rolling hills, and monstrous mountains gave home to creatures like griffons and unicorns. Mermaids swam the waterways and dragons glided among the clouds. His massive castle of carved obsidian sat atop a verdant plateau, the number of rooms too numerous to count.

No one had ever seen it, other than Will, but he didn't care. This was more of a home than his apartment in the waking world.

Will called this great mead hall the Valhalla Room, and Billy had no reason to change it. Again, it was for only the two of them to enjoy, but Billy took advantage of the size and cast upon the wall a ridiculously large monitor that displayed the images he saw in other people's dreams. The monitor was so large, he could simply walk right into it and the dream he watched whenever he desired.

This current search led him nowhere. But what else could he do? To give his mind a rest from peeking into random people's dreams, he strolled toward the ten-foot square window, open to the outside world of his dreamscape. He summoned a breeze, the air cool and calming.

"Come outside," whispered a voice in the wind. A girl's voice. A young girl's voice.

What the Hell?

Even in his dreamscape, the icy fingers of fear gripped his spine. The chill deepened when the far away horizon lightened, the sun shining brighter as the mountains turned to dust and floated away on the wind. The trees farthest away disappeared into the ground as if some giant beast slurped them from underneath with a straw.

By the time Billy formulated another *What the fuck?* thought, the madness outside the window ceased. As if a curtain had been drawn, a sunnier world existed beyond a line of thick-trunked trees, a definitive border between his world and a strange new one.

A tiny, mysterious voice had invited him outside. With no other option but to find an answer to whom the voice belonged, Billy stepped through the window, levitating from his castle to the newly formed tree line. He could have teleported had he chosen to, but then he'd miss the journey. Teleportation only took a fraction of a second for him to get where he wanted to go, and to his chagrin, it only took a fraction of a second for his dreamworld to change.

Past the trees, a blue ocean gleamed so bright that it temporarily blinded him. White sand beach with tall palm trees lay between the ocean and Billy's forest. He didn't like the brightness of this scene, the sun shining a hot light on his anxiety.

A girl sat on the beach. She looked about eight years old and wore a simple yellow sun dress. Her appearance gave him pause. She was so young.

The likeness of a small girl was easy enough to conjure and manipulate. He could look exactly like her if he wished. If this girl were a mere avatar, a glamour used by a vile monster in order to deceive, Billy would have felt it. She was no avatar or glamour. This was who she was in the waking world. The thought of turning into a mirror image of her crossed his mind, but he felt it would do no good. It wouldn't unnerve her. However, she unnerved him.

Billy stepped forward, bringing the forest with him. He circled around the girl to view her from all sides. An unseen border divided his dreamscape behind him, hers behind her. This realm was half his, half hers. Both dreamscapes altered as he walked, every step adding more to his in the direction he moved, while losing the direct proportion from the area he left. No matter how hard he tried to assert himself, the fifty-fifty split remained. This dreamscape had always been *his*. His and Will's.

After making one full revolution around her, Billy stopped. He had never encountered anyone like her before, so he was uncertain as to what to do, other than conjure a dozen dragons and hide them among the many trees behind him, ready to burst through should he call upon them.

"You've been looking for me, no? Quite a few nights now," the girl said.

"I have. How did you know?"

"Before we continue, shall we invite your other self? I would hate to repeat myself and it would save you from being the middleman."

"My other self?" She knew about Will. How? This wasn't good and getting worse by the second. Billy made more dragons, bigger ones. "That isn't possible."

"Sure, it is. We simply have to invite him."

Her gesture was simple, moving her hand with the elegance of a practiced dancer. As if collecting wisps of silk floating on a breeze, her fingers played the air. Billy felt her on his skin, though she didn't touch him. A caress at first, then a tug. Pinching. Pulling. Strands of his flesh flowed from the left side of his body. It burned; the pain was too great for Billy to call forth his dragon army. He screamed as ribbons of his skin swirled together. The experience was brief and before Billy could gather his wits to retaliate, Will stood next to him, shrieking.

"The fuck just happened?" Will yelled, looking around. "How'd I get here?"

Billy placed his hands on his knees to keep from fainting. He had never needed to catch his breath in this realm before. "We're in our dreamscape together."

Will spun slowly, taking in the sights, pausing when he saw the girl in yellow. "We haven't been in the dreamscape together. Since… since…"

The death of their parents.

"I know," Billy said as he stood straight, apprehensive, angry, concerned. He was human and liked to believe himself to be a god. This girl had the air of a god pretending to be human.

"How?"

"Her."

Will crossed his arms over his chest and chuckled. "Does she have a name?"

"You may call me Maya." There was a sadness in her eyes, and something more. The tone of her answer told Billy she guarded her secrets, and they were dangerous.

"So, we found the other one like us who has been killing innocent people in their dreams," Will said. He started to pace along the forest border.

Maya giggled, the sort of cherubic laughter expected from a younger girl in the waking world, not from a being with enormous power. "I have killed many people, often upon the urging of those who possess my waking body, but none were innocent. You might be thinking of the other dream eater."

"Dream eater?" Billy asked. "Who is that? Wait, do you mean us? Is that how you refer to us?"

Too agitated by the new information, Will's pacing quickened. "Jesus, I thought we were the only ones who could do this, now we discover Maya, *and* she tells us that there's *another* one like us."

Maya cocked her head. "Did you truly think you were the only one? Oh, that's right. You were raised Catholic. Mono-theological religions always teach their followers that there is 'only one.' I guess you absorbed more of their teachings than you'd like to think."

Billy didn't believe Maya meant her words to be cruel, but they struck many a nerve within Will. A rabid animal breaking free from its cage, Will rushed from the forest confines. His body swelled and doubled, then tripled in size. Spikes sprouted from his pores while thick shells formed over his skin and interlocked into biological armor. Long blades slid from his elbows, flesh turning to metal.

Will took three steps, maybe four, onto the beach, and Maya waved a hand. Will's metal skin clinked and clanged off his body and the two knives fell from his elbows to the sand. In a slimy display of anatomy, Will dropped to his knees and screamed, his flesh sliding off him in lengths of crimson, bared muscles twitching.

Billy reached out with his mind and yanked Will from the beach back to the safety of the forest. He replaced Will's skin, new and unblemished. Wild-eyed, Will continued to scream as he felt his face, chest, arms, and legs, verifying his flesh was where it should be.

Satisfied that Will was unharmed, other than now saddled with the horrific knowledge of what it felt like to be flayed, Billy turned his attention back to Maya.

"You shouldn't make an enemy of me," Maya said, her voice stern.

Careful not to cross the border, Billy asked, "Then why come here? Why introduce yourself if you aren't the one we're looking for?"

"To ask for help. And to give you a warning."

"You sure have a funny way of asking for a favor," Will said as he joined Billy.

Maya didn't respond to Will's comment. Instead, she held out her hand, an earthly globe floating above it. The Earth spun while the western part of the Pacific rim expanded, as if a camera filming the area zoomed in. The Philippines and Indonesia grew until the individual islands between the two countries became visible. Finally, they stopped changing size and one island glowed with a halo of light around it. "I want to go home."

"I'm assuming you can't. Did you imply earlier that you're being held captive?"

The image of the islands disappeared, replaced by a man in his fifties, gray mixing with the brown of his hair. "For two weeks now by this man. His name is Picasso."

"Picasso?" Will asked. "Isn't he that mafia guy?"

"He is."

"You're very powerful," Billy said, choosing his words wisely and tempering his thoughts and emotions. "Are you not able to enter his dreams and free yourself that way?"

"The waking world is unkind to me, so I need a guardian."

Will glared at her. "Too bad about your luck." Then he turned his back on her, and said, "I think I'd like to wake up now, Billy."

Billy wanted more time to process this information – something she had said made him curious. "You mentioned a warning?"

Yume's image was interchanged with Picasso's. "She will be your downfall."

Fists clenched, Will turned back around to storm toward Maya again. "If you hurt Yume—"

Billy reached out and grabbed the elbow of his other self and said to Maya, "Please elaborate."

Yume's image shimmered and changed to an older version of herself. Billy had seen this woman before, pictures of her throughout Yume's apartment. "Her mother? How will she be our downfall?"

This time, the image moved. Yume's mother drew a katana and sliced through faceless men who appeared out of nowhere. The image of Yume's mother split into two and they fought with sword-wielding individuals. Each image of Yume's mother split into two again, and this time she wore the black garb of a ninja. More images of Yume's mother stemmed from the existing ones. However, each image fought with opponents or killed men in business suits.

"Yume's mother is a ninja?" Will said, disgusted by the lack of creativity in what he assumed were false images. "Come on, Billy. She's trying to fuck with our heads. No way this is real."

Will had dismissed Maya once she said she was being held captive. Obviously, he thought she was going to die in the waking world, thus ending whatever threat she posed in the dreamscape.

Billy, on the other hand, believed her. With her air of omnipotence, it was beneath her to lie. Billy did not assume she was going to die by the hands of her captor. She said that he didn't want to make an enemy of her, but her very existence already made her an enemy, no matter her intensions.

Will was right. It was time to wake up.

Billy waved his hand, and a black rectangle tore through the fabric of this dreamscape. A doorway.

Will walked through without a glance back.

Billy looked back, though. Maya remained on the beach in the same spot she had sat this entire time with the slightest smile on her face, one unbefitting her station. Billy stepped through the doorway and woke up.

Sitting up in bed, Billy wiped his sheet over his sweat-drenched face. He needed to confer with Will about a way to kill Maya, but a nebulous idea already started to take shape. And it involved Yume's mother.

CHAPTER 16

Yume loved this part of the dream. She really shouldn't take as much joy in messing with her roommate, but Sloan had been such a bitch lately – between increased militancy of the bathroom's cleanliness and how she treated Shanna two weeks ago – that Yume couldn't stop herself.

Lounging on the couch and flipping through a magazine with no pictures or words, Yume smiled at Sloan as she walked into the living room from her bedroom. She frowned at Yume. "Why are you smiling at me?"

"It's a good day," Yume answered. "My semester grades were pretty good."

She had printed out her grades and left the paper on the half wall separating the kitchenette from the small dining area, the perfect place for viewing. When Sloan saw them, her frown deepened into a scowl.

"You got a 99 in Art History?" Sloan asked.

Sloan was in school to become a lawyer, so she and Yume had few opportunities to take the same courses. Art History 135 was of those occasions. Sloan had zero regard for art, and even less for creating it, so she chose to absorb and regurgitate for her Art requirements. Yume loved art, but had no skill at it, so she decided to learn about its impact on the world. Even though Sloan didn't care about the subject, she still wanted to do better than Yume. In the waking world, she did, earning a 98 to Yume's 95. But here, in Sloan's dream, the outcome was different.

"I did," Yume said. "The professor loved my paper about the three Carracci brothers' impact on the Renaissance."

Standing in front of the refrigerator, Sloan snipped, "First of all, they are High Baroque. Second of all, not all three were brothers. Lodovico was the *cousin* to Agostino and Annibale!"

Yume shrugged. "Huh. I never knew that. Anyway... I ate one of your strawberry yogurts."

Strawberry yogurt. Another nonstop source of consternation. Yume hated strawberries – it was a texture thing – but Sloan *always* blamed her whenever a yogurt went missing.

"Yume!" Sloan yelled, stomping her foot for emphasis. "How many times have I told you that those are mine?"

"But I replaced it."

"That doesn't matter! It's the principle of boundaries, and how you have a complete and utter disrespect for others." Sloan took a breath, ready to continue her scolding, but cut herself short when she opened the refrigerator. Small, single serve cups of strawberry yogurt tumbled from the refrigerator. And didn't stop.

"What the fuck?" Sloan shrieked a yogurt kept pouring from the fridge. "What the fuck?"

The containers piled at Sloan's feet and when they reached her knees, Yume hopped from the couch and moved to the back of the room where Billy waited.

He asked, "Think it'll work?"

Yume smirked. "If she accuses me of eating her yogurt again, we'll just revisit with more yogurts."

"Sounds like a plan." He gently held her cheek as he kissed her lips. Soft. Warm. Romantic. "Shall we head out?"

Yume glanced back at Sloan one last time. Her roommate cried as she threw dozens of yogurt containers around the kitchenette. "Yep. We're done here."

Billy waved his hand and a black door-shaped rectangle appeared. "Sounds good. I'm going to let Will run the show today. I'll see you tomorrow?"

"Yes, please. I love you."

"I love you, too."

Yume stepped through the door and woke up in her bed, two minutes before her alarm was set to go off. *Perfect timing.*

Yume got out of bed and felt great. The last two weeks had been amazing. She was glad Billy opened up to her the way he did. It freaked her out at first, but she equated it to driving – the first time behind the wheel of a two-ton death machine was terrifying, but with experience came a sense of vision. A whole new world ready for her to explore.

Each night, Billy escorted her through dreams – his own, other people's – and it brought them closer together. It was impossible for her not to fall in love with a man who allowed her into his mind, literally. And the sex was amazing, both in the dreamscape and the waking world.

She had yet to meet Will, though. The three of them decided to wait for the right time. It was more than just meeting a close family member. Yume was still learning about the dreamscape, and her feelings for Billy, so no one wanted to rush the situation. She was also learning to rationalize how she and Billy intended to use the dreamscape regarding the monsters of the world.

Killing a person disturbed her. Billy had done it more than once, which gave her a major sense of unease. He spun it as a form of doling out justice, and he gave her the names of the people – the men – he had killed. She researched them, learned what they had done and saw how the justice system failed the victims. Much like Gus.

At first, Millie was upset. A piece of shit or not, Gus was still her husband. But with each passing day, her remorse decreased. Shanna said that a couple nights ago, she and her mother went out to dinner together for the first time in years and had an amazing time. The world was now a better place without Gus. Yume believed in her heart that similar experiences were shared by the families of those who had their oppressors removed by Billy. And she wanted to help.

Last week Yume became a volunteer at a woman's shelter. Once the people running the shelter found out about her major, they allowed her to shadow the shelter's therapist, Margaret, and told her it was not an internship position. She didn't care about that. She wanted to meet those who needed help.

It broke her heart to see how many women needed the shelter. A few reminded her of Millie; they thought they needed to stay with their husbands, no matter the level of abuse. Even after arriving at the shelter with too many bruises to count, some went right back home. Many followed Margaret's advice, though, and proceeded to get the necessary help, either legal support to help start divorce proceedings, or support from the law to make their abusers pay.

Yume was happy when women accepted the help, but she wasn't there for them. She was there for the others. Like Lynette McDougall.

Yume followed Margret into a large room where Lynette and her two sons waited. It was a comfortable room, carpeted with soft pink walls and a bin of toys in the corner. The shelter was a house like any other on the street, one room in the back for administration, every other room converted to a safe space. Yume and Margaret sat on wooden chairs while Lynette and her sons sat on a loveseat, the boys showing no interest in the toys, the youngest refusing to leave his mother's lap. Neither boy fussed, content to sit as close as possible to their mother.

As with all other first-time meetings, Yume sat beside Margaret and remained quiet, unless she was directly addressed.

"Hi, I'm Margaret, and this is Yume. What brings you here today, Lynette?"

Margaret was always pure comfort. The faintest hint of a smile to let everyone else in the room know she was friendly. She modulated the tone of her voice as the interview went along, changing it to meet perceived emotional needs. First and foremost, she listened, asking questions only when she needed to, without prying. Toward the end of the process, Margaret made suggestions, from calling the police, contacting a lawyer, or spending a few nights at a secret property owned by the shelter.

"My husband, Rob," Lynette said with a hitch in her voice. As she told her story, Yume became madder and madder. She always got angry when listening to these stories from the women, disgusted by the way the men in their lives treated them. She was an expert at hiding her feelings, though, keeping her expressions like Margaret's: focused, inviting, calm.

"He never hit the boys before. Never, other than a good paddling if they deserved it." This was the third time Yume had heard that phrase that week. The other two times ended in an eventual call to the police. But something about Lynette made her think this wasn't going in that direction.

Lynette told her story about her husband getting drunk last night, and smacking the older boy, and she immediately started to make excuses for him. "He's having a rough time at his job." Too many bills to pay. He was the sole income source, after all. He turned to whiskey instead of beer, which he rarely did, and that made him meaner.

"What do you have there?" Margaret asked the youngest. She wanted to hear from the children about their home lives. Bad news, good news. She nodded toward the folded piece of paper clutched in his hand. The paper was a photo of his father. The bad news: Lynette didn't seem committed to leaving, and after seeing the picture crumpled in her little one's hand, it became obvious to everyone in the room that she intended to head home after she left this place. The good news: she made an emotional connection.

Yume looked into Lynette's eyes. Deeply. And into the boys' eyes.

Billy had explained to Yume that the eyes were the windows to the soul, as well as to the human brain. Once he looked into someone's eyes, then he could visit them that night with ease. If that person looked into the eyes of someone during the last couple of days, then Billy could jump into their dreams (but no guarantee). Add another layer, like Yume looking into Lynette's eyes to jump into the bastard husband's dreams, and the chances became slimmer, the dilution too great. However, emotional connection was a big plus. It helped the process, increased the chances of jumping from one to another successfully.

"Are you sure?" Margaret asked one final time as Lynette gathered her children and headed to the door. She had refused all aid Margaret offered.

"I'm sure," Lynette replied.

"We're always here when you need us."

"Thank you. Bye."

Yume took the opportunity to look into the eyes of each family member one final time, adding her own emotions to the mix. Billy should have no problems finding that bastard husband tonight.

And she couldn't wait to tell him.

CHAPTER 17

This party was like every other frat party Shanna attended. Thumping music from one of the rooms. Exuberant laughter occasionally heard over the thrum of voices. A whoop. A holler. Sensory overload. Everything a blur of color and noise. All she wanted to do was hook up. How difficult could that be?

Shanna took a drink. Something with an indistinguishable flavor from a red plastic cup. *Nothing but the best here*, she thought as she leaned against the nearest wall.

Then he came over.

Never taking his eyes off her, he made his way through a small crowd of people. She couldn't tell if he plowed his way through them, or if they parted to get out of his way like commoners with royalty. He certainly looked like a prince.

Tall, but not too tall, and his perfectly crooked smile, one side a hint higher than the other, turned Shanna's insides to jelly.

"Hey," he said.

"Hey," she replied, tone flirtatious. If that wasn't enough, she gave him bedroom eyes.

He leaned in for a kiss and she reciprocated. His fingers glided across her face and along her neck. Men never did that enough, but God, she loved when they did. The party noise moved to the background, behind the beating of her heart, and faded away completely.

When they stopped kissing to remove their clothes, she found herself in a bed. *How did I get to his bedroom? Did he carry me? Did we walk up the stairs while kissing the whole time? It doesn't fucking matter, dummy! Stop thinking about travel logistics and focus on the hottie dropping his pants!*

His body was everything she hoped for; tight with rippling muscles, not so big that veins popped out everywhere. But... When she looked up into his face and he smiled, she saw a flash of silver. He had a silver tooth! How did she not notice that before? *Doesn't matter. Makes him bad ass.*

Naked and ready, she gestured for him to join her, but he moved to the door and opened it. "Mind if a couple of my friends join us?"

Two naked men entered the room, both doppelgangers of Mr. Hottie. Except one wore a blue top hat – slightly bent in the middle and a bit crumpled, and the other had on blue cape draped across his shoulders and down his back, the edges tattered and frayed. Shanna giggled at the silly spectacle, and at the excitement of living out a fantasy.

"Wow," she said, "You three look alike."

"This is a frat and we're frat brothers."

"But you all look *exactly* alike."

"You've often said that all frat boys look alike."

Shanna chuckled. She didn't remember saying that. She had thought it plenty of times, and most definitely shared that thought with Yume, but she never said it in front of... *What was his name? Oh, it doesn't fucking matter!*

Shanna eased back on to the bed as the three men converged. Her hands wandered over smooth muscles, chests, shoulders, backs, glutes, thighs, overly thrilled at all the silk covered steel.

Three wet mouths moved across her body, lips indistinguishable from tongues, along her thighs, over her hips, across her chest. Yes! They touched her tits exactly how she liked. No biting, pinching, twisting, or squeezing. Just perfect caresses. Legs spread, she released a gasp when one of them slid inside her. Perfect fit. Large enough to send electricity through her body with every glide, not too large to cause discomfort. He thrust at the right pace without turning it into a race. Fingers on her skin, mouths on her body, the pleasure building and her vision blurred. She couldn't make out faces any more, couldn't tell who touched her or where, didn't care as the thrusting sped up.

A hand slid to the back of her head and then clasped and tugged at a full clump of hair. A blast of lightning ran from the base of her skull and stuck right between her thighs. Grunts and squeals of ecstasy escaped her mouth; she lost control as he took her where she wanted to go.

Then another hand moved up her chest and stopped on her neck. And squeezed. At first it was just another experience, something she had never done before, and she liked it. Until his fingers tightened. And tightened a little more. More. Breathing became difficult, but she was so close to finishing. Until she couldn't breathe at all.

"Not... into... this..."

She tried gasping for air, but couldn't as his grip tightened. Shanna smacked at his chest and punched his arms. Couldn't inhale. Couldn't exhale.

She thought she heard a snap in her neck right before she woke up in her bed, riding the wave of an orgasm blasting through her whole body, moaning as her legs twitched. When she finished, still panting, she was stunned that her right hand was inside her panties while her left clutched her throat just under her chin.

Laughing, she uncurled her fingers from her neck. *Of course, it was only a dream! No man was that perfect.* "Although, I might be more of a freaky bitch than I realized," she mumbled. She slid her fingers out of her vagina, wondering if her throes had been loud enough to be overheard through the walls. Holding her breath, she listened for her mother. Had she heard? After a minute with the house still quiet, she realized she felt too relaxed to care, and decided to start her day.

Showered and dressed, Shanna padded her way into the kitchen to fix breakfast. Her mother sat at the table, smoking a cigarette and staring at a piece of paper.

"Whatchyu got there, Mom?"

"Umm...? It's... It's... Uhhh..."

Shanna looked over her shoulder. "Whoa!"

It wasn't any ol' piece of paper. It was a life insurance check.

For one hundred thousand dollars.

"Whoa is right." Her mother's voice quaked, on the verge of tears.

Gus repeatedly proved his stupidity by the choices he made. Like signing up for a term-life policy. He had started with a fifty-thousand-dollar policy and thought he was set. Shanna tried to explain that he'd be better off with a whole life policy. He didn't understand the differences and the conversation ended in a screaming match and him buying another fifty thousand because in his little mind the additional insurance made him righter than he originally thought. Shanna never thought she'd thank God for another human's stupidity. "Sweet baby Jesus, thank you and blessed be."

"Amen," her mother finished, the word shattering the dam holding back her emotions. Tears ushered way to gulping sobs powerful enough to shake her shoulders. "I don't know how to feel! I don't know how to feel!"

Shanna bent over and wrapped her arms around her mother, fighting hard not to say, "Fucking amazing!" Instead, she tried, "Loved, because he thought to do this."

It was a necessary lie. Her mother squeezed back until she finished crying. Then she let go and asked, "What are we going to do with this?"

Shanna sat the table and put her hands on her mother's. "I think it's obvious, Mom. We do what we know Gus would have wanted us to do – we give the whole thing to the starving children in Africa."

Horrified wasn't a strong enough word to describe the initial expression on her mother's face, until she registered her daughter's sarcasm.

Her mother put her hand over her heart. "What the fuck is wrong with you, girl? Gus would have slapped you across the room if you said that to him."

"I know," Shanna whispered. She tilted her head and gave her mom a look that implied, *Think about what you just said, Mom.* The look worked.

Shanna's mother gave a little head shake and sat straighter. "There'll be no more tears from me." Then she muttered, "That grump never had much of a sense of humor. But... What do we do with this?" This time, her words held excitement.

"A hundred thou is more than enough to pay off the mortgage." Gus had ruined her mother's credit, after ruining his own. Their home wasn't much, but the high interest payments on the mortgage didn't reflect that. "Without a crazy high mortgage payment crippling your paycheck, you could save money and repair your credit. In five years or so, look for a better place. Hell, maybe gentrification will come knocking and make a nice offer."

Shanna's mother beamed, the pride not only seen but felt. "You are so right. You're smart and so right. I will deposit this tomorrow and ask about paying off the mortgage. But first, I want to take you out to a really nice place for dinner. Oh, how about the Chinese restaurant in the city that we used to go to?"

"The Dragon's Blessing? It's closed. Something weird happened there a couple weeks ago."

"Oh, that's a shame. Okay, you pick. In fact, call Yume and invite her along. It's been too long since I've seen her. I know Gus made her uncomfortable. He made a lot of people uncomfortable."

"I will, but I'm gonna make us some breakfast first."

Shanna smiled as she gathered flour and eggs and sugar, and pans. Her mother was slowly opening her eyes to life without Gus, and it was going to be awesome to be able to include Yume in more family things!

Yume.

Shanna thought about her dream and debated telling Yume about it. After her dream about Gus, Yume had insisted that Shanna share any nightmares or intense dreams she had. A kinky sex dream hardly seemed the kind of thing to worry about. It would only embarrass Yume anyway, so no point mentioning it. After all, it was just a dream.

CHAPTER 18

Yume briskly walked from the women's shelter to Billy's apartment, struggling with this moral concept: forgiveness was the harbinger to redemption, but if someone committed an unforgivable act, could they ever find the path to redemption?

Lynette and her children needed help. Rob needed to be stopped, and to be punished.

But her excitement at serving justice waned in the cool March air. The farther she got from the shelter, the further she removed herself from the situation. Who was she to decide what was right or wrong for Lynette and her family? She was weighing the pros and cons of taking a father away from two young boys, for God's sake!

A father who abused them. A father who beat their mother.

Yume chose to study psychiatry in order to help people. A mental health illness was a disease and this disease could be cured. Getting to that level of wellness took time and patience. So did relationships. What Yume planned on doing would take away Rob's opportunity to get well, for the two of them to repair and renew their relationship.

Yes, he needed to be punished. Yes, Lynette and her children needed help. Was Billy's solution right, though? It was the most permanent, so it should be the last option, not the first. Maybe Billy could haunt Lynette's husband's dreams? Give him nightmares that guide him into doing the right thing, like the ghosts with Ebenezer Scrooge. Still, Scrooge had to choose to do the right thing for himself. What were the odds that Lynette's husband would want to fix himself or work on their relationship?

Yume kept going back to the text conversation she had with Shanna earlier in the day. Her mother received a life insurance check. Money was never the motivation behind what Billy did to Gus, but money was going to help Millie improve her life. Billy had taken forgiveness and reconciliation away from Gus, and nothing but good things had come Millie and Shanna's way ever since. Although Billy had a narrower scope of view than Yume, they both saw the same point of the picture.

Yume wanted to discuss this decision with Billy first. Although Yume felt nothing but anger toward Lynette's husband when she told her stories, they owed it to him to explore other options first. That was what she intended to say to Billy.

That all fell out of her mind when she unlocked Billy's door and entered his apartment. He was standing in the middle of the living room with a towel wrapped around his hips. Wheelchair nowhere in sight.

Neither good thoughts (it was a miracle!) nor bad thoughts (he'd been lying to her!) formed in her head. She was too stunned. Billy was standing!

Smiling, he crossed the room to greet her, and extended his hand. "Hi, Yume! I'm Will."

Will? Billy's other personality. Technically the root personality that created Billy. Who was standing.

Yume didn't know how to respond. Billy had discussed Will with her plenty of times, answering any question she asked.

It was a stupid thought, but she assumed he'd look different. He was Billy's twin. No, he was Billy! No, not quite that either. It was Billy's body, but... He *did* look different in small ways. His eyes held nothing but exuberance while Billy's eyes held intensity, yet both were infectious. Their smiles were different; Will's mouth curved on the right while Billy's curved left. And Will's body... Yume had seen Billy naked, a few afternoons blissfully slipping by where they didn't leave the bed, but... Will's was different. They were the same size, shape, and build. Both were thin, but Will looked almost athletic with tighter, bulging muscles.

"I'm... uhhh... Yume... You're... You're Will? You look just like him. I mean, you are him, but... not? Am I being offensive? I feel like I'm being a dick. I mean, I know you, but don't know you, and... you're standing and walking, and you're taller than I am, and you have eight-pack abs!" The more she talked, the hotter the fire within her cheeks burned. Yume hid her face in her hands and mumbled, "God, I'm such an asshole."

Will laughed. "No, you're not. Billy and I hoped you and I could meet under different circumstances. Tell you what, follow me."

"I'm being an idiot. And insensitive. An insensitive idiot," Yume said. Flustered, she followed him, not realizing it was to his bedroom. She stopped at the threshold and then turned away, covering her eyes. She looked over her shoulder, but quickly turned back when he dropped his towel.

Will laughed again. "You weren't being insensitive before, but you are now. You've seen me naked before."

"I know, but... I haven't seen *you* naked. I don't want to give the wrong impression."

"So, Billy didn't tell you?"

Yume turned to face Will as he slipped a pair of nylon shorts over his boxers. Billy preferred briefs. "He told me a few things, but not everything."

Will grabbed a Metallica tee shirt from the closet.

Billy usually wore plain tees or nice golf shirts. Admittedly, the printed tee shirts taking up half the closet struck Yume as curious.

"He's a great guy like that, isn't he? You don't have to worry about the presumptions that come with nakedness. Billy can't walk, and I can't... perform. Like Billy, I, too, have a body part that doesn't work."

Skin going clammy, Yume slouched as if deflating from her soul leaving her body. "I... I'm sorry." She knew Will had suffered extensive and prolonged childhood trauma, but now that he confessed to having performance issues stemming from psychological issues – not physical issues – she deduced that those childhood abuses were sexual in nature. "I'm *very* sorry."

"No need to apologize but thank you for the sentiment. I did what any rational person would do – I created a superhero, made a whole separate personality, and killed my abusers."

The cavalier way he talked about this made Yume freeze in place and hold her breath. The justice system failed him by allowing his predators to abuse him, so he did what he did in self-defense. When discussing this with Billy, they were talking about a different person. In her mind, Will had a different life, different place to live, different face. But she couldn't help thinking that this was Billy standing in Billy's bedroom making flippant remarks about killing people.

Will must have seen the reservation on her face because a quivering smirk replaced his smile. He waved his hands in front of him, mocking an erasure of his words. "Apologies. I often use dark humor inappropriately, as a coping mechanism. Clearly, I'm being creepy and creeping you out with my creepy words. I'm just really nervous about meeting you."

Will had been through more than any human being, let alone a child, should endure. Him living as a functioning adult without the aid of medication was a minor miracle, so she figured he had a right to use whatever coping mechanisms he needed, no matter how off-putting they might seem at first. Then Yume laughed. "You're nervous about meeting me?"

"Well, yeah. From what Billy told me about you, you're rather amazing. I wanted to make a better impression than creepy shower guy making creepy jokes."

"Trust me, I've had worst first impressions. I met this one guy online, had great conversations with him multiple times, but when we met in person, this dude-bro showed up wearing a tee shirt that read: 'Who sharted?'"

Will smirked and shook his head. "That's... that's... I have no words."

"My date had plenty. He spent the entire dinner bragging about himself and how he made his 'nerdy roommate' converse with me online, convinced I wouldn't be able to resist him once I saw him."

"I'm confident you were able to resist. But did anyone solve the mystery of who sharted?"

"Pretty sure it was him after I stood up and loudly professed that he got me pregnant and refused to pay for anything. That was after I paid for the dinner and gave the server a generous tip."

Will laughed and gave a golf clap. "Nicely done."

"Thank you, thank you," Yume replied, curtsying. "So... You said you only know of me through what Billy tells you? He said you two don't share time, not even in the dreamscape, so you've never seen me?"

"No. Well, twice. It is *extremely* rare when both our personalities are awake at the same time, and when we are, it's very painful."

"Really? If it's so painful, then why do it?"

"To spend time with you."

"Me?"

"Yeah. Totally worth it. You're intelligent, funny, compassionate, quick witted. It's no wonder that Billy is in... ummm... in awe of you." Will put his hands in his pockets and gave her a look of innocent sincerity. "Honestly, I'm in awe of you, too. You're an amazing human being."

Yume tucked a lock of hair behind her ear as she glanced to the floor while blushing. Two men were in love with her. She was in a rom-com, and it felt... weird. It really was two men, wasn't it? Will's word choice and speech pattern were different. Billy used a broader vocabulary, but Will's delivery was bolder. But it was one body! Sure, there were slight physical differences – other than ambulation and impotence – but it was the same body, the same face. Yume looked to Will, and said, "I am in awe of Billy as well. And you, too."

Will moved closer, and Yume's heart sped up.

Smirking, he said, "But you technically don't know me."

"Billy talks very kindly about you, and you're a part of him. I guess he's a part of you since you made him."

Will chuckled. He had an easy-going, understanding spirit that made her feel like her mistakes were natural. Part of her wanted to crawl under the bed and hide until she could function like a woman capable of not freaking out, but Will showed no evidence of being offended. "I didn't make him like I made Bigby, but he is a part of me. I needed help and he came along."

"Okay. That's how I'll look at it. But... Who is Bigby?"

At first Will gave her an incredulous squint, then rolled his eyes. "Billy didn't tell you about Bigby, did he? He should have."

Will went to the closet and fished around through the blankets and boxes. He pulled out a thick sketchbook and gestured for Yume to have a look. "This is Bigby. He's a superhero I created about two years before Billy came along. My parents ignored my issues and appeased me by giving me all the comic books I could read and letting me watch all the movies and television I wanted to. I gravitated to stories of heroes rescuing victims. Surprise, surprise, right? Even though I have no need for him anymore, I still draw him from time to time."

Her jaw fell open – the illustrations were stunning. "I didn't know you were so talented." Of course, she realized it was Will who drew the illustrations, so she wasn't sure if Billy had any artistic talent or not.

The subject was... odd. He was large, the stereotypical high muscle, low body fat ideal of the fit male body, but he wasn't in traditional super-hero spandex. He wore a blue cape with a dapper vest, bow tie, slacks, and a top hat as blue as the cape. Not the superhero look Yume expected. What struck her as most unusual, though, were his teeth. Every picture depicted a rictus with razor blades instead of teeth. "I have questions."

"I knew you would."

"Bigby?"

"Not the most heroic name, I admit. He started as Big Bill, then I shortened his name to Big B, and finally Bigby. I was only twelve at the time, so I hadn't hit the peak of my creativity."

"Makes sense. The cape I get, but the top hat?"

"I wanted him to be suave."

"Excellent. He is. The razor blade teeth?"

"When a priest is shoving his dick in your mouth, razor blade teeth is the superpower you want."

Yume slapped her hands over her mouth just as she and Will said at the same time, "Oh my God, I did it again."

"I'm so sorry," Yume said hurriedly. "I keep saying awkward things!"

"I apologize for being gross!"

They stared at each other in wide-eyed silence. Yume's whole face felt as bright red as Will's cheeks. They each took a deep, cleansing breath and eventually found a breathing rhythm together.

After a few minutes, Will asked, "Have I screwed everything up?"

"Oh, hell no. I was too busy wondering if I had."

"God, no." He then held up an index finger, Yume assuming he meant that he had a great idea. She wasn't sure what it might be, but if it helped them move beyond the embarrassment, then it was the greatest idea the world had ever known. He strode past her and said, "Follow me."

In the living room, he gestured for her to sit on the couch as he went into the kitchen. Two glasses, one bottle of Pinot noir, and he took a seat beside her on the couch. As he poured the wine, he said, "Okay, this is a weird situation. A relationship like ours is weird, only made weirder by what Billy and I can do. So, instead of trying to follow social norms, how about we embrace the weirdness. You ask any questions you like, but you can't feel bad about them no matter how awkward society says they are, and I will make dark jokes with reckless abandon no matter how inappropriate they're deemed by the general public. Deal?"

Will offered a glass of wine to her. She took it by the stem and clinked it against his glass. "Yes, yes, all kinds of yes."

After a gulping pull from his glass, Will said, "Okay, now we're free to be weird."

"Excellent. I like this rule."

"As much as I'm happy to finally meet you, I thought you were volunteering at the women's shelter today?"

"I was. I left early to talk to Billy about a woman who came in with her sons."

Will shifted in his seat, moving closer to Yume. His eyes glimmered with excitement. "You found a candidate for one of us to visit?"

"I think so."

A cherubic smile appeared on Will's face as he leaned back and slouched, his body limp from relief. Looking at the ceiling, he said, "I'm sure Billy will exact the justice. It should be him since I haven't escorted you into the dreamscape yet. It will feel good to save kids from a monster. Good to rescue victims."

Yume originally wanted to talk to Billy about alternate methods to modifying bad behavior, and killing should be the last resort. What happened to Will as a child hadn't been "bad behavior," and those who were able to stop it, didn't. She worried about taking a father from two young boys, but they didn't have a father to begin with and she'd be opening an opportunity for their mother to find them one. Maybe one who could help them rescue themselves, so they wouldn't have to fabricate a savior from their imaginations, wishes, or dreams. She had come to the apartment for a philosophical back-and-forth with Billy, to come to a conclusion that they both agreed upon.

But thanks to meeting Will, she got to understand the potential future for Lynette's sons. Time to send the trolly down the other set of tracks.

Yume smiled and took a lip-smacking gulp of wine. "Yes. Yes, we will be rescuing a few victims."

CHAPTER 19

Shinko was the darkness, the shadow gliding silently over the alley wall. Aika stood close by, so quiet that Shinko often lost track of her. Fumiko's description of Aika's ability had not been understated; not one to aggrandize, but this skill level in one so young was nothing short of impressive.

The two stalked along the side of the building. Before the night ended, they would be like the specter of death: unsuspecting, unyielding, unheard. After all, they were to confront members of Heaven's Palisade, the same organization that had employed Karin as a housekeeper to protect Mr. Tanaka.

Shinigami's Helper made no pretenses as to who they were. Killers. They were paid for their services, but they had rules. A code. They were far from ignorant to the ramifications of their deeds. Should a request be deemed too detrimental to the world, they refused the assignment. When such requests arose, they used their expertise to alter the nature of the situation.

Shinko joined Shinigami's Helper twenty-six years ago. A little more than a year later, a particularly dangerous request had come, and then she understood the full scope of the organization. The cold war heated up, and a guerrilla government in South America – funded primarily from the drug trade – wanted to fan the flames of tension. They approached Shinigami's Helper with names of men to kill and a list of what to steal so their new country could begin a nuclear war among the worlds' superpower nations. Japan was enjoying a flourishing economy, so there was no benefit for the country, nor the world, should this upstart nation get their wish.

At first, Shinigami's Helper declined the offer. The warlords listened to their egos and became insistent. Shinigami's Helper accepted the assignment, and then handed everything over to the new government. As soon as the money transferred, Shinigami's Helper eradicated every member of the new government. Neither the government nor the names of anyone involved remained, not even as a story or a rumor. That was when Shinko determined she belonged with Shinigami's Helper.

Heaven's Palisade, on the other hand, operated in the complete opposite manner.

They offered protection and touted their kills as an "up sale" service. Those *they* protected were far less scrupulous than those seeking the services of Shinigami's Helper.

As a result, if an opportunity arose to disrupt a Heaven's Palisade assignment, Shinigami's Helper accepted it without a financial benefactor. Such was the case for this assignment.

Shinigami's Helper learned about a weapon stolen from an island between Indonesia and Philippines, and they traced the offenders to a Chinese crime organization. Fumiko had downplayed their mission, but Shinko assumed that if Heaven's Palisade was hired by the Chinese to protect the weapon and if Shinigami's Helper wished to find it, then the weapon was powerful enough to change the world. Now, she and Aika were tasked to retrieve it.

Three in the morning, the tiny slice of time when the city slept – after the bars had closed and a couple hours before the early risers started their day. The buzz of the streetlights was broken up by a dog barking a few blocks away, or by a homeless person coughing in a neighboring alley. Clanging from nearby trashcans, rats rummaging for food.

Shinko and Aika reached the end of the alley between The Dragon's Blessing and its neighbor. As expected, a small security camera was attached to the façade of each building. The nearest streetlight was too bright for them to continue. Shinko doubted the camera worked but wasn't foolish enough to disregard it. Wearing traditional ninja-yoroi – thick soles modified to endure bottle caps, nails, shards of broken glass, and other potentially jagged city terrain – her garb offered places to hide weapons, like the blow gun she pulled from her sleeve. Loading it with a plastic pellet, similar to a paint-gun round with a thinner casing, Shinko brought the gun to her lips and blew sharply. The pellet's black paint splattered the security camera lens monitoring

The Dragon's Blessing. Aika blinded the other camera in similar fashion. Two more pellets for the streetlight, dimming it enough to shroud their way toward the front door. Locked and strung with yellow crime scene tape.

Shinko appreciated tradition, opting to wear the clothes of those who had come before her; however, modern technology was now necessary for her to continue. She withdrew her automated lock-picking device from her breast pocket, the pick small enough to fit in her palm, and opened the door within a few whisper-quiet seconds. She pushed the door only as far as needed to slip inside; Aika shut it behind them.

When her eyes adjusted to the darkness, she gasped at the scene before her. Overturned tables. Scattered chairs. Broken pieces of furniture. What happened here?

Right hand on the hilt of her ninjato, the short-sword strapped to her back, Shinko crept close to Aika and lowered her face covering. Her mouth almost touching Aika's ear, she spoke, her words almost inaudible, "I was not expecting this."

Aika mimicked Shinko. "Are we too late?"

As if on cue, the lights popped on; Shinko squinted in the brightness. The women stepped away from each other, faced opposite directions, and drew their swords.

"Senpai," Aika whispered.

Shinko looked over her shoulder and her eyes widened in disbelief. Six figures dressed in ninja-yoroi – undoubtedly members of Heaven's Palisade – had entered the restaurant's dining room from the kitchen doors. Shinko had expected them, but didn't expect the different rainbow colors of each ninja-yoroi: red, orange, yellow, green, blue, purple.

"A tactic to confuse us?" Aika asked.

"Possibly," Shinko replied. If so, it had certainly worked. Traditionally, ninja-yoroi were black, except for white should snow call for camouflage. She'd never heard of any practical need for garments colored brighter than peacock feathers.

As the Heaven's Palisade members shuffled farther into the room, they split into two groups of three, one trio darted to the left side of the room, the other darted right. Each member of the trio had a different weapon. One held a ninjato, one wielded a pair of sai, the third twirled two tethered kunai.

Shinko faced off against Red, Orange, and Yellow. Red twirled the kunai – dagger-shaped blades tied to the ends of cords – and Shinko focused on this enemy first. Red planted his feet and spun both kunai faster, ready to strike. Shinko provided him with a target by kicking the closest chair into the air. The tactic worked, but...

Red flung the kunai at the chair, both blades piercing it. Shinko hoped that would be the end of the weapon, but to her dismay the blades were retractable. The kunai brought the chair back with them, and Red knocked it away with his foot.

Green tossed his kunai at Aika, and she dodged them with ease. Aika wasted no time going on the offensive.

Shinko decided Aika needed no assistance and started to advance, knees bent, both hands on her sword hilt close to her right ear, blade tip toward the ceiling.

As she moved closer to Orange, the one with the ninjato, she stepped to the side, placing him between her and Red. That didn't stop either color from attacking. Orange raced forward with his sword over his head when Red released the kunai. They shot past Orange on either side, and Shinko turned sideways as they passed in front of and behind her while she blocked Orange's downward strike.

She wanted to look into her opponent's eyes to judge, to measure, but for the second time tonight, the outfit confused her. Orange's face covering was pulled high while the hood hung low over his head. She couldn't see his eyes and wondered how her opponent's vision wasn't hindered. No matter. She'd kill him just the same.

Orange continued to strike after her initial block, and the clang of metal hitting metal rang loudly. His speed was impressive, almost terrifying, but his sloppy technique was all hacks and slashes.

Clang. Clang. Clang.

He attacked with nothing but pure speed, the way a westerner would. Easily blocked, but because of the speed, Shinko had difficultly shifting from defense to offense.

Clang. Clang.

Red and Yellow danced behind Orange, trying to find an opening to attack. The kunai shot past Shinko's head and sank into the wall with a thunk. This gave her an idea.

She had to make a dangerous assumption about Yellow, but she hoped to turn the tide of this attack, and needed to act. With every sword strike from Orange, she backed away, toward a wall with booths.

Clang. Clang. Clang.

The hits remained fast and strong, each impact jolting her shoulders. She stayed in front of Orange with Yellow attempting to time his attack with her backward steps. Another step and another, edging closer to the booths. All of Orange's slices swung downward, like an ax instead of a sword. Timing it perfectly, Shinko sidestepped his next swing, and his blade cleaved the booth's table, getting stuck. Yellow took advantage of Shinko exposing herself and lunged. As Shinko suspected – Yellow had no finesse with the sai, using them as implements to stab hard and fast. Shinko stepped in front of Orange as he struggled to dislodge the sword. His struggles ended with his partner skewering him.

Yellow also employed speed over precision. Two weapons instead of one, but the same lack of discipline, merely stabbing with them. Shinko used her sword to block one while dodging the other. Loosening the grip of her ninjato, she tried a different tactic – she blocked his next strike, though not as forceful. As she had hoped, the prongs of his sai caught her sword and he twisted his wrists, pulling it from her hands. Clearly, he lost focus of his surroundings. Shinko did not. Once the sword left her hand, she grabbed him by the shirt with both hands and pulled, dropping to the floor. Momentum brought his head down on Orange's stuck sword in the table, driving his skull into the tip with a sickening slurp of a ripe skewered melon.

Shinko launched herself toward the center of the restaurant, out in the open. Red threw both kunai. She dodged them, but then grabbed them on their way back to their owner. She jumped, the retracting kunai taking her along with them.

The retracting mechanism was strong enough to pull her through the air and Red was defenseless to stop her knee from jamming into his chest. She released his weapons and as she completed a shoulder roll, she slid her hands into a pair of weapons strapped to her thighs. Back on her feet and facing Red, she readied her shuko – hooked metal bands referred to as tiger claws – around her hands. Fast as lightning, she swiped at his head – and quickly wished she hadn't.

The claws ripped away his hood and face covering to reveal the head of a snake. Pale gray with steaks of black running along the sides over its eyes, the triangular head of a mamushi – Japanese pit viper – opened its mouth and hissed, exposing glistening fangs. More from impulse, Shinko raked her shuko over its face repeatedly until the body went limp. Shinko stared at the bloody mess on the floor, the body of a man with the shredded head of a snake.

Her reverie was interrupted by Aika's scream.

Fearing the worst, Shinko launched herself toward her protégé. Aika, alive and seemingly uninjured, lay on the floor in the fetal position while Green, Blue, and Purple surrounded her. Their hoods were drawn, their exposed snake heads hissing at her.

Arms extended and fingers splayed, Shinko rushed toward them ready to shred their faces like she had done with Red, until a voice boomed from everywhere, "Stop!"

Green, Blue, and Purple backed away from Aika toward the kitchen doors where the owner of the voice stood. A little girl with southeast Asian features, maybe eight or nine years old. Shinko guessed the girl to be from Indonesia or Philippines. The three snake-headed ninjas disappeared through the door behind her.

To Shinko and Aika the girl yelled, "Be gone!"

Shinko crouched beside her unmoving apprentice, and felt her racing pulse. Shinko stood and asked the girl, "Who are you?"

"My name is Maya. I am whom you seek."

"Impossible. I'm looking for a weapon."

The little girl smirked, and Shinko's stomach lurched. The girl held an unnatural glint in her eye, the flash of a star being born, then the flare of it dying. The smirk was unbefitting the face of a small child; it belonged on a person much older, much more ruthless. She waved her hand with the flourish of a stage actor, and the kitchen doors opened. Six snake-headed men in colorful ninja-yoroi entered the restaurant dining room. A dozen more. Twenty. "I am the weapon. Now leave."

Maya obviously controlled these snake creatures, but they lacked skill. Shinko could kill them, but she needed to compensate for their numbers.

"I can't leave without completing my mission."

"Then you will die."

The creatures walked toward Shinko as one. Slowly at first but picking up speed.

Shinko glanced around for a weapon. Anything! A discarded menu laid at her feet, a booklet of clear plastic. As expected, the restaurant's food offerings were followed by a description. The images of each dish were perfectly clear, but the words were squiggles and lines of gibberish. A once useless bit of information struck her like a lightning bolt: Most people can't read in their dreams.

"Wake up!" Shinko screamed as a dozen bodies slammed into her. "Wake up!"

Shinko jolted awake in a full body flail, disoriented. Aika's face was the first thing she saw, the young woman a portrait of worry. "Senpai? Senpai, are you okay?"

"Ye... yes. Yes."

"Oh my God, we were so worried," said a woman kneeling beside her. She wore a light blue blouse and a navy skirt. A flight attendant? Yes, a flight attendant. The fog lifted from Shinko's mind; she'd been on a plane, first class, with Aika occupying the seat next to hers. "You were having a nightmare, and your daughter couldn't wake you up."

"Yes, nightmare," Shinko repeated.

"Are you okay? You're so wet with perspiration. No offense, but I've never seen anyone sweat so much."

Shinko's drenched shirt felt heavy, weighed down with perspiration. She waved the flight attendant off. "Menopause. Hot flash."

A sympathetic yet worried smile crossed the younger woman's face. "Okay. As long as you're okay. We're landing in Philadelphia in about ten minutes, so make sure you're buckled." She hurried away as if menopause were contagious.

Aika stared with big, earnest eyes, a hundred questions behind them, but her mouth acted as gatekeeper, keeping them locked in.

"I'm okay," Shinko said. "Just a nightmare."

"It seemed like more than that."

It certainly did. Everything about it felt real. The ringing of metal against metal, the smell of old food in the restaurant, the burst of pain in her wrists and forearms from blocking the sword strikes. The adrenaline. The fear. Was it more than a mere dream? "Tell me something, Aika. Are you afraid of snakes?"

Aika blinked, taken aback by such an odd question. "No, Senpai. I… I'm actually fond of them."

"Very well," Shinko sighed, rolling the soreness from her shoulders. "Then it was only a nightmare."

CHAPTER 20

Billy awoke on his couch. Surprised to find himself there, but not as surprised at finding Yume asleep in his arms, her head on his chest. He looked around, trying his best not to disturb her.

No wheelchair. *Where's my wheelchair?*

He pinched the skin between his eyes – she must have finally met Will. The fact that Yume was still here meant it had gone well. The note on the coffee table, close enough to reach, proved it.

Billy grabbed it and read, "She's awesome!" in Will's handwriting. "I am. I really am," in Yume's.

Billy put the note to his forehead and smiled, the warmth of the words and their connotation going directly into his mind through osmosis. An impromptu meeting between his girlfriend and his other-self had gone well. As did his latest dream.

Transforming his shape had been uncomfortable, but he needed to pose as Maya to warn away Yume's mother. From what little he knew about her, he was confident the threat acted as an incentive for Shinko to hunt down Maya. The way she handled herself in the face of the unknown impressed and disturbed Billy. No matter how many ninjas he threw at Shinko, she remained unfazed, even when exposed to the snake-headed creatures. Should she become a foe, she'd be a challenge, exactly why Billy used Maya as a deflection. He was curious to see what Yume's mother would do, once she arrived in America, hoping she'd now want to find Maya. He was also curious about meeting Shinko in the waking world. Maybe that was why Yume had come over to his apartment unannounced? But since she was asleep…

Billy closed his eyes and slipped into his dreamscape, into his castle. He pulled up Yume's dream on the wall – the interior of her apartment – and stepped into it.

"Oh, hi!" she said, ice cream and chocolate sauce rimming her mouth. She sat on her couch with a heaping chocolate sundae in a giant bowl. "I came to your apartment looking for you and met Will."

Smiling, he sat next to her on the couch. He gently slid his thumb across her lips and then put it in his mouth. Unapologetically, she continued eating while he said, "I saw the note. I love that you dream about food."

After sliding the spoon from her mouth, she mashed her lips with exaggerated noises. "Same great taste and literally none of the calories. Now that I'm getting better at controlling my dreams, there's nothing more awesome to dream about."

"No riches and power and super-hot guys?"

Yume shrugged and then kissed him, her lips cold. "I'll eventually get riches and power in the waking world, and I already have my super-hot guy."

Billy's smile grew. "Does that mean I get to meet your mother?"

"Of course."

"Is that why you came to the apartment today?"

Yume wrinkled her brow. "No." She took one last bite of ice cream. Then the bowl, along with the chocolate smudges on her lips, disappeared. She turned to face Billy and took his hands. "I found our first candidate."

"Oh yeah?"

"Bastard named Rob who beats his wife regularly and recently moved onto his kids. Her name is Lynette. She and her kids came into the shelter and talked to one of our counselors. Unfortunately, she went right back to him."

"I certainly agree with your assessment. Were you able to look into her eyes?"

"Better. Her eyes, both of her kids' eyes, and the youngest had a picture of him."

Yume was resourceful and intelligent, but to increase the chances of finding the candidate like that? Impressive. "Wow! That's amazing, Yume."

"Can we go tonight? Can we go *now*? Wait... Is it tonight right now?"

Billy smiled and stood up. "Yes, it's tonight right now. There's a good chance he might be sleeping."

"Yes!" Yume pumped her fist.

With a wave of his hand, Billy created a doorway back to his dreamscape. Before he stepped through, he took Yume's hand in his and looked deeply into her eyes. "There's something I want to show you first."

She squeezed his hand and smiled. "Okay. What is it?"

Backing into the doorway, he encouraged her to follow. "My dreamscape castle. Specifically, the Valhalla Room."

"The Valhalla Room? What's the—?" Her words disappeared like her ice cream the moment she stepped through the doorway. "Whoa!"

Billy let go of her so she could explore the room.

Mouth agape, she studied the ten-foot-tall tapestries on the roughly hewn stone wall, and then ran a hand over one of the massive wooden pillars supporting a lintel. She looked out a window and Billy's heart lodged in his throat. What was she going to see? His world as he had created it, or a scene of Maya's making?

"So beautiful," Yume whispered.

That sounded promising, but Billy wasn't satisfied until he stood behind her.

The thick canopy of the rich, verdant forest blanketed the rolling hills. Relief set his heartbeat back to normal.

A winged unicorn flew by, and Yume asked, "Did you do that for my benefit?"

"Will and I had set a bunch of parameters in our subconscious and the wildlife kind of does whatever it wants. Sort of like a randomized screen saver."

Yume smirked and nodded. She looked back into the room, pointedly at the table. "So, the thirty people you hold feasts for... Are they from your subconscious, too? Or the deeper realms of your unconscious? Or are there orcs and dwarves who live in the side of the mountain out back?"

Billy and Will had spent countless hours over the years discussing such things. What rules to set, how detailed to make the background. The landscape and how often to change it. The creatures that resided there. It tickled him to talk to someone else about his private world. "We have never held a feast for anyone. We were teenagers when we designed this world, so style took precedence over substance. There's no practical purpose for a table that seats thirty, but we've had it here for so long that it's now part of our home. Unless Will did something without telling me – which is doubtful – there are neither orcs nor dwarves living in the mountains, or anywhere else in our dreamscape."

Yume nodded as she strolled around the table, her fingers gliding across the backs of the chairs. She continued to look around the room. "Fair enough. I don't blame you. I've always heard that orcs make the worst neighbors, shitting in your lawn and whatnot."

There was something special about Yume. She had been skeptical and resistant at first, like everyone before her, but she was willing to listen with an open mind, to take information and examine it. And then draw proper conclusions.

After her final lap around the table, Yume walked back to Billy, and kissed his cheek. "This is awesome, it really is. So, how do we go from here into Rob's dream?"

"Glad you asked." Billy turned to the wall with no windows or artwork, and waved his hand. A display of various scenes appeared, playing out in an arranged six by eight grid.

"I'm assuming these are other people's dreams happening right now?"

"You would assume correctly."

"I'm also assuming only a fraction of everyone who's dreaming right now."

Billy waved his hand; he didn't need to, but he enjoyed the theatrics of the action. The scene on each viewer changed as if flipping a channel. "Also correct. A tiny fraction of random people nearby."

"Amazing. How far can you reach?"

"I don't know the exact distance. Quite a few miles, but there are dependencies." Though not a complete lie, he downplayed his reach.

Yume nodded as if she understood. "Dependencies like... If you looked into the person's eyes versus if I looked into their eyes, and et-cetera."

"Correct."

Yume took a deep breath and exhaled slowly. She turned to Billy and grabbed his hands. "Okay, I'm ready. Are you ready? I'm nervous. Why am I nervous? What do we do next? What do I need to do?"

"It's okay to be nervous. We're going to exact justice. We're going to add to the betterment of the world by subtracting from it. Just relax and think of Lynette and her children." Billy released one of her hands and placed it on the viewer at the bottom corner, to help Yume conceptualize. "Think of the looks in their eyes. Look deeply into their eyes until all you see is Rob."

Yume nodded and breathed deeply, rhythmically. Billy stared into her eyes, wide and unblinking. He saw Lynette, the children. Felt them. He saw Rob. Then the scene on the viewer changed and portrayed four older men sitting on folding chairs around a small card table. Rob was one of them. The scene expanded to show them in an automotive garage. Dirty black stains streaked across the floor. A car on each of the three hydraulic lifts. All three bay doors open.

The neighboring viewers switched to the same portrayal of the men around the table. Then the next set of viewers, until all the viewers depicted that same scene.

"That's him," Yume whispered. She gulped audibly and then cleared her throat. "That's him."

The viewers merged, one into the next, until only one took up the entire wall. Without pomp and circumstance, Billy escorted Yume through the doorway by her hand.

Yume looked around and tightened her grip when Rob laughed. "Four aces!"

"Don't worry," Billy said to her. "He can't hear us or see us. Yet."

Not letting go of his hand, Yume pulled him along as she walked closer. "This is so fucking real. I can smell the oil. I can feel the air move from the fans."

Billy nodded. "Yep. He's dreaming about this place. I bet it's where he works. He must have a deep connection to it, meaning he either loves it here or hates it."

All four men wore dark blue work shirts with their names embroidered on their chests. Rob, Vince, Mack, Sam. Their backs had the same oval patch with a green and red logo, "Fratenelli's Garage" in the middle. The men played another quick round, ending with Rob howling, "I won again! I'm just taking your money tonight!"

"I'm assuming he loses at poker in real life," Yume said. "Or at least has an inferiority complex around his boss, coworkers, and friends, which is probably the impetus of him taking out his frustrations on his wife and kids. Sorry, Rob, you should find ways to raise yourself up, not drag others down."

Billy was falling in love with Yume; she understood him. She recognized how monsters like Rob were made, yet she didn't excuse them. Neither did he.

"This ain't the first time I took your money neither." Rob laughed as he eyed Mack. "You remember last month when the boss said he was coming by to audit your books, the books of a bookie? And you got nervous and checked your books and saw you were ten K short? And had to sell your new car quick for cash so he didn't find out? Yeah, that was me! I skimmed you, skimmed you so fucking bad! The best part is, if you ever had enough brains to dig into the missing money, you wouldn't even know that I made it look like Sam took it!"

"Boss? Bookie? Sounds like these guys are into more than running a garage," Yume said.

"Certainly seems that way," Billy said. Dreams stripped away the falsehoods to expose the reality underneath.

"And you, Vince Fratenelli, I got one for you," Rob said, his mouth oozing into a wicked smile. "I fucked your daughter. Yeah, Vince, I fucked Jenny last week." Rob guffawed, slapping his leg. "Went right into the strip club she works at and fucked her tits off in the champagne room!"

None of the other men moved, stunned by Rob's confession.

Vince shook as if fighting against invisible binds.

The men's eyes flicked from side to side, angry at Rob, fearful of what Vince might do next.

"Ten bucks!" Rob said. "All it took was ten bucks and I blew a load so deep in her, she's gonna taste me the next time she belches. I mean, she's almost forty and still working as a stripper? C'mon, man. I did her a favor."

The other three men at the table remained paralyzed while Rob laughed so hard, he snorted.

Yume turned to Billy, her face contorted with disgust. "Can we end this?"

"With pleasure," Billy replied. "You're good to go."

That was all she needed to hear. "Hey, asshole!" Yume shouted. "I hoped to see something different than what I expected, but you're worse. So much worse."

Eyes wide, stunned, Rob looked at Yume. Chuckling, he looked around to his tablemates. "One of you guys order me a Tai whore?"

"I'm Japanese, you no-dick inbred."

Every one of Billy's ex-girlfriends had been unsure, timid the first time he brought them along to exact justice. Not Yume. She had done her due diligence, and now that she was certain Rob was an asshole, she didn't back down, didn't waffle, or change her mind, didn't hide behind Billy. Instead, she stepped up closer to the condemned.

Rob finally stopped smiling; Yume had struck a nerve. He snapped his fingers and pointed to her. "All right you assholes, take care of her."

Vince, Mack, and Sam stood and shuffled toward the dream interlopers like puppets on strings. Before they got too close, Billy waved his hand to cut their strings, and they collapsed into a heap of tangled limbs. Yume gasped and Billy reminded her, "This is Rob's dream, not theirs. They're still alive in the waking world."

Yume set her jaw and frowned, then nodded. "Right."

Rob stood and started toward Billy and Yume, not bothering to acknowledge his friends on the floor. "I don't know what the fuck this is about, but I'm gonna end it."

"This is about your wife and kids, Rob," Yume said.

"What do they have to do with anything?"

"They're everything, Rob."

"They're nothing. They're the reason I have to work here and take shitty side jobs and deal drugs with these assholes. What are you to them anyway?"

"We're their justice."

Billy took her cue and waved his hand again.

Rob clutched his chest and collapsed.

The only noise was Yume's breathing. Hard. Rapid.

Billy had kept it simple, quick. Usually, he liked to make sure his target knew his motivations, like with Gus, but this was Yume's first time and she'd have a lot to process. He didn't want to add any unnecessary layers of emotional drama.

As soon as Rob hit the floor, Billy took over his dreamscape and kept it going, so he and Yume wouldn't be propelled back into the Valhalla Room. He wanted to make sure she was comfortable with what had happened.

Nostrils flaring, she marched over to Rob's corpse. She stared at his body for a few seconds and whispered, "Now what?"

"Whenever you're ready to go, I'll take us back to the Valhalla Room and then we can wake up."

With her breathing now under control, she moved away from Rob and walked over to his three friends. Billy didn't know why or what she was looking for, and he remained quiet as she took her time examining the bodies. Whatever spell she was under finally broke. Looking satisfied, she glanced around the garage, then walked back to Billy. She kissed his cheek and said, "Let's go."

CHAPTER 21

The sound of sizzling meat pulled Shinko from her daydream – a recollection and analysis of last night's nightmare – as the Fiesta De La Vida waiter passed by her booth with a fajita plate. A rumble rolled through her stomach; the delectable smells of lightly charred meat mingling with the thick cuts of onions and green peppers teased her hunger. She was definitely going to order that for lunch.

Shinko's flight landed in Philadelphia early in the morning. A quick text exchange with Yume to let her know she had arrived safely, and they set up a time and place to meet for lunch. After a cab ride to The Four Seasons, Shinko and Aika checked in and immediately planned their assignment. They indulged in freshening up from their flight, and then Shinko sent Aika on her way. Another cab ride to Fiesta De La Vida. Those very fajitas had taken her back to the dream she had on the plane.

The food aromas, the clattering of plates and cutlery. In her dream, the smells told her she was in Chinese restaurant. The metal against metal of the swords also sounded real, as did the thumps and thuds and cracks of the punches and kicks. Muscles in her arms were sore and her shoulders were stiff. How could they be sore from a dream?

Shinko rolled her neck. Aika had mentioned that she was twitching while asleep. Maybe she flexed rigidly in her dream?

Her phone buzzed. I found The Dragon's Blessing.

Aika. Shinko had instructed her to find the restaurant, but not to engage in other reconnaissance. Wonderful news. Please remember – do NOT enter.

Confirmed. Although, it is closed.

That was odd. When she researched the place two weeks ago, their website indicated they were open for lunch. Closed?

Yes. There is police tape over the entrance.

Shinko fumbled with her phone, almost dropping it. What kind of coincidence was this? Was it a warning? She heard stories of premonitions coming in the form of dreams, but those stories came from folklore or charlatans. Right?

Shinko gripped her phone and texted, Very well. We will reconvene tonight. In the meantime, enjoy the city. Confirmed.

Setting her phone aside, Shinko smirked while imagining Aika, grave and determined, in kitschy sunglasses, a baggy tee shirt, an oversized ballcap drenched in red, white, and blue while wandering up and down the streets of Philadelphia on a mission to see all the sites the city offered. Shinko remembered what it was like to be her age, so serious and dire. There was a lot to learn about people and the world, knowledge the one true advantage the aged had over youth.

Yume's birth added to Shinko's desire to absorb knowledge. The world was a dangerous place and its residents only made it more so. She had always wanted to learn about everything and to excel in her chosen career, but then her goal shifted to protect her daughter. To create a safe place where her daughter had options and didn't feel the need to follow in her footsteps. Unlike Aika, orphaned at eleven, plucked from the alleys at thirteen by Shinigami's Helper. Hopefully Aika would someday be confident and comfortable enough to look beyond the dangers of the world and see the beauty, wonder, and love. Of course, Shinko saw none of that in life until she had a child.

Those wonderful feelings rushed through her when Yume entered the restaurant.

Shinko stood from the table to get Yume's attention. No need to be showy by waving. After a few seconds scanning the restaurant, Yume saw her and rushed over, her glee culminating in a bone-crushing hug. Normally, Shinko found public displays of attention distasteful, but she was in a country where it was customary, so she accepted it and wrapped her arms around her only child. And, God, it felt good!

"It's sooooo good to see you!" Yume's words were muffled as her face pressed into the crook of Shinko's neck.

"You, too, My Dream." Shinko was content to hold her daughter but noticed Shanna and a young man in a wheelchair approaching.

"But I don't want to appear like an overbearing mother in front of your friends."

Yume chuckled as she untangled her arms from her mother. Wiping away a stray tear, she said, "You know Shanna. And this is Billy, my boyfriend."

"Hi, Ms. Dangan," Shanna said as she came in for a hug. "It's good to see you again."

The hug was brief, but no less crushing. There was a desperation to it, matching the subtle worry in her tired eyes. Shanna's smile was as limp as wet tissue, and she carried her weariness in the bags under her eyes.

Shinko had met Shanna twice before and spent time with her, finding her to be the typical American teenager. All present, no future; all words, no meaning. But she had always radiated light, an exuberance that made the people in her presence feel excited about themselves. That light was missing. Did all of that disappear when she crossed the threshold of adulthood, leaving her teens behind? "It's wonderful to see you, too, Shanna. How are you?"

"Good," she said. She stood straighter as if trying to mimic attentiveness. "Great, actually. A lot going on after... Gus... Ummm...?"

"It's okay. Yume told me what happened. I'm sorry for your and your mother's loss." Shinko wasn't entirely sure she believed her own words. Yume had never shined a favorable light upon Gus whenever she discussed him, and when she explained that he had died, she did not seem the least bit upset. But Shinko reached out and touched Shanna's hand, an uncomfortable gesture, but thought it might help.

It seemed to. Shanna squeezed her hand and said, "Thank you. I'll let her know you said that."

Turning her attention to the young man, Shinko stifled a gasp when she looked into his eyes. Deep wells of intelligence and... something she couldn't explain. Her dream from last night asserted itself again, confounding her. What was it about Billy that reminded her of her dream? What was it about him that reminded her of Maya? "You must be Billy? I've heard so much about you."

His smile was kind, his handshake firm yet warm. "I am. I've heard many wonderful things about you, too. How was your flight?"

Courteous. Smart. Handsome in a sleek sort of way. Able to make Yume smile and laugh. What about him was so off-putting? "Uneventful."

"Uneventful flights are perfect flights."

"Very true." Shinko gestured for everyone to join her. "Thank you for indulging me in the lunch venue. Mexican cuisine is not readily available in Japan."

To a chorus of "no problem," everyone took their place around the table.

"How has work been?" Yume asked.

"Nothing very exciting in the world of Human Resources. Much like plane rides; that's a good thing." She hated lying to her daughter, but Yume had such a bright future, and she didn't want to jeopardize it. Her cover as a low-level Vice President for the world's largest insurance company wasn't too far from the truth, especially the gallows humor accompanying the act of terminating someone. "My job is so boring that I just summed up all the events of the past year with one sentence. Please, tell me all about this school year."

Conversation flowed nicely around the table, Yume doing most of the talking, but with a good deal of input from Shanna, though Shanna's words were anemic, her delivery less effervescent than Shinko had expected. Though clearly focused on her schooling while happy that her mother now had an opportunity for growth, she seemed... tired. Not just from lack of sleep but weary of the person she saw in the mirror every day. Odd for a twenty-one-year-old.

Billy added to the conversation when appropriate, in a polite way. Astute, but carful to allow mother and daughter to catch up. However, Shinko and Yume planned to spend the rest of the day together, and she wanted to learn more about the young man who was the topic of her daughter's affections. "So, Billy, Yume told me that you, too, are majoring in psychology?"

"Yes. Though she and I share the same ultimate desire to help people, she wants to pursue therapy and help the individual with their mental health as a whole, while I focus on dreams and hope to land in a clinical setting."

Shinko raised her brows, appraising him. She smiled. "Fascinating. I'm sure your parents are proud of your goals."

A chill passed over the table; six pairs of eyes looked down and away. Yume explained, "Unfortunately, he lost both parents when he was a teenager."

"Oh! I'm sorry to hear that. I didn't mean to stir up unpleasant emotions."

With a poise unbefitting his age, Billy smiled and casually waved his hand, wiping away her unintentional faux pas. "No apology necessary. They were involved in things they shouldn't have been and paid a steep price because of that."

That was an unusual statement, but Shinko pursued the topic no further.

Once the food arrived, everyone's mood lifted, even the sleepiness disappeared from Shanna. The conversation shifted to fielding questions from Shanna and Billy about Japanese cuisine and other cultural differences. However, Yume didn't participate, her eyes constantly drifting to a small television over the restaurant's bar. A news channel.

"Something happening in the world more interesting than spending time with your mother?" Shinko asked, a bit of mirth to her words.

"Huh?" Yume's attention came back to the table. "Oh, sorry. There was... I heard there was an unusual death recently and I was curious if there was any news about it."

"Oh. Will this disrupt our day together? Is this something we need to be cautious about?"

Yume shrugged. "Nah. This is Philadelphia. People get dead all the time here."

Yume and Billy chuckled at her sarcasm.

Shanna asked, "Are you talking about the Chinese restaurant?"

"Chinese restaurant?" Shinko repeated.

"A couple weeks ago, an owner of a Chinese restaurant and his staff were killed after hours. Rumor has it that he was an organized crime member, and it was a hit from another criminal organization," Billy explained.

"What was the name of the place again?" Shanna asked.

"The Dragon's Blessing. They had the *best* Kung Pao chicken."

Shinko dropped her fork.

"You okay, Mom?"

"Yes, My Dream. I'm just surprised that I'm sending you to school in such a dangerous place."

Yume's expression flattened, a silent way of letting Shinko know she was overreacting. To put a finer point on it, she added more sarcasm. "Danger is my middle name, especially since I'm head of a crime syndicate myself, formed mostly of psychologists. Anytime the police start sniffing around, we start asking them questions about their mothers and then sneak away. We call that maneuver the Freudian Slip."

Dabbing the corners of her mouth with a napkin and then setting in on her plate, Shinko said, "It's not nice to be sarcastic to your doddering, old mother."

Yume rolled her eyes. "Oh, pah-leez! Old and doddering? Now who's being sarcastic? The woman who's always the hottest person in the room, that's who."

Shanna shrugged, putting her napkin on her empty plate. "She's not wrong, Ms. Dangan."

"Let's all pretend that I said something eloquent and charming, a sophisticated compliment while remaining within the boundaries of decorum," Billy added.

"Well, thank you all, especially Billy with his sophisticated compliment, but I'm a mother and it's my right, duty, and reflex to worry about my daughter."

"You have nothing to worry about, Ms. Dangan," Billy said. "Yume is a capable woman, able to take care of herself."

Shinko heard an experiential tone to Billy's statement, as if he had personally seen her get out of a bad situation. This, too, didn't sit well with her.

Yume smiled and grabbed Shinko's hand. "It's okay, Mom. We're going to have fun today. I promise we'll stay out of the bad parts of town, say no to drugs, and look both ways before crossing the street."

Patting her daughter's hand, Shinko replied, "I know we will, My Dream."

Shanna stood from the table and gestured toward the exit. "That's our cue, Billy."

"I do believe you are correct," he said as he wheeled back from the table.

After a few pleasantries and hugs, Billy and Shanna left. Halfway to the exit, Billy turned and smiled at Shinko with an unnatural glint in his eye, the flash of a star being born, then the flare of it dying.

CHAPTER 22

The star pulsed; random flares of light plumed from its surface like bright, white feathers. The corona shimmered opalescent, striking colors shifting rhythmically on the surface. It pulsed faster, and bursts of fire escaped while the roiling surface bubbled. The rhythm increased until the star passed the point of no return, its fate inevitable. Then all at once, it exploded, releasing its light and warmth into the universe.

Perfect description of Yume's orgasm, and she loved the visual metaphors.

Dreamscape sex was the best, touching upon pleasures not available any other way. Sex with Billy in the waking world was amazing, but the dreamscape offered the ability to do it on a cloud while floating through the center of a dying galaxy. After a few minutes spent enjoying the residual sensations of release, a kaleidoscope of blue winged butterflies fluttered by, leaving a trail of sparkling gold dust in their wakes. Nice touch.

As in tune with each other as they were in the waking world, the dreamscape amplified the experience. Thankfully, Billy never gave her giant anime or hentai boobs, nor did anything equally weird to his body parts. Directly linked in each other's minds and to all the fun sensory centers of the brain, the dreamscape allowed them to reach pleasures known to few individuals, assuming any others even existed.

Yume had limited dream manipulation ability. She could control her own dreams and jump into Sloan's dreams without help only because of close physical proximity and intense emotional reaction when thinking about her. But her control of Sloan's dreams was limited to nothing more than a tsunami of strawberry yogurt from the dream fridge. But Billy? A master at this, whatever "this" was. Billy was born from Will, and Will could do what Billy could do. Who developed the ability first? How was it developed in the first place? Were there others? Questions for another time. Now time to bask in the warm tingles of afterglow.

Laying side by side and sharing a pillow made of fluffy, pink cloud, Billy nuzzled his head against Yume's. She giggled. He reached upward and swiped away the twinkling remains of the exploded gold star to expose the cosmos behind it. A billion pinholes of light on a black canvas. The isolation of floating through the enormity of space struck her, and a slight chill skittered down her spine. She had to remind herself that this was just a dream.

"Have you ever done this before?" Billy asked, turning to face Yume. "Just lay around and look at the stars?"

Yume regarded Billy. Or was he Will? Mussed hair and an impish smile made him look like Will. If Billy could walk in his dreams, then it stands to reason that the biological shortcomings Will experienced in the waking world would be in working order here. She had to pay attention to speech pattern and mannerisms, but she was certain she had been with Billy this whole time. Would it matter? In the waking world, they shared the same body, so the answer became more ambiguous. But here? They were completely different people. Again, questions for a different time.

Smiling, she looked back up to the stars, then hooked her arm in his. "I have. When I was fourteen."

"Was it with a boy?" Billy asked, the tone of his words playful.

"It was. He and I found a grassy hill on a cloudless night."

"Ooooh, sounds romantic."

"The grass was wet, I got bitten by bugs, and his breath was so bad that when he kissed me, I swore he used his tongue to wipe his own ass."

"Ooooh, sounds romantic."

Yume swatted his shoulder and they laughed.

The stars varied in size and brightness as they twinkled. "I could never see the constellations. So, most of that special night was me saying, 'no,' every time he asked if I saw some constellation or another."

"Clearly, you didn't have the right guide to the stars." Billy pointed to a cluster of stars and moved his finger, tracing lines from one to another. The stars grew brighter and the lines connecting them glowed. "This is Orion."

"Ahh, that one, I know."

"Most people can find him. He's my favorite."

"Yeah?"

As Billy talked, he continued to trace other constellations. Like with Orion, the stars and lines became brighter to highlight their existence. Slowly, faint images of monochromatic white formed around the outlines. Orion turned into a muscled man wearing armor and helmet traditionally found on ancient Greek soldiers. Other figures filled the sky: a crab, a scorpion, a snake-like dragon, a bull.

"Orion is the hero of the sky. Sure, the tales of him are like many Greek myths – misogynistic and carrying the undertone of permission to cast aside all form of self-governance, since the instigator was allowed to seek revenge because the party that they wronged sought justice. But, you know, that's what happens when angry men oversee theology. Sorry, that's neither here nor there."

Armed with a short-sword and shield, Orion fought the crab – the same size as he – ultimately winning by cutting it in half. "There were different tales about Orion, but nothing as heroic or notable as Perseus or Odysseus, just a hunter with a few stories. But up in the sky, he's the hero. He's facing off against Taurus while danger is all around him. He's the constellation that everyone can find, even while he's standing next to Hercules."

Another well-muscled man with a sword jumped through the sky, swiping his weapon at the scorpion and dragon. None of his strikes connected, but he kept attacking until a bear lunged at him from behind and tore him in half. Orion ran across the sky and decapitated the bear. What happened next made Yume feel the need to brush up on her mythology; Orion took the head of the bear and placed it over his own before he went on to kill the hydra and scorpion.

"That was intense," Yume mumbled.

"Umm, yeah?" Billy's voice hitched, like he was just as surprised by Orion's actions. He swiped his hand and the images faded away, the stars returning to normal.

What was that about? Had Will taken control for a moment? Long enough to mess around and then move on? He certainly seemed like a prankster, and not outside the realm of possibility.

Billy turned to the side and gently pressed his forehead against hers. "I hate to ruin such an amazing time, but I have to wake up soon. The professor needs my help today."

Yume smiled and stroked his cheek, wondering if she could tell his soft flushed flesh apart from Will's, as if there were a form of trans-mutation. No difference. Same soft skin, same angles from cheek to chin. "That's okay. I'm going to hang out with Shanna today."

"Sounds good. Call me later?"

"Absolutely."

As they kissed, they faded until Yume woke up, warm and content, but her alarm clock's glowing red numbers let her know that she could catch a few more minutes of sleep. Shanna wouldn't be awake yet anyway.

Yume rolled onto her side, pulled the covers up to ward off the early Spring chill, and closed her eyes. It was going to be good to hang out with her sister. It felt like forever since it had just been the two of them.

During dinner with her mom four nights ago, Shanna had looked fatigued, blaming it on unsatisfactory sleep. What if it was bad dreams? If that were the case, then Yume knew just the person who could help.

Shanna was about a mile away, much farther than the short trip across the living room to get inside Sloan's head, but they had a much stronger emotional connection. *Focus on that. Focus on her eyes. Her pretty blue eyes.*

Yume visualized her sister's eyes as if she was nose-to-nose with her. Her eyes grew rounder and wider, her iris's disappearing beyond Yume's peripheral vision until the blackness of her pupil was all that remained. After a few heartbeats, a pinprick of light winked alive in the distance. Yume floated closer; the light grew larger. She saw a shape. A door. A closed door with light spilling out from behind all four sides.

Yume was standing now, in Shanna's dream, her hand on the doorknob. Excited about popping into her dream, she turned the knob and stepped inside.

Into an orgy.

No, not quite that. A lot of naked muscular men glistening from sweat, but Shanna was the only woman. Had Yume paused outside the door to listen, she might have recognized the moans and groans of pleasure coming from the other side before barging in.

Too stunned to move, think, or even breathe, Yume unblinkingly watched as six, seven, eight men (that she could count), undulated in a circle around Shanna on a small bed. On her back, feet in the air. The man between her legs threw his head back, howled with joyful release, and then moved away. The next man wasted no time taking his place.

After the next guy whooped to climax and moved out of the way, Yume snapped out of her stupor. A blast of heat flowed through her cheeks, embarrassed by her voyeurism. All the men looked exactly alike, and three of them wore blue top hats. Yume wasn't sure who he was – probably a guy in one of Shanna's classes – and she didn't understand the significance of the hats. She was confident that she didn't want to know the answer to either mystery. Taking a step backward, she suppressed the urge to apologize. She wanted to leave her sister in peace, until one of the men closest to her head shifted aside.

She made eye contact with Shanna.

At first, Yume didn't know what to say. Did she even need to say anything? As far as Shanna was concerned, this was just a dream; Yume wasn't real. But Shanna couldn't speak, her mouth full and cheek distended. And there was pure fear in her eyes.

Yume swiped her hand through the air and yelled, "Wake up!"

Jolting upright in bed, Yume looked around the room. Her bedroom. No naked men. No top hats. No sister.

She lunged across her bed and grabbed her phone from the nightstand, thumb primed to tap Shanna's number. No. That'd be weird, too difficult to explain why she was calling for no reason this early in the morning. 7:07AM. Not super early, but it might be construed as obnoxious to call and say, "I hope you're okay from the crazy sex dream I woke you from."

Yume returned her phone to the nightstand and got out of bed. They'd be meeting for breakfast in a few hours anyway.

She did her best to avoid Sloan, who had been awake for almost two hours now, going about her morning routine and catching up on schoolwork.

An hour later, the energy in the Grain-N-Bean café hummed, the unseasonably warm day bringing about conversations of optimism and hope for a magical spring. The change in seasons had as much to do with people and mood as it did weather and nature. Yume preferred spring and autumn; the moderate weather and the refreshing feeling of waking from a good sleep. That along with the comfort of snuggling in for a long slumber.

Yume took her regular seat with a warm cup of chai tea with lots of milk. Chai tea tasted great, no matter what season.

Yume's cheeks started burning as soon as Shanna entered the café. They burned hotter when Shanna sat down. After all, an hour ago, her sister had more than one dick in her. *Just a dream. Just a dream.*

She was fifteen minutes late, looking… plain. Nothing wrong with that, but for Shanna to be in public in a baggy sweatshirt and loose-fitting jeans was akin to heresy.

"Hey, Sis," Shanna said.

"Hey. How are you doing?"

"Good, I…" Shanna looked into Yume's eyes and paused. "Are…? Are you blushing? I never knew you could do that."

Yume laughed off Shanna's comment. "Racist."

With an exaggerated eye roll, Shanna replied, "Not what I meant, jerk."

"The tea was hotter than I expected. Caught me by surprise." To add credence to her statement, Yume slurped long and loud from her cup.

They shared a laugh and slipped into easy banter, each taking turns discussing their mothers; how Shanna's handled life post-Gus, how Yume's liked her visit in the States. Their conversation was nice, but Yume kept waiting for its usual turn toward Shanna's dating life so she could manipulate the conversation toward Shanna's dream. If Yume asked, "How are you sleeping?" then Shanna would just shrug it off. If she asked, "Any good dates lately?" then it'd be too jarring, out of character for her. So, she rolled along waiting for an opportunity, but as time drifted from breakfast into the realm of late lunch, the opportunity never occurred.

"I heard about this food truck. They serve a mean lobster mac," Shanna said as they left the café.

"Lobster mac? From a roach coach?" Yume laughed.

"Dude, where have you been? Here in 2006, food trucks are evolving past the old rolling grease pit stereotype."

With that, the women walked from campus farther into the city, Shanna texting friends and piecing together information about the food truck's whereabouts. Three blocks this way, four blocks that way, five blocks up, two blocks over. They finally found it. Not in the nicest neighborhood, one ripe for gentrification. On the edge of a tiny park, they stepped into a line of hungry people murmuring about the unique food options. Shanna and Yume stuck with their original choice of lobster mac.

As they used a tiny plastic fork to shovel the delicious gooey cheese treat from the plastic container into their mouths, they wandered around aimlessly. Shanna tossed her empty container away, then yawned.

Finally, something Yume could work with. She nudged Shanna. "Exciting night last night, sleepyhead?"

Shanna slouched and shook her head demurely. "Haven't been going out lately."

"Oh. Getting enough sleep?"

Shanna shrugged, not looking up.

Yume continued, "If you're not sleeping well because of bad dreams, we can figure out why and what they mean. Sleep is important—"

"Please, don't."

"Don't? Don't... what?"

Shanna looked up at Yume, her fatigue on display in bloodshot eyes. "Analyze me."

"Shanna, I'm not analyzing you."

"You are, and you do. I get it, I really do. It's your chosen career and that's great, but right now I'm trying to make big changes in my life and I'm helping my mom and that's been giving me... weird... dreams. That's it. That's all. I don't need a shrink to tell me that, but I do need a sister to cheer me on. Please."

Are your dreams recurring? Are you having fun in them? Have you done any of that in the waking world? Who is the guy? What's with the top hat? Why does that top hat look familiar? Why don't you want to talk about it? Damn it! "I'm always here for you, Shanna, no matter what you need. Always. And I'm beyond happy to cheer you on."

Shanna's smile was limp, but she grabbed Yume's hand and squeezed. "Thank you."

"Of course. Any time." Yume internally debated visiting Shanna's dreams tonight, but when she threw her plastic container away, something caught her eye. The trashcan was on the corner cut through street barely bigger than an alley. A red and green oval sign with hints of rust along the edges poked from one of the buildings.

Fratenelli's Garage.

"Just like my dream," Yume whispered. This was amazing! Not like déjà vu and more than a feeling. She had been here before even though she had never been here before. She headed toward the shop.

"Yume?" Shanna asked, following close behind. "Where are we going?"

"Just want to see something real quick."

The smell of old grease and used oil hit Yume's nose, but when she got to the open bay doors, she knew what to expect. Three men with their names embroidered on their work shirts.

Vince.

Mack.

Sam.

Reclining in a folding chair, fingers folded together over his chest, Vince watched the other men work on the engine of a hoodless car. "Still can't believe that fucker had a heart attack. Now we gotta find another guy. Think Rico would be interested in workin' for Picasso?"

"Fuck Rico and fuck Rob," Mack said. "We don't need a fourth. It's been what? Like four or five days or whatever, and we're doin' fine without him."

"What he said. Rob was the weak link. Trust me, that guy was worse than no good." Sam punctuated his statement by spitting on the floor.

"Yeah, Fuck Rob," Yume said.

Shanna gasped.

Yume pointed to Mack. "He stole ten thousand dollars from you...," and then pointed to Sam. "...and blamed it on you."

Vince stood while Sam and Mack turned toward Yume, their fists clenched. Through gritted teeth, Vince growled, "I don't know who you are—"

"But I know you," Yume interrupted. "You're the guy who has a stripper daughter. And I know that Rob fucked her."

Shanna pressed into Yume's back and whispered. "I think we should get out of here now."

"No, blondie," Mack said. "I think you two need to stay awhile."

Yume had them where she wanted them – stunned and wide-eyed, staring at her. She looked deeply into their eyes, studying every-thing about them. Rob was a piece of human garbage that needed to be removed from this world, and no doubt in her mind that his associ-ates were similar ilk, if not worse. In Rob's dream, he confessed to run-ning numbers and dealing drugs, and a minute ago they had men-tioned someone named Picasso. Satisfied with a clear enough pathway to follow over the next few nights, she reached in her pocket while Shanna reached into her purse. They both whipped out pepper spray at the same time. "Odds are, we'll hit your eyes, but just in case we miss, rest assured, we know where your balls are and how to kick the living hell out of them."

The men stopped and exchanged nervous glances with each other.

Backing away, Yume said, "That's what I thought."

The women walked backwards until they made it out of the through street. The main street sidewalk was crowded enough for them to feel somewhat at ease, but not enough for them to put away their pepper spray.

"Care to tell me what the fuck that was all about?" Shanna snapped, her words hot from anger.

"Not yet. I will, I promise, but not yet."

Shanna snorted and shook her head. "Okay. But let's get back to campus."

They jogged the rest of the way, Yume excited to tell Billy they had more candidates.

CHAPTER 23

Shinko watched The Dragon's Blessing from the abandoned convenience store across the street, the shelves picked clean by urban scavengers, the walls tagged with graffiti. She sat cross-legged on a counter along the side wall close to the front of the store. From the darkness, she watched the happenings along the nearly empty city sidewalks, aglow under the streetlights.

Miraculously, vandals had not shattered the windows, and there were no plywood coverings, just the standard cage-like bars.

A man and a woman walked into view, hands in coat pockets and their pace brisk. Heads down, the couple didn't give The Dragon's Blessing a second glance as they passed by. At almost three in the morning, Shinko assumed they lived nearby and were heading home after a night out. They belonged.

However, ten minutes later, she saw a man strolling down the street towards the restaurant.

Tall, wearing loose black pants and top and no jacket, the casual observer would hardly notice that he did *not* belong. As he passed in front of The Dragon's Blessing, he looked everywhere other than the restaurant. Then he turned down the next alleyway, disappearing into the shadows.

"Obviously a member of Heaven's Palisade," Aika whispered through Shinko's earpiece. Aika occupied a vacant, third-floor apartment farther down the street. A different angle, but she could see everything Shiko saw. "Shall we move in?"

Shinko peered into the store's depths to investigate the darkness for anything suspicious before answering. "Not yet. I suspect we'll see more members soon enough."

It took less than five minutes. A woman this time, wearing the same black clothing as the man before her, very similar to the ninja-yoroi Shinko and Aika wore. The woman approached from the other direction, but her path also took her behind the restaurant.

Shinko waited a few minutes, then said to Aika, "Let's go."

Having studied the area for the past few hours, Shinko slipped out the back of the convenience store and hurried around front. She crossed the street like a breeze, using her blowgun to shoot black paint pellets at every camera along the way. Just like her dream.

Aika joined her at the front door of The Dragon's Blessing right as Shinko inserted her automated lock-picking device. The streetlight's buzz could be heard, a dog barked a few blocks away, a homeless person coughed from a neighboring alley. Clangs and rummaging from nearby trashcans, rats scurrying for food. The sounds of a slumbering city. Exactly like her dream.

A quick headshake brought her back in the moment, and she chided herself about losing focus, even for a fraction of a second. Door open. Slide in. Door closed. Eyes adjusted to the darkness. Overturned tables. Scattered chairs. Broken pieces of furniture. "Just like my dream."

"Senpai?" Aika whispered.

"Nothing," Shinko whispered back, but drew her sword. Two members of Heaven's Palisade lurked somewhere in this building. No – there were more, she sensed them. Or was her dream making her think this?

Her assignment was to find a weapon, and that search led her here to The Dragon's Blessing. But *something* made her hesitate. She saw the yellow police tape across the front entrance – the dream had affected her decisiveness.

Plenty of things in this world defied explanation, and Shinko had always left those conjectures to theorists and philosophers. But now? Not only did she have tingly-warning goosebumps while laying eyes upon the restaurant, but that sensation echoed the ones she had experienced in her dream. What she heard, saw, smelled. Everything. Those with limited imagination used coincidence as an explanation. Far as Shinko was concerned, there had to be another reason behind her cautionary feelings. And what of Maya, the self-proclaimed weapon she sought? Was the mission truly to find a waifish girl? The answers lay within this building.

Following Shinko's lead, Aika unsheathed her sword, holding it over her head with both hands. She kept perfect pace with Shinko, step for step, as they moved through the dining room.

The kitchen doors flew open and shurikens zipped through the air, glinting from the ambient light.

Though different from her dream, Shinko was ready for an attack. Launching herself to the right, she landed on her shoulder, rolling to her feet with ease. Aika jumped to the left. The thunks of shurikens sinking into the wall echoed in the quiet restaurant.

Throwing stars were inaccurate weapons, designed to force the enemy off balance or slow pursuers. In this instance, separate partners. Four figures – two men, two women judging from shape and size – rushed from the kitchen toward the center of the room and split into pairs, one man and one woman each.

A bit of relief flitted through Shinko's chest; at least *this* differed from her dream. And all four members of Heaven's Palisade wore black and wasted no time with theatrical posturing. They attacked with urgency, without pretense. Also, unlike her dream, her adversaries were more proficient with their weapons. The man had two kunai and showed his accuracy, Shinko barely avoiding them by leaning back parallel to the floor as they zipped by her face. Had she not needed her ninjato to block a sword strike from the woman, she would have sliced the kunai's retractable cords.

Swords hummed a tinny tune while slashing through the air and ended with a reverberating crescendo when they clanged together. Block. Slice. Block. Dodge a kunai. Block. Slice. Block. Block. The next sword struck too close, and Shinko had to dodge another kunai strike.

The Heaven's Palisade pair were coordinated and fast. In between ducking the kunai and side-stepping the woman, a ridiculous thought struck Shinko. Cornered, she had no other choice but to act on it. She prayed she was right, that she had indeed fought in this arena before and therefore knew the secrets it held.

Clang. Clang. Jump back. *Clang.* Dodge. *Clang.*

She took one big step backward and blindly stomped. Success! She had brought her foot down on the leg of an overturned chair, launching it toward the woman. The move distracted her enemies enough that when the man threw both kunai his aim was off, and the woman had to pull up. Shinko swung twice; her first cut severed the kunai's tethers, her second sliced the woman's lateral side. Shinko had no time for a finishing blow; the man advanced on her while the woman fell back, passing the sword off to him.

Again, Shinko found herself blocking sword-strikes, his assaults harder than the woman's. Without needing to dodge projectiles, though, she was able to control her movements as she backed toward the kitchen. Since he was larger, she expected the confined space would be to her advantage.

The thin doors flung open, hitting hard enough to bounce closed again, Shinko timing her backward leap so the thin doors slapped against the man. A half second was all she had to analyze her surroundings. In the center of the kitchen a long prep counter stood behind her, a myriad of pots, pans, and utensils dangling over it. The man burst into the kitchen and Shinko sliced downward. Damn! He had expected the move and blocked her attack with a slicing motion of his own, hard enough to knock the sword from her hands.

Left hand on the counter behind her as a pivot point, she leapt and swung her feet with enough force to slide over the stainless steel surface. As she had hoped, he lunged with a hurried strike. His sword clanged impotently against the hanging cookware, his face now close to the counter. Too close. She boxed his head between two cast-iron pans with the satisfying crack of metal against bone. The man shook it off, swiftly recovered, and followed her, taking the same path over the counter.

Shinko backed away, the prep counter on her right, a line of deep friers, pantries, and more counters on her left. She scanned the area for an effective weapon. The air was heavy with the smell of peanut and sesame oil in the fryers, but... She caught a strong whiff of something else. Gasoline? In a kitchen? No time to ponder that. Running out of room, she opted for a pan and a massive ladle. Wielding the cooking gear like an ersatz sword and shield, she was ready to stand her ground.

Stopping a few meters in front of her, the man sheathed his sword and grabbed a rectangular can from the counter. He pulled a lighter from a tiny pant pocket and lit it. He squeezed the can and Shinko had to jump to avoid the stream of flame. One foot on the prep counter, her other on the edge of a deep fryer, a woosh of conflagration followed a wall of intense heat at her back. No time to look, think, or assess, only react. She tossed the ladle, but the man dodged it. He dropped the can and lighter to draw his sword and rushed toward Shinko.

Her heavy pan blocked his sword strike, and she threw it at his head as a diversion, allowing her enough opportunity to jump and flip over him. Landing on his other side gave her a better view of the fire claiming part of the wall. No matter. She had what she needed to end this – at least a dozen knives clung to a magnetic strip on the wall by the large cutting board. A few backward paces were all she needed. One by one, she threw them at the man's chest and head as he advanced. Either he dodged or blocked them with his sword. Down to three knives.

Shinko developed a rhythm in her knife throws, lulling the man into a false sense of predictiveness. He slashed with his sword as she threw the tenth knife, but not at his head. Into his foot. He kicked back in pain, a reflex, and stumbled, his head moving forward. With a tight grip on knives eleven and twelve, Shinko jammed them into his eyes; his eyeballs sickeningly squelched like wet gelatin and spattered red and yellow goo over her hands. His body stiffened, and she gave him one final push backwards, toward the burgeoning inferno. Whatever plans she had about gathering information literally went up in smoke.

She circled the prep counter to grab her sword, then burst through the doors.

As she ran into the dining room, the female adversary Shinko had fought lay dead on her back with two sai jammed into her, one in a bloodied eye socket, one in her wide-open mouth. The other woman was dead, pinned through her torso to the wall by a ninjato.

Wielding a pair of claw-like shuko traditionally worn for scaling walls, Aika swiped her fists of metal so fast her hands were blurs. The man had lost his weapon and backed away, blocking her with his shredded and bloodied forearms and shins. He didn't stand a chance. One final slice to his belly and his innards bulged out of the dark red opening; he doubled over, the fight within him gone.

"Don't kill him!" Shinko yelled as she ran over to help.

Aika threw him to the ground.

"And don't let him bite down on his tooth!"

As soon as he hit the floor, Aika ripped off his face covering and jammed her fingers in his mouth, her metal claws acting as mouth-spreaders. Blood ran down the corners of his lips from his torn inner cheeks, his grunts turned to gags, and with one pull, she plucked the gray false molar where the cyanide pill was hidden.

With no more struggle, Shinko knelt on his left arm, Aika on his right.

"You're going to die," Shinko said. "And I doubt your bosses will be waiting for you in the afterlife with a paycheck. The best way to avenge yourself is with a quick death after telling us what we want to know. Make no mistake, though, we will get answers. If not from you, then from another member. Up to you how many we will have to kill. So, if you have any close connections within your organization, imagine the whispers of their final words."

The storm behind the man's eyes diminished and a fine mist of blood accompanied each breath as he pondered her words. His expression softened to acceptance – all Shinko needed.

"Where is the weapon?" she asked.

"Gone." The man coughed and hacked up a bloody oyster-glob. "Taken."

"From here? Is that why this place was destroyed?"

"Yes. A group of men came, killed Chen and his family, took the weapon. Maybe another criminal organization."

"If the weapon is gone and your client is dead, why come back?"

"We came to burn the place down."

"Why didn't you do it earlier? Right after the weapon was taken?"

He chuckled, his laughter gurgling. "Politics and bureaucracy exist in every organization, no matter the size."

Shinko looked at Aika and raised her brow.

Aika asked, "What is the weapon?"

Shinko did not ask because she already knew the answer.

The man coughed again, then answered, "A girl."

"A girl? How could a girl be a weapon?"

Shinko fought the urge to laugh at the irony. Aika was often mistakenly viewed as just "a girl," and here she asked that same question.

The man shook his head. "They say she can enter and control dreams. Chen had been using her to eliminate his enemies."

Aika turned to Shinko with an unspoken question – is the interrogation over?

Shinko nodded, and made good on her promise.

CHAPTER 24

Picasso hobbled into his office and plopped into the chair behind his dark cherry desk. He sighed with relief, the pressure finally off his throbbing leg. The small 8th Street Gallery office had a standard feel to it. Decent desk, shitty subordinate chair across from it, metal file cabinet with a potted aloe plant on top, paneled walls, an oval coffee table large enough to support the pot of succulents, and a larger potted tree-like clementine in the corner. Justin, the gallery manager, brought them in and maintained them to "add life to this dreary dungeon." Justin hated the dark paneling, but Picasso liked the classic office look.

Dark cherry gave his desk a nice appeal. Picasso didn't use it for much. Stored a few forms in the hanging file-folder drawer, those files which made the business legitimate enough to survive legal scrutiny. Tucked back behind the file folders was a small bottle of mid-priced Johnny Walker. He didn't require fancy whiskey, just a hit or two… or three… to settle the tremors in his hands. He wasn't the fidgety type, unless things got dangerous, then his nerves acted up.

He was about to lie to his boss, after all.

Hell with it; a fourth swig from the bottle and back in the drawer. Deep breath. *I've been doin' this job longer than this kid has been alive*, he reminded himself as he tightened his tie and straightened his jacket. This office was where it started, four years ago when the kid took over the business from his father. However, he'd been on the other side of the desk and the kid had sat in this chair. The trip down memory lane calmed him enough, until he heard a knock on the door.

He licked dry lips and put on his game face, the heavy-lidded look of apathy. "Come in."

Maxwell Templeton entered the office and shut the door behind him.

Yup, a not even thirty-year-old kid who looked every bit like a seasoned tycoon. Thick brown hair matched any given cover of men's magazines and gave him an affable look, yet his square jawed face housed the dark eyes of a shark. The kid could be downright terrifying when pissed off. His light gray Armani shimmered as he walked, so pristine that he looked like he donned it fresh off the laundry press, even though Picasso knew there'd been a flight and a car ride between the start of the day and now. Picasso wasn't a jealous man by nature, so he tried not to dwell too long on this kid's age and what all he had.

"Afternoon, Harold," Maxwell said as he took a seat in the chair in front of the desk.

Picasso admired the kid for having no issues sitting in a pilled up-holstered chair for a business meeting. Thankfully, he didn't need to stand yet, his right leg still a painful mess from rescuing Maya. "How are things going?"

"Good. Thanks for asking, Mr. Templeton."

Maxwell chuckled. "You've always been fond of making under-statements. Unless it's your clever way of finding out who's paying attention."

Hopefully, not paying attention too closely. "I think you know I'm clever enough not to be too clever."

Nodding, Maxwell said, "Can't disagree with that. I scheduled this meeting to make sure you knew I noticed what you were doing."

"With… the Russians?"

Show no emotion. Don't react. Feign ignorance. Key tactics Picasso followed for conversational deception. On occasion, he'd nudge the conversation.

Sitting back in the chair, Maxwell crossed his legs and placed his elbows on the armrests, fingers folded together. When he smiled, he looked like a model, inviting and ready to sell. "Yes, Harold. The Russians. I noticed a few mysterious deaths with alleged members of the Agapov organization. One fellow walked in front of a bus. One man jumped from his fifth story apartment balcony. Another shot himself in the head. Rumor has it they're in quite a state of disarray. I don't know how you did it but taking out three key members in about two weeks is impressive."

With the slightest of smirks, Picasso gave a nod of appreciation. "Thanks. I do the best I can."

"You do. Though, usually you just make people disappear. On occasion, you go traditional, like The Dragon's Blessing a few weeks ago."

"On occasion, you need to send the right message."

"I agree. So, what was going on there?"

Remain calm. "Chen was getting bold. Bolder than I thought reasonable. The competition needed to be taken down a notch or two."

Maxwell's posture and gestures made it seem like he was talking to a buddy. But he was studying, judging; Picasso saw it in his eyes. "I can't disagree with that. So, the Russians. How'd you do it? I mean, pushing a person off a balcony is one thing, but making someone walk in front of a bus? Shoot themselves? That's next level, Harold."

Picasso tilted his head, raised a brow, and shrugged a shoulder – his variation of playing coy. "After the loud and messy Chinese place, I wanted quiet and clean. Let our competition know we can do either."

"That's it? Making hit jobs look like suicides?"

"Hit jobs to look like suicides."

"Then how about our guys?"

Picasso shifted in his seat and looked away, a normal reaction to a sensitive question. Looking back to his boss, he frowned, another natural reaction. "I got no answer for that."

"Two heart attacks, a brain aneurism, and a multiple organ failure, all while they slept. All four men from the Fratenelli crew."

Picasso blinked, impressed the king knew so much about the peasants. "A really weird coincidence."

"Could it have been poisoning?"

"All of the autopsies said they were clean. Other than the booze, cigarettes, and recreational shit they took. No poison. Nothing chemical."

Maxwell shifted in his seat. Feet on the floor, he leaned forward and rested his elbows on his knees. His stare bore deep into Picasso, as if he looked directly into his hidden thoughts. "I've seen some pretty weird things, Harold, and this is right up the top of the list."

Unflinching, Picasso said, "I agree. I have no explanation for what could have happened."

That was the truth. Picasso didn't know what happened to those four numb nuts at Fratenelli's.

But he had a suspicion he wanted to investigate, and needed to hide that from Maxwell, needed to remain steadfast when Maxwell asked, "Are you sure?"

Picasso nodded. "No explanation, yet."

Maxwell jutted his jaw and nodded, pursing his lips. Finally, he sat back. "A month ago, you said you might have a lead about something interesting."

Picasso gave a sad chuckle and shook his head. "Sorry, but nothin' panned out. Just another desperate soul named Yanni tryin' to get out of payin' us what he owes."

"It's a shame when people get desperate."

If his words had been any more pointed Picasso would be bleeding from his ears. *Hold it together, old man. Hold it together.* "It is."

Picasso heard the tick, tick, tick of a clock even though his office didn't have one. He had never once lied to his boss until now, so he hoped that degree of honesty would carry him through the meeting.

Tick. Tick. Tick.

His heart kept time with the non-existent clock.

Thump. Thump. Thump.

Maxwell clapped his hands and stood. Picasso fought the urge to jump out of his skin, but thanks to many years in a line of work that included gunshots and abrupt outbursts, he'd become used to sudden noises. "Well, this was a good meeting. Always good to see my number one employee."

Picasso forced a smirk, another perfectly normal reaction under the circumstances. Ready for the screaming pain from his right leg, he stood and shook his boss' hand before escorting him to the door. After a few more pleasantries, Maxwell Templeton left the gallery.

An hour later, Picasso was home.

His house was bigger than necessary, but smaller than the mansions in other parts of Philly. A long driveway off a wooded road led to a two-story six-bedroom brick beauty, gated for privacy. The master bedroom was no longer his, willingly surrendered to Maya.

The frail little girl looked even tinier lying on his king-sized bed, so heartbreakingly sweet, fragile. Soldier straight on her back, she slept. Her long black hair lay fanned beside her, but not a single strand on her earnest face. Even in sleep, she looked serious. Doing what made her special required a lot of energy; to recoup, she needed sleep, but ironically, she did what made her special during sleep. It was difficult to fathom such a little twig as the most powerful person in the world, capable of killing a man with a single thought. A little twig that could be easily broken.

Picasso slapped himself for that. The stray, meaningless thought should have never crossed his mind. Too many years as a thug, a killer, a monster hiding underneath the skin of an old man. He wanted to wake her and apologize for the thought. No, she needed her sleep.

His heart yearned for him to crawl into bed and curl up next to her, like he had done with his daughter. Read her bedtime stories. Give her a new stuffed animal. Let her know he'd always be there for her. Wouldn't be right if he did that, though. Maya wasn't his daughter.

Picasso crossed the bedroom to an armchair. He removed his tie and jacket and let them drop to the floor. Comfortable in the chair, he undid the top two buttons of his shirt. Eyes closed, he slowed his breathing. *Heh, after lying to my boss, all I gotta do is not worry about him putting a hit out on me.* Breathe. Control the breathing. Beach. Just another day at the beach. Just another day at... the...

Beach. The sand was so fine it felt like he was walking on satin. Perfect heat from the sun without the sweat. Maya walked next to him, looking up with her serious little face.

Warm ocean water splashing at his feet, Picasso looked down at a healthy kid who was full of life, dramatically more so than the wisp sleeping on his king-sized bed. He smiled.

"I'm surprised to see you here on the beach," she said.

Her voice sounded like a little girl, but her tone came from an older woman. Despite that, Picasso kept his tone soft and even, calm. No doubt in his mind she was only a child. "I had a tense meeting with my boss and the sound of the waves and the warm sand between my toes helps me unwind."

"Why was the meeting tense?"

"He's noticed what we're doing."

"And that's bad?"

"I don't want him to find out about you."

"No?"

"No. He would abuse your powers."

"How is that unlike what you're doing?"

Picasso exhaled slowly. "It is different. As soon as I rescued you, the Agapov organization moved into the territory and tried to capitalize on us taking out Chen. But you know this. All we need to do is remove a few more key members and they will leave us alone. Then I will take you home."

"A few more removals and then you'll take me home?"

"As long as nothing unforeseen happens. And as long as the mysterious loss of my men doesn't get any worse. I've lost four men. All four died in their sleep."

"Oh. I know who's doing that."

Picasso stopped in his tracks. Cold goosebumps prickled his skin as he processed her words. "You... *know*... who's killing my employees?"

Maya stopped walking and turned to him, cocking her head as if confused by his confusion. "I do. His name is William, but he is either Billy or Will."

Wobbling on jelly legs at her words, he asked, "There are more of you? Other people who can do what you do?"

Maya shrugged like a girl her age, quick and whimsical. "Why wouldn't there be?"

Valid question. Why did Picasso assume Maya was the only person who could travel into dreams, affect them, use them as lethal weapons? In his line of work, failing to consider the angles was how people wound up dead.

Another individual out there like Maya was knocking off his men. It made perfect sense that Picasso could be moving to the top of a list he didn't want to be on, but he didn't know any William who went by Billy or Will. Well, there was "Fork-Flip" Bill who worked in a warehouse close to the docks, but that putz gained fame for stupidly filming himself popping wheelies on a forklift. The numb-nuts flipped it over and the video went viral. No way that idiot could be the "William" in question.

Picasso wiped his hand over his face and raked his fingers through his hair a few times, a physical tic that helped alleviate deep frowns. Satisfied that he no longer looked angry, he crouched in front of Maya. "Can you show me this William?"

"He's sometimes Billy, sometimes Will," she said as she waved her hand through the air.

A static image of a young man appeared a little farther along the beach. Very young, early twenties maybe. Handsome enough kid, but kinda thin. Unassuming. The kind of guy who could walk from one end of a crowded airport to the other without anyone noticing him.

"You know how to contact him?"

"Through the dreamscape."

Picasso nodded and stroked his chin. "I think maybe I need to meet him."

CHAPTER 25

Billy sat in his Valhalla room, watching a dozen "screens" while lethargically swiping through them. He leaned back and propped his feet on the table, but immediately moved them back to the floor, the memory of Yume's farcical scolding still fresh.

"This is a castle, not some hunting lodge," she had said right before they slid into Vince Fratenelli's dreamscape. "What's wrong with you? Orcs and wizards have to eat off this table, and you're putting your feet all over it. Do you know how many hours dream-dwarves spent hand-crafting this beautiful table, and you just put your feet all over it?"

He couldn't help laughing out loud alone in his own dreamscape. He was in love. And so was Will. Most people wouldn't understand having a relationship with someone who had one body and two minds, but Yume nurtured it. She always added a little something extra to the notes he and Will left each other in the waking world, everything from cartoonish doodles to fun asides like, "It totally was *not* me who ate all the ice cream."

Billy admired how effortlessly she seemed to handle life. Earning high grades. Doing everything she could to help her headcase "sister," Shanna. Dealing with a shitty roommate. Being the best daughter possible. Helping Billy and Will tip the scales of justice to the side of the angels.

Though he was upset that she put herself in danger by going to Fratenelli's garage in the waking world, she impressed him by looking into the eyes of three more men who needed to be removed from society. Will referred to her as brave.

Yume's instincts were spot on. She was the only one Billy and Will had met who could affect other people's dreams. At least she was showing signs that she could. Filling her roommate's dreams with strawberry yogurt cups was better than nothing.

A few of his ex-girlfriends could break the chains of waking world physics within their own dreamscapes, but most of them didn't know if they were dreaming or not. Yume's skills surpassed them all, making her dreamscape as malleable as warm clay.

The proud feeling was fleeting as the thought of Maya entered his mind.

Not only did Maya share his abilities, she was more powerful. She invaded and altered his dreamscape with ease and was able to pull forth Will. He wanted to look for her again, but didn't think he could with any more stealth than last time. Undoubtedly, she'd discover any further attempts. That was the whole point of showing Yume's mother who Maya was. But that plan had not worked.

After spending two weeks in America, Shinko was scheduled to return to Japan tomorrow. Yume had visited her every night this week, yet still had the energy to hunt down and remove Fratenelli, Mack, and Sam. Fratenelli had a boss, someone named Picasso, but neither Billy nor Yume saw him in Fratenelli's dream. If he was higher on the organized crime food chain, they'd find him soon enough. They killed four of Picasso's men and he needed to fill the vacancies.

Billy was disappointed that Shinko hadn't dealt with Maya. At least, he didn't think she did? There was a fire at The Dragon's Blessing a week ago. Maybe there was a connection? There had to be. When he posed as Maya, Shinko had been thinking about The Dragon's Blessing enough to dream about it. He assumed Shinko was hunting Maya, but didn't know for certain. It wasn't like he could talk to Yume about it. "Hey, sweety, did you know your mom is a ninja assassin? Yeah, a really good one, too." Billy shivered thinking about how angry she would be and the impending wrath that would surely follow.

No, he decided to go back to scanning dreams, searching for maleficence.

A paper airplane glided into the Valhalla Room from the window. It could have come from only one source. Billy got out of his chair and reached for it, but it banked left, avoiding his grasp. Looping around the room, the plane transformed into a tiny dragon. With a smoky puff of fire from its nostrils and a flap of its wings, it sailed out the window.

If she wants a dragon, I'll give her a dragon. Billy jumped out the window and landed comfortably in a leather saddle strapped to a fifty-foot, green-scaled dragon. Using a set of heavy reins, he guided the beast through the air, following the smaller dragon to the same scenery from the last time Maya visited.

Billy flew his dragon above the thick tree canopy until the forest abruptly terminated, giving way to a white sandy beach and the bluest ocean. Like last time, Maya stood by herself on the beach. Unlike last time, Billy crossed the threshold.

The dragon landed in a swirling sand cloud as it flapped its grand wings. When the sand settled, Billy dismounted the beast and approached Maya. Should she try anything aggressive, Billy readied spikes to burst from the sand, a kraken to attack from the ocean, and meteors to fall from the sky. "I'm assuming you want something since you invaded my dreamscape."

The little girl possessed an adult mind, evident by her smirk and the gleam behind her eyes. That unnerved Billy.

"Interesting choice of words, Billy, since you're the one standing in *my* dreamscape. I merely sent an invitation."

"Semantics don't conceal intent."

"Humph. I invited you because someone wants to meet you."

"Someone who?"

Maya waved a hand and ripped a hole in the air. She didn't take part in unnecessary conjecture. That, Billy appreciated. The hole grew, stretching and widening large enough for a man to walk effortlessly through. An older man, entrenched somewhere within his fifties. His black hair held as much white in a style akin to the nineteen forties. He carried weight in his midsection the way many men his age did, but his three-piece, gray suit was cut nicely enough to serve as camouflage. The kind of man that should have spats, a fedora, and Cuban cigar.

"Good evening. My name is Harold Varvaro," he said, voice smokey and gravely.

Billy answered with a steely-eyed glare. He wasn't sure what game Maya, or this Harold Varvaro, were playing, but it was undoubtedly rigged in their favor.

Harold turned to Maya. "You said sometimes Billy, sometimes Will. What did you mean by that?"

Just like when Billy asked her a question, Maya wasted no time with words, she simply waved her hand again.

"No!" Billy yelled, the pain as searing as the last time she extracted Will from his body with the sensation of burning flesh being ripped away. By the time he could react, the ordeal ended, and he was too drained to do anything about it.

"Mother fucker!" Will screamed in an exhale, on his hands and knees next to Billy. His fingers curled to fists when he looked up at Maya. "You!"

Will launched himself at Maya, his body tripling in size, changing shape. Muscles grew while his skin turned to stone. Wings sprouted from his back as his face twisted into the gnarled folds of a gargoyle. Fire consumed his clawed hands as he reached for the little brat on the beach.

Maya flicked her hand as if shooing away a fly, pushing Will backwards while the monstrosity he had become crumbled into pebbles, a crushed statue.

Billy reached down and helped Will to his feet. At least he still had his skin this time. "We're in her dreamscape."

Will spun in a circle, looking around. Fists still clenched, he nodded and looked back at Maya. "All right, I'll bite. Why?"

Hands behind his back, Harold stepped closer to Billy and Will, eyes slightly closed, relaxed yet irritated, as if he were waiting to board a plane. "So, I get to meet you two."

"And you are?"

The older man glanced between Billy and Will, clearly wondering why he had to repeat himself. "My name is Harold Varvaro. I wanted to discuss your recent activities."

"Yeah?" Will chuckled as he asked. "Which ones?"

"The ones where you're killing my men."

The tone in his voice unnerved Billy, simply miffed as if a bit of mud had splashed his shoes. "We don't know what you're talking about."

"Don't play coy. It's unbefitting of intelligent men like you two."

His words were like the waters of the ocean that Billy stood next to, nice on the surface, rough and dangerous when deeper.

Will gave an overly exaggerated shrug, and said, "You'll just have to tell your men to stop doing nasty shit... Picasso."

Billy placed his hand on Will's arm, an unspoken message to take it down a notch. Billy tried a different approach. "What he means to say is that we're on a mission. Obviously, we'd like to honor your request, so how about you give us a complete list of who you'd rather us not kill, and we'll see to it that we leave them be."

His comment elicited a coarse chuckle that sounded just like he imagined. Harold pointed at Billy but spoke to Will. "He's clearly the smart one."

Will smirked as his body changed again. Staying human, he grew a couple feet taller, and his body tripled in muscle mass, veins pressing against skin. "Yep, he's the brains of the operation, which means I'm the muscle."

Countenance shifting back to aggressive apathy, Harold turned and walked back toward the portal he had come through. "Yeah, I've seen your muscle, kid. To be honest, I'm putting money on my girl."

Will started to run toward Harold, but Maya stepped in front of him and waved her hand.

Billy jolted up in his bed, drenched in sweat, panting as if he sprinted a marathon.

After gulping a glass of water from his nightstand he flopped back on his bed. He was certain Will would be fired up and leave angrily written pages on the notepad tomorrow. He'd calm Will down. But now that they had a name, it would only take a little research to find Picasso.

CHAPTER 26

The 8th Street Gallery hummed with subdued excitement, whispered conversations about how *this* artist captured the meaninglessness of meaning, or how *that* artist offered catharsis through existential crisis.

Yume smirked at the pretentiousness she overheard, thinking that when the time came for a thesis paper, she could write about the desire to be accepted, humankind adding perceived value by manufacturing something out of nothing. Like peacocks strutting around in full plume, many people prattled about topics which they held some form of expertise, or so they thought. An attempt to impress. An exertion of dominance. Applying recently learned knowledge.

Yume enjoyed art, but she never dissected it or gave meaning where it wasn't warranted. If she liked a piece, it was because it appealed to her, not because she could apply a checklist of vocabulary terms.

Tonight, she found herself lingering around six paintings displayed on one of the temporary walls toward the rear of the gallery. Bright, smooth colors flowed together with bursts of complimentary colors to enhance the imagination. Like being on foreign planets with alien skies. Or traversing the human subconscious.

"Do they look like the dreamscape to you? Or am I being a whackadoodle?" Yume asked, sipping her wine.

Billy shoved a stuffed mushroom into his mouth and wiped his fingers on the tiny cocktail napkin as he chewed. When finished, he answered, "First of all, you are always a whackadoodle, the number one reason why I love you. Second of all, I too, feel as though we could easily see these images in any given dreamscape. Or on any given album cover of a psychedelic seventies progressive rock band."

Yume chuckled and lightly bumped her hip against his shoulder. "Wise guy."

"I think, technically, we're here to investigate a wise guy."

Yume snorted and shook her head.

The gallery was beautiful, a surprising front for a man involved in organized crime. The artwork was mostly paintings hanging on moveable walls within the space, creatively accessible and intriguing even to an eye unattuned to the finer points of the craft. Whenever a space could accommodate one, a sculpture of some sort occupied it in a non-aggressive way. A few cases of handcrafted jewelry and other trinkets lined the wall closest to the door, a cash register on top of one of the cases. The prices for the merchandise were ridiculous, very few items with a listing price less than four digits, making the space prohibitive for Temple students and most people living near the college. As tempting as free high-quality wine and hors d'oeuvres for a new artist's opening night might be, she and Billy were the only students there. Yume guessed that they were the only two under the age of forty in attendance, though more than a few women obviously had a decade or so removed through the miracle of modern science.

Thanks to the egocentricity of the other attendees, no one paid attention to the underdressed young couple milling about. Billy wore a coordinated shirt and tie combination with a nice pair of slacks while Yume's form-fitting little black dress complimented her modest silver earrings and silver necklace. Going unnoticed suited her just fine.

There was, however, one person whose attention she wanted. The proprietor of the gallery.

"Unfortunately, I don't think we'll find the wise guy back here," Yume said.

"I agree. Judging by the noises coming from the front, the guest of honor has arrived."

Yume took one last, longing gaze at the six paintings she liked, each with a ten-thousand-dollar price tag, before gulping down the rest of her wine. She and Billy made their way toward the front of the gallery, staying near the edge of the aisleway formed by two rows of moveable walls. Observing the circus from the peanut gallery.

Exhibition designers had arranged the gallery to display a dozen of the featured artist's paintings, leaving enough open space for him to strut before a crowd of two dozen. The artist had the look and air of a failed rockstar: mussed hair, leopard print shirt unbuttoned to his sternum, shiny, black leather pants, pink snakeskin boots, and every piece of jewelry had either a skull or an eagle. Never once during his speech did he remove his sunglasses, nor put down his wine glass, emptying it one gulp at a time between conceited interpretations of his artwork. He rambled on about a painting divided into four equal quadrants, two black and two white. A tiny white dot was in the center of each black section, a tiny black dot in the center of the white sections. "They are a visceral reminder about the hope within nihilism," he said. "And the nihilism within hope and how they eat at us while eating each other like an ouroboros."

As the crowd released ohs and ahs, Yume leaned over and whispered to Billy, "I think he learned that word yesterday and has been dying to use it."

Billy laughed into his fist.

Yume regretted foregoing another glass of wine needed to tolerate the artist. He rivaled Narcissus himself. She tuned him out and thought about her mom's visit.

Warmth bloomed within her chest. It felt so good to spend time with her. Though, she couldn't help thinking that her mother had been distracted, not a hundred percent in the moment. She hoped that whatever preoccupied the other percentage of her time wasn't critical. Sure, she downplayed her working role as "only" human resources, but she was a vice president of a major company. There had to be a backbreaking level of stress placed upon her shoulders. Whenever she talked to her next, she'd take more interest in her mother's career. Ask for an honest answer to the question, "How are things at work?"

Soft applause brought her back to the gallery. The featured artist bowed with flourish, signifying he had finished spewing nonsense. "Thank God," Yume moaned. "What an insufferable windbag. I don't understand how this Harold Varvaro tolerates this."

"He doesn't," came from behind them.

Harold Varvaro.

Hands in the pockets of his perfectly tailored suit, he looked every bit how Billy had described him, including the bored look in his slightly shut eyes.

Billy and Yume backed out of the aisleway and into the open area of the gallery. Harold followed them and gestured with his head toward the featured artist's painting on the side wall. "That's why I have a gallery manager, to deal with insufferable windbags. Plus, I make a nice living from insufferable windbags."

Justin had greeted Yume and Billy when they first arrived. Now, the gallery manager placed a circular red sticker on the description card below the painting with the four black and white squares, signifying it had been sold.

For forty thousand dollars.

"Extortion," Yume mumbled.

Harold shrugged and made the, "Eh, what can you do?" facial expression. He then said, "I'm not taking advantage of anyone. Other than you two and my staff, everyone here has big wallets and little brains. I'm Harold Varvaro, by the way."

"Oh, I know who you are," Yume said with a growl.

Harold looked at Billy but spoke to Yume. "You do, do you?"

"Yes," Yume answered. "We have no secrets."

Harold rolled his eyes. "Kids nowadays."

This man rankled Yume. His kind were exactly what was wrong with the world. In his mind, wealth equaled priority; since he had more money, he was more important. No one poorer than him mattered, other than to serve him. It burned Yume up that adults accused her generation of having a false sense of entitlement, when this man's generation invented it. "We may be kids, but we did some damage."

Harold chuckled, but without the mirth. "You think you did some damage?"

"We must have, or you wouldn't have sent your attack dog, Maya, to threaten Billy and Will."

Yume was over-the-top with mouthiness, but she wanted to get under Harold's skin, wanted him to talk and expose a weaknesses. She wondered if her plan was working when he looked over his shoulders and took one large step closer to them.

"I may not look it, but I know a thing or two about a thing or two, and believe it or not, art is one of them. I'm not going to insult you by asking if you know the story of Icarus. Of course, you do. And if I asked you what it's about, you'd regurgitate the answer you'd been taught over there at that university. Hubris. But I think there's another point to that story, maybe a deeper meaning."

Harold took another step closer, hands still in his pockets. He leaned into their personal space, lowering his voice as he continued. "Futility. Icarus tried something he shouldn't have. He knew it, but he did it anyway. It wasn't hubris because he got cocky. It's hubris because he ignored the futility of his impending actions. Then there was the futility of trying to correct his mistake. That's the second meaning no one talks about. There are many artistic depictions of him – trust me, I've seen most of them. The one that sticks out to me is *The Lament of Icarus* by Draper. There's Icarus lying dead on the ground with a big, beautiful, full set of wings. They didn't burn away – he got *just* close enough to the sun for it to melt away *just* enough wax. Imagine poor Icarus falling with his big, beautiful, full set of wings flapping, flapping, flapping his ass off, and *still* falling. Imagine the futility."

Harold rolled his shoulders and addressed them both. "I feel like you two are smart. How about you prove it and head on back to your dorms and put your noses back in them books, where they belong. Or else…" Harold walked in between them, toward the featured artist while whispering, "Flap, flap. Flap, flap. Flap, flap." And then he merged into the throng of art revelers.

Billy took a deep inhale. "Ironically, a man who blatantly throws around the power of another person as if it were his own uses the story of Icarus to make a threat."

"Couldn't agree more," Yume said. "But he gave me an idea. Is there a way for us to take that power from him?"

Smirking, Billy answered, "Believe it or not, Will is looking for that as we speak."

CHAPTER 27

The house was a monastery to the West's religion of greed and power. A long driveway snuck between a pair of manicured bushes and led from the tree-lined road to a horseshoe drive in front of the house, decorative lights low to the ground lining the way. Various lights made the house gleam like the devil's diamond on the moonless night. Shinko moved along the perimeter, careful not to trip any motion sensors. She had yet to see guards, unless they were all on the inside. After all, this was the house of...

Whose house was this?

What is my mission?

Where is Aika?

Shinko paused and looked around, trying to assess her situation, regain any form of memory about where she was or what she needed to do.

This was highly unlike her. She never forgot an iota of information about any of her missions, let alone the entirety of the mission itself! Aika. She would have to swallow her pride and subject herself to inquisition from Fumiko, but she needed to complete this mission with her life intact first, and the only way to do that was to find Aika.

Back against the house, Shinko moved around the side to the rear, her steps perfectly placed without disrupting a single blade of grass on the manicured lawn. The soft light from the house didn't extend far into the backyard, and Shinko wondered why her heart beat so fast as she pondered the darkness beyond. This wasn't right, didn't feel right. Why was her mind so muddled? Had she been drugged? If so, by whom and when?

No, that wasn't right. Her training within Shinigami's Helper had exposed her to many different drugs to understand how her body reacted, and then how to counteract their effects. This didn't feel like any she had been exposed to. This felt more like... like...

A dream.

Yes! Shinko was dreaming.

Wake up.

Wait... Not yet. Much like when she dreamt about being in The Dragon's Blessing, this felt real. Too real. Crouching down, she removed a glove. Fingers through the grass. Every blade felt cool against her fingers, the smell fresh. If this was a dream, like the one about The Dragon's Blessing, then that meant Maya was controlling it. That meant she was still alive, still a viable weapon at use. Shinko needed to stay in the dream to learn more about the girl.

Shinko put on her glove and continued to move around the building, mentally preparing herself for the fantastical, like more snake-creatures. *This is just a dream.* But she knew the different theories regarding dreams, especially about dying in a dream. *It doesn't matter if dying in a dream means I die in the real world, because if I die in the real world, I'd still be dead.* The possibility of death had never stopped her from a mission.

Shinko hated not knowing anything about the enemy. Did Maya know she was here? How was she able to control dreams? Was she asleep and dreaming?

The Heaven's Palisade member she had killed in the restaurant gave little information other than what Shinko already knew about Maya, only confirming that she was indeed the weapon. Shinko assumed Maya knew she was here, maybe even observed her at this very moment. Safer to assume the enemy had the most information possible.

At the rear of the house, she made her way along the gray stone patio wall, up the patio stairs, and across the patio. Glass back doors showed an impossibly dark room, blackness obscuring what might lie beyond. No matter. Shinko picked the lock and slipped inside.

By the looks of everything from outside made Shinko believe she would walk into a modern home with open floor plans and stylish décor, at the very least a contemporary look with a living room, dining room, and kitchen. Not a long abandoned Victorian mansion.

Slivers of moonlight from behind cast glowing rectangles over the marble floor and dark wood walls of the expansive foyer. With two gryphons perched on either side, a massive staircase led to the second floor, a banister of squat posts securing the perimeter. Cobwebs and thick layers of dust clung to every surface while bits of random debris were scattered across the floor. Strips of plastic hung from the stair's banister, tables along the walls, and the oak grandfather clock beside the staircase.

Shinko crept farther into the house, wondering why it looked like it hadn't been lived in for decades.

The door slammed shut behind her. No longer glass patio doors, rather a slab of wood with strange faces carved into the grain supported by twisted iron hinges.

The home's interior looked like a scene from a movie set. Shinko drew her sword and tiptoed through the room, careful to avoid stepping under the chandelier's concentric circles of crystal and chain.

Two open doorways to the left of the foyer, two to the right, all four rooms shrouded in darkness and mystery. The stairs seemed to be the logical choice to take. Why do people instinctually want to go up in dangerous situations? She didn't know what she was looking for and if Maya were setting a path for her to take, why take it? Her instincts told her to remain stealthy, stay silent, and glide among the shadows, but this was a dream and the host was aware of her presence. Fighting against what she had been taught, Shinko stepped into the brightest square of moonlight and yelled, "Show yourself!"

"Why have you defied me?" Maya asked in multiple voices from around the room.

Sword over her head, Shinko remained at the ready. "In what way have I defied you?"

"I told you not to challenge me." The words came from different sources, but gathered as she spoke, pooling together at the top of the stairs. Like a belle from the antebellum south, Maya appeared at the top of the stairs in a voluminous tiered gown and slowly descended. "Yet, here you are."

Warry of her surroundings, Shinko padded closer to the stairs. "You brought me here."

"When you realized you were in a dream, you could have woken up at any time you wanted. Instead, you continued. You came to hunt me."

"I came to learn about you."

"You came to kill me."

"You have been referred to as a weapon, including by your own admission."

Maya smiled broad with too many teeth made even more unsettling on a cherubic face. Palms up, she extended her arms from her sides, ready to bear the weight of the world upon her shoulders. "I am the queen of dreams, after all."

Without so much as a tremor, the room split apart into various sizes. The stairs remained intact while the floor around Shinko fragmented into half meter by half meter squares, floating away from each other. The second floor separated from the first, the banister posts floated freely and independently as if a child had blown upon a dandelion puff. Unhinged doors toppled drunkenly through the air. As the pieces moved farther apart from each other, they exposed blue and purple streaks upon a backdrop of black, dotted with myriad specks of light. Shinko felt like she stood in the center of the universe, one grain of sand floating alone in the middle of a calm ocean.

Only a dream, she reminded herself. Fiction or not, the small square of floor she stood upon floated away from the stairs. Maya was a threat, a weapon, and Shinko needed to stop her. She needed answers, and she wasn't ready to awaken until she received them.

Leaping from one square to the next started easy enough, but they began to move in different directions at different speeds. Each jump required longer strides, and she found herself on a piece with no floor-square within reach. *This is only a dream*. It didn't matter if this was her dream or Maya's or a combination of both, the environment around her reacted to a child's whim.

Shinko had to be able to control some element of this place. Focus.

She crouched and stared at a chunk of floor drifting in front of her, about five meters away. At first, she tightened her muscles and readied herself for the jump but recognized that wasn't the proper thinking. Maya deconstructed the interior of a house into hundreds of pieces without physical means. Shinko had no experience manipulating anything within her dreams, but if Maya could do it, then it meant manipulation was possible.

Without thinking about the push or how much effort to put into her legs, Shinko focused on where she wanted to go. In a dream, jumping and landing on the piece of floor five meters away was no different than a piece one meter away.

As softly as a snowflake on an eyelash, she landed on the floor piece. Success! Hardly considering herself a master, Shinko was pleased that she could affect how she moved about her surroundings. With less effort, she leapt to another piece, and then another, getting closer to the stairs, to Maya. Close enough to see the girl frown.

Maya waved her hands and the floor pieces changed direction, tipped and flipped. Shinko slid off the one she stood upon, grabbing ahold of the edge with her hand, feet dangling in free space. Options streamed through her mind, none good. Sheathing her sword, she used both hands to grab the edge as it rotated, glancing around to see how many pieces floated below and beside her. Dream or not, fear dried her mouth and her pulse beat hard in her throat.

Fear always cut deeper than the enemy's sword.

Think! Where was she going to fall?

Wait... *Why* fall? Why continue applying real-world veneers on a fake world? If everything around her was floating, then why shouldn't she?

She let go.

And floated with the house debris.

Instead of contemplating what she didn't know, she focused on what she did. *Feet on the floor, feet on the floor,* she repeated as she stared at the nearest piece. It didn't matter if it were sideways or not, she cleared away all thoughts other than getting her feet onto the floor piece. Moving through the space, she floated toward her target. Physics be damned, she was standing on a piece of floor languidly rotating in space. As natural as hopping over a mud puddle on the sidewalk, she jumped to an upside-down patch of floor, then to another one that lay sideways and twenty meters away. Getting closer to the staircase, she pushed aside a freestanding door summersaulting lazily through the space.

"No!" Maya yelled and swiped her hands through the air like a conductor in an orchestra of chaos. In unison, five doors not attached to any frame or wall, just languidly summersaulting through space, flipped open to nothingness. Lizard-headed ninjas in colorful outfits clawed their way out of the black, like devils escaping from Hell. One, two, three from each door, armed with a weapon, just as Shinko remembered from her prior dream.

Some jumped along the pieces of debris while others floated, closing in on her. They moved more efficiently in this environment than she, but they still couldn't match her fighting skills or weapons prowess.

A lizard man in blue struck first. Leaping from one chunk of stone to another, he lunged at Shinko with a sai extended like a jousting lance. Dodging the sloppy attack was easy and decapitating him was easier – a quick spin to avoid the sai and a downward slice of her ninjato to remove his head, blood flowing from the body like crimson water from a hose.

The sai twirled through the air in front of Shinko. With the ease of plucking a flower, she snatched it and threw it into the eye of next lizard creature. Blobs of gelatinous ooze burst from the socket, floating in all directions. The creature released its grip on a set of nunchakus, easily accessible to Shinko should she want them. They weren't her preferred weapon.

A lizard creature in red had what she was looking for.

Leaping across the field of debris became almost second nature to Shinko, no matter what orientation she found herself in.

The lizard in red continued to make its way to her, whirling the tethered kunai over his head like a helicopter blade. As with her earlier dream involving these creatures, Red had limited skill. Like before, the kunai was retractable. Shinko gripped the cord after the projectile missed and allowed momentum to bring her to him. A simple twist and the kunai sunk deep into his eye while she sliced his neck with her sword.

Now, to show Maya how to use the kunai.

Shinko stood firm on a dark patch of wood that used to be part of the foyer's wall and tossed the kunai at her closest opponent. The blade went exactly where she aimed, into the lizard creature's neck, right under the jaw. The creature fell limp as red liquid orbs flowed out of its wound.

Like a bolt of silver lightning, the kunai flashed from her hand to the next target and the next, felling them with single strikes. She continued to stop her attackers one at a time, no matter the direction they came from. In less than a minute, fifteen scaly corpses floated among the foyer pieces, their blood like red globs of oil bobbing through water.

Stone gryphons guarding the base of the stairs were no longer static. They shifted, sounds of rocks grinding together as they took flight from their pedestals. Faced with another impossible attack from Maya, Shinko came up with her own impossible answer.

Bounding across the rubble, she headed towards the closest door. She didn't know how a door attached to nothing could open to something beyond, but that didn't matter; she just knew it would. She jumped from a piece of ceiling tile to the chandelier still hanging from an invisible hook, and then to the door oriented as if it led to a cellar. The stone creature from myth swooped in as she jumped, and it crashed into the chandelier, glass breaking, brass twisting. The creature struggled to escape as thrust carried it forward, toward the open door. It shrieked like a wounded bird as it glided into the door's nothingness. Shinko slammed the door and stood on it, readying herself for the second stone creature.

Maya's anger and frustration manifested into a prolonged and echoing scream. The more she screamed, the more the second gryphon changed. No longer stone, the limbs and wings gave way to green shaded scales. The claws on its front legs resembled fingers while a reptilian tail sprouted from its lower back. The wingspan grew with every flap, surpassing fifty meters. Boney nubs protruded along the cranial ridge of its lizard-like face. The gryphon had turned into a dragon.

A thought had been tickling Shinko's mind ever since entering the house, a faint voice louder and louder until she understood what it was trying to say.

Maya was not who she said she was.

In Asia, few mansions looked like part of Victorian era England. Gryphons were found in European myths, not Asian. And East Asian dragons were beautiful creatures, as graceful as the air they glided through or the currents of water they swam in, not brutish beasts with wings and horns and talons. No denizen of Southeast Asia would populate their dream world with these things. Maya might exist, and she might be a powerful weapon, but the little girl on the staircase was not Maya.

Whoever the adversary, they still had the advantage. Experience led to mastery, and Shinko had neither. She was comfortable enough with this reality's workings, but she needed to push past what she saw. *Focus. Believe. Manifest.*

The dragon's ugly blasting roar vibrated Shinko's bones. It served as an announcement of its intent to strike. Mouth opened for devouring, it straightened its diamond shaped serpent's head and gave a flap of its mighty wings. Diving like a raptor chasing after a field mouse, the dragon sped toward Shinko. *Focus. Believe. Manifest.*

She watched and waited to time her maneuver perfectly. Now! Shinko threw the kunai at the staircase floating thirty meters away. Logic dictated there was not enough cord attached to it, but she pushed that thought aside and fought against real world limitations. The blade sank deep into the bottom step. Shinko leapt and activated the retracting mechanism a second before the dragon snapped its jaws shut on the door she had been standing upon.

Her trip through the space was brief and as soon as she reached the stairs, she climbed them two at a time. Before the little girl could call upon any other monsters from fantasy, Shinko slammed into her. Kneeling on the girl's legs, fingers wrapped around her pencil thin throat, she actively told herself that nothing was as it seemed. She was *not* choking a helpless waif. "Show yourself! Show me your true self!"

Maya's face changed to that of a white man in his fifties.

Shocked, Shinko loosened her grip, giving him a window of opportunity. His hands turned into knife blades, and he slashed her arms.

Shinko woke up screaming, crossing her arms over her chest, pressing her hands against her shoulders. They were wet.

Blood.

She was sitting in her hotel bed bleeding.

Breathe. Focus. Calm.

Her room's interior lights were off, but enough ambient light from outside seeped past the curtains. Her shoulders burned and ached, but the pain was far from paralyzing. Rivulets flowed past her fingers and down her arms, not gushing cuts. With no concern of losing too much blood, she took a moment to close her eyes and regain control of her breathing. Focus. Calm.

Tonight, she had garnered a few painful answers about how the dream world worked. She got out of bed and went to the bathroom to clean her wounds, and as the cold water ran, a new question took precedent: Who was the man posing as Maya?

CHAPTER 28

The microwave dinged and Shanna took her breakfast to the couch, setting it on the coffee table. Yume had given her the apartment key and permission to come and go as she pleased. And to eat her food.

A tremor in Shanna's hand had led to a large piece of eggshell dropping into her breakfast cup while preparing it. *Fuck it. I'll just have a little extra crunch with breakfast,* she thought as she spooned the steaming egg and potato concoction to her mouth.

Time for a Red Bull. A quick sip to make room for the contents of a 5 Hour Energy. All-nighters were difficult, but she couldn't bear to sleep and deal with any more dreams. Or nightmares, depending how she wanted to view them, considering she was on twenty-five hours of no sleep and actually felt more rested than she had for over a week.

A gulp from her drink and she set the can on the coffee table, making sure she used a coaster lest she face the wrath of Sloan. It was too early for that, and she was too tired.

A few bites of hot egg mash and another chug of Red Bull. She sighed and leaned her head back, luxuriating in the couch's softness. The apartment was small, but Yume spared no expense on a quality couch. Shanna's eyes burned and the time between closing them and opening them got longer and longer. *Nope!* She snapped her head off the couch-back in a jolt. *Not having a crazy sex dream on my sister's couch.*

Shanna didn't hate the dreams, or how freakishly realistic they were. Okay, the realism unnerved her at times, especially when they went from "kinky" to "nasty." Too much pleasure became painful. And it affected her waking hours. She'd been waking up more tired than when she went to sleep, exhausted from constant activity, and drenched in sweat. Throbbing from between her legs. And bruises. She had real, honest to God bruises on her neck, chest, ass, and inner thighs. What the hell was she doing to herself in her sleep? How hard did she grope her own tits to leave marks? Did she slap her own ass?

Her warm breakfast wasn't enough to chase away the sudden chill along her spine.

"What the hell are you doing here?" Sloan asked exiting her bedroom, brows furrowed so deep that it looked like she tried to make her hairline touch her nose.

"Good morning to you, too, Sloan," Shanna replied, and then finished her Red Bull.

"That cup in your hands better not be one of my yogurts," Sloan snapped as she made a beeline to the refrigerator. She yanked open the door and grabbed one of her strawberry yogurts. Studying it, her frown softened, disappeared, her expression giving way to confusion. Her brow now going the opposite direction, her eyes widening, she looked... scared? Faster than the situation called for, she tossed the yogurt back into the fridge and slammed the door. "Just... umm... Just checking to make sure you didn't take one."

Shanna gave her a salute. "I know the rules. Yume gave me permission to eat her food and to come by whenever I wanted."

"At least it's a decent hour. But Yume's not here. I'm assuming she's with Billy."

"Yeah, I kinda figured."

There must have been something unintentional in Shanna's voice – a tone, a quiver – that she didn't notice but Sloan did. Yume's roommate grabbed a meal replacement shake from the refrigerator and stalked closer to the couch. "Do I detect a hint of jealousy?"

Had she been able to get any form of restful sleep, Shanna could have crafted a snappy comeback. Instead, her muddled mind offered, "No."

"Oh, I think there is. Mr. Perfect is stealing your lover from you, so how couldn't you be jealous?"

Was she having a bad dream? Did she actually fall asleep on the couch? "Lover? Do you *really* think Yume and I are a couple?"

"Aren't you?"

Sloan's cloying smile verged on wickedness, and Shanna knew better than to engage, but she wasn't fast enough to stop her mouth. "No! Why would you think that?"

Sloan made the face that everyone made, the one that implied they were dealing with an idiot. But it rankled Shanna deep within her chest. "It's *obvious* why I would think that with all your... proclivities."

"Not that it's any of your business, I'm hetero. And just because I have a healthy appetite doesn't mean I'll jump into bed with anyone." *Despite what my dreams have been telling me.* "You know what? Maybe you should get laid once in a while. You obviously need it."

Sloan crossed her arms over her chest and cocked her hip. "I would, but I don't want any of your sloppy seconds, so that doesn't leave me much."

"God, you're such a bitch."

"Yeah? Well, you and your 'sister' and her boyfriend made me that way. You're constant nuisances with your dramas and disruptions and late-night hours. No wonder I can't get any good sleep."

"Hold on... You're not sleeping?"

"Not that it's any of your business."

"I... I'm not getting sleep either. Are you concerned?"

"What?" Sloan's face was back to full frown-of-angry-gods mode. "What the hell kind of question is that? Are you making fun of me?"

"No! I'm serious. I've been having crazy, crazy dreams so real that they're scaring me. It's a heck of a coincidence that you're not sleeping well either. We should ask Yume if she's sleeping."

"Is this your trailer trash version of a game?" Sloan yelled, reminding Shanna of a rabid junk yard dog baring its teeth and frothing at the mouth. "Some fun prank you're trying to pull because you're jealous of me? If you think you can... No. You know what, I'm *not* going to stoop to your level. But I will say this – fuck you. Fuck Yume, too."

Sloan punctuated her statement by storming to her room and slamming her door.

Yume had said that Sloan was under a lot of pressure, from herself and from her parents. Pressure stemmed from lack of control, which was why Sloan was always quick to enforce the rules of the apartment, the one element she felt she could control. What if there was more to her stress, her lack of control? What if she was plagued by intense dreams?

The bedroom door opened, and Sloan emerged, dressed for class and backpack slung over her shoulder. Shanna felt Sloan's anger knock into her like a bulldozer, but still had to try to connect with her, let her know she wasn't alone. "Sloan, I—"

The slamming apartment door cut her off.

"Nice job, moron." Shanna scolded herself for not taking the right approach, for not seeing what should have been obvious, for not trying harder. She was frustrated for not cutting Sloan the same slack that Yume did. Maybe when Yume got back—?

The door opened and Yume hurried to the couch beside Shanna. "Hey, are you okay? I passed Sloan in the hallway and she looked nuclear level pissed. She didn't even hurl a pass-aggressive snide comment when I said, 'Good morning.' Did you two fight?"

"No? Yes? I don't know, maybe?" Shanna didn't want to make the situation worse by adding more strain to the tenuous relationship between Yume and her roommate. She had already done enough of that with her stepfather drama. "No. She and I were both a little off today. She mentioned she wasn't sleeping well, and I wondered if she had bad dreams."

A fleeting expression of acknowledgement swept across Yume's face, followed by concern and attention. "Okay. How about you? You seem like you're not sleeping well either. Is that why you've been a little off as well?"

Shanna shrugged. "Just a few weird dreams here and there."

Yume leaned forward and placed a hand on Shanna's. With a tone as severe as if Shanna had said she found a lump in her breast, Yume said, "Sleep is important to your health. Just as important as diet and exercise. I know, I know, you asked me not to analyze you, and I swear I'm not. I'm concerned about the physical ramifications of you not getting enough sleep."

"I get that. But it's coming off as nagging."

"If I'm nagging, it's because I'm concerned. Billy and I have been doing a lot of research about sleep and dreams. Some of his theories and experiences are rather eye opening."

There it was. The reason Shanna wanted a heart-to-heart with Yume. As she tried to think of the right words, her body spoke for her. Her posture stiffened as she looked away and shifted in her seat. Yume immediately reacted to the message. "You... You don't like Billy?"

"I like Billy," Shanna said. True. Billy was kind and smart and charming. But... "You've been really, I don't know, wrapped up in him lately."

"What do you mean?"

"Like, I get he's into dreams and interpreting them and stuff, and that's cool, but you've been kind of obsessed about it."

Yume frowned. "That's because they're an interesting look into our own psyches, an unexplored landscape of who we are. Billy has many interesting thoughts and ideas about them."

"What about *your* thoughts and ideas? And *your* time? Before you met him, you'd talk to me about your classes, even the ones you didn't like had something interesting about them. Now, I barely even know what classes you're taking. It's always Billy this and dreams that."

"Don't. Please, Shanna, please don't be the jealous, paranoid sister."

"But you've been acting erratic."

"I haven't done—"

"The side street a week and a half ago." She didn't like when people cut her off, so Shanna was mindful of her place in conversations. She hated to do it, but she couldn't let Yume gain the upper hand. Shanna wasn't entirely sure she'd describe herself as an enlightened individual, but she knew enough about herself to admit that Yume was smarter. Way smarter. Sometimes Shanna felt like an unfortunate cow wandering onto the tracks when Yume's train of thought picked up steam. "What was up with you wandering down a very unsafe side street to peek at a skeevy garage?"

"It... I thought I saw the garage in a dream. I saw their sign from the street and wanted to check it out."

"It was more than that, Yume. It's been bothering me. I should have brought it up sooner, you talking to the guys in the garage. You called them *by name* and accused them of stealing money."

Yume looked away, her eyebrows knitting worry lines across her face as if debating what to tell Shanna. Eyes slicked with tears, Yume looked back and said, "It's nothing. Like I said, I saw it in a dream and… I got weird, okay? It was a weird situation, and I didn't handle it with any level of appropriateness."

Yume hadn't been part of Shanna's life since the beginning, like a biological sister, but she had been during her formative years, through the tear-filled talks and idle discussions about hopes of the future and silly conversations about impossible fantasies. They had a bond, a strong one where they knew things about each other, even things the other one didn't. Yume was hiding something. "There's something more."

"There's nothing more."

"What's going on, Yume? Is it… Is it drugs?"

"No! God, no, not even close."

"Close? That means there's something going on? What are you and Billy up to?"

"Nothing!"

"What is it with Billy? Are you protecting him? Are you obsessed with him? Are you two in danger? Are you two, I don't fucking know, running some kind of underground, illegal night club? Talk to me!"

Yume sat straight and turned away from Shanna. Wiping away tears with her sleeve, she said, "I can't talk to you like this. Please go."

Shanna's heart broke. Even though there had been arguments before – effervescent debates as Yume referred to them – they were few and far between. Since Yume was so smart, fun, cool, witty, Shanna usually went along with whatever she said. In the rare occasions she disagreed, she still acquiesced to Yume's wishes, opinions, ideas. Life was awesome that way. But Shanna didn't know what to do now. She hurt her sister; her sister hurt her. Words were never Shanna's strong suit, always abandoning her in her times of need. Just like now.

Wondering if she'd ever see her sister again, Shanna stood up, grabbed her empty can and half eaten breakfast, tossed them in the trash, and left.

CHAPTER 29

Billy looked at the notepad, at the words taking up half the legal sized, yellow paper. He was just getting started. Yesterday, he and Yume met Harold Varvaro, the man who used Maya as a weapon. He needed to let Will know the details, but writing it out on a notepad wasn't good enough. He had to share the information first, then offer his opinion, and ask Will for his. There'd be questions and another exchange for answers. By the time all that happened, the situation could change, and the information would be stale. He tore the page from the pad, crumbled it into a ball, and tossed it into the wastebasket by his desk. Typing it on the computer would make the necessary exchange no faster. There was no other choice. He needed to contact Will directly.

In preparation, he wheeled from his desk to his bathroom and grabbed two ibuprofen from the medicine cabinet. Better make it three. No, four. He then went to the living room and situated himself on his couch. Good chance he was going to want to lie down after this. Of course, he didn't exactly know how "this" worked. Up until meeting Yume, he hadn't talked directly to Will since they were teenagers, when Will killed his parents. Here goes nothing.

Will?

Nothing indeed. Billy shifted around on the couch, getting as comfortable and relaxed as possible.

Will?

Empty silence. Will had first communicated with Billy when he met Yume. Maybe she was the invitation Will needed? Billy cleared his throat and slouched down, allowing the softness of the couch to ease his muscles. He relaxed his vision, his living room blurring, and overloaded his mind with thoughts of Yume.

Will?

"Ow! What? You don't have to yell."

Ow! Neither do you.

"Ugh, sorry. Oooh, this hurts. How are you feeling?"

We're probably sharing the same headache.

"Yeah, I don't doubt it. I'm glad you called, though."

Really? Why?

"Last night, I jumped into Yume's mom's dream to do what we discussed."

How'd it go?

"Crazy! Like, she's crazy skilled. She knows how to move. I mean really move!"

Ow!

"Sorry. She learns fast. And nothing freaks her out. I threw lizard men and stone gryphons and a dragon at her. I posed as Maya, and she kept coming after me. I then showed her Harold."

Think she'll find him?

"She's smart. She figured out that Maya wasn't the one running the dream."

Did you let her see you?

"No. I was still disguised as Maya when she figured it out. That's when I turned into Harold to let her get a good look at him."

I wish we had a better plan. Or time to make a better plan.

"Yeah, me, too. But she and Yume said their goodbyes, so we needed to do this before she got on the plane back to Japan."

Do we think it'll be enough to keep her here? Make her look for Harold?

"I hope so. I hate to admit it, but I'm not sure if either you or I are strong enough to take on Maya in a head-to-head battle."

To be fair, we thought we were the only two who could traverse the dreamscape.

"Yeah. Yume's been doing great, though."

As if following a cue, Yume entered the apartment. Billy hadn't been expecting her, and he sat up straight with a jolt.

"Oh! Sorry," she said. "Didn't mean to startle you."

"She's here?" Will asked. His questions didn't stop. "You weren't expecting her, were you? Why is she here? It looks like she's been crying! Why was she crying?"

Ow! Damn it, stop yelling!

"Ow! Sorry. I'm just upset that she's been crying."

"No worries," Billy said to Yume. "Are you okay?"

Yume shut the door and sat next to him on the couch. "I was going to ask you the same thing. You look like you're in pain."

You have to go, Will.

"Come on, let me stay," Will said. "I want to make sure she's okay. I promise I'll stay quiet."

"Yeah, no, I'm okay," Billy said to Yume as he scooted closer to her. He put his hand on her knee and she replied in kind. "Just a headache. I took some Ibuprofen and closed my eyes. Must have dozed off. How about you? You've been crying?"

Yume released a deflating sigh, slouching as if too weary to sit up straight. "Yeah. Shanna and I got into an argument. Disagreement? It was weird and unusual for us."

"About what?" Will asked Billy.

"About what?" Billy asked Yume.

"She and Sloan got into a tiff, I think, but I wasn't there for that," Yume said. "She said it happened because neither of them is getting sleep, which I knew about, and part of that is my fault."

"Your fault?"

"Yeah! I mean, I've been messing with Sloan's dreams."

Billy shook his head. "You've been going into her dreamscape and dumping yogurt on her. How many times have you done that?"

Yume shrugged. "I don't know. Maybe three times? Four?"

"Right. One dream every few nights is hardly enough to disrupt her sleep. Are you doing anything else to her?"

"No. Not saying I wouldn't if I had the ability to alter her dreamscape with more than just yogurt avalanches, because she's a bitch, but I'm not doing anything else to mess with her."

"And Shanna?"

"Me messing with her dreams? Oh, hell no! But she's been having some intense ones. Today she seemed kind of shaky, like she had too much caffeine."

"Should we visit her dreamscape tonight?"

Yume folded her hands on her lap and went rigid. Looking away, she said. "I jumped inside of her dream the other night and... I feel weird even talking about it. I love her and I invaded her privacy."

Do you know what she's talking about? Billy asked Will.

"No," Will answered. "Do you?"

No.

"I understand," Billy said. "But if her dreams are ruining her sleep and you have the opportunity to help her, shouldn't you take it?"

Yume worked her jaw as she chewed her thoughts. She turned to face Billy. Sitting cross-legged, she said, "You're right. She's been having sex dreams. Not like 'normal' sex dreams, but... really kind of intense. In the dream that I visited, she was... Oh, God, this is so weird. She was in a gang bang. With a lot of guys."

A warmth bloomed within Billy's cheeks. "Oh! Well, people... I mean, *some* people... have dreams about—"

"She didn't look like she was having fun. In fact, quite the opposite. Like she wanted to wake up but couldn't. I freaked out and woke her up. I think she's having a lot of these dreams and it's messing with her. I keep trying to get her to talk about it, but she accuses me of trying to analyze her. Today it came to a head, I guess."

"Oh. Okay. That's... That is a lot to unpack."

"Wait!" Will yelled, causing Billy to wince. "She said that Shanna came to her apartment. Ask her why Shanna came over."

"So... You said Shanna came over to see you, but it wasn't about her dreams..."

Billy let the statement hang in the air between them, hoping he came across as concerned, not prying. He started to get worried when she frowned, and he felt Will pacing around in his head. "She said she was worried about me. That I've... changed, I guess... since meeting you."

"She's jealous of us," Will said.

Don't make assumptions.

"Do you feel like you've changed?" Billy asked.

"Yeah! There's no way to do what you and Will and I have been doing without changing, without challenging my ideals and goals and biases. But that's what you need to do to grow, right? Challenge yourself and your views of the world and how you fit into that world. If you don't grow, you die, and you can't grow without changing."

"But?"

"But I get what she's talking about. I'm keeping a secret from her. A big, huge, massive secret and I must be doing something, even subliminally hinting at that, which is probably why she isn't willing to tell me about her dreams. I think it's some form of unconscious, 'If you're not going to talk to me, then I'm not going to talk to you,' sort of thing. So… I think I need to tell her."

"Noooooooo. Bad idea," Will said. "Just in case you can't see what I'm doing right this very second in your mind, I'm flashing red lights to go along with the klaxons."

I agree, bad idea. Please stop yelling.

Billy took her hand into his. This would be the measuring stick. However hard she yanked her hand from his would let him know her anger level. "I really don't think that's a good idea."

She squeezed. Not to the point of pain, but clearly she was going to argue. "Why not? It would help her understand what I've been doing… what we've been doing. I think she'd understand."

"That's a heck of a risk, Yume. Remember how you reacted? And – no offense to Shanna – you are far more capable on many cognitive levels. Even if she wrapped her head around what we can do, how do you think she'd react to why we're doing it? I killed Gus. I killed her stepfather. Yes, I know fate smiled on her and her mother because of it, and you and I both know in our hearts that I did the right thing, but…"

Again, he let the idea dangle like ripened fruit, hoping Yume would pluck it. "But he was still her stepfather. No matter how despicable he was, he was still a part of her life, and a decision was made that she wasn't a part of."

"Exactly."

Yume threw herself against the back of the couch. Growling with frustration, she ground the heels of hands against her eyes. "I just feel so awful that she's in pain and isn't letting me help, and I don't know how to help without going into her dreams."

"We'll figure something out. You consider yourselves sisters, so I'm sure there's a way to get her to confide in you."

"I need to do something. I hate not doing anything."

"I understand, but I don't know if pushing her would—"

Yume waved her hands to bat away his words. "No, sorry, not about Shanna. I'm changing subjects." She tapped her index finger against her forehead. "The monkeys in the circus of my mind are screeching and flinging poo, so it's very chaotic in there. But I need to do something."

"Uh-oh," Will said. Wide like plates, her eyes were borderline maniacal, her irises all but pushed away by diluted pupils. "I don't like the look in her eyes."

"Would you like to go to the woman's shelter to find more candidates?" Billy asked. "I could scan local dreams tonight."

"No." A sly twist of a smile played at her lips. "I want Varvaro."

"Whoa," Will said.

"Whoa," Billy said. "Will and I haven't figured out Maya yet."

"Doesn't matter," Yume said. "We'll go in tonight."

Billy sighed. "Yume, we *really* need to think about this."

"I have thought about it. A lot. And here's my conclusion: When a man holds a gun, he's still a man – he hasn't changed one bit. Same weaknesses, same thought process, same size, and shape. You're not afraid of the man; you're afraid of the gun. If you can't get the gun away from the man, then you must get to him before he can use the gun."

"An ambush?"

"Exactly!"

"I'm not entirely sure how to set up a dream ambush."

"We literally do it every time we go into someone's dream. They don't know we're there until we reveal ourselves."

"She has a good point," Will said.

Not you, too!

"She's going to think you're trying to hold her back," Will said.

I'm not trying to do that at all. I just want her to wait so her mother has a chance to find and kill Maya.

"Now who's keeping secrets from whom?" Will asked Billy.

There is no way we can let her know that her mother is a killer for hire.

"Dude, we gave her a piece of God and you're telling her to set it aside and admire it from afar. Because of us, she now has the power to help, and *also* because of us, we're telling her not to use it how she sees fit. Only how we tell her to use it. We have to give her something. Either we attack Varvaro tonight, or we let her tell Shanna what's going on."

"What if we wait a day or two to come up with a plan?" Billy asked Yume.

"Then that's a day or two Maya and Varvaro get to plan," Yume said. "Do you believe his whole 'if you leave me alone, I'll leave you alone' nonsense? I don't. I'm sure Maya could get into my dreams any time she wants. We go into his dreams tonight. If we kill him, then yay good guys. If not, if things get too intense, then we wake up and try again tomorrow. Maybe we can get them to slip up? Maybe we can discover who his enemies are? Or loved ones? Or where he lives in the waking world?"

"I can't argue against her," Will said.

This is dangerous.

"It's dangerous every time we do it," Will said. "But she gave me an idea."

God help us.

"He won't need to, Billy. Trust me."

Fine!

"Okay," Billy said to Yume. "We'll go in tonight."

CHAPTER 30

The house was a monastery to the West's religion of greed and power. A long driveway twisted between a pair of manicured bushes and led to a horseshoe drive in front of the house, ground-level decorative lights lining the way. Various forms of lighting made the house gleam like the devil's diamond on this moonless night. As expected, three guards were stationed on the patio attached to the rear of the house. After all, this was the house of…

Harold Varvaro.

This morning, as soon as she woke, Shinko sketched the man pretending to be a little girl named Maya. She then attached the image to an encrypted email to Fumiko. Shinko explained that she saw this man with the weapon stolen from the Chinese syndicate. Within an hour she received the name "Harold Varvaro" and pertinent information about him. He and his underlings dealt in weapons, debt management, gambling, and drugs. Shinigami's Helper suspected that he was only a puppet and someone powerful pulled his strings, though no educated or speculatory guesses as to whom. Harold's status wasn't important, though. The weapon was.

Not only did she receive the blessing to pursue, but Shinigami's Helper also gave her a direct order to eliminate Harold and anyone standing in her way to capture the weapon.

From the darkness of the forest border, Shinko and Aika crouched on the ground, observing the back of the house. All the windows were barred. The front door was guarded.

Three guards, all dressed alike in black suits, white shirts, no ties, semi-automatics slung over their shoulders by a strap. One slowly paced the length of the patio, both hands on his weapon while puffing a cigarette. The others took relaxed postures; Number Two leaned against the wall next to the glass patio doors, Number Three reclined in a cushioned chair with his feet propped up on a sturdy patio table.

A flash of movement from behind the glass doors let Shinko know that more people actively moved within the house. She took a deep breath, her exhale shaky.

"Senpai?" Aika whispered from next to her. "Are you okay? You seem... hesitant."

Indeed. Shinko was hesitant about moving forward. Hesitant about telling Aika why.

Aika had remained reticent all day, never once asking Shinko how she came upon Varvaro's image; she communicated her suspicions with steely glances. Without question she had followed Shinko's orders to research Harold Varvaro and his art gallery, and spoke only when she had information to share.

Alas, there'd be ramifications if Shinko didn't share her secret. "I fear if I tell you, Aika, you will think sensibility has abandoned me."

Just enough moonlight cut through the trees to illuminate Aika's eyes. Cold black like unignited coal, with just as much potential to blaze should they be sparked. Shinko watched them weaken with a moment of doubt. Shinko almost gave her permission to speak freely, until Aika's eyes once again reflected stern confidence. "You saw this house in a dream."

She wondered if the Aika she had interacted within her dream had been the real one. "How did you know?"

"Shinigami's Helper preaches observation, does it not? Your nightmare on the plane seemed far more intense than normal. At The Dragon's Blessing, you accepted the man's words. The cuts on your arms this morning – you tried to hide them, but I saw the bandages. Unless you went on a solo mission last night, which I don't believe you did, then you must have received them from a dream."

"You believe what happens in dreams can happen in the real world?"

Aika offered the slightest shrug. "I can't think of a reason why not?"

"There is no science to back it up."

"Many actions, thoughts, and feelings can't be explained by science, so why should dreams be any different."

Cognizant that they were on a mission, Shinko stifled a chuckle. "Fair point."

Aika nodded toward Shinko's arms. "Evidence leans toward proof of a theory or idea. You've seen this place in a dream, and have cuts on your arms from being wounded in a dream."

"Again, fair point."

As quickly and quietly as possible, Shinko shared her experiences in the dreams. She also shared her suspicions about Maya, and whether or not she even existed.

Aika nodded and asked, "Does this change our mission?"

"No. It's doubtful that the house's interior will resemble a Victorian mansion, nor do I believe we'll face snake-headed creatures. We shall treat this like every mission. Our objective is to eliminate Harold Varvaro, and capture Maya the weapon, if she actually exists."

Aika nodded once more and disappeared into the forest. A bright future was in store for her within Shinigami's Helper.

Shinko waited for her ward to sneak toward the house and position herself on the roof before gliding through the shadows to cross the lawn. She easily avoided the obvious security cameras as she crept along the side of the house. Padding up the stairs to the patio, she readied her blow gun. Three guards, three darts.

As soon as the pacing guard came into view, she blew a dart. His hand went to his neck, and he dropped to the ground. She reloaded, blew again, hitting the exposed neck of the reclined guard. The guard leaning against the wall hurried over to his fallen comrades, drawing attention from inside the house. Stupidly, he crouched down to investigate, making him an easy target for Shinko's third dart. The poison worked fast; it seized their hearts in seconds.

The glass door slid open and another man in a suit ran out. Two steps onto the patio and he jerked back, his hands at his neck. The fiber-thin garrote Aika held cut deeply into the guard's skin, under his chin. He clawed at his throat, fingers bleeding, unable to twist away.

Aika lay flat on the roof, at the lowest point, and didn't budge even though the man probably outweighed her by fifty kilograms. Leverage and gravity worked against him, draining his life away, face bulging, neck bloodied. Once he stopped squirming, Aika silently lowered his corpse to the patio. She dropped from the roof as Shinko finished ascending the stairs. They slipped through the opened door into the main room of Harold's house.

Far more modern than a Victorian mansion. She figured it was unlikely that the interior would match her dreamscape where she had battled Maya, but the decor still surprised her. The space in front of her was one massive open room. Couches, tables, bookshelves, television, even a pool table at the far end. A load bearing wall ran the length of the house; more rooms on the other side of it and a staircase to the second floor. Upstairs had to lead to Harold's bedroom.

Shinko gasped – a spiral lamp on a side table startled her. She first thought the slim S shaped metal base was a snake ready to strike. It emitted a soft LED light, dim yet white, more of a nightlight than anything else. Too bright for Shinko's taste. They needed to hurry. Get to the stairs before…

Men in suits sprang out from a doorway under the stairs. She and Aika retreated into the room – fleeing the house was not an option as more men ran in from the far end. Seven in total, armed with handguns. They formed an uneven line and moved toward Shinko and Aika.

"I'll take the three on the left," Shinko whispered. "You take the three on the right. The one in the middle we'll save for last. He won't know which half of his comrades to help."

A couch ran lengthwise between Shinko and Harold's goons. She took a step forward, then jumped left, sailing over the back of the couch. The three closest men moved their aim in unison; two shot, their bullets hitting the wall. She took another step forward and jumped back over the couch. The three men retargeted – three bullets, the window shattering. One more step forward and she feigned a jump left. Another gunshot, and something that sounded expensive shattered behind Shinko. Overcompensating, the guard who shot swung his hand back, but blocked the sightline for the two guards next to him.

This time, Shinko leapt over the couch and quickly took a step forward only to jump back. All three goons waved their guns wildly, leaving Shiko close enough to chop downward on a goon's wrist with one hand while slamming the bottom of the gun with her other, popping it from his grip. The gun tumbled upward and she smacked it from the air, bouncing it off the head of the next closest thug.

A quick spin and she was behind the guard she disarmed, using him as a shield from the third goon; the second goon crouched and held both hands against his bleeding forehead. She poked her head out from behind her human shield, one side and then the other, enticing the third guard to shoot.

Hands out as if they'd stop bullets, Shield yelled, "Don't! Don't fucking shoot!"

Taking advantage of the confusion, she used Shield's shoulders as a pivot point and leapt from behind him, her feet landing hard on the third man's outstretched arms, knocking him off balance. She sidestepped out of his way as he fell forward and crashed into her Shield, dropping him to the floor. A spin and the heel of her foot to his chin took him out of the fight.

The goon who had a gun ricochet off his head got back to his feet, blood from his forehead painting his face. Before he took aim, Shinko snatched his weapon, popped out the magazine, and threw it at him. Different pistol, same target – his head. This time he crumbled to the floor. Shield didn't stay down long either. Shinko took care of that by crushing his nose with the palm of her hand.

The room amplified the pop of a fired gun. The goon in the middle had chosen to focus on Shinko, but missed. A few backflips landed her next to the pool table. She whipped the eight ball and the blue two ball. They crushed his knuckles and he dropped the gun, but he snatched a pool stick lying on the pool table. He gave it a dramatic twirl before taking a swing at Shinko's head. Missed. His swings wild, yet fast, forcing Shinko into a strange dance – lifting her feet when he attacked low, stepping to the side when he attacked high. With his final assault, he swung the pool stick like a baseball bat, aiming for her ribcage. She spun and brought her arms down, trapping the pool stick between her biceps and back. With a twist, she yanked it from his grasp. She struck the goon across the bridge of his nose with the sound of a pop, much like the gun. An explosion of blood and he dropped to the floor.

Anguished grunts and wet snaps of bones breaking let Shinko know that Aika was handling her three goons, so she hurried across the room and glided up the stairs as if skating on shadows. Aware of the various rooms on either side of her, she drew her ninjato and padded down the hall to the open door at the end. Harold Varvaro's bedroom.

Standing at the doorway, back against the frame, Shinko exhaled slowly. *Focus.* Did it feel like she was alone? *Listen.* Were there any noises? *Watch for movement.* Nothing.

She slipped into the dark bedroom. Two people sleeping on top of the blankets, breathing in rhythm. No sense of anyone else in the room.

Shinko turned on the lights, sword held high. Neither body moved, nor reacted to the sudden brightness. Shinko crossed the room to Harold Varvaro, set to end his life. Until she realized the other person in the king-sized bed was a child. A little girl. Maya.

The center if her floral nightgown bloomed red; blood from a fresh wound. Panic tore through Shinko, a feeling she hadn't experienced in over a decade when Yume had been hospitalized with flu related encephalitis.

Her panic demanded action, and so she rushed to the other side of the bed and removed her gloves. Maya had a pulse, a strong one in fact. Confused, Shinko gently pulled the gown up to expose Maya's belly, and gasped.

Two cuts marked either side of her abdomen. Shinko's eyes widened and she held her breath, watching the wounds shrink. Slowly, the enflamed skin softened in color.

Maya's eyes moved back and forth under closed lids. She was dreaming. Maybe she had been stabbed in her dream and could heal herself? If that were the case, then Shinko dared not wake her up, yet. Shinko thought about her own wounds, the cuts throbbing and burning on her arms, and wondered why *her* previous abrasions had not healed in *her* dreams. Maybe because she was no dream hopper, no magical interloper.

Shinko regarded the child. The girl-weapon. She might have been powerful in the dreamscape, but on the huge bed she looked so frail, innocent. This was no longer about retrieving or neutralizing a weapon. This was about rescuing a little girl from a cruel captor.

She shifted her eyes to the door, then Varvaro, glancing occasionally at Maya's cuts. *Hurry, hurry.* Eight-centimeter slashes became four centimeters in length, then two. One. Soon as they vanished, Shinko ran her fingers through the girl's hair, and whispered, "Maya? I'm here. Let's leave this place."

Harold gurgled.

Shinko's hand gripped the hilt of her sword.

The man spasmed, went rigid, then limp. She considered checking his vitals, but Maya sat up. Shinko swallowed hard, stunned by the little girl's eyes. Earnest. Old. Filled with knowledge.

"Will you take me home?" Maya asked.

"Yes."

"Who would you like me to kill?"

At Yume's age, Aika's age, Shinko had killed for the first time and hadn't stopped taking lives since. But when Maya asked her question with the coldness of a killer more seasoned than herself? It broke her heart.

She wasn't thinking about what Maya would do or how dangerous she could have been, Shinko just reacted to what her spirit told her to do. She hugged Maya and said, "No one."

After a few thumping heart beats, Maya wrapped her arms around Shinko, returning her hug. "Thank you."

Scooping Maya up in her arms felt like lifting a bag of feathers. She didn't know where she was taking the girl. She just wanted to get her out of here.

"Thank you," Maya whispered once more, her words triggering tears.

CHAPTER 31

Yume finished her valerian root tea and set the empty cup on her nightstand. Billy told her not to use any medications or sleep aids, but a little valerian root wouldn't hurt. A few low effort yoga poses, light stretching with her eyes closed to help her connect her mind, body, and spirit. Lights out, she slipped into bed.

Relaxing thoughts. The whole reason she wasn't at Billy's right now – her bedroom was more relaxing. She needed to calm herself, a little difficult as she felt her heart beat through her entire body, including her toes. *I've done this before. No big deal.* But it was a big deal, with a high potential of coming face-to-face with a dream manipulator that possibly surpassed Billy and Will in skill and power. *Stop focusing on that!*

She was lying on her back. Dumb. She was a side sleeper. And why so rigid, like this was a formal affair with a scripted routine? Grunting, she rolled over on her side, one hand curled under her pillow, the other on it, close to her face. Much better. She decided to try a technique that her mother had taught her. Easy to do and comfortable in this position. Using her thumb to block her right nostril, she inhaled through her nose. She shifted her thumb to block her left nostril and exhaled. She then inhaled deeply and moved her thumb to her right nostril and exhaled. Inhale. Move thumb. Exhale. Inhale. Move thumb. Exhale. Inhale...

The Valhalla Room.

Hands behind his back, Billy paced the length of the table. A deep frown carved pensive lines in his face. Yume knew him well enough to know he was trying to think of a dozen ways to counter every possible scenario.

The monitors on the wall were black.

"Hey, you," Yume said as she approached. To hide her nervousness, she added, "Fancy meeting you here."

Billy stopped pacing and smiled. The worry retreated from his face but remained firmly entrenched in his eyes. "Hey, gorgeous! Come here often?"

Yume grabbed the sides of his shirt while he draped his arms over her shoulders. "Only when you're here."

After a soft, extended kiss, they hugged. Yume savored moments like this, their love too raw to be anything other than true. Foreheads pressed together, Billy whispered, "Are we ready for this?"

They had removed evil from the world, a quartet of disgusting worms that burrowed through the fabric of dignity and virtue in the form of Fratenelli and his crew. They were just puppets, though, and it was time to start going after the puppet master, Harold Varvaro. Yume pulled back and smiled. "Absolutely."

Billy turned to the monitors, his face all business. A wave of his hand brought them from dead black to a glowing blue. "Okay, this is going to be a little different than the others. We've been over this before, but when we appear in his dreamscape, we kill him on sight. No discussion or monologuing."

"Agreed. Do the deed before he or Maya can react. If they somehow get the jump on us, we'll fight back, but if it's too much, then we retreat."

"Correct. Ready?"

No. The thought of someone more powerful than Billy terrified her. So did the dreams of an organized crime boss. But as she said, if it got too crazy, they had to wake up, an act that took only the speed of thought. After all, if they died in the dreamscape, they died in the waking world.

Usure how she could possibly feel her heartbeat in a dreamworld that wasn't her own, it revved, her pulse speeding through her entire body. Bouncing from foot to foot, she blew out a deep breath and shook her hands as if air drying them. She nodded and said, "This is it. Let's do this."

The monitors merged, forming one large screen of glowing blue. It flickered, and it took Yume a beat to realize they now looked into Harold's dream.

Billy and Yume jumped into the image as easily as walking through an opened door. On a beach of soft sand bordered by crystal blue ocean, Harold Varvaro reclined in a chaise lounge chair. Who knew that a dirtbag crime lord would dream about a day at the beach?

Running toward him, Yume extended her hands; fire plumed from her fingertips. Knives, swords, and axes fell from above Harold like rain.

As if protected by an invisible shell, the fire flowed on either side of him and the edged weaponry gathered in piles in a five-foot perimeter around him. He looked over his shoulder and lowered his sunglasses, regarding Yume and Billy like resort staff calling his name.

Adjusting her stance, foot long metal nails flew from Yume's hands, while Billy summoned lava from below Harold. The nails bounce away, hitting nothing; the glowing orange lava pooled around the invisible perimeter and cooled to dull black.

Harold stood and removed his sunglasses, a look of mild consternation on his face as if more upset about them ruining his lounging session than attempting to kill him. "So, you kids didn't take my advice."

No messing around, no discussion back-and-forth. Yume extended her arms toward Harold again, shooting dozens of melon-sized fire balls at him. Billy waved his hands around like a wizard working a complicated spell – columns of sand erupted, breaking through the dried lava crust and forming giant fingers. Three, four, five hands reached for Harold.

"Nothing is touching him," Yume said.

The fireballs fizzled to harmless puffs of steam while the hands exploded into clouds of fine sand. As the nebula dissipated, Harold's triumphant figure, him standing with his hands behind his back, came into view. After a few more heartbeats, Yume saw a second person.

Maya.

Yume knew she was a little girl, a child, but to see her for the first time was truly unsettling. The girl stood in front of Harold, hands out as if her little body was enough to stop a charging beast. And she was more than capable.

Billy launched house-sized boulders at her from all directions. A mere finger wiggle from the girl and the stones disappeared in a swirl of dust.

Yume extended her hands and hundreds of arrows fired from her fingertips. They all turned to blue-winged butterflies and fluttered away.

But Maya looked confused when serpent-like vines sprouted from the sands and wrapped around her.

The little girl whispered, "No," and the vines fell to the ground as shriveled black husks. Fingertips dancing with each other as if making origami from tissue paper, her feet left the ground. As Maya floated higher, Yume's stomach lurched as she, too, defied the confines of gravity.

Yume couldn't move, her arms stuck by her side, legs straight, feet pinned together. Billy floated next to her in the same position.

Maya drifted closer, composed with her hands behind her back. Yume didn't like feeling as if she had disappointed her favorite teacher. Maya's long, black hair danced freely as if she were underwater, her endless eyes too intense.

Maya then backed away. Addressing Billy, she said, "You split your attack to make it appear as if Yume was powerful enough to manipulate the dreamscape. Very clever. But she has no power here."

"I do!" Yume snapped, brow furrowing with a headache-inducing frown. Instead of concentrating on fire, lava, comets, and volcanos, Yume called forth the only thing she could in someone else's dreamscape.

Yogurt.

Dozens of strawberry yogurt cups dropped from above, cascading between Yume and Maya.

A glint of mirth flashed within Maya's eyes. "Clearly, I was mistaken."

Yume felt like a child, but this was one aspect of the plan, and she played her part accordingly.

Jaw clenched shut, Billy glared at Maya while she regarded him with the dark, empty eyes of a shark. Streams of arcing blue electricity danced along his body. He twitched and moaned, but the experience was brief, simple jolts to show everyone who was in control. She was the apex here.

"I told you to stay away," she said.

"You're protecting a killer," Billy snarled.

"You're a killer."

"I kill for justice. I kill to make the world a better place. He kills for money and power. He ruins lives while I protect lives."

"You're still a killer."

"And so are you. Both he and you need to be stopped."

"Not by you. I admire your ploy, though. It did confuse me briefly, but it was just an illusion."

Billy smirked, knowing the joke's punchline before it was finished. "Yes. But this isn't."

With sword blades instead of hands, Will burst from Billy's chest – also part of the plan even though Billy screamed in agony. Will drove both blades into Maya's sides.

Maya screamed and extended her hands to push herself away. Even under duress, she exhibited mastery of the environment, launching herself backwards. Once far enough away, she ran her hands over waist, and her wounds began to heal. Anger reflected in her face.

Their plan wasn't enough to stop her, but Maya had released her invisible grip on them. They still had a chance to beat her!

As Yume continued floating, she hoped she wouldn't plummet back to the ground. The soft sandy beach was not soft enough to prevent injury, or worse.

Billy and Will navigated the dreamscape, flying in different directions through the air, trying to put Maya between them.

"Sorry about the painful entrance," Will said to Billy.

"No worries," Billy replied. "Let's end this."

Billy and Will made broad, sweeping movements with their hands in unison, like witches summoning dark and wicked spirits over a boiling cauldron. They succeeded in calling forth beasts from nothingness.

A dozen different colored dragons, their scales vibrant and beautiful, armored by gemstones. With sharp horns ready to pierce, they flapped massive, spiked wings. Large enough to swallow a person whole, they swooped in figure eights around Maya while belching liquid flames.

Maya waved her hand at each attack, diverting the fire or turning it to steam. With every swipe of her hands, she looked as if she gained more control. She then said, "Yes, let's end this."

Maya pointed to a green dragon, and it exploded like a gore-filled balloon, its wings falling to the beach. Maya pointed to a dragon closest to Yume. It also exploded, blood dousing Yume and pelting her with chunks of raw meat. Maya continued pointing at dragons, a bloody firework display. Their entrails twirled through the air like slimy streamers, bathing Yume, Billy, and Will in syrupy, crimson liquid.

Yume's stomach twisted with the raw smell, her skin and hair covered in sticky, warm blood; it was too alarming for her to concentrate. "Need to wake up," she whispered to herself. She looked at Billy and Will, ready to yell at them to retreat, but before she formed the words, the sky broke.

Like a window shattered by a brick, the clear blue sky broke into hundreds of pieces. The beach and the ocean as well, fragments slowly toppling across an endless, black background. Then squares of white appeared, creating a checkerboard pattern. The pattern began to swirl.

Yume floated among the broken pieces of the world while the universe behind it twisted in on itself. Disoriented. Too disoriented to wake up. The people. *Focus on Billy. Will. Find Harold and Maya.*

Billy and Will both spun through the churning insanity just as she did. Billy was too far away to make eye contact while Will screamed vicious profanities. Harold, expressionless as usual, kept his eyes closed. Maya stayed in control. This was her environment, her universe.

Dread seeped into Yume as she toppled about. Their plan had been so close to working, but she couldn't focus, couldn't calm herself enough to wake up. Then everything stopped.

No longer flipping and flopping around, she floated among the shards of shattered beach and ocean and sky along with Billy and Will. The pieces stopped tumbling, but more importantly, the background became devoid of the white checkered pattern, no swirls of madness.

Just black. Yume slowed her breathing. But something was wrong with Maya.

Not wrong. Different.

Maya floated in the center of everything, looking over her shoulder, enthralled with something only she could see. Was this the opportunity Billy and Will needed to end this?

No.

Maya turned away from Yume, Billy, and Will, and focused on Harold. She waved her hand and he flickered and faded, slowly disappearing. Once he was gone, she addressed Yume and said, "Your friends are in danger."

Maya winked out of existence.

Wake up!

Yume sat up straight in her bed, sweat flowing over her body. Shaking, she touched her face, arms, legs. Throat as scratchy as if she swallowed sandpaper, she scrabbled across her bed, and chugged the glass of water from her nightstand. Gasping and clutching at her chest, she hugged her body to stop shaking until her hands felt steady enough to call Billy.

"Hello," his voice dry and raspy.

"Did we win?" Yume asked.

Silence, then the distinct sound of him gulping water. With a clearer voice, he answered, "I don't know."

CHAPTER 32

The restaurant was dark and quiet. Shanna sat alone at a round table designed for two, thick white tablecloth almost reaching the floor. The air smelled like freshly smoked cigarettes, abundantly more than what came from the stogy in her hand. Four crushed butts laid in the ashtray. She had been here for a while. She liked this place.

Miniature lamps on the tables and the single spotlight above the stage created hard shadows, giving a monochrome feel, as if Shanna had stepped directly into a black and white 1940s movie. A lone singer stood firm in the center of the stage. A piano accompanied her dusky vocals, its silhouette at the back of the stage. She belonged on a New Orleans riverboat with her Brenda Lee voice and floor length form-fitting, sparkling black gown. Her combed blonde hair rested in swirls on her shoulders.

Shanna twisted the ends of her hair round her finger, admiring her. Could she carry that same look with her own hair? And then the spotlight moved and she saw the singer's face.

It was her.

Startled, she wondered how she could be sitting at a table enjoying a martini while watching herself sing on stage. Where did the drink come from? Oh, yeah. This was a dream. Only a dream. She already knew where this dream was going and what would eventually happen next. So, she tried pushing it from her mind, determined to enjoy the show and her drink, the gin burning all the way from her mouth to her soul.

She sensed the presence of other patrons, but they could have been anyone. Family. Teachers. Classmates, old or new. She didn't bother pondering who they were. If she were having a nightmare, they'd be monsters or ghosts or partially dismembered people. Had she seen any zombie movies recently? No, and she wasn't going to look around, content to stare ahead at the stage. At herself.

The elegant woman on stage was everything she wanted to be. Stylish. Classy. Noticed. In control. Beautiful because she wanted to be, not because she had to be. It pissed her off to think she could be this version of herself. It would only take a few changes; a couple big, a couple small. Yes. Starting tomorrow, she would figure out how to become like this woman on stage, in command of who she was.

A figure from the shadows approached her table, a man wearing a blue top hat and opera cape. He smiled, his teeth shining silver in the dull candlelight. Were they *actually* metal? She couldn't tell.

He gestured to the empty seat beside her and said, "I couldn't help but notice how beautiful you are. I would be remiss if I didn't meet you. May I join you?"

Sometimes he was nice, playful like tonight, and he always smelled like warm cinnamon. Sometimes he was more direct, he and his friends feasting on her like city rats with a block of cheese. She wasn't in the mood for him tonight, but she smiled, happy that he was solo. Maybe if she showed appreciation, then it'd remain just the two of them. She pushed the chair out with her foot and smirked.

After a slight bow, he sat. "Thank you. My name is—"

Still smirking, Shanna brought her index finger to her lips. "Shhhh." Forget waiting to wake up; time to take control of her life starting now. She gave a kittenish wink, and then pointed to the stage.

With a silver grin, he turned to the stage. Then sat beside her.

She was mildly impressed that he lasted three songs before leaning in and whispering, "She seems very familiar."

Shanna's eyebrow peaked. "Does she now?"

The man of her dreams turned in his chair, giving her his full attention. "She looks like someone I've seen before."

Shanna sat back and ran her finger along the lip of her martini glass. "Actually, she's someone you have yet to see."

"Really?"

"Yes. She is a woman in control of her life. In control of everything. I will be her soon enough."

"That certainly seems exciting." Shanna wanted to focus on anything other than his silver smile. Not that she didn't appreciate its uniqueness, but it stirred a primal feeling deep within her chest, one that served as a warning.

More dark figures emerged from the shadows. Once upon a time, Shanna had fantasized about being the center of attention for a group of hot men who prioritized her needs over theirs. The first few fantasies were exciting, her dreams playing out every way she had hoped. But the adage about "too much of a good thing" held true, as most general adages do. And this was *her* dream after all, and her priorities had changed.

Shanna raised her palm. "Not tonight, boys."

The shadow figures halted.

The man in the top hat frowned and turned to glance at his comrades, then turned back to Shanna, his brow raised. "When you said, 'take control,' you certainly meant it."

"It is my dream, my life, right? My sister and her boyfriend yammer on and on about lucid dreaming, about taking control of your dream while in it. Figured I'd give it a try."

He cocked his head and smiled, the lamplight reflecting timidly off his metallic teeth. "A woman in control is very sexy. So, what will you do when I do this?"

Standing, the man in the top hat raised his arm, gesturing like a ringmaster bringing the circus to life. Light shined from above, casting away the darkness behind him, exposing a beige and white wallpaper pattern. Two similar walls sprouted forward from that one, and the night club disappeared. The tables turned to dust. The stage faded away. The singer vanished. Shanna stood from her chair just as it disintegrated.

No longer in a swanky nightclub, she stood next to a king-size bed in a hotel room. Clean, but bland.

In the night club, she had exerted control, made the world around her respond to her wants. And she'd do it again.

Mimicking his same grand gesture, she waved her arms, and the room changed. Nothing about the structure altered, she just wanted to make it a little classier. Hidden ornate sconces slid from the walls as if the objects realized it was safe to make an appearance. Posts sprouted from the four corners of the bed; once they hit the ceiling wispy mesh dropped and flowed from post to post. The wallpaper color deepened to scarlet, and gold filagree appeared as if scrawled by ghosts. A claw-foot bathtub arose from the floor.

The lights dimmed and Shanna crawled onto the bed. Kneeling, she swiped her hands once to make her clothes fly off her body, then again to make his clothes disappear. "Still think a woman in control is sexy?"

He replied with his silver smile and put his warm hands on her waist. Leaning in for a kiss, he guided her to lay on the bed. She gently placed her fingers on his lips, then grabbed his shoulders and turned him. Once he caught onto what she wanted, he lay back. She straddled him, then chuckled. He had an issue with her dominating him, because his manhood was bigger than it had ever been before. And it kept growing.

Thighs squeezing his hips, she started to grind. "You're threatened by me?"

"Oh, my dear Shanna, I'm not."

His size continued to increase, approaching her threshold of comfort. "You're getting bigger."

"Because I just realized something."

"Yeah? What?"

"They appeared at the same time to fight Maya. Even though the two of them failed to kill her, they now coexist. I've been hiding from them, but now I can free myself. The three of us can exist simultaneously and now is my time to *take control*."

Confused, Shanna stopped grinding. "What are you talking about? Who appeared at the same time?"

Cheeks, chin, and forehead rippled as his face changed. The transformation was brief, but his face morphed into someone she recognized. "Billy?"

"Not quite." He smiled, his silver grin no longer teeth, now razor blades.

Was this Will? Yume had told her Billy had another personality, one distinctly different. Was this him? If so, why was she dreaming about him? Why was she dreaming about Billy or Will? She tried to wake up but couldn't. She tried to get off him, but his member had grown too big to dismount. His fingers dug into her hips while he thrusted. He kept getting bigger. "Stop! Let me go!"

"No!"

Skin stretching, her insides shifted to make room for his growing penis, moving deeper with each thrust. "Why? Why are you doing this?"

"To punish you."

Shanna struggled to breathe and wanted to vomit. Hot pain radiated from her crotch up her spine. "Punish me? Why? For what?"

"For being a terrible mother!"

"I'm not… I'm not a mother! I don't want to be!"

"I know! You're a whore! A fucking whore who will get pregnant and have a child you don't want. You'll resent your child, let your child fall prey to wicked adults, willfully ignore your child's cries and pleas as they fall victim to teachers, priests, doctors!"

Shanna tried to reply, tried begging him to stop, to convince him that he had the wrong person, but the thrusting bulge moved beyond her belly. Beyond her chest. Into her throat.

No! This was her dream. She should be able to stop this madness, to wake up and free herself. But if this was her dream, then why couldn't she stop him? Why was she hearing her skin rip, her hip bones break? Why did her stomach protrude as if pregnant, then tear open with her organs flopping down on him through a sluice of blood? Why was the world going black?

CHAPTER 33

The diner bustled with dawn's early morning life. Men and women wearing stained jeans, flannel shirts, and trucker caps ate next to people in khakis, dress shirts, and ties. This was the magic time when the locals finished their breakfasts and swapped places with college kids.

Yume had beat her peers to the punch. Alone in a booth, she stared into coffee cup number four, her overly caffeinated hands shaking. The "Working Man's Special" – an eloquent label for three eggs, three pancakes, three slices of bacon, and three pieces of toast – had gone easily down her gullet. She had never consumed a meal so large, let alone breakfast. And now she was eyeing up the French toast. Maybe a slice of pie. She was so hungry from last night. Last night was… No idea. Exhilarating? Terrifying? Enlightening? Draining. She wasn't sure about the other feelings, but last night had definitely been draining.

"Anything else?" the waitress asked, stopping by her table, bill in hand.

Yume lapped at the last of her coffee. "Another one, please."

"You sure?" She punctuated her question by pointedly looking at Yume's shaking hands.

Yume folded her hands and hid them under the table. She smiled and said, "Yes. A big test coming up. I need the energy."

The waitress had probably heard every lame excuse while working at a diner with Temple nearby. Lips drawn tight, she grunted and poured from the pot she carried around with her.

"Thank you," Yume said, positive her words went unheard as the waitress slapped the bill on her table and moved along to the next. A weird sense of superiority and guilt played through her mind. She had looked into the waitress' eyes, deep enough and long enough, confident she could easily slip into the woman's dreams tonight if she wished.

As evidenced by last night's embarrassing yogurt attack against Maya, Yume still couldn't control much in other people's dreams. However, she could observe, possibly influence. Not like the woman was a closed book, but after some time, Yume would be able to piece her life together. Everything that led her to become a sixty-something diner waitress would be on full display for Yume. This omniscient power was Godlike, wasn't it? Choosing to manipulate another person. Choosing to do something no one else could do.

"Hi, sorry I'm late," Billy said as he approached.

Yume jolted in her seat, then chuckled at the waitress' earlier spot-on assessment – maybe she shouldn't have that fifth coffee. "No worries. I should apologize for eating without you. I had a Working Man's Special and gallons of coffee."

Billy wheeled his chair to face the table and looked at her with a goofy smile. After last night's experience, which she was anxious to analyze, his silly smile seemed out of place. "So... The school play is *Alice in Wonderland* and you're auditioning for the Cheshire cat?"

"Not exactly. I'm smiling because of why I'm late."

This had better be good, because she was in no mood for coy games. "And the reason why you're late is...?"

"Will and I discovered something interesting this morning. Something we find very exciting, and hope you do, too."

"Interesting and exciting. Okay. Would you two like to share your little secret?"

Billy's smile changed subtly, from enthusiastic to confident, borderline cocky. The look in his eyes, too. From bright and focused to fiery and adventuress.

Then he stood from his wheelchair! Yume's mouth fell open. Billy slid into the booth across the table from her, his smile never wavering. "What do you think?"

Yume had witnessed fantastical dragons appearing out of thin air, a little girl blowing them apart with the wave of her hand, and the universe disassembling mere hours ago. But this? This was akin to miraculous. "Billy?"

He jerked his head back and snorted. "No. It's me, Will."

Yume snapped her jaw shut and leaned forward for a better look. He sat straighter than Billy. His smile. The look in his eyes. All three differences could go unnoticed, even under scrutiny. "Will?"

Slouching back, he extended his arms, a stage magician proud of his newest trick. "Well, what do you think?"

Yume smiled, though it might have been forced. "That's... that's... How?"

Almost humming with energy, he sat back up and snatched the last bit of crust from Yume's toast, running it through the leftover pancake syrup. He tossed it in his mouth and said, "We don't know. This is just conjecture, but I think when we willingly split apart and coexisted in Harold's dreamscape, it unlocked something within our psyches. Billy isn't one hundred percent sure, but he says it sounds plausible. And now, we can switch from one to the other, like this."

As he chewed the syrup coated crust of rye bread, his expression changed. Billy didn't like overly sugared foods and he never ate syrup. A slight sneer formed as he finished swallowing. "Ugh. I hope he doesn't turn this into a thing."

"Billy?"

"Yes. I apologize for his antics, but Will is very excited that we can now switch easily. I have to confess; I, too, am excited by this notion. We still have a little pain when we 'talk' to each other, but it's a lot more tolerable."

"Can... Can he hear me now?"

"Yes. And see you."

Yume leaned forward, squinting. She looked into Billy's eyes, expecting to see Will living in his head. "That's really cool."

Billy leaned in and touched his nose to hers. Eyes exaggeratedly wide, he said, "He's waving. Can you see him?"

Yume crinkled her nose and pinched his cheeks. "You're so cute when you're a smartass."

They shared a chuckle as they leaned back.

She pursed her lips. "It's awesome, but one rule – when we're together, always tell me when you switch. I can tell you two apart, but it takes me a minute. And no pretending to be the other. That won't sit well with me."

Billy nodded. "Understandable. We both agree. Those are valid requests."

"Good. At the risk of sounding impatient, can we talk about last night?"

"Yes, definitely."

"Have you or Will ever experienced anything like that before?"

"No, not until Maya."

The tremor increased in Yume's hands. "It was like... like she tore the entire universe to shreds."

"For all intents and purposes, she did."

Yume wished she could get control of herself, but her breathing quickened as she thought about what lay behind a universe. Every time she blinked, vertigo tickled her mind, a spiraling black and white checkerboard in the momentary darkness. "It was... It was... It was..."

Billy reached out and squeezed her hand, bringing her back to the diner, like nudging the needle on a skipping record. "It's okay. It freaked out Will and me, too. We never experienced anything like that either, and we never tried anything like that, because we never conceptualized anything like that."

Yume rarely felt afraid. She wasn't even sure if she was actually afraid, or if her adrenaline levels were still elevated, or if the caffeine had her on anxiety overload, but Billy's hand felt good in hers, the tight grip comforting. "Okay. Good to know I wasn't freaking out because of my noob status."

Billy smiled, and it was *Billy* smiling, she could tell. "You are perfectly justified in your feelings."

"Good. Okay. Good. So... Did we win?"

"Technically, yes. We escaped with our lives, and we were able to hurt Maya. Will seems to think we won't hear from her again. He believes she has no more interest in us, which was why she left before killing us. But moving forward we need to be wary of her, or others like her."

"Others like her. God, I haven't even thought of that." Yume's heart raced, but Billy squeezed her hand again. "How about Varvaro? Do you think he's dead?"

"Will does, because it goes with the theory of never seeing Maya again, but I'm not so sure Varvaro's dead." Billy's right eye closed and he cocked his head, a sudden wince of pain. "He's yelling into my brain, 'Why else would he have disappeared?' I'm not disagreeing with him, I just don't see any evidence."

"Okay. I guess the best we can do is head to the gallery and see if he's there. If he's not, then maybe ask for him?"

Billy exhaled, looking up as if pleading to the heavens. After a minute of contemplation, he looked at Yume and shrugged. "I'm not thrilled with this idea, but I can't imagine waiting around for the news to report missing mobsters."

Yume didn't like it either. There were a lot of unknowns and too many variables, but she allowed herself a sense of serenity. This was something new for both Billy and Will, and she appreciated their honesty and vulnerability in sharing that information with her. Facing someone like Maya and cohabitating one body more easily.

Yume almost giggled at how the idea of having two boyfriends had unexpectedly become more exacerbated. It'd be weird, and another adjustment, but she was confident that they'd find ways to control the active personality, and make it work. She was excited to tell Shanna...

Yume frowned and slouched back in her seat.

"What's wrong?" Billy asked.

"It's Shanna. It's our argument. We've always shared everything with each other. She sensed that there was something going on – the whole point of our argument. I'd love to be able to tell her something."

Billy cocked his head. He looked contemplative, but Yume knew he was conferring with Will. His hangdog expression let her know the drawn conclusion. "Too dangerous. Especially after last night. If we figure out what happened to Maya, *then* maybe you can let Shanna know we can traverse the dreamscape."

Yume looked away. Arguing would only be a waste of words. He was right. But...

She sat up higher, unable to hide the excitement in her voice. "Can I at least tell her about the new thing you and Will can do? She knows about you two, and I don't have to tell her your theories about why you're able to switch upon command now. If she asks, I'll gladly take the credit. It's because of me. You two love me so much that you're willing to share the lead personality. Makes perfect sense to me."

Billy laughed. "Both Will and I agree; our love for you could be the reason we now effortlessly and consciously switch. So, yes, share this news with her."

"You two are the collective best." Yume stood from the booth and dropped cash on the table. "Sorry to ditch, but I don't like arguing with her, so I really want to go see her now."

"Nothing to be sorry about. Tell her we both say hi."

After a kiss and a hug, Yume left the diner and headed toward Shanna's. It was a hike, but she felt invigorated. She had survived her first encounter with a dream demon in the guise of a little girl. *Uncool, dream demon. Uncool.* There was a chance that she and her boyfriend – boyfriends? Okay, they'd have to figure that out later – removed a crime boss from this world, making it a better and safer place. When should they find another candidate? Was it safe to try now, or should they wait? Yume debated with herself for the next half hour, until she got to Shanna's house.

Almost nine in the morning, still early for Shanna, so Yume lightly knocked on the door. Millie answered in an ankle length silk robe, coffee in hand. Parts of her hair reached in stunning directions, but she had a happy look on her face. "Oh, hi, Yume. Very surprised to see you so early."

"Sorry for waking you, but is it okay if I see Shanna?"

"No worries, I've been up long enough to make coffee. I'm sure Shanna's still sleeping, but feel free to wake her, if you dare."

Yume glided to Shanna's room and knocked on her door, barely hard enough to hear her knuckles make contact. She whispered, "Shanna?"

Nothing.

Yume took a deep breath and knocked a little louder. One more knock yielded more silence. Turning the doorknob and cracking the door ajar, Yume announced herself. "Shanna? Sorry for our misunderstanding, but I have exciting news. I'm... I'm coming in—"

Yume froze and forgot how to breathe.

Shanna was in her bed. Naked. Twisted. Bent in half on crimson-soaked sheets, her entire right arm hidden inside of her. A portion of her lower spine poked out from her skin.

Her lifeless eyes wide open and staring at Yume.

Millie screamed from behind Yume and collapsed.

CHAPTER 34

After breakfast with Yume, Billy went home. Thanks to spending much of the early morning with Will, he was exhausted. Soon as he sat on the couch, he fell asleep.

In the dreamscape, Billy's feet dangled over a plateau; his hands folded together on his chest while lying on the dry, packed dirt ground. The sky, various shades of purple, blended and mixed as the stars twinkled at different speeds and intensity. Most of them moved. Some at a lethargic pace, others streaking along and leaving a trail of white fire behind them. Turning his head to the right, he watched an entire galaxy form, the millions of stars pulling apart the gossamer fabric of the nebula gasses. The dreamscape made him feel insanely powerful, yet mind-numbingly insignificant.

"Hey," Will said, walking up beside him. He sat down as Billy sat up.

"Hello," Billy said.

Now that they sat next to each other, Billy felt like he was looking into a slightly distorted reflection. Will's hair and energy were a bit wilder than his own, his facial expressions more dramatic. Eyes just as soulful, though. "This is nice. It's been a while since we've been able to do this. Together, I mean."

Billy rested his hands on his lap and looked over the alien landscape, nothing but tall plateaus and barren lands, except for a few trees made from twisted blue vines. "I agree. Until recently, the last time we occupied the dreamscape together was before..."

Will finished Billy's statement, "Before I killed our parents."

"Right after you created me."

Will put his hand on Billy's shoulder and squeezed. "I didn't 'create' you. You've always been a part of me."

"I'm not sure that's true."

"You have memories of our childhood, right?"

Billy nodded. He remembered the priest and the taste of his communion. He remembered his guidance counselor making unreasonable demands and his therapist prescribing drugs and trying to convince him that his abuses weren't real. He remembered his parents berating him when they weren't ignoring him, telling him he wasn't trying hard enough in between calling him a liar. He remembered the sting of Dad's belt. He remembered everything. The sadness. The fear. The guilt. The loneliness. The anger. The anger that grew. The anger that mutated and twisted into something beyond the confines of rage. Then one day, he felt... different.

Powerful. That was the only way to describe the new feeling. Powerful. Enough to change the world around him with a single thought. At the time, he hadn't known he was dreaming. Until he met Will.

They both shared the same psychiatrist, the pustule of a man who introduced the two. Only then, upon meeting each other as teenagers, did he realize he was dreaming. The memories felt different, as if he hadn't lived through them the same way Will had. The anger still existed, but not the unadulterated hatred. It felt like someone had surgically removed a prehensile organ, though he remembered having it.

Billy had taught Will how to control his dreams, and how to go into other people's dreams. At the time, it was easy to blur the lines between dream and reality, easy to confuse their dreamscape with their existence in the waking world. Billy had a trick, though. He coated a quarter with gold paint to make it special, memorable. He put it in his pajama pocket before bed, taking it out immediately after waking up. If he had it, then he was still dreaming. It was about making it a part of the subconscious. Just like ghosts were usually portrayed in clothing that they were wearing when they died, never naked, people often wore in their dreams what they had been wearing that day. So, Billy made the gold quarter a part of his outfit. He also taught this trick to Will. One day, Will slaughtered their parents, priest, and psychiatrist in a dream, only to discover no quarter in his pocket. Luckily, the police investigation found plenty of evidence to substantiate Will's claims of abuse. However, from that point forward, they had not been able to exist in the dreamscape at the same time. Until their encounters with Maya.

Billy answered after a moment of silence. "I do remember our childhood, but it's as if it were merely a nightmare I had awoken from."

A shoulder squeeze. "Me, too. Ever since I killed our parents, my feelings and memories seemed a little different."

Billy turned his attention to his other self. "I never knew that. Maybe a bit of catharsis from enacting justice?"

Will shrugged. It was his turn to look out upon the alien landscape. He waved his hand and sighed. Trees and plants slowly sprouted from the dry, flat ground of every plateau, the trunks and stalks the same blue hue of the existing flora. "Maybe. Sounds as good as any other explanation. Or maybe the pain was divided between the two of us? That's why we couldn't be in the dreamscape at the same time, because our subconsciouses were afraid of uniting the pain again."

Billy nodded. It was his turn to wave his hand at the landscape. Leaves and flowers sprouted from Will's creations, pinks and reds and yellows so vibrant they almost glowed. "Your theory is sound. Maybe we can now be in the dreamscape together because we've moved on. We found love."

"Or maybe because we had to fight a new villain?"

There was anger in Will's tone, obviously upset by the ambiguous outcome versus Maya and Varvaro. More than just anger, though. Billy heard guilt. Nila came to mind, as did the other ex-girlfriends who had joined Billy and Will on their crusade to rid the world of monsters. They had all been driven mad, accusing Billy or Will of killing the monster's innocent family members. Ultimately, each relationship ended the same way. "Is Maya the villain? Did she kill the family members of the men who we've exacted our brand of justice upon?"

"She must be. The first time we met, she openly admitted that she's killed people before."

"She also said she wasn't who we accused her to be. She said there was another – how did she put it? – dream eater."

Frustration shot the words out of Will's mouth. "Course it was her. Guilty people have the habit of blaming other people. Or it's pass-through blame, like it's Picasso's fault, not hers."

"I can't believe Picasso would have her slaughter the families of men we killed. What are the odds?"

"I don't know, Billy! Maybe she's like a genie. Whoever holds the bottle gets the wish."

"Do you really think she's dead?"

Will worked his jaw, chewing on the question. "I do. I believe Yume's mother got to her. She got to her and Harold Varvaro and killed them both. I keep replaying what happened. Maya had us, had all three of us. She was ready to tear us apart atom by atom, but something distracted her. The way she looked away from us? Something happened in the waking world. She and Harold both disappeared from the dreamscape. At the very least, Yume's mother killed Picasso and freed Maya."

"I tried looking for Shinko, but I couldn't find her."

"Me, too. She's gotta asleep sometime, right?"

"Unless she's back on a plane to Japan and out of reach."

"You think? It's only been four or five hours."

"Don't forget what she *actually* does for a living. She told Yume she left a couple of days ago. I'm sure when she's on assignment, she goes where she needs to, does what she needs to, and then leaves as soon as possible."

Will nodded. "Get in, get done, get out. Makes sense. So, now what?"

Silence as Billy mulled over the question. He and Will took turns adding to their dream world. Billy started with mountains teasing the horizon, then Will brought forth rivers branching off to pass the plateau where they sat. Billy added colorful fish with long, flowing fins. Will added smaller animals to cavort among the trees. Billy added birds and Will added dragons. Will *always* added dragons.

"I think we stick with what we told Yume at breakfast," Billy said.

"Go to the gallery today and ask for the owner? They're not going to come out and say he's dead. Hell, probably none of his employees even knows he's dead. If he's dead."

"True, but if he comes out to greet us, then we know he's alive."

"If not, then we have to wait a day or two or three while we keep checking the obituaries like a couple of old people." Will added a farcical creakiness to his voice, "Oh, look Esther, poor Mildred made the obituaries. Poor girl taken too soon at a young ninety-seven. She was so spry and crocheted the best babushkas."

Billy laughed. "Clearly, you don't know what a babushka is."

"I don't. I just like saying babushka. But I don't like waiting."

"You don't like decision making without variable knowledge."

"That, too."

"We need a little patience, that's all. Once we—"

Billy and Will shuddered and looked at each other, eyes narrow. They took a deep breath and looked around.

Billy shook his head. "There's nothing new in the dreamscape, but—"

"I feel... something," Will said.

"So do I. In the waking world, maybe?"

"If that's true, then that means someone is in our apartment!"

Billy opened his eyes. Fully awake, from the couch where he lay, he heard sniffling.

Yume.

Stiff muscles protested with him, but he forced them to do his bidding and he sat up. Once upright, his blurry vision cleared. Yume sat in the armchair, knees pulled to her chest, arms hugging her shins, face glistening with tear tracks and twisted in agony. She was crying.

"Oh my God, Yume. What's wrong? What happened?"

"It's... It's..." Her words hitched in between chest rattling sobs. "It's Shanna. She's... She's... She's... Dead! Shanna's dead! Maya killed her!"

CHAPTER 35

The woman shelter's bedroom was smaller than the one in Yume's apartment. She helped Margaret settle a young woman named Alicia into the small room, and then forbade herself from ever complaining about her apartment again.

Alicia had shown up a half hour ago with a black eye. Thankfully, Margaret convinced her to stay the night.

Even though Yume didn't say a word throughout Alicia's sign-in process, she hung around long enough to look deeply into her eyes. Finding her dirtbag boyfriend in his dreams would be easy. No... *Would have* been easy, if it weren't for Will's moratorium on jumping into other people's dreams.

Will was certain Maya was dead. He couldn't add any more other than "she could have killed us, but she disappeared" as his reasoning.

Billy made no assumptions. Neither did Yume. However, it was Will who said there would be no jumping into other people's dreams until Yume was comfortable. He wanted to search the general dreamscape with Billy for evidence of Maya, dead or alive. Billy agreed.

After Alicia's abuse story, Yume decided she was more than comfortable jumping into dreams. And turning them into nightmares.

It had been three emotionally grueling weeks since Shanna died. Understandably, Millie suffered a breakdown and needed time in the hospital. She came home a week ago, bottles of medication in hand.

Yume was distraught, but at least she had the support of Billy and Will, and knew how her sister had died. Poor Millie had no clue. Neither did anyone else. Police badgered Millie every other day since two deaths involving extreme sexual violence happened in the same residence within a month. Their best guess was two or more men broke in and brutalized Shanna, despite no evidence supporting that theory. No sign of anyone else being in the room. No hairs, no bodily fluids, not even a rogue skin cell from anyone other than Shanna, Millie, or

Yume. The toxicology report revealed nothing stronger than alcohol and uppers in Shanna's system.

After helping Millie get settled, Yume decided to visit the women's shelter. Part of her felt like she needed the services; her sister had been murdered in a horrific manner after all, and she found solace in trying to help others. And frustration. Alicia had been the third woman this week with a story about an abusive relationship. "Enough," Yume said to herself.

Billy and Will weren't jumping into other people's dreams, but they were actively exploring the dreamscape and observing, searching for signs of Maya. Yume and Billy visited the 8th Street Gallery every other day to get a beat on Harold Varvaro. They finally received confirmation – he had disappeared. They were even there when the gallery's owner was there – a big shot businessman named Maxwell Templeton. Neither Yume nor Billy had a chance to look into his eyes, but after internet research, he seemed up-and-up.

Will was dubious, stating, "The more innocent a millionaire looks, the more guilty he is." He also wondered how Varvaro could run criminal activities out of the gallery without Templeton's knowledge. At the time, Yume was in no mood to think about it. Now, angry enough to think about jumping into dreams, she decided to discuss furthering the research on Maxwell Templeton.

Margaret thanked Yume for her help with getting Alicia settled, and then sent her home for the evening.

At her apartment and done for the day – wearing thin shorts and cotton top, hair pulled back into her sleep-time ponytail – she called Billy to say goodnight.

"How are you feeling?" he asked.

Sitting on the couch with a glass of Pinot Noir in hand, "Good. Actually, really good. Still angry about everything that happened, but... I want to use those feelings as motivations."

"Okay."

Yume took a sip of wine, and then lowered her voice. Sloan's door was closed, but she might storm out at any second. "Tomorrow I'd like to talk to you two about going back into people's dreams, about revisiting what we've been doing."

"Oh! Wow, okay. That's great. Are you sure?"

"I think so. That's why I want to talk about it *tomorrow. Tonight*, I want a good night's sleep, no dreamscape. We should also talk about Templeton. I agree with Will; no way he's not involved in some criminal enterprise."

"Sounds great. Will and I will do another search for Maya tonight."

"Okay. Love you both. Good night."

"We love you, too. Bye."

Yume pulled from her glass again and tucked her feet under, staring absently at the wall. Even if Maya were gone, that didn't mean there weren't other monsters out there. Someone, or some*thing*, had murdered Shanna. Another item to put on tomorrow's discussion agenda. There were too many other kinds of monsters out there, though, the non-supernatural ones on hindlegs who thought they were entitled to abuse whomever they wanted. *Those* monsters she and Billy and Will could hunt. *Those* monsters they could stop. Speaking of different monsters…

Sloan's bedroom door opened. Dressed much like Yume in shorts and a tank top, hair up, she hurried to the kitchen and grabbed a glass from the cabinet. Good thing Billy wasn't here, or Sloan would undoubtedly launch into a diatribe about respecting her sleep needs and to shut up for the rest of the night. As she retrieved the container of purified water from the fridge, she said, "Still hitting the booze to cope with Shanna, I see."

Yume took an exaggerated sip and then licked her lips. "Yep."

Water glass full, fridge closed, Sloan headed back to her bedroom. "Too bad it wasn't me, huh? You'd at least have gotten all A's this semester."

"Why do you have to be such a bitch?"

"Why do you have to distract me all the time with your drama?"

"My drama? Seriously, you—"

Sloan slammed her door shut, cutting Yume off.

A week or two ago, Yume would have sat there and taken it, too empty from the loss of her sister to do anything. Not today. Not now. Fists clenched, she popped up from the couch and started toward

Sloan's bedroom, knuckles ready to pound. But when she got to the door, she heard a sniffle, and stopped.

Surprised and curious, Yume leaned closer to the door and held her breath. An exasperated sob. Sloan was crying.

Yume was all for standing up for herself, but she couldn't bring herself to tear into someone who was crying, even someone as nasty as Sloan. There had to be a reason for her nastiness, right? That was the whole point of psychology – understanding behavioral pattern and motivation. Humans didn't act without a reason, even if the act was unreasonable. Sloan was a bitch, and she had a reason. Sloan was alone in her room crying, and there was a reason.

Yume closed her eyes and leaned her forehead against the door. The sobbing became more pronounced. Then she heard Sloan whisper, "Please, God, let me get some fucking sleep tonight. Please."

One of the last things Shanna had mentioned to Yume – *God, that was our last conversation* – was about Sloan having bad dreams.

Yume's turn to cry. She went back to the couch and slugged back the rest of the wine. She washed the empty glass before she went to bed.

Mere minutes ago, she had told Billy she wanted no dreamscape tonight, but that was before her interaction with Sloan, before realizing she might have an opportunity to help her.

Falling asleep was easy, as was finding Sloan's dreamscape, where it was easy to see why Sloan hadn't been sleeping.

It had been a month since she last entered Sloan's dreamscape and it now seemed so... different. Alien. Intense. A small arena. No, more like under the main tent of a circus, bleachers surrounding the packed dirt center. Sloan stood in the middle and Yume cautiously approached. The stands were filled, but instead of hundreds of different people, they were hundreds of copies of two people – Sloan's parents. Yume never met them, but she had seen enough pictures to recognize the angry, screaming faces as they hurled insults and aspersions at their daughter.

A giant glass case protected a trophy, a golden "A+." Sloan pounded against the six-foot tall casing hard enough to shake the trophy within. She had been at it for a while, judging by the cracks radiating from the impact points, watery crimson following along many of the crystalline webs. Crying and screaming, Sloan continued to pound her fists against the glass.

Yume had always known that Sloan's parents put pressure on her, but not how much. How harsh were they? Or was this Sloan's perception of their words and actions? Either way, Yume saw this as an endless loop. The pressure caused her nightmares, which interrupted her sleep, which created extra pressure. Yume doubted her help would cure Sloan's bitchiness, but she felt bad that Sloan's dream tortured her like this.

Yume called out over the crowd noise, "Sloan! Sloan, it's Yume! Can you hear me?"

Sloan kept pounding on the glass. Each hit yielded more cracks. And more blood. "I'm almost there!"

"You don't have to do this. You don't have to hurt yourself to achieve your goals. You don't—"

The glass wall shattered. Pieces, pebbles, and chunks of glass crashed to the ground. Laughing, Sloan looked at Yume with the eyes of a maniac. Blood poured from her hands. "I did it! Yume, did you see that? I did it!"

"Have you broken through the glass before?"

Sloan extended her wounded hands and walked toward her reward. "No. Never."

Yume wasn't sure if she had helped; maybe her presence was enough to alter the dream. She almost clapped when Sloan reached for the trophy.

But her hands slid right through the golden A+ as if it were a mirage.

Sloan reached for it again and again, each swipe more exaggerated than the other. Shaking, she looked at her bleeding hands. "What's wrong with them, Yume? Why can't I grab the A?"

Yume marched closer as Sloan tried again and again for her prize, each attempt as impotent as the prior. Her screams louder but warbled. Crying, she dropped to her knees and stared at her hands. "Why, Yume? Why can't I get the A?"

Yume knelt next to Sloan, trying to conjure encouraging words or appropriate questions. The blood flowed from Sloan's cuts faster and her skin started to pale. "What's happening?" Yume muttered.

Blood now pooled around their knees.

Laughter from the stands, instead of taunts or insults, the same laugh from dozens of mouths. Yume looked up to the crowd, but instead of Sloan's parents, she saw only one face replicated. A man with twisted skin and hollow eyes. Each copy of him wore a blue top hat and smiled through a mouth full of razor blade teeth.

"Why can't I get it?" Sloan asked one last time.

Yume awoke and leapt from her bed. A bit disoriented by the darkness of her bedroom, she slammed into her door. For the briefest moment, she thought about how mad Sloan would be at her for making so much noise.

"Sloan!" Yume called as she rushed into the living room. "Sloan! Are you—?"

She skidded to a stop, collapsing, her legs going weak when she saw the body. Bloody strips of skin and mangled meat where Sloan's hands used to be. Large splashes of red between her and the sink, the garbage disposal whirring.

Yume screamed.

CHAPTER 36

The temperature slowly dropped in the small room. The evening air pushing away the stuffiness from the unseasonably warm day, the window the only form of climate control. Maya slept beside Shinko on her back with her arms crossed over her chest.

Shinko thought about shutting the window but cutting off the ambient city noises so abruptly would be jarring. And she liked the sounds, thought of them as white noise, like a fan. She was content to lay in the shoddy bed with the threadbare mattress and stroke Maya's hair.

Right after their flight landed in Jakarta, Shinko ordered Aika back to Japan to report to Shinigami's Helper. She also ordered Aika to tell Fumiko everything, including Shinko's personal mission to return Maya to her people.

Once they left the Soekarno-Hatta International Airport, Maya instructed Shinko where to go – a no name motel in a less than savory part of Jakarta. Shinko offered to take Maya to a nicer hotel, extoling the virtues of luxury after everything the little girl had to endure. She refused, saying that her people would feel more comfortable retrieving her here. Shinko acquiesced, and Maya crawled into the feeble bed and fell asleep as soon as her head hit the pillow.

Shinko felt obligated to guard Maya but had little to guard in the cramped motel room. Bare of everything except the necessities: a bed, a window, one ceiling light bulb, a working sink, and a toilet. The building was quiet, and they were four stories above the bustling streets. So, Shinko lay next to the girl and watched her sleep.

A gust of cool wind brought in a chill and Shinko no longer thought it wise to keep the window open. Without so much as a creak, she got up from the bed and shut the window. However, when she turned around, Maya was awake and sitting up, her dark eyes fixed on Shinko. She looked noticeably healthier. "Thank you for rescuing me."

Shinko smiled and bowed. "You're very welcome."

"My people will be coming for me soon. You should get some rest."

"I'm not tired." Shinko paused and looked around the room. Smiling, she said, "I'm already asleep and this is a dream."

"Why do you think that?"

"Nothing specific. A feeling. A sense. If you have a deep affinity for a painting and someone hands you a forgery, you can tell the difference, even if you don't know why."

Maya hopped out of bed and approached Shinko. She held out her hand, ready to sweep it through the air. Before she did, she smiled softly. "Very perceptive and impressive. No surprise. In your chosen career, you need to be both. If you were deficient in either, I don't believe I'd be here. Since you rescued me, I wanted to thank you properly before I left. Now, I'll leave you and when you awake, you'll feel refreshed."

"Wait! Before you do, could you answer a few questions?"

Maya's face wrinkled in contemplation. The city noises were muffled behind the shut window. She waved her hand at the window, reducing the noises to nothingness, and folded her hands together behind her back. "Yes. I shall answer anything you ask."

Shinko bowed. "Thank you. You are a very powerful individual, so I was wondering how Harold Varvaro came to be your captor?"

"Like you, he rescued me from my prior captor. And like Harold Varvaro, Mr. Chen was involved in organized crime. Both men had bosses they wished to escape from, though Harold Varvaro respected his. It could not be said that Mr. Chen felt the same way about his boss. Like all men, he wanted power."

Shinko shrugged. "Women want power, too."

"Women want power over themselves. Men want power over others and they achieve it by conquering. What is the saying? When the only tool you have is a hammer, you see everything in the world as a nail. Men are *born* with a spear."

"When the first tool you have is a weapon, you see the world as a battlefield."

"Yes," Maya said. "Mr. Chen heard stories about my people and then spent great expense, time, and energy researching our island. He came offering gold and gems, enough to entice my reclusive people from their hiding places, and told a tale of woe, of his ruined life. My people summoned me into this frail vessel."

"Summon you? You're not human?"

"I am not."

"What are you?"

"A being. There are beings that live in water. Beings that spend more time in the air than anywhere else. Beings under the ground and on the ground. In the coldest parts of the planet's poles and in the hottest deserts. Beings of different sizes, shapes, and powers live in different realms. I come from one of the many realms you are unfamiliar with.

"Even though I had been kind and subservient, my people hindered me in the waking world, so I wouldn't have the strength to move freely."

Shinko was torn by that statement – indignant over Maya being restrained, yet she understood their need to hamper unlimited power.

"Would you do me the honor of showing your true form?"

Maya smiled as her eyes sparkled. Shinko wondered if anyone had ever made that request of her.

"I cannot show you what your mind cannot comprehend." Taking a step back, Maya glanced around the room. The ceiling and walls disappeared in a blink. The floor started to rise, floating free from the building, and ascended into the sky. Once they hovered above the tallest buildings of the city, Maya morphed into an adult – taller, a mature face befitting her new stature. But she kept growing beyond the confines of an adult woman. Her long hair fanned out and flowed along a breeze, growing to an impossible length, a thick net capable of ensnaring the entire city. Her golden skin glowed and entire galaxies floated within her eyes. The rags she wore as clothing turned into a gauze kaleidoscope. Twice as tall as Shinko, she said, "This likeness is for you."

Shinko gasped. Even if this was a fragmented version of her true self, Maya was awe-inspiring. She was more than just another being. Shinko now understood humankind's desire to worship.

"Maya, I had a dream I was hunting Harold Varvaro, but you attacked me. At least, it was someone who looked exactly like you, but afterward, I didn't believe that it was you. Are there others who have your power?"

Maya gave the look of a proud teacher. "Impressive – you deduced it wasn't me. The entity you engaged was human. He was imbued with a being like myself, but one not from my realm."

"Another realm I'm unfamiliar with?"

An earnest expression swept across Maya's face. The sky went cold black, filled with fire, flames dancing aggressively. Shinko caught a strong repulsive whiff of sulfur.

"This is the realm humans are more familiar with."

"Hell? The being is from Hell?"

The sky of fire disappeared, replaced by a field of eternal purple filled with chromatic nebulas and individual stars of brilliant colors. "Your term for the realm is not inaccurate. The individual who posed as me is human, at least one of him is. But I do not know how he obtained the ability to eat dreams the way he does."

"Who is he?"

Awash with sadness, Maya turned her face away from Shinko. "You will find this information upsetting."

Surprised by Maya's statement, Shinko asked, "Why?"

"Because you know him."

"Then that's all the more reason to tell me."

Maya arced her arm, and her flowing sleeves revealed a figure as if he had been hiding behind a curtain. A young man. Billy.

Shinko gasped, incredulous that the nice young man dating her daughter was capable of – How did Maya put it? – eating dreams. Did Yume know? No matter. Yume was in danger and Shinko had to save her.

"Billy?" Shinko felt daft for asking, but she was too shocked to stop herself. "Billy is a dream eater?"

"Yes. He enters and manipulates the dreamscape of others to kill them."

Shinko knew she was in a dream, but it felt real in every way, including how her heart beat hard against her ribs. "He killed people while they sleep, using their own dreams as a weapon. That means a prevailing theory is true – if I die in my dreamscape, then I die in the waking world."

"If you die in any dreamscape, you die in the waking world. Unless your body dies while you're in someone else's dreamscape. Then your consciousness will be trapped in their dreamscape until their body dies. Unless you move into a different dreamscape."

The monster had her daughter. It wasn't often Shinko felt true anger, but Billy had been inside *her* dreams, *her*… dreamscape. She needed to return to America and hunt him down. "All I need to do is kill Billy."

"That is not so simple. The dream eater has another personality within him. If you kill the physical body, you only kill one personality. The surviving personality can simply move from dreamscape to dreamscape. Unless, of course, you kill the person whose dreamscape he inhabits."

"Then I must kill Billy *and* his other personality. Teach me."

Maya chuckled. "No need to teach you what you already know how to do. You know how to kill."

"Teach me how to do what you do, how to do what he does. I need to kill them both in the dreamscape, so teach me how to be a dream eater. Teach me the science behind the magic."

Maya seemed distressed, an unusual look for a being with such power. "It would take time."

"I'm willing to make any sacrifice to save my daughter. Please. I beg you."

Shinko never imagined seeing a goddess woeful, yet the look upon Maya's face was one of sorrow. "Very well. As with any new endeavor, we must begin small."

A shimmering ball appeared before Shinko, no larger than a plum. It pulsed and crackled with electricity. "What is this?"

Maya offered a knowing smile and moved her hand over top of it. As she did, the pulsing slowed, then the shell of the object started to fade, until Shinko realized that it was no shell at all. A tiny pellet had been moving around a sphere at a high speed, giving the appearance of a spherical shell. An atom. Maya moved her hand the opposite direction and the hydrogen atom returned to its natural state. "Practice moving it without touching it."

Shinko stared at the atom, and mentally demanded that it move. It did not. Frowning, she envisioned moving the floating ball to the right. It remained unchanged, hovering in front of her.

"Come now," Maya said, a whimsy in her voice. "Don't tell me you've forgotten how to focus."

Focus. Her training began with focus. Closing her eyes – a silly act to do while asleep – she focused her breathing, her mind. She brought her palms together and touched her forehead. Sliding her fingertips down her face, she opened her eyes and spread her hands over her chin. Right hand in front of her chest, she looked to her left and extended her left arm in that direction. Inhaling as if she used her whole body to draw in air, she slowly looked to the right and brought her left hand to her chest while extending her right. On the exhale, she blew away all thought, relying on feeling and instinct. She continued looking left and then right, slowly breathing and becoming one with her environment. The hydrogen atom followed her lead, floating in the direction she was looking. Soon, she directed its movements, the sphere dancing through the space around her as she changed her motions, gaining more and more control over it.

"You're correct, there is a science behind this," Maya said with affirmation in her tone. "Everything in the universe is made of atoms, including us. Including our thoughts, memories, feelings, and dreams. Atoms move around in our brains. Everything we see, say, touch, think, do – nothing more than one set of atoms controlling another set of atoms."

A wistful hand gesture from Maya and two more spheres appeared; one identical to the hydrogen atom, the other significantly larger. Shinko continued to move her body, her arms flowing like water, guiding the three atoms around each other. Water. The larger of the three atoms was oxygen. Moving her hands, she guided the atoms together to form a water molecule.

"Are you beginning to understand?" Maya asked.

"I believe I am," Shinko replied.

"Let's find out." Maya glided through the air, her arms moving as if they were paintbrushes and the universe was her canvass. More spheres appeared in her wake. Shinko continued to focus, but expanded her mind, reaching for the new atoms, combing two hydrogens to each oxygen. But the molecules started to shrink in size. No matter, Shinko realized. They're still water molecules no matter their size, and she treated them as such.

A sweep of her arm, a twist of her hand and the water molecules pooled together at a central point. More atoms appeared; more molecules formed. Shinko made a drop of water.

Continuing the cycle of atoms to molecules to the droplet, she made it bigger.

Something was a bit different, though. Maya simply floated in front of her, hands behind her back, wearing a prideful smile.

Maya was no longer making the atoms; Shinko was.

Gaining confidence, experience, Shinko skipped creating atoms and created water molecules from nothingness. The pool of water was spherical, now the size of a basketball. And she made it grow, no longer needing to create molecules. "I'm doing it. I'm doing it!"

"Yes, Shinko Dangan, you are," Maya said. "And this is only the beginning."

*

Volcanoes erupted, spewing lava with such force the liquid rock cooled as it left the atmosphere. Shinko waved her hands and created hundreds more. Elevated pits of bubbling fire sprouted all over the planet's surface within seconds. From where she stood, it was like a full moon spewing flame. It took but a mere gesture to pull the planet closer, doubling, tripling in size as it floated toward her through the cosmos.

Satisfied with everything she saw, she moved her fingers as if unscrewing a lightbulb and the planet rotated accordingly. The planet surface was jagged with hues of red, orange, and black. Nothing but broken mountains and discontent volcanoes. *Perfect*, she thought. *Ex-*

actly how I intended. A flick of her wrist sent it farther away from her, into the depths of space.

"It seems that you are ready." Standing behind Shinko, Maya had an encouraging lilt to her voice.

Wriggling her fingers, Shinko kept the planet spinning. She then reached out with her other hand to regain control of three other planets she had recently crafted: one of water and storms, one a blissful green filled with flora, and one a dull silver from endless landscapes of iron. She slapped her hands together and all four planets collided with each other, the colors spiraling before reforming and splitting into two shapes: a phoenix and a dragon. The two creatures chased each other through the night sky. "I believe I am."

"Then this is where we must part," Maya said.

Shinko turned to her sensei and bowed deeply. "I am forever indebted to you and will always be in your service."

Maya waved her hand, the human reaction to dismissing Shinko's words. "Nonsense. You rescued me. It was the least I could do."

"Then I promise that I will get you back to your people when we awaken."

Maya giggled, almost a titter. "No need. My people have come and taken me home."

"Taken you home?"

"They have completed the ritual to release me from the child-vessel they had put me in. Once we say our farewells, I will return to my realm."

A chill skittered down Shinko's spine. She assumed that time worked differently in the dreamscape than in the waking world and didn't know if she had been there for an hour or a decade. "How much time has passed in the waking world?"

"Three months."

"Three? How have I been able to stay alive in the waking world?"

With a wistful smile, Maya touched the center of Shinko's forehead. "The human brain is capable of so much more than it is used for. While we trained, your physical body adjusted to meet the needs of your mind and spirit. For simplicity's sake, I'll call it a form of hibernation. When you wake, you'll be a little stiff, but no worse for wear. Plus, you had a caregiver."

"But—"

As Maya faded away into a radiant halo of stars, she bowed and said, "Farewell, Shinko Dangan."

Awake. Shinko blinked to adjust her eyes to the surrounding gloom and moaned.

"Senpai?" came from the corner of the room. Neck muscles tight, Shinko turned to Aika. The younger woman was dragging a man by his ankles. Another body lay on the floor. Bloody streaks around the bodies, visible even from the outside's weak lights, told Shinko that they were dead.

"Aika?" Voice as dry as sandpaper scraping brick, Shinko swallowed and tried again. "What... happened...?"

Aika dropped the man's feet and hurried over to Shinko. She picked up a glass of water from the floor and lifted it to her. As she gulped it down, Aika explained, "I went to Fumiko and told her everything. Giving us the full support of Shinigami's Helper, she ordered me to find you and assist in your goodwill mission. I found you like this. Fumiko assumed you were on a journey and instructed me to protect you."

"The dead men?" Shinko croaked, throat still raw and dry.

Aika shrugged. "Every once in a while, a man or two notices a room rented by two women. You know how men can be."

"Men are born with a spear. When the first tool you have is a weapon, you see the world as a battleground," Shinko whispered as she sat up with Aika's help.

"Excuse me?" Aika asked.

"Doesn't matter." As she rested to catch her breath, she admired Aika's resourcefulness. Electro-stimulation pads to prevent atrophy. An I.V. A bed pan.

"We need to get to America and kill my daughter's boyfriend."

Unphased, Aika said, "Yes, senpai."

CHAPTER 37

The suburban neighborhood was quiet, a sunny day with not a cloud in the sky. Most of the two-bedroom houses were starter homes or ender homes. Moving here was either the first step after leaving an apartment, or the last step before entering an assisted living facility. The veneer of hope layered onto the dread of inevitability.

Yume walked along the sidewalk toward the only house displaying activity. The one with the nagging wife henpecking a husband sitting in a chair on the porch. Her name was Marianne. His was Leonard, but thanks to his antiquated view of masculinity, he went by Butch.

Yume walked across the lawn and stood before their porch, an audience of one watching a sad drama play out upon a white banister stage. Another Marianne stepped out from the house to join in the domestic heckling. Then a third. And a fourth. They all said the same thing, berating Butch for being a failure, lazy, weak. Yume had seen enough.

"So, this is how you view your wife, Butch? Has she *ever said* any of these words to you?"

The Mariannes froze, their statue-stiff bodies in mid-scold. Butch rose from his rocking chair and approached the edge of his porch. "What comes out of her mouth is just as bad."

"What comes out of her mouth are words of encouragement that your insecurities twist into nagging impediments. Instead of growing with her, you break her down to your level of... I don't know... Laziness? Ineptitude? Entitled view of a misogynistic lifestyle? All of the above?"

"Who are you? This ain't none of your business. You got no right telling me how I ought to advise my woman on her wifely affairs."

All of the above. Marianne had visited the women's shelter three times. First time she arrived with a bruised right cheek for getting accepted to the community college for night classes – he said it was her way of telling him he was stupid. Second time she visited with a black eye because the fertility clinic told them Butch had a low sperm count – he blamed her cooking. Third time she had a fat lip for receiving a promotion from admin assistant to executive admin assistant – her way of reminding him that he was a failure at work.

Yume had asked her why she didn't get a divorce, and Marianne replied, "I took an oath, and an oath comes from the soul. If I break my oath, I'd break my soul."

Posture stiff, lips pursed, Yume regarded Butch. "Do you even hear how fucking stupid you sound? And yet you want to procreate. If you can't stop being a dirtbag who lashes out at his loving wife every time you feel your machismo slighted in the least, how the hell would you imagine yourself a good father?"

Face reddening, Butch screamed, "I'd be a *great* father! I'd teach that boy how to be a man and how not to take shit from no one!"

"That boy?" Yume smirked. "Like there's no possibility you could sire a girl. A daughter. God, that poor girl, if you had one. You'd re-sent her, ignore her, let her fall prey to wicked adults, willfully ignore her cries and pleas as she falls victim to teachers, priests, doctors. And I honestly believe it'd be worse for your son, because you'd project all your failings onto him and use 'love' as a form of currency, ultimately leaving him emotionally broke and in debt."

Butch glowered, chest puffed out, ready to enact his God-given right as a man to defend his castle and his property. Property like his wife. Pointing at Yume, spit flew from his mouth as he screamed, "You listen here—"

Yume held out her "talk to the hand" – palm toward him and fin-gers splayed. "You've spewed enough filth. No more."

Yume curled her fingers into a fist and Butch's head collapsed in on itself like a deflated balloon, slimy glops of blood and red goo squirting from his nostrils and ears and mouth as his skull crumpled like mylar. Marianne didn't believe in divorce, refused to break her oath. No one at the women's shelter could get her to reprioritize her ideals, to understand that she was in danger. In the morning, she'd wake up to a dead husband, a "victim" of an aneurism.

Yume stared at the bloody mess of Butch's pulped head and thanked God that Marianne wouldn't wake up to that. Crushed skulls and exploding brains in the dreamworld translated into non-gory aneurisms and strokes in the waking world. Whenever Billy or Will ripped out a heart or caved in someone's chest, the autopsy revealed a heart attack. They had the power to manipulate a person's body in the waking world, but it took a great deal of effort, so they did it sparingly, like with Gus. Though, Billy admitted to getting a little carried away.

"Nicely done," Billy said from behind Yume, clapping as he approached. Billy had taken control of Butch's dreamscape so they didn't have to hurry.

Yume smiled and curtsied. "Why, thank you, thank you."

This had been the fourth cleansing this month. She and Billy had removed seven monsters since moving into Billy's boyhood home in California two months ago, though Yume had handled the last four by herself. Billy or Will joined her, observing from the shadows should anything untoward happen. Even though the guys could exist in the dreamscape simultaneously, they opted to limit their time together, in case Maya returned.

Yume still had limited ability to alter someone else's dreamscape. She could move items around and make herself float – weak forms of telekinesis. And, of course, crushing people's heads with a mere thought as if squeezing overripened fruit proved effective and efficient, but if she couldn't use her mind to fling sharp objects hard enough to pierce skin and bone, then she'd continue to feel defenseless.

Looking back to Billy, Yume said, "I feel more in control, but it's taking so long to master anything else. I want to take the next step."

"The next step isn't laid out in a set of instructions. By moving slowly, you're perfecting each step."

Yume knew Billy was right, but she was growing impatient.

Billy created a doorway back to the Valhalla Room. Yume stepped through and made a beeline to the wall that displayed all sorts of medieval weaponry. Determined to figure out how to use the weapons, she singled out one that looked like a spear with an axe-head at the end. "What's this one called again?"

"Umm...? A halberd. Dare I ask why...?"

With no idea how to properly wield it, its weight significant in her biceps and shoulders, she gripped the middle with her right hand, her left clutching the pole's backend. Guiding it with her right hand, her left hand as support, she slowly waved it like a flag to understand how to maneuver it.

Concentrate. Focus.

Instead of flinging the object, she focused on the object while ignoring its weight. "Maybe I'm trying too hard to do what you do. Like you said, these steps aren't laid out. I think if I start small – not like the *small objects* I've been moving with my mind – but use my mind to *aid* the movement of other objects, like this!"

Focusing her energy, Yume swung the halberd downward at a high-backed chair – a blocky chunk of dark wood with a swirling pattern in the grain – one of thirty around the massive table. The clang of the metal blade hitting the stone floor followed the crack of wood splitting.

"Wow! Nice hit," Billy said.

Smiling, she took a step back to admire her work. "You can fix that, right?"

Billy waved his hand and the chair returned to its original state. "Successful experiment. Hey, it just dawned on me how much you look like your mother."

Confused, Yume turned to Billy and said, "That's an odd thing to say."

"I meant that you looked very poised and determined."

"Did you bring her up because you want me to reach out to her again? I get that you care about my relationship with her, but I haven't heard from her in three months. After she texted me that she landed in Japan, I got crickets, even after I left voicemails about Shanna. I don't know what the hell her problem is, but I'm not going to keep blowing up her phone if she doesn't want to talk to me. And she's making it clear that she doesn't want to." Yume punctuated her statement by driving the axe blade of the halberd through the chair again, the two halves clattering across the floor.

Another wave of his hand and Billy fixed the chair again. "Maybe if she knew that you dropped out of school and moved across the country to California—"

The chair flew apart from Yume's next swing, this time the pieces toppling neighboring chairs. Yume turned to Billy with a snort. "You and Will and I almost died in some kind of astral netherverse and then my sister and my roommate did die, murdered by either a strange dream child or by some other undiscovered dream monster who may or may not be currently hunting us. I need some fucking time off from school, okay?"

"I didn't mean… Actually, you're right. I care about your relationship with your mother, but it wasn't right of me to push. Take as much time as you need."

"Damn right I'm right," Yume said, liking the growl in her voice.

She stared at the wall of weapons and spied a gleaming ninjato. She extended her hand, reaching for it with her mind, imagining it weighing no more than a sheet of paper caught in the wind blowing in her direction. It rattled and then drifted away from the wall, languidly making its way to her hand. As soon as she gripped the hilt, she drove it through the back of the closest chair.

I'm liking this. I'm liking this a lot!

CHAPTER 38

When Shinko had finished her training with Maya and exited her dreamscape, even before she sated her intense hunger, she picked up her cellphone to call Yume.

Yume had filled Shinko's voicemail with messages, erratic at best, each one playing a different emotion. Concern. Fear. Panic. One message was pure sadness, Yume sobbing a story about Shanna dying. Frustration. Anger. Then two months of nothingness.

She called Yume's cell. A recording said that the number was no longer in service. Why would Yume have gotten rid of her cell phone? Shinko tried Yume's apartment landline but received a similar recording.

Shinko contacted the administration office of the university, and they informed her that Yume had withdrawn from school. No official explanation had been given by Yume, but the individual Shinko talked to said something about her roommate's death. At first, Shinko thought the admissions employee was confused about Shanna, but when she asked more questions, she learned that Sloan had also died.

Yume probably stayed just long enough to cooperate with the police investigation. After what Shinko had learned from Maya these past three months, she had suspicions as to what really happened to Sloan. And Shanna.

Now, Shinko stood in the administration office of the college, holding a box of her daughter's belongings. She wore black slacks and a white blouse and held her small clutch under her arm. She looked like a businesswoman on the go, yet genial; a woman accepting of information, not idle chit-chat. The college had cleaned out Yume's apartment. Shinko's first thought had been to examine the room herself, but the administrator mentioned they had used a crime scene cleaning service. "The room has been swept bare and repainted," the woman said when handing the box to Shinko. She was affable enough and tried to modulate her words upon Shinko's non-verbal cues. Without much else to go on, the woman continued. "I'm sorry you have to go through this. Even though she withdrew from this university, we would have happily mailed her things to her if she had left a forwarding address."

"Thank you," Shinko replied.

The woman folded her hands together, her thumbs fidgeting. "When you… uhhh… When you see Yume, please extend the school's condolences. She was a wonderful student and even a better person. Losing three people close to her… Everyone here understands why she'd want to leave."

Three? "You're referring to Shanna, Sloan, and…?"

So desperate to connect, to unburden her own feelings, the woman blurted, "Millie. Shanna's mother, Millie."

That explained why there was no answer when Shinko had tried to call. "Oh, that's dreadful. What happened to Millie?"

"No one has told us much of anything. Privacy, HIPPA. Anyway, her husband and then her daughter. Neighbors found Millie on the couch with a suicide note and empty pill bottles. As a mother and wife myself, I… Well, you know."

"I do." Realizing she'd garner no more useful information from this woman, Shinko turned to leave, offering a polite smile, nodding at the box in her hands. "Thank you again."

Once she got into the car, Shinko rummaged through the box on her lap. Aika watched in silence from the driver seat. Toiletries and school supplies. An empty CD case. One sock. A broken computer mouse. Drawing her breath and releasing a heavy sigh, she crumbled a stupid brochure, but noticed the address. Thinking it might have been someplace her daughter recently visited, she smoothed out the paper, and stared at it. A name at the bottom. Proprietor: Harold Varvaro. "We're going to the 8th Street Art Gallery."

Aika started the car and they drove away.

*

249

The gallery was in an unassuming building across the street from a pay parking lot, the art inside garish. Some pieces had potential, but few appealed to Shinko's sensibilities. If a piece of art had to be explained, then she had no interest in it. The meaning behind anything hanging on the walls didn't matter to Shinko, as she approached the front counter and asked to speak with Harold Varvaro. The young man's face turned a shade of white. This was the second time within an hour that she pulled forth a similar look from the person she talked to. "Unfortunately, Mr. Varvaro is no longer with us."

In this instance, since she had been in the room with him when he had died, she expected that answer. "Was he the owner of this gallery?"

"He wasn't. May I ask what this is regarding?"

She showed him the brochure. "I missed the showing, but a friend told me about a piece I might be interested in acquiring, if it's still available." A necessary lie.

The man's face lit up as he picked up the phone receiver. "Oh, okay. You're in luck. The gentleman who owns the gallery is actually in today. Let me see if he'd be willing to meet with you."

After a brief conversation in hushed tones, the young man hung up the phone and gestured toward the back of the gallery. "Mr. Templeton is through the door at the end of the hall, in his office."

Shinko didn't know what to expect, but she didn't expect a tall, fit man in his late twenties wearing a three-piece gray suit while sitting behind a modest desk in a small, wood paneled office. And she absolutely never expected his first words to her would be, "About time you showed up."

So taken aback, she uttered, "Excuse me?"

Out of formality, he stood and pulled out the chair in front of the desk. "Please have a seat, Shinko Dangan."

Instinctually, she reached into her clutch and placed her fingers on a small throwing knife. "Who are you and how do you know my name?"

He pointed to the seat before he returned to his. "Please. You have no need for whatever weapon you're reaching for. My name is Maxwell Templeton. I know who you are because my late father used to work with your brother."

Before joining Shinigami's Helper, her brother, Kamu, had spent time with a band of mercenaries. Their last mission together went poorly, resulting in the loss of two of his friends. The remaining mercenaries disbanded, and her brother returned home. As a suggestion from Shinko, he joined Shinigami's Helper and flourished. Every July fifteenth, on the anniversary of the failed mission, he flew to America and met with the surviving members of the defunct mercenary band. Six years ago was his last visit – he disappeared.

Shinko sat on the edge of the chair, her hand in her purse. "Your father?"

"Roger Templeton. I don't know how close you were with your brother, but if he ever shared stories with you from his time as a mercenary, he would have known my father as Hawke."

Shinko nodded. She knew the name. "Hawke was one of the two who died during their last mission together."

Maxwell looked away and chuckled, the sad sound of remembering a joke told in poor taste. "Yes and no. He was left for dead by his team. Instead of seeking revenge, though, he decided to change his identity and use his resources to build wealth and power."

"I'm assuming you now possess his wealth and power?"

Maxwell flashed the devil's smile. "I do."

"That doesn't explain why it seemed like you were expecting me."

Rolling his chair closer, he leaned his elbows on his desk. Time for the business Shinko hadn't been prepared for. "Your daughter has disappeared and you're trying to find her. I have an idea of where she is."

Shinko's grip tightened on her knife as she withdrew it, tip gleaming under the office lights.

Maxwell held up a hand, a silent request for her to let him finish before she jammed her weapon into his eye. "Before you kill me, you need to know I had nothing to do with her disappearance. She left willingly with her boyfriend, William Devereaux. Do you know who he is?"

"I do. Do you?"

Even though he looked a couple decades younger, she sensed his experience; his eyes saw things just as terrible and fantastical as hers.

"Oh, I do," he said. "This world is riddled with unexplainable phenomena and abilities that shouldn't be wielded by human beings. I make a point to learn about these phenomena. William is one such individual."

Shinko weighed her response carefully. Normally, she didn't like to share knowledge, but Maxwell admitted he knew what William could do. It would do Shinko no good to be coy or cagey, so she asked, "Did you know about the split personality, too?"

Maxwell smiled again.

It caused a dreadful stir within her belly. It wasn't often that she found herself lacking in information, but the chasm of knowledge between them was so great that closing the gap seemed insurmountable. "Good. That saves us both from explaining the impossible."

"That it does. However, I have something you might be interested in. His address. His childhood home address in California. Once I realized that William was… special… I started to dig. Needless to say, a man of my wealth can afford fancy enough shovels to dig deep into William's past. When he was a teenager, he killed his parents, his priest, and his therapist. His lawyer presented an overabundance of evidence proving self-defense. His parents had done well for themselves, and he inherited everything. He never sold the house, so I have a feeling he retreated there and took your daughter with him."

As Maxwell wrote the address on a sheet of paper, Shinko asked, "You are a man of means and willing to use your resources to get what you want. So, why have you not acted on this before now?"

"This is exactly how you and I operate, isn't it? I get others to kill for me, and you kill for others. Plus, I wanted to meet the woman who sliced and diced almost a dozen of my men and put Harold Varvaro in the hospital."

Shinko took the paper with William's address. She stuffed it in her purse along with her knife. "Are you saying Harold Varvaro isn't dead?"

"Apparently not. We thought he had a stroke, and we took him to a hospital. However, after he stabilized, he disappeared. At first, I thought you came back to finish the job, but your reaction says otherwise. He was one of my best employees, but he withheld quite a bit from me and went rogue. Whenever you finish killing William, give me a call. I might be interested in having you find Mr. Varvaro."

Shinko stood and glared at Maxwell. He had given her considerable information that she needed to assimilate. At the very least, she'd contact Fumiko and make her aware of Templeton and his proclivities toward the supernatural. "If you knew about William why only keep tabs on him?"

"Look at what happened to Varvaro. I can only surmise as to what he had gotten into, but it garnered your attention. William is a weapon; one I can't use. If there's a weapon I can't use, then I prefer no one can. I'm more than happy to help you get rid of that weapon."

With a nod, Shinko left the office.

CHAPTER 39

Billy swept his hand through the air and crystal trees sprouted from the iron ground. His superfluous gestures helped him focus. Will also made similar gestures, with more flourish, as if his fingers dug into the land itself. The metallic ground split and separated as Will spread his hands and fingers like he was pulling taffy, creating a sluice for a flow of bubbling lava. "There we go. Now the river from Mt. St. Motherfucker has someplace to go."

Billy chuckled. He would not have chosen such a crude name, but Will insisted on naming the crystal and steel volcano he had created. Like the last dozen planets they created together, this one would remain a marble floating around a distant star the next time they visited the dreamscape. After all, this was just exercise.

While wiggling his fingers Billy called forth fruit from the trees in the form of hearts. Human in nature and dangling from the glass-like branches by blue and red vessels, they beat asynchronously.

"Whoa," Will said from behind him. "Grim. Very creepy. A lot of awesome, though."

"We can create living creatures, but I wanted to see if we could blend fauna with flora. I don't know if it will come in handy if we face Maya again, but any new skill is a useful skill, right?"

"Agreed." Will extended his arms and moved his hands about like a conductor of a macabre orchestra. The ground rumbled, and a point of land elevated. The crystal trees changed, curling around the hearts to form a protective shell. As the peak of steel continued to rise, the trees merged together. Metal shifted around the crystal and formed a humanoid shape. With one foot in the newly created river, the lava flowed up the leg and into the hundred-foot-tall beast. Within the crystal chest, the lava ran like blood among the hundreds of pulsing hearts. "When that bitch comes back, we'll be ready."

Billy still wasn't sure about Maya's motivations. At first, he believed she had invaded their dreamscape because they were trying to kill Harold Varvaro. He had no idea what kind of power Varvaro held over her, but once Yume's mother killed the crime lord, why would Maya continue their feud? Why kill Shanna and Sloan? Revenge didn't seem like motivation for the stone-faced child. Billy shivered at the thought of in not being Maya, that a different entity infiltrated the dreamscape. In any case, it was good to train.

"Go ahead," Will said. "I'm ready."

Genuinely confused, Billy asked, "Ready for what?"

"Whatever it is you want to talk about. You're making the, 'I need to talk to Will about something' face."

Billy sighed. "It's Yume."

Moving his arms up and down like a puppet-master, Will's metal and crystal monster with lava veins stomped around the gray landscape. "She's been great lately! Don't you think?"

"She's slowly learning how to control other people's dreamscapes, but..."

"Billy, come on. This is the first time we have a girlfriend who is one hundred percent behind what we're doing to the point of doing it herself."

"But she killed a dozen men in ten nights, making a grand total of sixteen in a little over two months. The authorities must have noticed an outbreak of aneurisms and heart attacks among assholes. No doubt they're investigating chemical culprits, maybe even exploring the ideas of contagion, but how long until they start to think outside the box?"

"By that time, she'll have developed other techniques. She's getting close, I can feel it."

"I can, too. She's moved beyond popping heads and has started to use our weapons during the last few nights, but she's been more than a little bloodthirsty, don't you think? Like she's becoming addicted to the killing."

"Look, she lost someone very close to her and walked in on her roommate's murder scene. That's a lot to process, and three months isn't enough time to make a person good to go. She's working through the trauma as best she can, and she talks to us about it. So what if she's taking her frustrations out on dirtbags?"

"I don't know, Will. It feels like it's more than that. It's been ten nights *in a row*. Have you tried to talk to her about her mother recently?"

Eyes wide, Will shook his head. "Oh, hell no. She's sooooo pissed at her mom."

"I know, but… She doesn't know her mother the way we do."

"Is that a bad thing that she doesn't know her mom is a paid ninja assassin?"

"Maybe? She's mad at her mother for abandoning her when she might be in trouble, or worse."

"If we told her, then she might want to go to Japan to find her."

"What's wrong with going to Japan? If her mom is okay, then they can work on their relationship. If something happened to her mom, then we help her. It might help her find closure for at least one part of her life, which might help her move past Shanna and Sloan."

"I don't know, dude. There's a lot to—"

"Knock, knock!" came a voice from above.

Billy and Will looked up to see Yume poking her head through a hole in the sky. "May I join you?"

"Always," Billy and Will said in unison.

The hole in the sky closed behind Yume as she floated to the ground, landing between the guys. She did a full three-sixty to take in the view of the planet they had created. "Metal ground, lava rivers, and crystal trees. Big, giant-ass colossus made from the environment. Very cool! But… Are those beating human hearts hanging from the trees?"

"They are," Billy answered.

Yume crinkled her nose. "Eww! That's kind of gross. What is wrong with you two?"

Neither cracked a smile. Yume frowned and crossed her arms. "Okay, out with it," she said. "You both have that, 'I need to talk to Yume about something' face."

Billy and Will regarded each other. Billy assumed his face looked as nervous and guilty as Will's. Knowing that Will didn't one hundred percent agree with him, Billy shouldered the responsibility and said, "It's... It's about your mother."

Will cringed as Yume's frown deepened. "What about her?"

"There's something you don't know about her."

She squinted, and Billy's spine turned to cold jelly. "How could you know something about her that I don't?"

"Ummm... Will and I have been to her dreamscape."

Hands on her hips, Yume took a step forward. "That's fucking creepy! And a *huge* breach of trust!"

"We had to," Will said, stepping forward to shield Billy from Yume's wrath. "There's... more to the Varvaro/Maya story."

Nostrils flaring, Yume crossed her arms again over her chest. "More?"

"Yes. When we fought Maya in Varvaro's dreamscape, he disappeared. That's because he died in the waking world, killed by your mother."

Eyes blinking rapidly, Yume shook her head. "What in God's name are you talking about?"

Billy waved his hand and the world around them changed. They went from alien landscape to inside a Chinese restaurant, The Dragon's Blessing. The trio stood in the center while six individuals in traditional ninja garb fought amongst themselves. "This is what happened at The Dragon's Blessing."

Billy watched Yume digest the action around them. Two ninjas versus four. The fewer outmatched the greater. And one was Yume's mother.

Shinko and a girl who looked to be about Yume's age killed the last enemy after interrogating him. Then the images stopped, like a paused movie. Yume's expression changed from a red grimace to a pinched frustration. "I don't understand what you two are doing, but I *really* don't appreciate it."

"We're trying to tell you the truth," Will said. "We don't know why she hasn't contacted you for a while, but... Maybe she's in trouble? We know she was looking for Harold Varvaro. We don't know if he was an assignment or if Maya had something to do with him. If it's the latter..."

Will let his words trail away, leaving an obvious implication. Yume huffed and shook her head. "Stop. Stop, stop, stop. What you're saying makes zero sense. You're not only telling me *my mother* is a murderer, but she does this as a fucking ninja?"

"I know it's hard to believe," Billy said. He stepped closer to her and waited for her to look into his eyes before he continued. "Have either of us ever lied to you?"

Yume huffed again and looked away.

Billy continued. "Yes, we've withheld the truth, but only to make sure you were receptive. If we told you every truth immediately, you would have never believed us."

Yume turned back with the look of a bull ready to charge. "There's a difference between saying, 'Hey, I can go into people's dreams' and 'Oh yeah, your mom's a ninja assassin.' One is far more outlandish than the other."

"I understand, but is it really?"

The personification of anger, arms crossed over her chest, hip cocked, Yume's glare had the incendiary potential to turn the whole planet to ash. Billy felt bad for being thankful that her dreamscape power was limited, then struggled to fight through the buzz of guilt to create a coherent roadmap to guide her to acceptance. Wait... The buzz wasn't guilt.

Billy turned to Will, his face mimicking the skin-tingling concern he felt. A wave of his hand, and the restaurant turned to dust. As it fell away, they stood back on the metal and crystal landscape they had created earlier. They both looked to the sky as if God had said something.

Will mumbled, "I feel it, too."

Yume followed their gaze. "Feel what?"

"As if someone locked a door," Billy said. "Will...? I can't wake up."

"Neither can I."

"Yume, where are you?"

"I'm lying right next to you in our bed," she answered. The fire behind her eyes flared as she continued, "I'm going to wake up and see what's going on."

"Be careful," Will and Billy said in unison, though she had disappeared before they finished.

Billy and Will remained silent. They could speculate about their situation, but that would do more harm than good at the moment. Instead, they both continued to concentrate, continued to try to wake up.

After a few minutes and with no result, Will exhaled and looked down at his feet. He paced. Billy watched the sky as if it held the answer and he simply had to puzzle it free.

Suddenly a doorway opened between them, and Yume stumbled through. Eyes as wide as a spooked horse, she blurted, "You're right. You're both right. My mother is a ninja assassin. And she's here!"

CHAPTER 40

"I feel exposed," Aika whispered to Shinko. "Are you sure we shouldn't wait until nighttime?"

It wasn't often they went on a mission during the day, let alone in a suburban American middle-class neighborhood in the state of California. Walking side by side down the sidewalk, Shinko glanced at the streetlights, nodding at Aika, encouraging her to be observant. "When those streetlights go on, there will be no place for us to hide. If we tried to sneak around the back of these houses, motion sensors will trigger floodlights. Dogs would bark. Curious eyes never sleep. Right now, we're just regular people taking a stroll."

Across the street a man and a woman approached from the opposite direction, walking their Yorkshire terrier. Both had thick white hair and wore blue pastel collared shirts. Neither of them had any issues gawking at the strangers.

Aika huffed. "Regular people who don't belong here. When the police find William's body tomorrow, that older couple will definitely mention us."

Shinko chuckled. "This is America, Aika. To them, you and I look no different than the other millions of Asian descent women living among them. When the police ask them if they saw anything suspicious, they'll say two Chinese women – or judging by their age they'll say two Orientals – were walking down the sidewalk. You and I are wearing the best disguise: no disguise at all."

"I would hate to live here," Aika mumbled as they continued deeper into the neighborhood.

Shinko agreed, but she also thought of all the glowing commentary from her daughter about her experiences in this country, when she was a college student in Philadelphia. Now she was...? Shinko blinked away a tear – she had no idea what her own daughter was doing in California. She considered herself observant, but if she were, then she would have recognized that Yume was in trouble. She would have known that she was involved with a dream eater. Even though Shinko received three months of intensive training from a goddess-like being, she wondered if her time would have been better spent in the waking world with her daughter.

She raised her chin. No second guessing the past. *I'm now better equipped to help her out of this bad situation.*

William's house was a modest two-story with sky blue siding and white shutters. The only thing setting it apart from the others was the complete lack of landscaping. Just a plain carpet of short grass. No hedges or bushes, no mulch work or decorative stone, no lawn ornaments or fencing. A short driveway led to the garage and a brick path ran to the front door.

Shinko used her automatic lockpick on the front door, and whispered to Aika, "Are you ready?"

Clutching her small purse, Aika unzipped it and reached her hand inside. "Yes."

No wasted movement; once the lock clicked, Shinko opened the door far enough for the two ninjas to slip inside. They closed it without a sound.

Silence and the dryness of dust greeted them. Shinko raised her brow once she heard a ticking clock deeper within. A faint intermittent drip came from the kitchen. The house had no basement, so she and Aika skulked about the first floor with no fear of creaking floorboards. Living room, kitchen, dining room, computer room. No signs of anyone home.

Dust outlines showed that pictures once hung on the walls. If what Shinko had heard about William's parents had been true, no wonder he had taken them down. In fact, Shinko understood his anger. The pain. Killing those in power quelled those emotions, but only for a short time. She had researched the deaths from the past couple of years, the ones that occurred while the victims slept. Most were criminals and their deaths seemed natural; heart-attacks, strokes, and aneurysms. But their family members – siblings, spouses, and children – suffered fates more brutal and more mysterious. Bones broken while asleep. Sleepwalking into deadly situations. Their deaths much like

Gus, Shanna, Sloan. That was the work of a monster and Shinko could not let a monster like that live, especially if he was involved with Yume.

They kept close to the wall as they ascended the stairs, avoiding the center where the creaks and groans dwelled. Once they reached the top, Shinko paused to listen. She heard beathing. Soft, rhythmic. Two people in one of the rooms.

The ninjas followed the shadows from the stairs to the bedroom.

Yume and William were lying in bed next to each other, on their backs and clothed, almost business like. The onset of tears tingled behind Shinko's cheeks. She had failed her daughter and fought the urge to reach down and stroke Yume's cheek or tuck a stray lock of hair behind her ear. *Not yet.*

Hand buried in her purse, Aika moved to William's side of the bed and awaited orders. Shinko nodded and Aika removed a damp cloth, placing it gently over William's nose and mouth. The chloroform should keep him from waking once Shinko entered the dreamscape. First, she had to save her daughter.

Shinko reached down, but as soon as her fingers touched her daughter's cheek, Yume reached up in a flash and grabbed her wrist.

"Mother? What are you doing here." Yume sat up and glared at Aika. "And who's that? What is she...? I smell something sweet – hey, is that a rag soaked in chloroform? What's happening?"

Placing hands on her daughter's cheek, Shinko guided Yume's face toward hers. "Aika and I are here to rescue you."

"Rescue me? That's a strange choice of words. Rescue me like I'm some sort of mission?"

"Yume, William is dangerous and needs to be stopped."

Yume pushed her mother's hands away. "Dangerous? Stopped? Oh my God! Are they right? You... You aren't who you say you are. You've been lying to me!"

"Yume, I'll explain everything after we get you out of here."

"Explain? You know what I'm talking about, don't you? Oh, God. You... You *really* are a ninja? You *really* kill people for money, don't you?"

"It's..." Shinko struggled with what to say. "It's complicated."

"Ninja assassin is a pretty simple concept."

Shinko glared at her daughter. "When I remove someone, it makes the world a better place."

"Yeah? We do the same thing, so this sounds like the pot preaching to the kettle."

The sudden weight of her daughter's words pressed against Shinko's throat. Not only did she know what William was doing, she participated. Blinking away tears before they could form, she continued. "Yume, now is not the time to joke. I am in no position to debate moral ambiguity, but what William has done goes beyond that. He's killed innocent family members of those people. And what about Shanna? Sloan?"

"We didn't do that! That was a bitch named Maya."

"No, Yume, it wasn't. I've been with Maya for the last three months. That's why I couldn't answer your calls. Let's go, now. Let's get out of here."

Shinko reached for her daughter again, but Yume recoiled, a snarling look of shock and disgust on her face. "You're working with Maya?"

"She's not the enemy."

"Yes, she absolutely is! You don't know what she's capable of! You haven't seen what she's done. What she did to Shanna, to Sloan!"

"That wasn't—"

"No! You've been lying to me my whole life! I won't listen to you anymore! You're a *murderer* and you're working with *a monster*. Is that why you and your pretend daughter are here? To murder Billy and Will?"

Shinko couldn't bear to lie to her daughter again. Instead, she grabbed Yume's wrist and pulled her to a stand. "We don't have time for this. We have to—"

"No!" Yume yelled as she yanked free. Tears pooling in her eyes, she glared at her mother as she extended her index finger and middle finger on each hand. Fast as a cobra, her fingers struck pressure points at the back of her own head, just below her skull. Her eyes fluttered closed, and she fell back onto the bed.

"Yume?" Shinko grabbed her daughter's shoulders and shook. "Yume!"

"Should we abort?" Aika asked.

"No." Shinko looked around the room and decided there was no better place to deal with her daughter than in the dream world. She sat on the floor and crossed her legs. After a quick stretch to relax her neck, back, and shoulders, she folded her hands on her lap. "I'll go into the dreamscape and do what I need to do."

Aika dropped to the floor on the other side of the room and assumed the same position as her mentor. "I will join you."

"Nonsense! You have no experience or power in the dreamscape and would be a liability."

"I will be a surprise, and therefore an asset. I have been trained by Shinigami's Helper, just as you. I will not bring disgrace to their name by abandoning you on this assignment."

"Very well, but if I command you to leave the dreamscape, then you leave. Understood?"

"Yes."

As Aika closed her eyes and altered her breathing with long and slow breaths to induce relaxation, Shinko couldn't help but see her daughter in Aika, the young women so close in age and proximity to each other. Disgust and disappointment over her own hypocrisy twisted within her gut to the point of pain. She had trained a woman Yume's age to be the exact thing she didn't want Yume to become.

No. Not now. Save that philosophical debate for later.

Shinko closed her eyes.

CHAPTER 41

Billy didn't know what to do. He had to defend himself and Will. But against his girlfriend's mother? Yume didn't say Shinko was coming to kill him and Will, but she didn't have to. Her twisted face and wringing hands said enough.

"Do you think we could expel her from the dreamscape when she shows up?" Billy asked Will.

"Doubtful."

Billy turned to Yume. "Why can't we wake up?"

"She and another ninja bitch named Aika used chloroform on you," Yume answered.

"Whoa," Will said. "That's fucking intense. Okay. This is Billy's dreamscape. We have home field advantage."

"She spent the last three months training with Maya."

"So," Will said. Fire engulfed his hands as they turned to metal. "I mean, three months is a long time, but we've been doing this for years."

"We need to be ready for anything," Billy said. He desperately wanted Yume to tell Will and him what their objective should be. They stood on a world of iron and lava with flora made from sharp crystal. They had created a one-hundred-foot golem from steel and crystal with liquid fire running through its veins. Billy was prepared to use his environment, but wasn't sure in what capacity – defend or attack, capture or… kill.

A hole formed in the sky and Shinko dressed in black ninja robes shot through like a bullet, aiming for Billy with her ninjato raised over her head.

Billy turned to face her, planning to erect a steel barrier from the ground.

"Move!" a voice called out and an unseen force pushed Billy aside. He hit the ground just as a young woman in black rushed by, her ninjato slashing right where he had stood.

Shinko had been a distraction. This other woman had been the real attack.

The other ninja had to be Aika, and she joined Shinko, but stayed behind her.

Shinko didn't let up her attack. On the ground now, she pulled a shuriken from her pocket and threw it at Billy, but as soon as it left her hand, one turned into a thousand.

Billy swiped his hand upward and a wall formed from the metal ground in front of him, just large enough to hide behind. The machine-gun clangs of the throwing stars hitting the wall and ground beside him sounded like hail against a tin roof.

The wall curled toward him, and he leapt backwards before it crushed him, but as soon as he dodged the wall, a dozen metallic hands sprouted from the ground, grabbing at his ankles. He turned them to powder with a thought, but more hands took their place. *Get off the ground!*

With the slightest bend to his knees, he launched into the sky. He needed a second to get his bearings. To plan an attack. To think!

Only twenty feet in the air, he watched Will launch a plume of fire from his hands at Shinko. She was prepared for the attack – undoubtedly because Will's hands had been on fire this whole time – and extended her left hand. The fire ended before it even got close to her, as if hitting an invisible wall.

"Mother!" Yume yelled. "Mom! Stop this!"

Shinko didn't acknowledge her daughter. Instead, she launched a thousand shuriken at Will. None hit him as they turned to puffs of smoke.

Billy had no eye on the other ninja, Aika. *Where is she?*

"Move!" The mysterious voice again. Something invisible slammed into Billy and pushed him out of the sky, saving his life again.

Aika had been cloaked from his sight, visible only after swinging her sword at the spot where he had hovered. Billy landed on his back, hitting the metal ground with a thud. Aika floated to the ground, her landing butterfly-soft.

He sat up, grateful to be alive, and quickly healed his bruises and sprains, the pain disappearing with a mere thought.

Shinko had her right hand extended toward the other ninja. Obviously she must have developed the skill to make Aika disappear from view.

Billy didn't know where the voice was coming from, or how it knew to save his life, but it wasn't Will, who was too busy deflecting all of Shinko's attacks.

Her attacks were relentless, allowing Will no opportunity to mount any offensive beyond taking to the sky and throwing impotent plumes of fire. She paused a mere breath as she sheathed her sword and clapped. Globs of liquid metal shot up from the ground and formed a sphere hundreds of feet in diameter around Will. And started to shrink.

"No!" Billy shouted as he pressed his palms to the ground. He could no longer wait for direction from Yume; he needed to stop her mother using any means necessary before she hurt Will.

A fissure ripped along the ground next to Shinko. The crack widened with the echoing squeals of twisting metal, followed by a gush of lava. She didn't run or jump or fly away from the wave of lava ready to crash down on her. Displaying Maya-levels of power, Shinko flicked her fingers and the roiling lava turned to red confetti and rose petals. She snapped her fingers and the canyon slammed closed as if it had never existed.

Billy wanted to help free Will from the metal sphere, but the second he took his eyes off Shinko and her partner it'd be all over for him. Neither of them would sneak up behind him again. This was his planet, his dreamscape. He should've been ready for anything, but Shinko was so fast.

She reached behind her back, and then thrust her hands forward. Dozens of chains and braided cables sprung from the ground, each tipped with a pernicious hook.

Yume jumped in front of Billy and yelled, "Stop!"

In a blink, the weapons turned into gray streamers, the thin papers floating to the ground. At first, Billy thought Yume did it, but Shinko snapped, "Yume! If I hadn't stopped my attack, you would be dead!"

"Then stop your attack."

"No. He is a monster and needs to be dealt with."

"He's no monster. I love him. I love him and Will! Let Will go and get out of here. Leave us alone."

The sphere holding Will continued to shrink.

"I can not and will not leave my daughter in the hands of a monster. I will not let him turn *you* into a monster."

Yume started to walk toward her mother, her gestures quick and short, pantomiming her frustrations. "He and I do the same thing you do, so how can you possibly be such a hypocrite?"

"Because this is no life for you! I do things that are distasteful for the betterment of the world, but more importantly, so you don't have to. So you can lead a safe and secure life."

"But it's perfectly okay for you to teach *her* how to be a killer?" Yume yelled as she pointed to the young woman standing behind her mother. "She looks like she's my age. How many people has *she* killed? How is that okay?"

"Because Aika isn't my daughter!"

Billy thought the harsh words would garner a reaction from Aika, but she gave no twitch or frown or look of sadness. Aika watched Shinko with a perfectly emotion-free face.

Shinko's expression softened as she took a step closer to Yume. "He is abusing his power. He doesn't stop with the bad men. He wipes out their families. He's killing innocent people."

A banging noise reverberated from the sphere. Will was hitting the sphere wall, trying to break out.

"Neither Billy nor Will committed those murders," Yume continued, no longer yelling, now pleading. "It was Maya."

"What possible motivation would she have to kill innocent spouses and children of common street thugs?"

"She worked for Harold Varvaro. He's a crime boss, mother. She did terrible things for a terrible person."

"I've spent time with her, and she had little choice to do his bidding, and even then, those she killed were far from innocent."

"She's a monster, mother! You spent time with a monster."

"She's a being who was tricked and trapped. She had been in America for only a month before I rescued her and returned her to her home. The atrocities your boyfriend committed have been going on for almost two years."

The sphere thumped and shook. Will hit it harder and harder.

"Stop using your eyes!" The voice again. Where was it coming from and who did it belong to? It sounded muffled. Was it coming from inside the sphere? Was it inside with Will?

Billy had been watching Shinko and Aika. But the voice told him not to. Twice now Aika had snuck behind him. Even though he was a god in the dreamscape, he wasn't acting like it. The ninjas had used speed to keep him and Will off balance. They also preyed on his weakness, knowing that even though he was a god, he still thought like a human. He still relied on his five senses.

A crack formed in the sphere, and then another. Will's struggles yielded results, but Billy couldn't wait for him.

Stop using your eyes.

Everyone in the dreamscape had form, but a person's form was just a representation of who they were. A representation of their energy. Billy needed to "see" the energy.

A particularly solid hit inside the sphere added more cracks.

Don't think about Will, he's fine. Focus. Focus on everyone's energy. Start with Yume.

Billy concentrated on Yume, watching her argue with her mother, clenching her fists, yelling.

Concentrate. Focus on her. Her energy.

Bright white light glowed within her chest and a shimmering gold halo formed around her body. Yes! Yes, it worked.

A hit from inside the sphere made the ground shake even though the metal globe still hovered above the planet's metallic surface. Cracks spider-webbed along the face of the sphere. Will would make an opening soon enough.

Aika had been invisible twice now, so Billy stared at her and concentrated like he did with Yume. A glow emanated from within her, and light surrounded her. That proved to Billy that she was in front of him, not behind him. Next was Shinko.

One final hit and the sphere exploded into metal chunks. Will was free! But when Billy looked at Will, he saw two sources of energy. One from Will, and one from beside him, an incorporeal glow. There was another being in the dreamscape, the mysterious voice that had been protecting him. From his peripheral vision, he noticed that Shinko's body had no glow to it. The woman that Yume was arguing with was a mirage! That meant...

Billy turned just in time to see Shinko's sword slice cleanly through his neck.

CHAPTER 42

Yume watched her mother decapitate one of the men she loved.

The blood flowing between her ears to the beat of her heart muffled Will's rage-filled screams.

No, that couldn't be her mother. The murderer wore her mother's face but dressed in loose black clothing and wielded a ninja's sword. That woman couldn't have been the same woman who tucked her in after reading a bedtime story. Couldn't have been the same woman who helped her with her schoolwork. Or the same woman who listened to her woes and gave her advice. Who taught her how to dress, bathe, feed herself. Supported her dreams. No, that woman could not be her mother. Her mother wasn't the warmest individual, but she was no killer. That woman murdered without hesitation. That woman already had a daughter named Aika who dressed and acted just like her. That woman took the love of Yume's life.

"He was evil, Yume. He was killing children." Lies from the look-alike mother.

Billy and Will were abused as children. They were created by evil. Yume could never truly understand the horrors those two had witnessed, had been subjected to, but she understood what evil was. And the woman who looked like her mother, who murdered Billy, was the very evil that needed to be eradicated.

Extending her arm, fingers spread wide, Yume knew what she had to do.

Will and Billy had been training her how to manipulate the dreamscape. The one thing she learned how to do with ease – reach out and crush a person's head by closing her hand. Looking at that… monster… who took the form of her mother, that lie created to hinder her thoughts and toy with her emotions, Yume closed her hand.

Time stopped.

Yume couldn't move, her arm out and hand balled into a fist. She couldn't turn, shift, breathe, or scream. All she could do was watch. No, time didn't stop, but slowed to expose what she was trying to do. A vaporous hand extended from her own, wavy like the air above hot asphalt. It slowly glided toward her target, fingers reaching for the woman's head.

She must have seen the same thing Yume saw, because when time returned to normal speed, the woman slashed twice, and the hand turned into harmless mist.

In a blink, the woman was standing in front of Yume. That woman who looked like her mother but couldn't be, grabbed Yume's shoulders. In a voice identical to her mother's she said, "Yume! Yume, wake up and leave this place."

"Senpai!" Aika screamed.

The Mother-Imposter looked to the sky in time to see, and stop, a plume of fire. In theory, she saved Yume, but Yume smiled, confident that Will wouldn't have harmed her.

The woman who looked like her mother disappeared.

Pain twisted Will's screams, turning them to incomprehensible vowels, and he clapped his hands. The colors of the universe inverted. The sky flipped to a milk white, speckled with the bursts of black stars. The blue-gray ground shimmered orange while the molten red rivers of lava now flowed green. Aika and Will appeared as featureless masses of rippling purple.

The woman posing as Yume's mother, no longer invisible, was streaking skyward toward Will. She saw another featureless mass of rippling purple next to Will. What was it? Maya? Some other being? Yume opened her mouth to call out, but Will screamed and clapped again. The colors returned to normal and the Mother-Imposter shot backwards, toward the ground.

A controlled flip and the woman landed on her feet, but immediately punched the ground. Right under Will, a column of steel shot upward. Will spun and extended his arms toward the woman. This was his planet; he regained control of the chunk she had used in her attack and turned it back on her in the form of thousands of spears.

Moving like dancing water, the woman's body flowed, her hands gliding through the air. The spears turned to butterflies. A river of chromatic wings crashed down upon her, but when the butterflies fluttered away, the woman was nowhere to be found.

"No!" Will shouted and clapped his hands again. This time the discoloration happened in a wave, washing over everything and exposing what couldn't be seen by the naked eye. The colors returned to normal after the ripple passed and when the band of negative colors hit the woman, it blasted her from the sky again. Yume saw the other shape next to Will again, but it disappeared when the colors returned to normal.

The Mother-Imposter fell from the sky, but when she slammed into the ground, there were dozens of her. Will roared as he curled his fingers and slowly raised them over his head. Hundreds of tiny mounds formed along the metallic ground, growing bigger. A few feet in diameter, they stopped growing and started to pop, a blast of green ooze flowing from them like bursting pimples. Followed by hands reaching skyward.

Zombies.

Will had summoned hundreds of zombies to deal with the dozens of ninjas who looked like Yume's mother. Unshaken by the army of animated corpses rising out of the ground, the ninjas attacked them with speed and precision. Sword slices yielded decapitations. The undead had numbers, though. A wall of zombies surrounded one of the ninjas and like a wave of dead flesh, the horde crashed down upon her. This happened to a second ninja, then a third. But more ninjas appeared with swords large enough and long enough to slice through two and three zombies at once.

How was this possible? That the woman who looked so much like Yume's mother – an uptight businesswoman from Japan, who spent her day pouring over new laws and regulations regarding the hiring practices for the company she worked for – could master the dreamscape? Intelligent? Yes. Aggressive? Yes. Fearsome? Yes. But a ninja? A murderer? Someone capable of mastering the dreamscape? Yume couldn't believe that it was her mother doing this. But she knew someone who was a dreamscape master and had no compunction against killing.

Maya.

This Mother-Imposter said she spent time with Maya. Yume was more inclined to believe that this was Maya herself, wearing the face of her mother.

"Move!"

From behind Yume, the other ninja, Aika, lunged forward and swung her sword. Yume jumped back and raised her hands to cover her head, but quickly realized that Aika hadn't attacked her. She saved her.

Yume had broken the first rule of life – never let your guard down. So focused on trying to figure out who intruded Billy's dreamscape – Will's dreamscape now – and murdered him, she hadn't been aware of what was happening around her. The zombie army wasn't localized to the Mother-imposter – Maya? – and what had started as hundreds were now thousands. They were everywhere and didn't discriminate about their targets.

As Aika dropped two, three, five, ten more, Yume yelled up to Will, still hovering in the sky. "Will! Will, I'm here!"

"Madness has deafened him," Aika said as she felled two more zombies with one slice.

The young ninja was right. Will was close enough for Yume to see his face, his eyes. His rage.

Yume focused on the zombie in front of her and reached out. She balled her hand into a fist to crush its head. Nothing happened. She tried again, opening, and closing her hand. When the Mother-Imposter slowed time, Yume saw how her trick worked, but a magic trick was no longer magic once exposed, instead becoming a learned and practice set of maneuvers. Yume overthought the process to make the magic work to the point of feeling like every step she needed to follow suddenly becoming a foreign concept. Now helpless, she clutched her hands to her chest and screamed.

Aika saved her again, cleaving the zombie's head in half, through its neck and into its sternum. As she extricated her sword, Aika yelled, "Is there any element of the dreamscape you can control?"

"I could… I used to be able…" Aika sliced the hands off two zombies reaching for Yume, then beheaded them both. Yume turned and saw nothing but curtains of decaying flesh dangling from bony hands reaching for her. This was too much. Too much! "I… I…"

"Can you fly?"

Fly? Not like a bird or a superhero, but Yume could float into the sky. Tapping into a skill she had mastered, her feet started to leave the ground. Aika put her left arm around Yume's shoulders and then hooked her left leg with Yume's right, supporting herself while hacking away at the reaching zombies.

"Let go of me!" Yume screamed at Aika.

"Your mother and I are here to help you."

"I don't know you! And she's *not* my mother!"

"Yume, the woman who brought me here is Shinko Dangan, your mother. The woman who is fighting the dream eater is Shinko Dangan, your mother. There is no parent who harbors in her heart more pride for a child than she does with you. There is no parent who would sacrifice more for their child than she would for you."

"She murdered my boyfriend!"

"She slayed a monster."

"No! My mother wouldn't do this! It's Maya. This is Maya seeking revenge."

"Maya is a *goddess*. Her followers imprisoned her and sold her to a man seeking power. She has no care for concepts like revenge, and if she did it would be toward those who imprisoned her. Your mother rescued her and spent three months learning from her to rescue *you*. All of this is *for you*!"

Yume cried, big gulping sobs from Aika's words ringing true. The woman dressed like a ninja was indeed her mother, doing this as a misguided attempt to save her. She clamped her mouth shut when she noticed that the goliath Billy and Will had created started to move. The ten-story tall creature made of steel and crystal had been standing dormant behind Will, but now it reached for him. Will abruptly dodged to the side, narrowly avoiding the creature's grasp, as if pushed by an invisible hand. Billy had moved like that, as if acted upon by an unseen force. Was there another entity at play? Was that who she had seen next to Will?

Screaming, Will extended his right hand and the air rippled from his fingertips to the monster. His creation blew apart; twists of metal and crystal shards crashed to the ground. Will hovered in the air but reached out with both hands, closed his fists, and then pulled them back to his chest. The ground rumbled as the volcano in the distance came to life.

The mountain grew from the land followed by two clawed hands. The arms pressed against the ground and pushed as the rest of the thing's body unearthed itself. The opening of the volcano tipped forward, the glowing orange mouth of the great beast, as other mountains formed its shoulders. It roared, and the metallic reverberations of a struck gong shook the ground hard enough to shatter the crystal trees, the human hearts falling to the ground in scarlet splatters. As the great beast of metal and lava lurched forward, the opening of its mouth grew wider and dark shapes stirred from within. It lurched again and spewed…

Dragons.

Will always turned to monsters and dragons, great beasts of fantasy, when faced with insurmountable stress, anger, and fear. Coping mechanisms. He once told Yume that he prayed and dreamed about conjuring monsters to kill his parents, but the most effective conjuring was Billy. Billy was dead, and Will went back to what he knew. First zombies, now dragons.

Dozens of cobalt blue dragons flew from the volcano-monster's mouth, splashing lava from their metal wings and bodies. Screeching like unoiled machinery, they blew fire from their mouths, a deadly portent of things to come.

The river of lava bubbled. The flow twisted in unnatural ways and then upward, out of the riverbed. Emerging from the curtain of lava came dozens of Asian dragons, their snakelike bodies and leonine heads made from fire. Some flew toward the metal dragons and engaged them with the fury of claws and teeth. Others circled around Will.

Flinging his arms about, Will yelled obscenities while conjuring giant hands from the ground below to grab the dragons, squeezing them hard enough to sever their bodies into two pieces. Shinko retaliated with tentacles bursting from the ground and wrapping themselves around the hands to hinder them.

This was all too much for Yume to follow let alone comprehend. Will remained in the sky, but spun in circles, desperately trying to maintain control over his dominion.

How was her mother able to combat him on so many fronts? Where was she?

Yume looked to the ground below, covered by a swarming mass of zombies being dismembered by an army of ninjas... who all looked like her mother. She was hiding in plain sight. One of those army members had to be her mother.

There! One figure was not paying attention to the chaos swirling around her. Instead, she focused on the heavens above, the battlefield of dragons, her hands moving as if sliding pieces along a grand gameboard. That one had to be her.

Yume floated closer and Aika offered no resistance.

"Mother!" Yume called out, but no response. Once her feet touched the ground, Yume pushed away from Aika, and ran to her mother. She didn't want to believe, didn't want to accept it, but Aika was right – this woman was her mother, Shinko Dangan. "Mother! Stop! He's a victim of abuse!"

Shinko didn't turn to face her daughter, her focus on the battle in the sky unwavering. Even when Yume stood mere inches from her, pleading. "Mother, please. I know what you think, but he's not evil. He's in pain. Most of his life has been a hell that neither you nor I could comprehend. Please, just stop and listen. Please." Yume reached out to grab her mother's shoulder. But her hand glided through as if her mother were a ghost. "No... No!"

Yume looked upward.

Before she could call to Will, her mother suddenly appeared behind him, her sword raised over her head.

With one swing, she sliced Will in half.

CHAPTER 43

The left and right halves of Will fell from the sky and splattered onto the ground with a messy splash, cleaved organs spilling out.

Chaos ended. The moving volcano stopped. The zombies and metal dragons disappeared in an unceremonious blink. Shinko descended gracefully to the ground, the lava dragons and multiple versions of herself vanishing. Reflecting upon what Maya had taught her, Shinko maintained the dreamscape, not wanting it to disappear and put her daughter through any more distress. Though, she wasn't sure if that was possible.

"No!" Yume shrieked as she dropped to her knees. "No!"

Shinko hurried over and knelt in front of Yume. Hands on her shoulders, she blocked her daughter's view of Will. "Yume, I know you don't believe me, but William was a monster. I understand he had been traumatized when he was younger and he lived through an abusive situation, but he murdered innocent people. Children, Yume. He killed children. Please wakeup so we can talk this through."

Yume cried uncontrollably and Shinko wondered if her daughter heard her, until she croaked through her sobs, "It wasn't him. It wasn't him."

"I'm sorry, but it was. We can discuss this in the waking world, but we must leave the dreamscape. I have control of it, but I don't know for how long now that the owner is dead."

Laughter filled the air. Raspy and endless, it echoed as it grew louder. Right at the point of madness, it stopped. A familiar voice boomed from everywhere and nowhere. A voice that sounded much like Billy's, Will's. "Oh, Shinko. You are wrong about two things..."

Billy's decapitated body stirred and stood. With shuffling steps, it ambled toward Will's body. It grabbed both halves and shook them as if snapping wrinkles from clothing. Bones and the remaining sausage-like organs slopped to the ground. As if putting on a costume, Billy's

278

body stepped into Will's skin. Hands pushed the two halves of Will's head together on top of the empty space over Billy's neck. The scarred face smiled, but instead of teeth, he exposed a mouthful of razor blades. He then spun, spattering blood through the air. When he stopped, a tattered blue cloak flowed around him and a bent blue top hat rested on his head.

"Oh my God," Yume whispered. "Bigby?"

Bigby bowed like an actor relishing audience applause. "First, this isn't Billy's or Will's dreamscape. It's *yours*, Hot Ninja Mama. Second, you're not in control here – I am!"

All light vanished from the universe.

Shinko floated in a darkness so black that she felt as if she had been reduced to disembodied consciousness. Unnerved by the concept, panic started to set in. No! It didn't matter if she had a body or not. That was linear thinking, the type that led to Billy and Will's downfall. They both reacted to what they saw in front of them. Even when they exposed Shinko's plot and disrupted her invisibility, they continued to think and act like human beings with unfathomable abilities instead of creatures with near infinite power. But now a few things made sense to Shinko.

When she attacked Billy and then Will, there were moments when she missed. At first, she thought they had dodged her attacks, but now it was clear that this creature – Bigby, as Yume called him? – had pushed them out of the way. Yume had mentioned that Billy and Will were different personalities inhabiting the same body. She seemed to know who this Bigby was. Maybe a third personality? Possible. Very likely. This personality had a better grasp on the dreamscape. She felt his presence everywhere. However, if Bigby were another personality, then he'd be human on some level. If she were to defeat him, then she needed to exploit that weakness.

First, she needed to find Yume and Aika. They were still in the dreamscape – her dreamscape – and they would be confused.

With a wave of her hand, she created light. To her surprise, she was indeed corporeal. And standing in the middle of a field of tall grasses and weeds. The sky was a cloudy twilight, muting the colors around her. A lone figure wore a hooded ninja garb. Aika. She slashed at people approaching her with a ninjato, each cut a killing blow, dropping the people faster than a farmer with a scythe cutting weeds. As she approached, Shinko called out, "Aika!"

No response, too focused on the threat in front of her. Shinko walked closer, ready to wave her hand and make the throng of people disappear, but she gasped when she got close enough to see their faces – people *she* had killed before. Varvaro's men she killed while rescuing Maya from his house, the ninjas she faced at The Dragon's Blessing, Karin and Tanaka from her last assignment, the man from the assignment before that, men from the assignment before that. Dozens of faces Shinko recognized gave one last twist of agony as Aika's sword stripped their lives away. Enough! She waved her hand and they disappeared. Close enough now, she grabbed Aika's shoulder and turned her, the hood falling.

It wasn't Aika.

It was Yume.

"No!" Shinko exclaimed.

"No?" came from behind Shinko. Yume. "You wanted her to be Aika and not me?"

Shinko turned back around to see that it was now Aika's shoulder that she clutched. "Aika?"

"Senpai? What is happening?" Aika had been the very definition of stolid and pragmatic ever since Shinko had first met her, nothing phasing her, but her voice had quivered when she asked the question.

"What's happening is this: my mother has chosen you over me."

"Yume, that is not true!" Shinko yelled.

Was this young woman actually Yume, or another one of Bigby's tricks? *Don't lose to the tactics you used to win.* Will had made the dreamscape change colors and Billy had looked around as if searching for Shinko while she was invisible. She was only invisible to the eye. Energy. They were looking for her energy. It made sense that everyone had some form of energy in the dreamscape to retain consciousness. Shinko focused on reading the energy around her. Yes, the young women who stood before her were Yume and Aika.

Yume rolled her shoulders. "Aika was the first person you looked for and when you saw my face, you were disappointed."

"No! I was shocked. Afraid. I never wanted you to follow in my footsteps. That is why I hid the truth from you. You living my life is my nightmare, Yume."

Nightmare. Yes, this was indeed a nightmare and she wasn't the one controlling it.

Before her daughter could rebut, Shinko yelled to the sky, "Reveal yourself, monster!"

"I'm no monster." The voice echoed. It sounded like William's, but deeper, more sinister. Hateful. "I was created by monsters. I kill monsters."

"You believe yourself to be a hero, but you are not. You are a coward who kills innocents!"

"Innocent?" Bigby cried out, as if offended by the word. "Those I killed would not stay innocent for long!"

Figures appeared before Shinko, Yume, and Aika. A man beating a woman while two young boys watched. Yume gasped and whispered, "Her name is Lynette. I know her."

"Yes, you do," Bigby said. "She came to the shelter. You recognized that her husband was a monster, so you and Billy killed him. But you didn't complete the mission."

The husband disappeared and then Lynette started to beat the children. The children rapidly grew, boys turning into men. They each found a woman to marry, and had children. Then those men abused their families, just like their father had.

"No," Yume said with impending tears, her words shaky. "No. That's not true! Billy, Will, and I saved those children from that future."

"There was nothing you could do to save them. But thanks to you leading me to them, I saved the truly innocent by stopping the cycle of abuse."

The scene reset to the father beating the mother. This time, after he disappeared, Bigby showed what he did to Lynette and children.

"No!" Yume cried, reaching out for them.

Shinko looked away. Even Aika gasped.

The scene changed again, a different man hitting a different woman, different children watching. Next to them appeared another family in the same situation. Then another family next to them. Family after family popped into view out of thin air, but the same actions happened – the father slapped, kicked, punched the mother in front of the children. Simultaneously, all the children grew older. The sons turned into their fathers, beating their wives and children while the daughters turned into different kinds of abusers, some striking their children, others ignoring them as other people in their lives abused them. As with before, those children grew older and repeated the cycle.

"No!" Yume shouted as she spun in circles, the unending horrors surrounding everyone. "This is not what happened!"

"You're right," Bigby said. "Thanks to you finding these monsters, I stopped their children from becoming like them."

Like the other scenario, Bigby showed what he did to the mothers and children.

Yume dropped to her knees, her body wracking from crying. "I did this. I did this! I killed them!"

"No!" Shinko shouted. "You did not kill the innocent, Yume. This monster did. He killed them all."

"I led him to them. I led…" She stopped crying, her eyes impossibly wide. She looked to the sky and asked, "Why did you kill Shanna? Why?"

"She would have turned into a monster." Multiple versions of Shanna appeared, looking as she had right before she died. Each version of Shanna grew older and a child or two appeared next to her. Every child was abused by Shanna, no matter the version.

"She'd never do that! Never!" Yume cried while on her hands and knees, the weight of the sights she witnessed crushing her.

Shinko dropped to her knees and threw her arms around her daughter.

"She would!" Bigby yelled back. The scene changed to Shanna in a bedroom, leading a man in a blue top hat to her bed. "I had no choice but to stop her."

"Noooo!" Yume howled as Shanna's death unfolded.

Shinko tried to maneuver herself between Yume and the events they witnessed, but her daughter pushed her away. "Why are you doing this? Why are you showing me this?"

The scene faded, leaving an endless barren landscape. Like an angel descending from Heaven, Bigby floated down from the sky. Once his feet hit the ground, he straightened his tie and cleared his throat. The skin of his face pulled tight, fold lines crisscrossing from head to chin, like he was wearing wrinkled clothes three sizes too small. "For you, Yume. Billy and Will weren't the only ones who loved you. And it's obvious you love me, or else you wouldn't have shown me all the monsters to kill."

"Yume, don't listen to him," Shinko begged, reaching out to her daughter only to have her hand slapped away.

Yume shook her head, but her whole body quaked as if stricken by palsy, tears dropping to the ground. "No. No, he's right. I made this happen. I wanted to help the world, but I made a monster. I should have been more like Aika, the daughter you wanted. You wanted me to be more like her and I failed. This is all my fault."

As she spoke, Yume faded until she was gone.

Assuming her daughter was now awake, Shinko swiped her hand in Bigby's direction, turning him into dust. Accompanied by omnipresent laughter, the dust swirled and reformed into Bigby. He floated in the air, his tattered cloak fluttering. Shinko blinked once, a simple close of her eyes, but by the time she reopened them, she had transported herself ten meters to the right to dodge his attack, a three-meter -wide hole right where she had been standing. "Aika! You need to wake up and kill William."

Bigby laughed. "You already did that. Will was the original personality. Once you killed him in his dreamscape, you killed him in the waking world. Before his pieces parts fell from the sky, I pulled us all into your dreamscape. Once I kill you, I'll just move to another. And another. And another!"

Shinko blinked again, this time ten meters on the other side of Bigby, her sword passing through his neck along the way.

The severed head bobbled as his left foot caught the fallen top hat. Bigby laughed. "Oops! Left hand, right hand. You need to work together now. No dropping me. Upsy daisy. Here we go." He screwed his head back on and he kicked his fallen hat back on top of his head.

Shinko repeated her maneuver, dodging another one of his silent attacks that left nothing but a crater, and delivered one of her own. She sliced through his head, a clean cut right above the bridge of his nose.

The cap of his skull slid off his head, red pulp oozing over his cheeks and necks. "You move so fast that you got my head spinning." He reached up and rotated the top of his skull a few times before returning it. "You know what else moves fast? Insects. And that's how I'll deal with you!"

In a heartbeat, he was taller than a city building. He lifted his leg to stomp Shinko with his foot, but Shinko dodged out of the way. Matching tactics, she grew in size as well, twice as tall as him and on her rise she slashed her sword upward, cleaving him from crotch to head, splitting that damn top hat in half.

In two separate voices, he said, "Worst first date, ever!"

The two halves mended together as he continued to grow taller. Then Shinko grew, slashing and hacking, but every cut body part regenerated.

Why wouldn't he die? William's body was dead, and she had killed both Will and Billy in the dreamscape. Yume seemed to know Bigby but was surprised to see him. Maybe neither Will nor Billy knew Bigby existed? The energy of being was tied directly to the brain, so it made sense that if one died, the other also died. If Billy and Will didn't know about Bigby, then he wasn't tethered to them, to their energies, to their shared body in the waking world. But Bigby was still energy. He might exist solely in dreamscapes, but he still had to obey the laws of the environment.

Bigby's torso consumed the sky. Was this an illusion? No. Shinko felt his malignant energy and it was growing. His fingers dug deeply through the metal ground of the planet and then he pulled it apart. If he was larger than an entire planet, then Shinko needed to be larger than him. As she grew in size, she waved her hand to form a protective bubble around Aika. She had a plan but needed Aika's help.

The two dream masters floated in space and continued to get bigger. Shinko slashed, and Bigby dodged, her sword cutting a nearby planet in half. In a flash of light, Bigby moved farther away and became even larger. He grabbed the closest star and threw it at her. With a wave of her hand, the gaseous ball of fire turned into butterflies.

"Not bad," Bigby said, continuing to grow.

"This is my reality," Shinko replied. She needed to keep playing his game, let him think he was in control.

"We'll see about that!"

The butterflies stopped flittering and collapsed in on themselves, each one creating a spot blacker than space itself. The universe tore into different directions like overstretched gauze, the fabric twisting and disappearing into the vortices created by each of the newly formed black holes. Planets, stars, whole galaxies pulled into the hundred points of emptiness. When there was nothing left, Shinko folded in on herself, her body twisting in unnatural ways. It was disorienting, but not enough to make her lose focus. This was her dreamscape after all, and no way she'd allow someone else to control it. With a simple thought, she restored the reality back to the point when the butterflies flitted away.

Bigby looked confused. Now it was time for her to act.

Shinko waved her hand and Bigby turned to dust. It wouldn't kill him, but…

His dust particles spread like talcum powder on a breezy day. When they dissipated to the point of disappearing, an image started to form. Little by little, Bigby's face and razor-blade smile came into view, large enough for stars to bounce off his cheeks. Exactly as Shinko had hoped.

Being of energy or not, he was formed by a human, and doomed to think like one, including the American pathos "Bigger is Better." Shinko planned to use that against him. She shrunk, taking Aika with her.

With Aika in front of her, they floated in darkness between a large sphere and a buzzing cloud. Confused with panic in her eyes, Aika looked around. "Senpai? Where are we? What is happening?"

"We are inside a hydrogen atom. We don't have long, so please listen."

Worry played across her face, but Aika shook herself to attention. Shinko placed her hands on her protégé's cheeks and said, "You need to wake up and kill me in the waking world."

"What?"

"This is my final assignment to you."

Tears formed in Aika's eyes. "I don't wish to do it."

"You must. Bigby is not tied to a body in the waking world, so he can simply travel from dreamscape to dreamscape. The only way to kill him is by killing the body of the person who owns the dreamscape he's in."

"But—"

"Aika, please. This is no different from any other mission the Shinigami's Helper assigns. It is for the greater good. It is to save the world. And I need you to promise me that you will keep Yume safe. She has been exposed to a world I had hoped she'd never think about, let alone live in. Please make sure she goes back to the path she had been on, the right path."

Aika stood straighter and gently removed Shinko's hands from her cheek. Squeezing her mentor's hands, she nodded.

Shinko looked up beyond the electron shell. Bigby was shrinking, searching for her. "Be ready, Aika."

Visualizing how she wanted her attack to go, she regulated her breathing to help her concentrate. Bigby continued to shrink: the size of a galaxy, then the size of a star, down to the size of a planet, down to a mountain. Smaller. Smaller. Now!

Shinko increased in size to match Bigby's height and formed a sphere of metal around him, just like she had done with Will. Inside, she created a black and white checker patterned universe that flowed and twisted in on itself. Bigby was powerful, maybe more so than Billy or Will, but he still thought like them, still relied on his eyesight. This should keep him disoriented for a while.

"Aika! Wake up now!"

*

286

Aika awoke with a start and shot across the room before she even realized what she had done. By the time she was oriented, her blade was through Shinko's chest, through her heart. Aika cried, a body wracking sob that expelled every emotion she never thought she had.

The assignment.

Feeling foolish for allowing her emotions to surface, she jumped to her feet and looked around the room. Nothing had changed since she first entered: William and Yume still lay on the bed. Bloodied sword raised over her head, she crept closer to William. His color had faded enough to indicate he was dead, but she checked his pulse anyway. Nothing.

Aika walked around the other side of the bed and placed a hand on Yume's shoulder. She knew Yume would not react well to being awoken by someone she didn't like, and finding her lover and mother both dead. But...

Shouldn't she have already been awake?

Aika shook Yume's shoulder. No response. She lightly slapped her cheek and gently used her thumb to open one of her eyes. No response. No pulse, but Yume was still warm and looked very much alive.

Closing her eyes, Aika turned to her training. Fumiko had taught her that everything in life was connected, all energy intertwining with the physical. Shinko took a more scientific approach to Fumiko's teachings, but Aika liked to believe there was some magic in the world. After all, she had just been inside the dreams of monsters. She leaned over and placed her ear against Yume's chest. A heartbeat. Faint. Slow. But steady.

Yume was in a coma of some sort. She had faded to nothingness in the dreamscape, and if her energy had left, then her body remained a shell. Where did she go?

And... Something else? A different kind of energy.

Aika lifted the bottom half of Yume's shirt. Placing her ear on Yume's belly, Aika closed her eyes and focused. Listened. Felt the energy. Gasping, she pulled back.

Yume was pregnant.

EPILOGUE

Aika went unnoticed in the hospital waiting room. She had been trained by Shinigami's Helper to blend in with her environment, but her anonymity went beyond her training. Shinko once told her that Asian women in America were often ignored, and that had been proven often during Aika's five months of living here.

Once she had learned Yume was pregnant, she contacted Fumiko and explained everything that had transpired in detail. Fumiko instructed Aika to leave the situation as is. There was no risk of exposing Shinigami's Helper, so leaving Shinko at the scene, despite the mystery, was acceptable. Aika called 911 and fled from the dream eaters' house, after saying her farewells to her *senpai*.

After only a few hours, Fumiko gave Aika new orders, a new mission. Her first, and possibly only, solo mission.

Her American citizenship came a week later via the assistance of Shinigami's Helper. Their pockets were deep, their reach endless.

Over the next five months, Aika learned and assimilated. More importantly, she maintained surveillance over the hospital where Yume stayed. The hospital had no choice but to keep her. A young, pregnant woman in a coma with no identification? The authorities had learned her identity, but she had no next of kin, her mother mysteriously dead in the same room. There was nowhere else to send her.

However, one man stepped forward, willing to foot the bill for her stay, for the baby's delivery when the time came, and for the future of her wellbeing. A businessman named Maxwell Templeton.

Aika knew there had to be more to Templeton. He had given Shinko the address to the dream eaters' house, after all.

Shinigami's Helper provided little information, though. The head of a small, organized crime organization, Templeton's father had died over five years ago. Maxwell picked up where his father left off, and that was all Fumiko was willing to share.

There was more to this man, though; Aika could feel it.

Fumiko forbade Aika from personal reconnaissance, her current mission superseding her desire to learn more about Maxwell. She stayed away from his properties, but she researched him, and asked the shadows what they were hiding. Just rumors. Rumors that Maxwell had a penchant for items and stories about the supernatural and unexplainable.

No wonder he sat in the hospital waiting room with a blond-haired couple in their mid-twenties.

"I'm still a little confused by this mission," Madison Fogelberg said to Maxwell. Her husband's name was Conner. At least that's what Maxwell put in the official system. They were a married couple and in Maxwell's employ. He, too, had deep pockets and unfathomable reach.

"It's simple," Conner replied. "We adopt a baby today and we raise him. If anything weird happens, we contact Mr. Templeton."

"That's what I don't get – how exactly are we defining 'weird?'"

"Anything out of the ordinary," Maxwell said with a placating smile. "If he starts to fly or shoots laser beams out of his eyes or... If when he's older, he can enter into people's dreams."

Being ignored gave Aika great power. How else could she describe sitting so close to the trio that not only could she hear every word they spoke but see Madison's face twist with confusion. "Laser beams? Entering people's dreams? What are you talking about? Do you honestly expect the child will do that?"

Conner squeezed her hand. "Trust me, sweety, if our kid is flying around the room or entering our dreams, we'll be more than happy to call Mr. Templeton."

Shinigami's Helper was able to dig under the pretty garden of information that Maxwell had planted. The Fogelberg couple were a part of his security team and had been trying to have a baby for the past few years. They were desperate enough to change their names and take this assignment. Even if the baby did fly around the room, Aika was certain Conner would hide it from Maxwell for as long as he could. Madison? Aika wasn't sure about her, seemingly along for the ride and willing to do anything, even turn a blind eye, to have a child.

"That's all you want us to do?" Madison asked. "Let you know if the kid does something weird."

Maxwell nodded. "Yes. I'll ask for a progress report every three or four months, but that's it."

"Okay. It—"

"Mr. and Mrs. Fogelberg?" a man in scrubs asked as he entered the waiting room, carrying a swaddled newborn. "Care to meet your new son? He joined us an hour ago."

All three stood, smiles taking up their faces. Conner extended his hands, and the nurse handed the baby to him.

While he and Madison cooed over the newborn, Maxwell pulled the nurse aside and asked, "How is the mother?"

A deep sadness washed over the man's face. "Unfortunately, she didn't make it. Her heart just… stopped."

Maxwell's smile disappeared. "That's unfortunate. I'll make arrangements to—"

A woman in scrubs rushed through the doors into the waiting room, headed toward the nurse talking to Maxwell. Nervous, she whispered to him, "The mother? She… Ummm… She's gone."

"Gone?" Maxwell and the nurse said at the same time.

"We… Umm… Security reviewed the videos and… An older man was seen carrying her out."

"An older man?" Maxwell asked. His gaze drifted away. Aika smiled. She knew exactly what had happened to Yume.

While researching the rumors about Maxwell, she heard another rumor. A rumor of a man named Harold Varvaro – the target of her very first assignment – disappearing. Aika knew every rumor had a reason to start. This time, the reason was the truth.

She found Varvaro and explained Yume's situation. His eyes held the desperation of either love or addiction. In this case, maybe a little of both. Despite treating Maya like a weapon, he seemed to have loved her. And he couldn't hide the fact that he enjoyed going into the dreamscape. If there was any chance he could someday do that again, then he'd do anything. Including stealing Yume from the hospital in hope of her becoming his new escort into the dreamscape.

The nurse offered a placating smile and said, "We'll notify the authorities immediately and keep you abreast of the situation as it develops. In the meantime, we'll let the happy couple enjoy the newest member of their family."

After a minute of glowering to himself, Maxwell turned his attention back to the Fogelbergs. Conner and Madison stood shoulder to shoulder, whispering promises of love, protection, and a grand future to their baby. Maxwell smiled and stroked the baby's cheek. "What do you think?"

"He's beautiful," Madison replied, wiping away a tear.

"Perfect in every way," Conner said. "Thank you."

"Have you thought of a name yet?" Maxwell asked.

Mother and father chuckled. "Actually, no. We were too busy thinking about everything we needed to do. Get a new car, move to a good school district, find a live-in nanny, figure out what our new careers will be, baby-proof the house."

Sometimes a ninja's best weapon was timing, and over the past five months, Aika had learned that few weapons sliced as deeply as an inviting smile. She stood and folded her hands together. As demurely as expected, she approached the trio, her practiced smile warm. "Hello? Sorry to interrupt, but I overheard you say you were looking for a live-in nanny?"

All three stared at her, confused as if she had splashed cold water in their faces.

"I have experience and am currently looking for a new job. That's why I'm here, to see what positions were available at the hospital."

Conner and Madison looked at each other, nervous about the perfect situation suddenly dropping right into their laps. Aika offered a slight bow. Her English was perfect, but her accent was thick, so she assuaged their obvious concerns. "I apologize for not mentioning that I am an American citizen and I have contact information for the last two families I worked with."

The happiness returned to the Fogelbergs. Even Maxwell seemed amenable. Since Conner held the baby, Madison extended her hand and said, "Thank you for your offer. We'd definitely like to contact your references, but after that checks out, there's no reason why we wouldn't accept your offer, Ms....?"

"Aika," she said as she shook Madison's hand. "Aika Dangan."

Aika could think of no better way to honor *senpai* than to carry on her family name. It didn't matter if Maxwell researched the coincidence of Aika sharing the same last name as Yume; he'd find no connection.

"Pleased to meet you. I'm Madison. This is my husband, Conner, and this is our... dear friend, Maxwell."

Aika leaned forward to look at the baby, her mouth and eyes going wide, the standard expression of joy when anyone looked at a sleeping baby, and said in a sing-song tone, "And this must be Orion."

Conner and Madison looked at each other, confused. Madison chuckled nervously and asked, "Orion? Why do you think his name is Orion?"

Aika glanced to each of them. "Oh, I apologize. I thought I heard one of you say that was his name."

Conner laughed. "We didn't, but... I gotta be honest, I really love that name!"

"Me, too!" Madison beamed.

"It sounds like he has a name now," Maxwell said.

Yes. Orion was his name. Aika didn't know why, but something inside her told her that was his name.

The story isn't over! Eighteen years later, Orion is being hunted by an assassin with a list of names. Trying to stay alive, he meets other people on the list and they must work together to uncover the sins of their parents in:

THE TRUTH
IN THEIR BLOOD

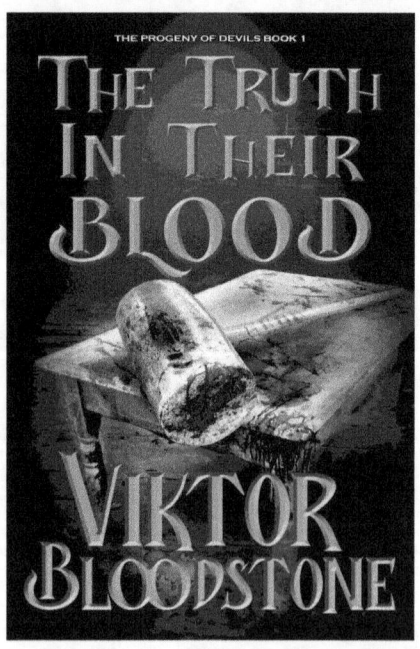

www.fortresspublishinginc.com

More from the *Legacy of Devils* series:

Hammer and Blood

www.fortresspublishinginc.com

Care to read about William's origin? His story can be found in ***Hellbent***, an anthology by Hellbender Books.

Viktor Bloodstone

is

Brian Koscienski

Chris Pisano

Jeff Young

www.novelguys.com